Lizzy Barber studied English at Cambridge and works as the head of brand and marketing for a restaurant group. Her debut novel, *My Name is Anna*, was the winner of the *Daily Mail* crime writing competition and she is currently hard at work on her next thriller. Lizzy lives in London with her husband.

@byLizzyBarber

MY NAME IS
ANNA

LIZZY BARBER

arrow books

13 5 7 9 10 8 6 4 2

Arrow Books
20 Vauxhall Bridge Road
London SW1V 2SA

Arrow Books is part of the Penguin Random House group of companies
whose addresses can be found at global.penguinrandomhouse.com.

Penguin
Random House
UK

First published in Great Britain by Century in 2018
First published in paperback by Arrow Books in 2019

www.penguin.co.uk

A CIP catalogue record for this book is available from the British Library.

ISBN 9781787460768

Typeset in 10.71/16.08 pt Palatino
by Integra Software Services Pvt. Ltd, Pondicherry

Printed and bound in Great Britain by Clays Ltd, Elcograf S.p.A.

Penguin Random House is committed to a sustain-
able future for our business, our readers and our
planet. This book is made from Forest Stewardship
Council® certified paper.

For Mummy: for the children's encyclopedias;
and for being my A–Z

I felt a cleavage in my mind
As if my brain had split;
I tried to match it, seam by seam,
But could not make them fit.

Emily Dickinson

He watches the silhouette of her body slicing through the dawn, until the horizon claims her completely. With the pads of his fingers touching, poised as if about to make the sign of the cross, he draws an errant grey hair away from his temple, smooths the waist of his white linen suit.

Behind him: chaos.

He can hear their moans, their undignified clamouring for help; praying for him, for his guidance, his command.

But he, at least, is immaculate.

As he turns his chin to the light, he allows a smile to illuminate his lips, as if echoing the sun on its rise. Because he cannot be sullied so easily.

Wherever she has gone, he will find her.

Wherever she is, she will remember him.

ANNA

1

Dirt has a way of falling through the smallest of cracks. You may think there is nothing there, but it will always be found eventually.

I raise my fingers through the cooling bathwater and check my nails, looking for the invisible fragments of dust I always fail to spot but Mamma hones in on with such definite aim. In my head, I rehearse the words I have whispered to myself so many times I see them written across my lids when I close my eyes.

Today is my eighteenth birthday and, for the first time, I am lying to my mother.

I sought out the comfort of the bath, hoping it would ease the tension. But even here I cannot shut out the remnants of my fractured sleep. The ghost of my dream floats on the water's clouded surface; the dream that has come before, that has grown more frequent as my anxiety has mounted, its creeping fingers reaching for me in the strangest of moments. A dream that feels so real I swear it isn't a dream at all.

It taps me on the shoulder now, revolving and gyrating just out of reach. A whirl of bright colours. Laughter, music. A face, the features blurred. And a voice, calling. I know it's me they're seeking, but something isn't right: the name they're calling isn't mine.

I pull the plug and the water begins to swirl around me, milky with the residue of peach-scented foam. My voice penetrates the silence of the bathroom, although I'm not sure if it's real or in my mind. 'No. My name is Anna.'

The bathwater drains, but the dream lingers.

In the bedroom, I situate myself. Take in the calico curtains that remain always drawn; a hermetic seal against the outside world. The pinewood dresser whose contents are neither numerous nor elaborate. The crucifix on the wall, under whose watchful limbs I say my nightly prayers. The bed. The chair. These things – these petty, everyday things – are the items that make me feel safe. These are the sights that tell me I am home, and happy, when my memory tries to convince me otherwise.

That name.

I peek through the curtains and turn my chin to the daylight, allowing it to wash away the last of the disquieting night. It's another beautiful morning in Alachua County.

I'm reminded of my favourite hymn, 'Morning Has Broken', and hum the opening notes as I tidy the bed and fold my nightdress under the pillow, making everything neat, precise. When not a speck remains out of place, I pull on the denim blue dress I know Mamma likes best, and release my hair from the knot that has been holding it, damp around the edges from where the bathwater has licked it.

'Happy birthday,' I tell the girl in the mirror as I rake a comb through the tangles. 'Today is your eighteenth birthday.' She smiles back, curious, uncertain, and I ask her, not for the first time, if I am pretty.

I asked Mamma once, but she shook her head and gave me a little laugh. Not cruel, just dismissive. 'Pride is a sin, Anna. We are all pretty, because we are all gifts from God.' I never asked her again.

I suppose I consider myself pretty enough. My face, though I always find it a little round, is free from marks or blemishes. I've never needed braces, which is good, because Mamma despises the dentist. My eyes are clear, and a soft brown like maple syrup, although not Mamma's enviable sparkling blue. My hair is the colour of wet sand, but it picks up blonde streaks in the summer, and falls about my shoulders in a thick curtain. Some of the girls at school, the so-called popular kids whose names all blur into one, have theirs dyed bleached-blonde and cut into sharp layers, but I know that even if I should have such an inclination, there is no way Mamma would allow it.

Mamma says we should be happy with what God gave us.

Dressed, I make my way down the stairs, mentally skimming through that string of words one final time: *We're driving to Ocala National Forest; we're going hiking; we're having a picnic.* My throat constricts – I swallow sharply. *Forest. Hiking. Picnic.* Nothing else.

Mamma's voice rises out of the kitchen as I go to greet her. She's singing, which means she's in a good mood. She loves to sing, even though her voice is a little thin and can come across a tad flat. But I'd take a chorus of tone-deaf, happy Mammas than one single, silent alternative.

The kitchen is my favourite room in the house. It has big French windows overlooking the backyard, the only ones that aren't suffocated by curtains, so that daylight streams right in. The big farmhouse table always has a vase of fresh flowers on it, grown by Mamma's own green-fingered hands. Today they're tulips, pink and red and yellow, their tight-lipped petals on the verge of spilling their secrets. On the far wall, next to the stern grandfather clock that stopped working years ago but that neither of us knows how to fix, are the little pencil scratchings which mark how I've grown, right back from when I was nigh on three years old and we first moved here, until last year: five foot four, and not likely to have much growing left in me. Mamma is taller; she must hit five eight, five nine, in bare feet, but she always seems to stoop, as if worried her height makes her conspicuous.

'Good morning, Mamma!' I call, hopeful that I have judged her mood correctly. She turns to me, gives me her best attempt at a smile – the one she saves for the really good days – and I am thankful that I'm right.

She opens herself out to me. 'Good morning, Anna dear.'

I step towards her, breathe in her familiar scent of lavender soap and Lysol. *A clean home and a clean body are the first steps to a clean soul.* I could pick Mamma out across a crowded room with my eyes closed, through just that scent. I want to throw my arms around her and kiss her cheek, like I've seen other girls do. But I know that wouldn't do.

Instead, Mamma holds me at arm's length, and I feel her taking me in, assessing me; her eyes searching me over for any sign of sin or contamination. She lets go with a satisfied nod. My arms drop to my sides. I've passed the test. 'Happy birthday, dear heart. May the Lord bless you and keep you well.' When she's content like this, all is right with the world.

She points to the vitamins laid out on the sideboard and I duly take them, wash them down with the glass of water waiting. She pulls out one of the chairs from around the kitchen table, motions for me to sit down. I obey, hearing the ping of the toaster and knowing it must be frozen waffles again. Mamma hates to cook, but she sure has a sweet tooth.

She sets a plate down before me bearing a dense, rectangular slab, a pat of butter and a drizzle of maple syrup slowly melting into each rectangular depression. Sometimes it feels as if Mamma would like to keep me frozen too, for ever her little girl. 'Thank you, Mamma,' I say quickly, and raise a hand to pick up my cutlery.

'*Anna.*'

My fork freezes in mid-air. I set it down, the waffle untouched, realising my mistake. Eighteenth birthdays aren't exempt from grace. I clasp my hands together and bow my head as Mamma takes a seat opposite, relieved as she starts to speak.

'Lord, we thank you for all that you give; for the food we see before us, and the home over our heads. Help us to live our lives with thanks and grace, and to always remember that, as long as we have You in our hearts and live pure lives, You will show us the way. Amen.'

'Amen,' I mumble into my hands, chastened as always, then open one eye to peek. Hers are squeezed shut, as I know they will be: continuing the secret, silent prayer she always adds on for herself, lips pursed in a thin, pious line. I've never asked what it is; never dared.

Before we eat we each pick up a fork, hold it to the light and then rub it carefully with our napkins. We do the same with the knife, scouring it for any speck of contamination. As always, Mamma leads, I follow. Before I even set the edge of my cutlery against the plate, I wait for the telltale sign: a slight tilt of her head, the barely audible 'hmm'. When her knife touches the rim of the plate, I can begin.

I'm so het up I can barely manage a quarter of it. My stomach plaits and unplaits itself as the acidic orange juice Mamma pours us from a carton bubbles against the waffle batter. I do my best to finish the whole thing, knowing how Mamma feels about wasting food, feeling the crunch of sugar against my teeth with each bite. She spies me agitating a piece around the plate and I quickly swallow it down in a swirl of syrup and butter.

'Delicious. Thank you, Mamma.'

'Good.'

To prove it, I reach across the table for the jug of maple syrup and drown the remaining mouthfuls. The syrup soaks through the batter and is so sickly-sweet I almost wince, but it helps the food slip down my throat with more ease.

When only crumbs remain on our plates, Mamma surprises me by setting a package down in front of me, wrapped neatly and simply in plain blue paper. I eye it casually, but Mamma gives me an encouraging nod. 'Go on.'

She's not usually one to fuss over birthdays.

The package is soft to the touch. I unstick the Scotch tape neatly, cautious of Mamma's watchful eye, and take in the cream hessian that begins to reveal itself. It's a cushion, a perfect square I know has been sewn by Mamma: across its front is her distinct, careful stitching: *I prayed for this child, and the Lord answered my prayer. 1 Samuel 1:27.*

'Oh Mamma,' I breathe, turning the cushion in my hands. 'Thank you.'

'I thank the Lord for you, Anna.' She turns to look at the picture hanging on the wall, one of the few we have in the house: my parents on their wedding day. 'And I know your father would too.' I follow her head towards the picture I have studied so many times I no longer really see it. Mamma in a plain satin dress, a spray of calla lilies resting over the crook of her arm. My father next to her, his stiff grey suit a little too close-fitting, looking younger than his twenty-five years. I was only two years old when he died. A car crash – piled into by some drunken teenagers on their way home from a game. It was after that we moved here: a fresh start. Mamma always said she had no family to speak to, no ties to hold her, no reason to stay.

It's hard for me to get a clear picture of him, this shadowy figure who is more of an idea than a reality. Like Mamma, he's no stranger to height; there must've been a short ancestor in the distant past whose unlucky genes I was handed down. And he's clean-shaven; although somewhere, somehow, I see him with a beard. A whisper of my baby hands reaching out for the coarse hairs on his chin, and then it's gone. From the picture, it's hard to tell what features of his are mine. I want to ask Mamma what he was like, what he would think of me, what traits of mine are his. But whenever I ask questions like these, she clams up, keeping her pearls to herself.

'Let's clean up.' She severs the mood as quickly as she created it, moving across my vision and breaking my contact with the picture.

*

The sound of the doorbell wakes us both from our own private thoughts as we stack plates and wash dishes. We both step into the hallway and I can make out William's shape through the glass on the front door. His arrival makes this all seem alarmingly real, and I feel my breathing quicken, the centre of my palms moisten even as I chide myself to calm down. Just a few more minutes and we're in the clear.

Mamma goes to greet him, and his lanky frame slinks into the house, ducking to pass under the Tiffany chandelier – most definitely a relic of before Mamma's time here – threatening to upset the coloured glass and prompt rainbow shadows to ricochet off the walls.

'Good morning, Mrs Montgomery. Good morning, Anna.' He nods deferentially at my mother, a wisp of hair escaping onto his forehead, and then pulls a bright bouquet of wildflowers from behind his back. 'Happy birthday, Anna.'

'Oh William. They're beautiful.' I take them from him shyly, feeling the tops of my ears burn pink. 'I'll put them in water right away.'

He leans forward as if to kiss me on the cheek, but at the same time he eyes Mamma, pulls back and nods politely at me instead.

William and I have been dating for nearly a year. He's older than me, already in college, and Mamma only permits it because he's the son of Pastor Timothy, and therefore she couldn't bring herself to deny it. We met in the church choir when his daddy took over our local parish, and we've been seeing as much of each other as possible since then. Nothing fancy, just trips to the movies, bike rides on Saturday afternoons, helping out with church fundraisers – our time together carefully meted out by Mamma's exacting direction. We've talked, loosely, about getting married when he graduates next spring, but this isn't exactly a conversation I have shared with Mamma.

I parade the flowers into the kitchen and set them in a vase on the sideboard, ready to take up to my bedroom later. When I return, William has his hands in his pockets, his feet shuffling the way he does when he's running out of polite conversation. My secret squirms around me. We are so close to freedom. I stride over to William and take a strong grip of his hand.

'Mamma, we should probably be heading out now, if we want to make good time ... ?' I try to sound firm, but I can't stop the upward inflection of a question nudging its way into my voice. Always asking for permission. 'We'll be home in time for dinner, I promise.' I imagine kissing her on the cheek, wrapping her into a hug. Instead my hand reaches out, pats her upper arm. 'Thank you for breakfast. And for my present.'

We're nearly out the door when Mamma rests her hand on the frame, blocking my exit. 'Remind me where you two'll be again?'

My mind goes blank. Stupid, stupid.

'Just heading across to Ocala for a hike and a picnic, Mrs Montgomery.' William touches me lightly on my lower back, letting me know he's got me. 'I promise I'll have her back in one piece.'

She blinks, then gives him a tight-lipped smile. 'Yes, you did say that. Be careful on the hiking trail, Anna; it's easier than you think to slip and fall.' Her hand releases the door frame. 'You kids have fun.'

We watch the door creak shut behind us, and then finally we are released into the fresh air. I gulp it in as we make our way over to William's red Ford Focus, the beaten-up old car he is prouder of than almost anything else in the world. He opens the passenger door and waves me inside. 'Princess, your chariot awaits.'

With the doors shut, I rest my head against the seat back as William reverses out of the long drive, and turns in the direction of the I-75. With the roar of the engine in my ears, and the hot breeze fanning my face through the open window, I let go part of the tension I have unwittingly been storing up all morning. But although we seem to have escaped, a part of me does not feel entirely free. The residue of the dream still clings to me, stronger today than ever before.

I press my hand to the dial on the car stereo, trying to drown out the noise inside me, attempting instead to hum along to whatever lazy pop song is blaring from the station.

Because today is my eighteenth birthday, and I feel invincible.

Because we've made it this far, and nothing bad happened. We are really on our way, and no one has stopped us.

And we aren't going to Ocala. Or hiking. Or having a picnic. Or going to any other place Mamma would allow.

We're going to Astroland.

ROSIE

2

I rake through the pile of clean laundry. Cotton socks and T-shirts and pyjama bottoms spill out of the dryer and fan around me, bursting with the powdery smell of synthetic lavender. I rise, frustrated, and pluck a peach-coloured bra bristling with static from my thigh.

'Mum, have you seen my gym socks?' My voice ricochets through the house. 'Mum?'

No reply.

I pull out my phone from my jeans pocket and click the home button. My face, highlighted with purple glitter from last year's school disco, gurns back at me. Above it, the time flashes in neat, white letters. It's quarter to eight. The bus leaves in ten minutes. 'Muuuum!' I shout again, craning my neck towards the stairs.

We live in one of those stretched-out town houses off a backstreet in Islington: a basement kitchen, permanently at risk of damp; two interconnecting living rooms, one always empty, the other squashed; at least one too many floors. Dad calls it a triangular house, because the rooms get smaller as you go up it, so even though it looks big at the start, by the time you get to my room in the attic you're breathing in to get past people.

I shove the phone back in my pocket, about to give up and look upstairs, when a piece of paper on the kitchen counter catches my eye. It's an email to my parents, I notice, looking-but-not-looking. Odd, to have it printed out. And then I see the name of the sender, and edge closer.

Susanne, David,

I am concerned that I have still not received an answer from you regarding my email dated 3 March 2018. As you know, we only have funds to last us until the end of May, and unless anything happens to the contrary before then we will be forced to close the trust.

I in no way wish to burden you further at such a sensitive time, but I would be grateful if you could please let me know how you wish to proceed.

Kind regards,
Sarah Brown
Director

The end of May. That's six weeks away.

It's as if someone's pressed the mute button. Every petty urban chirrup, the beeps of cars outside, the whirr of the washing machine, the indistinct motions of the rest of the family have all been silenced. I reach for the paper, my fingers barely touching the space where the text finishes and the blankness begins. So few words, to say so much.

I hear the hurried *bump, bump, bump* of feet on the stairs, and Mum's head appears round the door. I swerve my eyes from the paper, take a step away from it.

'Are these what you're looking for, Rosie?' She dangles a pair of blue and white striped socks between her fingers.

'Yes, that's them.' I snatch them from her. 'Thanks.'

'They were in Rob's room,' she tells my back, following me up the stairs to the front door.

'Course they were.' I shove the socks into my kit bag, not wanting to look at her. Worrying that she'll read my face, and know instantly that I've seen it. Why did she have it out now? Is it because of the interview tomorrow – our last hope, a last-ditch plea, to keep the trust alive?

My backpack is where I left it last night, hanging on one of the hooks by the front door, textbooks on the brink of spilling out. I grab it, trying to ignore the words that feel as if they've been taped across the inside of my eyelids, so Mum won't know anything is amiss.

She watches me, her face wrinkled with concern. She's dressed in her usual work uniform – flared knee-length skirt, blouse, cardigan – but on her feet are the big fluffy slippers she swaps her heels for as soon as she walks in the door. She works in advertising, a huge corporate company that makes things like that Christmas supermarket ad that went viral last year, but I can't remember a single day when she hasn't been there to see me off in the morning, or welcome me home after school.

'You will be on time tonight, won't you, Rosie?' She works a strand of brown hair around her finger, waiting for an answer.

I am seconds from the door. From being able to think. 'Yes, of course I will.'

'You know it's important – to me and your dad. It's an early start tomorrow, to get to the studio, and we want to spend some time together tonight. To talk about her. As a family.'

'I know, Mum. I'll be on time. Early, even.' I puff my cheeks, jigging from foot to foot as I eye the door.

'Text me when you're off the bus, and when you get on this afternoon.'

'I will. I always do.'

'And if you need anything, anything at all, you can call me at the office. I'll always answer.'

'Yes, Mum.'

'OK,' she sighs, then opens the front door for me, holding on to the frame as I duck past her. She grabs me on the shoulder just before my foot touches the first step, pulling me into a hug I have to fight the urge to struggle out of. 'I love you. Be safe!'

'Yes, Mum. Love you too.'

She relinquishes her hold and I hurry down the steps.

When has she ever not ended a farewell like that? *Be safe.*

I try to do my Spanish homework on the bus next to Keira, but I can't help but play the words of the email in an endless loop: ... *only have funds to last us until the end of May* ... now it's nearly the end of April.

Keira sticks her feet up against the seat in front of us, balances the book on her knees. I see her watching me, caution in her eyes, but then she rests her iPhone on the wedge between our seats, the magenta sparkly case picking up the specks of the mottled purple and grey upholstery, and wedges one of her earbuds into my left ear, turning the volume up on the Drake song she knows I love.

'*¿Admíras a los famosos?*' she asks, reading from the maroon textbook in front of me.

It's like I've never heard the words in my life.

'*¿Admíras ... a ... los ... famosos?*' she asks again, nudging me. 'Come on, Rosie, it's an easy one.'

I see her features crinkle together, and I rub my eyes with the heels of my hands, forcing myself to scrub the email from my mind. *Do you admire celebrities?* The meaning comes to me at last. '*Sí, sí, admíro mucho. Liam Hemsworth es muy guapo,*' I joke. That's what I always do.

She giggles, thumps me on the head with the book, and I know I've struck the right note. It's always so much easier.

... *forced to close the trust.* That must be what it is. They'll use tomorrow's interview as an appeal – to see if the nation's ghoulish hunger for sympathy will invite a new wave of donations that'll allow us to keep the trust afloat a little longer. The interview will be the biggest piece of coverage we've had this year, and the fifteen-year anniversary is a big one – we're sure to pluck at the heartstrings of all those stay-at-home mums glued to the television set tomorrow morning, clutching a half-drunk mug of tea to their chest as they comfort themselves with the knowledge that their little Bobby or Jane is safe in bed.

The bus drops us in Highgate Village, where we pass the newsagent Keira got chased away from last week for trying to convince a man outside to buy her a bottle of vodka. I clock her smoothing down her nut-brown curls, turning her head in the opposite direction to avoid detection.

'Like they remember you, you twat.' I nudge her in the ribs. 'Can you imagine how many times someone's tried that on? You weren't even in uniform.'

She reaches a hand out as if to give me a shove, but then she stops, grabs hold of my hand and squeezes it hard. Her features whirl into a concerned frown. 'You're all right, yeah?'

I go cold. At first I wonder how she can know, replaying the morning's conversation to see if there's anything I could have said that betrayed me. Trying to work out if it's something my mum may have told Keira's. But then, why her and not me?

I open my mouth, about to ask how she knows, when it strikes me: she doesn't mean the email, she means the date. Of course: she knows that. 'Yeah, I'm fine.' I feel my shoulders tighten, and force them to unknit themselves from my spine. I've been told before I need to stop acting defensive. That my 'natural inclination to keep people at arm's length makes it hard to form true and meaningful attachments'.

But Keira's different. And she knows me too well to press me. Instead, she gives me a forced smile, hikes her bag over her shoulder as she turns to leave me. 'OK, cool. Save me a seat on the bus.' She blows me a kiss and weaves off down the hall through the anthill of navy uniforms.

At school I keep my head down, try to avoid the whispers. It's a big enough place that I can slip down the corridors without bumping into anyone I know, but of course they all know me. Even the younger ones – the ones who weren't even alive fifteen years ago – regard me with a rich mixture of horror and curious fascination. I see it in their faces – their eyes wide, their shoulders hitched back a little, as if it might be contagious – as they wonder to themselves, *What would I be like, if it happened to me?*

When I do my journey in reverse, get off the bus at the top of Highbury Corner, I switch on my phone, kept dark all day to avoid the inevitable barrage of alerts. The ones that now flood the screen. The messages of sympathy from people who barely know me, but feel like having me as a friend – even a virtual one – gives them a certain cachet. The running commentary from Mum, telling me about her day, asking me how mine's going, telling me she's just checking in. Each ping on the screen is heavy with her desperation to know I'm still at the other end.

At home I dodge past Rob, who's already in his usual position in the living room playing video games on full volume, and shout down to Mum in the kitchen. 'Home! Got an essay due for English!' I can't deal with it now – all of it, all of them. I crave the closed door of my room, the sanctuary it provides.

Upstairs I change into a pair of red tartan tracksuit bottoms and a grey T-shirt that reads, 'But First, Coffee', discarding my uniform on the bedroom floor like a body has melted from it. I tap methodically at my keyboard for an hour, trying to contemplate *How Austen's portrayal of Mr Darcy reflects the attitude towards men in the novel as a whole*, but the letters on the screen before me are meaningless.

Is the email still there in the kitchen? Or did she clock it after I left, secrete it away? Does she know that I know? Is tonight when they are planning on telling us? Prepping us for the interview tomorrow, so that we're primed to make our sob story even more compelling?

At half past six the distant sound of the front door opening and slamming shut, followed by the metallic *thunk* of a bike, signals Dad's return from work. He's a music producer – classical stuff mainly; good enough so that the press always trots out the same, well-rehearsed line, 'celebrated music producer David Archer', as if he has no right to complain about what happened because he's successful.

'Evening all!' I picture him unclipping his helmet from under his greying beard, removing his high-vis jacket and seeking out Mum; seeking out the reassurance that everyone is OK. Everyone who can be.

The smell of cooked meat rises up the stairs and curls around my room in fatty, salty tendrils. My stomach rumbles. I couldn't face lunch.

At ten to seven I scrape my hair into a high ponytail, trying to avoid looking at my reflection. If I do, I'll be compelled, tonight of all nights, to look for the similarities. Does my mouth curve the same way as hers? Are our eyes like Mum's, or Dad's? Is there something in our noses, our ears, our jawline, that I can look at and say, 'That's us'?

I don't want to talk about it. I don't want to sit there over dinner, and watch Mum screwing up the corner of her mouth, and Dad ripping his napkin into shreds, as we go over it and over it all again: every shred of every story they have, nothing to be forgotten. The muscles in my legs tense in resistance. I consider calling down, telling them I feel sick, I have to finish an essay, I'm not hungry. But I know no excuse is good enough tonight.

Instead, I ball my fists, take ten deep breaths. A doctor with a German-sounding surname once told me this is 'an excellent technique for self-reflection and relaxation'. That was after the time I punched the wall in my room so hard I broke a knuckle.

When it doesn't work, I stop by the bathroom and pop a couple of aspirin, curling my lip at the razor by the sink. Too like *The Bell Jar*, even for me. I turn towards the stairs, and the smell of cheese and tomato permeates the air – lasagne, I guess – and I place a foot on the topmost step.

I practise a smile, a nod. I'm OK. We all do our best to pretend we're OK.

And then, with nothing else for it, I make my way downstairs, each step bringing me closer to the moment I've spent all day dreading.

To dinner.

To my family.

To the past.

To Emily.

ANNA

3

I've never questioned why Mamma won't allow me to visit Astroland, the amusement park that opened up in the north of Florida nearly twenty years ago. I'd never dare to. It's one of those things I know instinctively is Off Limits, just like painting my nails, or owning a home computer, or any of the myriad things that others seem to have and do.

For my classmates, special occasions are usually spent on the highway, making the hour's drive to Astroland. They will compete for weeks beforehand as to who will get to dress up as which character from the wildly popular kids' movies. When I was really little, I'd come home clutching glittery invitations from children to join their special birthday trip. But the invitations were thrown straight in the trash. Eventually they stopped asking me.

The idea of Astroland wouldn't have come up at all if it weren't for William. His family moved to Alachua County from San Antonio, Texas, and he couldn't believe it when I told him I've never been. His family are all Astroland mad; they've seen all the films a bunch of times, and I think they even have a first edition copy of one of the books in their living room. Even William, who was already in college over in Gainesville when they moved, was thrilled at the prospect of a family season pass.

At first he wouldn't let it go, this fantasy of us going to Astroland together. He was convinced he would be able to win Mamma around. But that was before he really knew her, saw that even his charm couldn't sway her set mind. Which was why he ended up formulating a way to sneak me in. It started as a joke: 'I'll hide you in the trunk of my car; she'll never know you're gone. We'll get you a wig, a moustache.' But when my birthday started edging closer, it was all he could talk about. As if proving he could do this would demonstrate that we are unshakeable, showing me that Mamma's power isn't so absolute.

'Are you excited?' he asks me now, stroking the bare skin of my forearm underneath my sleeve.

'Uh-huh. Sure am.'

'You don't sound sure.'

'I am!' I look over at him, taking in his profile: his square jaw, with the two tiny puncture marks on it where he got bitten by a dog as a kid; the kink in his nose where it got broken by a badly landing basketball; his autumn-leaf hair blowing backwards from the wind, the exact same shade as his mother's. I never thought I'd know another person so distinctly. Apart from Mamma, of course. 'I'm *so* excited. I just can't believe we're really doing this.'

'It's going to be great. You trust me, don't you?'

'Of course.'

As we chug along to the sound of William's wheezing engine, the road widens out and becomes more populated with cars and trucks, all bound north, in the direction of Georgia. I see less and less of the grey stripe of asphalt as the cars shunt forward and grapple for space. A silver Mercedes honks loudly at our rear, then swerves to overtake us.

William tuts as the car speeds on ahead, but remains calm. He likes to drive precisely on the speed limit: not over it, not under it; on it. 'People hurrying like that never slow down to enjoy what's around them,' he says.

Dotted between a row of wide, white condos and brown scrubland, I spy a collection of thick orange trees. It's April, coming to the end of navel season, and the weather is particularly hot. The ground is thick with the fruit, fallen from the trees and left to rot in the sunshine. It reminds me of a time when I blithely started hand-juicing oranges from our tree, only to look down and realise with horror that they were full of maggots. Their bodies wriggled and writhed in the orange liquid. The juice was alive with them and I screamed, dropping the jug. When Mamma saw what had happened, I had to scrub the entire kitchen with bleach from top to bottom, and then she took my hands and scrubbed them too, up to the elbow. It made the skin around my fingers flake and peel for days, revealing the shiny pinkness underneath.

I turn the volume up on the stereo, now blasting out that eighties heavy guitar rock William loves, to drown out the memory. What will Mamma do if she finds out where we've been today?

The suburbs sweep around us, and the billboards that begin popping into our view tell us, in looping, ever-increasing hyperbole, that we're close. Is it too late to bail on the whole thing? My seat belt digs into my chest. I roll the window down further.

We pull up into the parking lot and jump on a shuttle bus to the park, painted silver and bearing the sign 'All aboard the Xelon 3000', the name of the movies' signature spaceship. The driver has identical white teeth and not a hair out of place, and asks us, with a wide, uncomplicated grin, 'Are you ready for take-off?'

Two little girls sit next to us, wearing costumes over their jeans and T-shirts, one in an emerald-green tiara and tutu, the other fiddling with a gold cowboy hat on her lap. They chatter excitedly to one another as their parents look on, and I wonder if I will have somehow missed the vital magic of seeing the park at that age.

'You're never too old for a gold lasso.' William nudges me with his shoulder, seeing where I'm looking.

I blush and fix my eyes instead on the road ahead.

The bus pulls up to a line of shuttles and we join the crowds heading to the bank of ticket barriers which flank the entrance to the park, and William pulls the tickets out of his pocket. Ahead, above our eyeline, a sleek, silver train pulls into a station below a sign that reads: 'This way to Mars Central.' Beyond it, I see the most famous icon of all: the green sparkling turrets of Princess Bianca's castle. There is noise; loud, jolly music booming from speakers and competing with the burble of crowds. I clench my fists in anticipation, and a shiver escapes down my spine: there is something unsettling, something almost hyperreal, about those iridescent green turrets.

We step out into The Time Before, the part of the park that depicts life on earth before the characters' adventures begin. A smell of fudge wafts from one of the open doors, and we stop by a glass window, decorated in fine gold lettering, to watch a woman in a white mop cap and frilled apron stirring a huge vat of sticky liquid with a long wooden stick. Up ahead, we scoot past an open-top fifties-style car that screeches to a halt, and a group of actors in retro-style silver space suits clamber out of it. Something about it strikes me as familiar, and I try to remember where I could have seen images of the park before. I quicken my step, eager to move on.

In Rocketland, with its twisted steampunk vision of the Kennedy Space Center, we're strapped into black shiny seats, launched upwards into the air through a dark metal tunnel so fast I shriek, gripping on to William's hand so hard that afterwards he shows me the line of red half-moons my fingertips make on his palm. Later, we eat hot, buttered corn on the cob from a wooden cart, even though it's nowhere near lunchtime, and William gives me a corn-ear smile, pressing the cob against his lips and tilting his face this way and that.

'Having fun?'

I reach up on tiptoes, give him a buttery kiss on the cheek. But then a vision of myself enters my head like a picture taken in aerial, and I imagine Mamma's face if she saw me, eating from a cart, licking melted butter off the sides of my hand as it drips over the paper napkins. I excuse myself, find a restroom and twist the taps on full, washing my hands two, three times until the smell of animal fat no longer lingers. When I rejoin William, he throws a lazy arm over my shoulder but I pull away. The thought of Mamma has unnerved me.

We stop for lunch, eat vast burgers and salty fries, drink vats of green Slush Puppies that course sugar through my veins. And then, finally, we reach the part I've been secretly the most excited about: Mars Central.

Despite Mamma's attempts to stop me going to the park, and her refusal to let me watch 'that trash' on television, she couldn't quite block out the existence of Astroland in my life. Over the years, be it snatched flickers between stations on Mamma's heavily manned television set, or stolen glances at my classmates' books, I managed to piece the stories together enough to get a sense of it all. Princess Bianca was always my favourite. I used to hang on to every word, carving out a picture in my mind of her gleaming castle in Mars Central, suspended above the ground by a blanket of fluffy blue clouds. The picture was so clear to me that when I first spotted the peak of turrets at the park entrance, it was as if I'd seen them before.

Around us, people eat vast mountains of blue cotton candy. It perfumes the air with its sugary smell. William finds my hand, gives it a squeeze. I let him. Seeing it all, it's as if every secret glimpse I've had has collided together into a technicolour reality: bigger and better than I could possibly imagine.

And yet. The more I look at it, the more something scratches around the corners of my mind; an unsettling half thought, like it's been softened over time, an oyster forming a pearl around a grain of sand. Was my childhood imagination really so strong that I could make the park come alive without seeing it in the flesh? The closer we get to the castle, the more a sense of anxiety washes over me.

'Come on, Anna, let's jump on the carousel!'

Part of me wants to resist, to pull away from him and flee, but William guides me carefully around the back of the castle, to what he promises is 'the best ride of all'. A giant green carousel looms into view, teeming with silver horses, made magical with illuminated neon hooves and reins. As the carousel whirls round, the horses bob up and down on their poles, as if they're racing each other on this never-ending loop. The colours spin together: pink and silver and yellow and silver and orange and silver, until they all blend together in a fantastical swirl.

As the horses dance in front of me, the scratch in my mind becomes a grip, tightening around every fibre of every muscle in my body. I stop in my path as the sickening spin of colours intensifies. Nausea hits me: I shouldn't have had all that food – perhaps I've eaten too much sugar?

But then I hear a voice in my head, and I know instantly it's the one from my unsettling dreams. It's calling me. That name. The one that clings to me with icy fingers, a little ghost child that won't let go. Only here the voice becomes alive and I feel as though I can see glimmers of a person attached to it; but who is it?

The dreams and my reality interlace as scenes play out as if in front of me, every whirl of neon bringing them more sharply into focus.

Where are you? The voice becomes more urgent, but as it does, it fades into the distance.

'William,' my weak voice calls through the passage of time, and I clutch the air until I feel his hands on me. My whole body has come out in a sweat, but I am freezing cold.

'Anna? What is it? You've gone white.' William draws his arms around me, and I feel myself sinking into him, giving way. We stumble over towards a bench and sit down. He takes my shoulders in his hands and stares desperately into my face, but I can't speak, I don't know how to answer.

And as blackness plays around the corners of my vision, I say the words that sound so unbelievable, so beyond reality, that even in the depths of this horror I know I sound crazy. 'William,' I swallow as the blackness takes over, 'I've been here before.'

ROSIE

4

The car arrives at 4.30 a.m. Dad tried to tell them we could drive ourselves, but *no, no,* they insisted, it was the least they could do. The interview is an exclusive, which does wonders for the expense accounts.

It's always this early, for morning TV. In the many interactions I've had with it over the years, I've got my routine down to a fine art. I decide on all my clothes the night before, down to my knickers and socks, and have them waiting for me on my desk chair. I set my alarm for four twenty, race to the bathroom before Rob gets a chance, and am ready at the front door by the time the doorbell rings.

It's a black Ford, with sliding doors and the acrid sweetness of fake cherry air freshener that emanates from two dangling red baubles on the rear-view mirror. The driver either doesn't know who we are or doesn't care. He mutters 'Good morning' and turns up LBC as we wind through Liverpool Road and the backstreets of Canonbury. Mum grimaces, prepared to hear our names; hers. Dad asks him to turn it off; not angrily, but with an authority that makes the driver's hand flick instantly to the volume control. Rob falls asleep in the front seat, his hoody pulled tight around his face.

I do my make-up in the car, balancing my compact on my knee as I rim my eyes in black.

'I don't know how you can do that.' Mum, next to me, rests her head on Dad's shoulder and closes her eyes. She won't have slept last night: I'd know that instinctively, even if I hadn't heard the creak of her footsteps on the landing below me. 'I'd get it all over my face.'

'Practice,' I shrug, not looking at her.

I don't know what I expected from dinner last night – the dinner Mum had so insisted upon, to mark the night before the Official Anniversary. I don't know why I thought they would have told us about the email, about the state of the trust, when they have always been so parsimonious with the information they give us. Instead, they shared stories of her. Stories that seem to grow stronger and more fixed each year, as they pass from reality into rote.

And the more obvious it became that they weren't going to reveal their secret, the more I felt the little stone of hardness grow inside me, the one that stops up the other, more frightening feelings that I have long ago learned to lock away.

I know she's not doing it on purpose, but I can't help the knot of anger I feel for Mum. I don't like secrets. Not when I already live my life under the shadow of one. Not after the last time.

Dad is nervously upbeat, talking in a jittery voice about anything he can think of. Anything but the reason we're in the car. Rob rouses himself long enough to ask, in a disgruntled tone, how long the filming will last, and Dad instantly pales, remaining silent for the rest of the journey.

The building is grey; a sixties hangover in some non-descript part of White City. It is bustling by the time we arrive, and I find myself wondering if people just develop a new routine for getting up this early, or if they're always disguising their tiredness with good concealer and lots of coffee. The lighting is fake; too white, illuminating the scurrying workers that edge their way past us and pull lanyards from their necks to swipe through the entrance gates.

At the reception desk, a woman with shiny red hair holds a turquoise fingertip up at us as she gabbles into a telephone headset. Eventually the finger comes down and she gives us a smile. 'How can I help?' Behind the desk, a woman's magazine is open on a double-page feature about some actress from a soap. I wonder what it's like to actively want to have your face known to the world. Everyone always seems so hungry for fame; they don't know how much I would swap it all in an instant to be anonymous.

As we sign in we are presented with plastic visitors' badges with metal clips at the top; Rob immediately starts fiddling with his. I stick mine in my pocket, where the laminated edge digs into my upper thigh. *Rosie Archer. Sister.* That about sums me up.

We wait on a collection of fuzzy black chairs positioned around a coffee table. The room smells of disinfectant and instant coffee. Mum flips through a magazine in front of her, but she can't disguise the tremble in her fingers as she reaches for a leaf of paper, and I can't help but think, what is the point of hashing it out again, of putting ourselves through it? What do we think will come up after so long, after so many years of nothing?

Eventually, a producer comes to greet us. 'Hi, hi.' Her voice wavers between cheery and professional, as if she's unsure of quite what tone to adopt. 'Thank you so much for being with us today.'

Dad goes through the motions of introducing everyone, even though it's entirely obvious who we all are. His voice is quieter now, more tentative, all that jitteriness washed away by the reality of actually being here, almost a year since the last time. It used to be more often, but after a certain amount of time there's only so much you can say. But this is special. The Anniversary. Our last hope, maybe, for people to be interested in us, for someone to remember something, *anything*, that could give us a lead.

She takes us upstairs and into a waiting room, asks if we want anything to eat or drink. I mindlessly tear apart a blueberry muffin, knowing that if my hands don't have something to do I'll be inclined to tear at myself. Dig my thumb into the bruise on my knee, perhaps, enjoying feeling out the edges of the injury; chew at the hangnail I know is loose on my right thumb, right down to the nailbed, until I make it bleed. Mum sits beside me, strokes my hair, smothering me with all the excess love she has, enough for three of us, not two. I want to pull away, still keen to punish her, but I can't help feeling soothed. I see her eye the muffin crumbs, and I know she knows why I'm doing it.

We wait in silence until a runner comes to collect us, rousing Rob awake from where he's curled up on a grey felt sofa, and following her out. She guides us through the corridors, a blonde ponytail bobbing at her back, to the studio where Gail Peters, the presenter, is already in position under the lights. She's wearing a white short-sleeved dress with fat, yellow daisies on it that shows off her cleavage in a way that blurs the line between provocative and morning-TV-appropriate, and a lipstick smile the same colour as the air freshener in the car that brought us. When she sees us, her smile opens up to showcase straight white teeth with her signature front-tooth gap, and she gives us a wave. She's interviewed us before; we're practically mates.

A team of crew members stop us in the sidelines and loop mic packs through our clothes. The black mic pack is heavy on the back of my jeans, the metal clip cool against my skin.

One of them holds the wire up towards me, but I take it from him. 'That's OK, I'll do it myself,' I mutter, threading the mic through my shirt and clipping it against one of my buttonholes. I don't like people I don't know touching me.

The wire is loose and traces my torso, reminding me of my presence here with every movement I make.

They guide us onto the set and into position: Dad, Mum, me, Rob. Gail smiles at us with professional sympathy. 'It's good to see you all today – I'm so glad you could join us.' Her teeth gleam against the studio lights.

Dad reaches across for Mum's hand, takes it in his lap. It looks limp and frail against the grey pinstripe of his suit. I know the statistics: most couples, when something major like this happens, divorce within a year. The pressure; the media attention. It's seen as a testament to their marriage that they are still so strong together, that they went on to have Rob and that, so far at least, I'm not a major fuck-up, bar a light dependency on picking at myself. I wonder if that's part of the reason we're such a continued source of interest; if people are just watching, waiting, for one or all of us to fall apart.

Gail pours water from a bulbous glass jug on the table in front of us. It has roundels of cucumber floating in it. She gestures to the collection of glasses. 'Please, help yourselves.' She beams at us, and I see the make-up crinkle at the corners of her eyes. Does she know about the state of the trust? Will she use it, like a bullet point to check off, to make the pitiful Archers even more pathetic?

The water tastes disinfected, like the smell of the waiting room, but it's cold, and it seems like the polite response to drink it.

'I promise this is going to be nice and easy. You guys just take your time.' As Gail says this, I feel the familiar compression in my throat, and know it's almost time to go on air. She's prepping us; using that well-worn media training to situate us without directly alerting us to the exterior world of the set.

She fixes her gaze in the distance and I hear the muffled counting of the producer. 'In five, four, three, two ...' Her gap-toothed, lipsticked smile hits the centre of the camera, and it's on; we're ready to begin; it's showtime.

'Before the break, we touched on a very important occasion: the fifteen-year anniversary of the Emily Archer case. Here in the studio today we are privileged to be joined by her family, Susanne and David Archer, and their children, Rosie, who was just one year old at the time of the incident, and Rob, who was born several years later. Sue, David, kids, thank you so much for joining us today. Now, tell us: what's going through your minds today, fifteen years on?'

Here goes. My sister Emily disappeared when I was a baby. Snatched from a ride at an American theme park, and never seen or heard of again. We say 'disappeared' as if it truly means something. Like one day she was a living, human creature, and the next day – *poof!* – she had vanished into thin air, a plot out of a science fiction movie.

In a way, I suppose 'disappeared' is apt: we don't truly know what has happened to her. We know the logistics, yes: they've been trotted out a million times in the papers, in blatant, formulaic detail that never really comprehends what it was like to go through it all; but there comes a point where our knowledge jumps off a cliff, leaving not even the tiniest sliver of a trail for us to follow.

There was never any body. No leads strong enough to follow. No succinct form of conclusion that would help my parents mourn her, or put searching for her to rest.

Instead we've been holding a rolling funeral for her for the past fifteen years.

I know that sounds harsh. I've been told over the years by various professionals that my 'apathetic attitude can come across as bitter'. That I indulge myself in behaviour that can be considered self-destructive. That particular chestnut after Mum first noticed my habit of pinching the skin on my upper arm so hard it left marks.

It's very difficult to feel anything for a sister you barely even met, except for a vague sense that if she hadn't gone … wherever it is she went … your life would be different. It's painful, but it's a fuzzy pain – the sort you get when you sleep in a funny position and wake up with a dead arm.

Instead, I live my life under the gaze of the Ultimate Older Sister, preserved for ever in perfection. There are pictures of her all over the house. Fewer than there used to be, but they're there. Her second birthday party, in an oversized, puff-sleeved dress they were probably hoping she would grow into, but never did. One of those classic professional baby photos taken in the back of a pharmacy, with the mottled grey background trying so hard to be velvet. And there's the one they used all over the media. Taken the same day she went missing: our first day at the park. We'd been down in the Keys for a wedding – some old university friend of Dad's (which is the only reason, Mum says when defending herself, she was mad enough to take a baby and a toddler on an eight-hour flight) – and had decided to round off the trip with a few days at Astroland, because it was so new, so shiny, so hyped up as one of the most innovative experiences the world had ever seen. So off we went.

Pink T-shirt. Gap-toothed grin. As familiar in our living room as it is on TV sets and in newspapers around the country.

Around the world.

She can do no wrong, whilst I am always trying to play catch-up.

Sometimes I manage to convince myself I have a memory of her, but the line is blurry as to whether it really is one, or if it is just me having looked at a picture of her so hard that I imagine it's true. I googled it: it's called a 'false memory'. *A false memory is a psychological phenomenon whereby a person recalls something that did not, in reality, occur.*

Rob wasn't even born then – he has no memories of her. But for me, it's like having a faint whisper of a sister, like the strands of translucent egg white in the chicken and sweetcorn soup at our local Chinese restaurant: definite, but indefinable.

Mum gets so frustrated if we don't remember something about Emily. As though we're doing it deliberately, as though we're doing our best to forget. 'You *must* remember the Christmas at Granny and Grandpa's, when Grandpa wore the Santa suit and Emily screamed the house down. You *must*.' I can hear the edge in her voice when she says stuff like this, and I know that a tiny part of her would like to shake the memory into us, but then Dad will place a hand on her wrist, and tell her that *he* remembers, and she'll become quiet, and apologise.

She cuts out each little memory of Emily and sticks them in a mental scrapbook, but to me and Rob they're only photocopies.

In the interview, they're showing the one image that is definitely not up anywhere; the one I hate seeing the most. A mock-up of Emily as she would look today. I've always been surprised, when they've shown this in the past, that we don't look more similar. Her hair is bobbed to her chin, like it was when she was a child, and very blonde, almost white. I can't discern any of my features in her nose, her mouth, her chin. Dad said, the one time I asked him about it, that it's because I look more like him, and she looks more like Mum. I accept that, but I can also imagine that as the gap widens and the years roll on, it gets harder and harder to morph a three-year-old's photo into someone who is now very nearly an adult.

She's there now, my sister: twenty-two inches high on the monitors in front of us, her missing front teeth filled in with an even, digitised white smile.

Gail has her head cocked to the left, with a lilting nod, her expertly tweezed eyebrows knitted together. She's using the proper interview voice now, not the one she speaks to the camera with. That one's clipped, and strong, and low, coming in after the chime of the clock, announcing the time: 'Good Mor. Ning. Britain. Today's. Top. Stories are.' This is more melodic, and softer, like a choreographed dance. 'Suuusanne. Daaayvid. I realise this must be increeedibly hard for you. Tell me your thoughts.'

Through the camera lens, I feel the eyes of thousands of households blinking back at us.

When the interview concludes, we're led out of the studio through a path of saccharine, sympathetic looks from the crew. Mum is shaky, but has managed not to cry. Dad's jaw is set, and he's winding his gold wedding ring around and around with the tip of his thumb. Rob ... is Rob, impervious as usual.

How do I look, to everyone else?

In the waiting room, we're unlaced from the mic packs, and I ask who mine will be leased to next.

'Sorry?' The runner pauses winding the wires around the packs to gawp up at me.

'Maybe a celebrity chef, or the presenter from that dance show everyone loves?' I'm trying to fill in the conversation, to close off the opportunity for him to ask the questions I don't want to answer. *What's it like? Do you remember her? What do you think happened?*

'Oh ...' His face scrunches up. 'I don't know.' He continues his methodical winding, and I wonder if he'll take this titbit home with him: *I met the Archer sister today; she was really weird. But then, I suppose something like that will make you a bit odd.*

But I'd rather he thinks I am odd than pitiful.

In the car, Dad's hands massage Mum's shoulders, and I see her blinking back the tears she has finally allowed to fall. 'I think that went really well?' There's an upward inflection in his voice; tentative, thoughtful.

She screws her mouth from side to side, a gesture I have come to recognise over the years as her trying to overcome her emotions, and bobs her head in the briefest of nods.

'It'll be on the website, YouTube. Imagine the amount of people who'll have seen it. I'm convinced, darling. This is it, I'm telling you. Someone will remember something. Someone will come forward. It's our chance. It's—'

'*David, shut up.*' Mum aspirates like hands pressing on a punctured tyre. And then she palms her eyes, pushing her head back against the headrest. 'I'm sorry. I didn't mean to snap. I'm just exhausted.'

I don't want to deal with this. I don't want to be trapped in this metal box with my parents' pain raw as a picked scab. I want to scream at them both, *Why didn't you say anything? Why didn't you beg? If you're going to do nothing about the trust, why don't you just tell the truth about it to the one daughter you have left?*

I flick on my phone, and with relief see a message from Keira flash up on the screen. *How did it go?*

OK, I type back, grateful for the easy distraction.

You looked really pretty.

I can't help letting a smile creep in. She's learned, over the years, how to edge her way around me; to show me she cares without prying. To show that the door of conversation is open, should I wish to enter. Which I never do.

I search for the picture of the girl flicking her hand to the side, press send, as if the act of pretending will somehow make my confidence real.

The car is thick with my parents' hurt. I can taste it, stale on my tongue. I have an urge to scratch, to pick at my skin; work that hangnail until it peels back in painful relief. But I know even that won't help. Nothing I can do to myself will be enough of a release from today.

I wait; I wait for them to say something. To mention the email. To say how the TV appearance will make something happen, make it all OK.

But no one says a word.

So I fish out my headphones, turn my music all the way up, and tune out our life for the rest of the drive home.

ANNA

5

On the drive home I am silent, trying to make sense of the jumbled jigsaw pieces of my day.

William doesn't ask many questions, but then what could I possibly say that would make sense? I tried to explain in the park: I remember it; I remember being there, that ride, so palpably. But if I've never been there, how can that be?

He listened, told me gently that there must be an explanation, and then, somehow, I let him lead me to the exit, back to the shuttle, whose silver shell and gurning driver now seemed a grotesque parody.

I know the whole thing sounds fantastical, unbelievable. But the more I poke and prod at the recesses of my mind, the more I feel as if, all these years, some tiny part of myself has been urging me to recall this forgotten memory.

Fragments of thoughts have slipped through my fingers before I could grasp hold of them. But now the park has made them stay.

William stretches his arm across to the passenger seat, rests a hand on my knee. But his thoughts have already moved on, focused on the reality ahead of us. 'We're nearly home now. We'll be back in time for dinner, don't worry. She'll never know.' He has practicality written all over him. He's a man built of facts and pragmatism, not feelings and recollections.

The thought of dinner sickens me. How can I sit there, making up stories about where I have and haven't been all day, as if nothing has happened?

But soon we turn down the long dirt drive, and our house, a white clapboard two-storey, austere but for Mamma's abundant gardening, looms into view. As we approach and William turns off the engine, I gaze up at it. How is it possible that it can still be standing here, unchanged, when my whole world is out of kilter?

The front door opens before we've stepped out of the car, and there's Mamma, waiting for us. I take her in, bordered by the white door frame like an old-fashioned Polaroid. The pleated navy skirt and blue checked shirt which are practically a uniform. A pair of house slippers on her feet, the same tongue-pink pair bought over and over from Walmart, as soon as the previous pair shows signs of wear. Tendrils of fair hair escaping from a fuzzy velvet headband. My mother.

I scour her face to try and read what sort of mood she is in. To try and work out what I can possibly say or ask of her that will make my muddled thoughts clearer. Does she know something that will explain it? That will make my fear go away?

'Anna, why are you gawking at me like that?'

Her voice startles me, and I flick my eyes to the ground. I feel William's hand brush ever so gently next to my own, in the guise of helping me up the porch step, giving it a light squeeze of reassurance.

'Sorry, Mamma. Just tired. How are you?'

'I think the caterpillars have been at the oleanders again. But I've finished planting the roses, and I've a pile of clothes ready to return.' Mamma takes in mending – alterations and repairs sent to her by post. It's the perfect job for her really; limiting the social interactions she would otherwise have to make. 'I hope you two had a nice time?' Her eyes flick down to my foot, poised at the threshold. 'Shoes, Anna.'

My body tightens, and I hurry to unlace my white trainers and twin them side by side in the entrance hall. We always take our shoes off before entering the house. Less chance for the dirt to follow us in. Mamma watches William quickly copy me, pursing her lips even though he's observing the rules without question. His presence is an intrusion on her carefully ordered home.

'Those shoes look very clean for a day's hiking?' Mamma inspects them, her eyes narrowing.

I hesitate, but William swoops in: 'We wore our hiking boots, Mrs Montgomery. Anna had left hers in my car from last weekend, when we went to Bolen Bluff.'

I clench, waiting for the blow of her response.

'Very well.' She nods, padding off down the hall. Her soft slippers mask the sound of her steps, so that she could creep up behind you and you wouldn't know until the last moment. 'Wash up for dinner.'

In the upstairs bathroom we run the tap, and I sink into the wicker chair beside the bath, resting my head against the cool white tiles.

'I don't understand what's going on, Will.' I hold my fingers under the tap, letting the cool water run over them, and then touch them to the pressure points on either side of my neck, before folding myself into my knees. 'I know for sure I've never been to that park. But the feeling I had was so strong.'

'Hey.' He sits on the edge of the bath beside me, and takes my shoulders between each of his palms. 'It's all going to be OK. Like I said before, I'm sure there's a simple explanation. Something you've read, or something else you're getting mixed up. It'll be nothing. We'll work it out. But it's not going to happen tonight, so, for now, come downstairs and enjoy your birthday.'

I swallow, splash cool water on my face and then scrub my hands clean, allowing William to take one in his as we make our way back down. The elements of the day whirl around me, begging me to catch hold of them, but at the same time William's right: I can't begin to make head or tail of it now. And Mamma is waiting.

She's there in the kitchen, emptying a packet of salad leaves into the cedarwood bowl we bought at a church fundraiser. She holds out her hands and without question I place mine into them. She raises my fingertips into the light and inspects each of my nails, turns my palms over and scours every line for any possible hidden indecencies. Only when she lets go do I make my way to the table.

'Time for grace.' It's a command, not a question, stretched across the tablecloth when we are all seated.

I look pointedly at William, and together we bow our heads.

I see him trying not to stare as Mamma and I clean our cutlery. A fork is poised in his hand, as if he's unsure whether to follow suit. The first time he saw me do it, at a church picnic last summer when we first started dating, I tried so hard to explain it to him: about the invisible specks, too small for the eye to see; the dirt and the dust just waiting to take root. He laughed, at first, but when he saw I was being serious he didn't question me again.

The food is dry in my mouth, sticking to the sides of my throat as I drink glass after glass of water to wash it down. A single pea seems the size of a potato. A salad leaf an entire tree. The carousel horses dance across my vision. A flash of someone's hand on mine. I turn my head, even though I know no one is there.

'You're very thirsty today, Anna.' Mamma's eyes flick to the glass in my hand.

'It was very hot today, Mamma. I think I'm a bit dehydrated, that's all.'

She raises an eyebrow. 'We'll have to keep an eye on that: thirst is one of the signs of diabetes. Have you been feeling particularly tired lately? Any blurred vision?' Mamma is suspicious of any potential disease, spending hours poring over the thick medical dictionary she keeps on the living room bookcase, punctuating our days with carefully timed vitamins. She knows the symptoms of most of the common medical diseases by rote, which is why I am hardly ever sick: she cuts any illness off at the pass.

'Nothing like that, Mamma; honest to goodness, I'm just thirsty's all.' I subtly push my glass away from me, and force myself to drink slower.

'Mrs Montgomery?' I hear the note of question in William's voice, feel the little hairs on my arms and the back of my neck quiver with the anticipation of what he's going to ask. 'Anna told me today that neither of you have ever been to Astroland.' He smiles, warm, encouraging. 'Is that really so?'

Across the table I see Mamma stiffen, shutters coming down over her face like a shop at closing time. 'Of course not, William. What a thing to ask.' She places her knife and fork in the exact centre of her plate, although her food is not yet finished. I try to catch his eye across the table. *Please, no.*

'My apologies, Mrs Montgomery. I didn't mean to be rude. I was just surprised, it being so close and all.'

'Well, we never have.' She picks up her napkin, dabbing ferociously at the corners of her mouth, at the specks of food that aren't there. 'Your father may be more lax on the subject, but our previous pastor was quite clear: all that talk of science and machinery – it's irreligious.'

'I see, Mrs Montgomery, I do. And you've never even walked inside? Not even, perhaps, when Anna was a little girl, just to see?'

Mamma stands abruptly, picks up her plate. 'You're upsetting me now, William. I've already told you, no. Neither Anna nor I have ever set foot in that godless place and we never plan to.' She stalks around the room, taking the cutlery from my hands and the plates from the table. 'Anna, I think it's time William is getting home.'

'Yes, Mamma.' I stand, not looking at either of them, wishing he'd never asked. He should know, by now, not to push. But all the same, the thought buzzes in my ear: *Why? Why that park? Why does it upset her so?*

I see him struggle, looking from her to me. 'I really am sorry, Mrs Montgomery. I didn't mean anything by it. I was just asking. I—' He sighs, bows his head. 'You're right, it's late: I should be going.'

Mamma turns her back to him. The dishes clatter into the sink as she begins to scrub. We hover, awaiting final dismissal.

At last she sighs, quoting at him without turning around, *'As the Lord freely forgave you, so you must forgive one another.'* In her own language, he is forgiven. 'Anna? See William out.'

In the porch light, William strokes the side of my face then takes my hands in his. The evening is dark, but balmy, and the humid air brings out the smell of the plants surrounding us; musky and sweet. On any other day it would be a beautiful night.

'Anna, we'll figure this out. I promise you. Come for dinner on Monday night, after school. You can tell your mom my parents have a birthday present for you. And we'll just ... try and talk it all through, one step at a time.'

'OK.' All the energy has drained out of me.

'Hey.' He lifts a hand to my chin and raises it with his fingertips so I'm looking directly into his oak-brown eyes. His other arm encircles me, pulling his body against me, his face into mine. 'One day I'm going to take care of you, Anna. Properly,' he murmurs into my hair. I feel his hot breath tickling my neck. 'Protect you. Take you away from ... from ...'

'I know, I know.' It's not the first time he's said this, over the last few months, but now more than ever I pull myself away from him, trying to calm the rising nausea that comes from any thought of leaving Mamma. I glance up at the closed door, terrified Mamma will hear. 'Will, please. Too much.'

I feel the frustration in his wilting limbs before he releases me. He is patient with me, accepting that even a simple touch is new and unfamiliar to me – not just from him but from anyone. But he is still human.

'I believe you, Will. I do.' I hold out my palm for him, inviting him to touch it back. Our gesture; the one we use when the thought of anything more is too much.

He presses his hand against mine, and now I curl my fingers over his, and kiss the knuckles lightly. See? See how far we've come?

'I love you, Anna.' He kisses me on the forehead, and then moves down off the porch step to go.

I watch him back out until the beam of his headlights disappears from the drive, and am about to turn inside when I hear a familiar metallic whine: the sound of our mailbox opening and shutting. But it's nearly nine o'clock – long after the mailman comes and goes. What could be arriving now? The hackles rise on the back of my neck. What could have been so important that it would escape the daily delivery?

I patter down the drive towards the grey tin mailbox that stands at the end of it, holding a tissue in my hand to open the flap.

A single envelope sits inside. On the uppermost corner I see my name, the letters handwritten in bold, black cursive: *Anna Montgomery*. The words curl themselves into a knot in my stomach. In all my life, I can't ever remember receiving anything addressed to me. Who would send it? Surely not Mamma in some flight of fancy – the thought of it almost makes me laugh – and not William. There is no one else.

And then I realise the package has no stamp. It must have been delivered by hand.

I scan the landscape around me, as if whoever sent it might be waiting, watching. In the distance, I spy a lone figure on the path, marked out against the moonlight by the white suit he's wearing.

'Hey!' I call to him, but he doesn't slow, or turn around. 'Excuse me?' I try, louder, even as the figure disappears around the bend in the road. I hesitate, consider running after him, but fear drives inertia into my veins and I hang back. What if he's dangerous? What does he want with me? I glance back at the house, feel Mamma's presence, even along the long stretch of drive and beyond the walls of the building. I should go to her; open it together.

And yet. There is something about the strangeness of this letter that makes me pause. Something dangerously alluring about being singled out. It's my daily task to fetch the mail for Mamma; every day the same: bills; the packages of clothes Mamma receives, to mend and return to her small but steady stream of clients; junk mail advertising car dealerships or warehouse sales. No letters from relatives, no postcards from friends abroad. Nothing, ever, for me. Until now.

I hook a finger underneath the edge of the envelope's flap, freeing the triangle of paper from its glue.

Inside, a small card; a watercolour spray of white lilies, their petals stretching to the top of the paper like they're trying to escape. My fingers find its edge. I open it up, read: *Happy birthday, Emily.*

That name.

I hear a voice calling now: *Emily? Emily? Where are you?*

I lose my grip on the envelope and it falls to the ground, spilling something that hits the gravel path with a metallic clink.

Forcing my shallow breaths to slow, I crouch down and take the object in my palm. A necklace. The thin chain drips over my fingers as I hold it out. A silver cross sits at its centre, its delicate points bowing slightly outwards. A flower is set around it – a single bloom whose petals curve around the cross, its stem twirling around the base, two silver leaves keeping it in place. A lily.

I look back at the card. No signature. No return address. No friendly clue to help me uncover its sender. A whisper of something stirs in me, its voice as soft as wind chimes in the soporific summer heat. That endless whirling, whirling. The pendant – something about it agitates my mind – where have I seen it before?

The carousel. I see it, spinning on its axis. The pendant glints in response.

Something happened in that park. Someone wants me to remember.

I should tell Mamma, but I fold the card back into the envelope and carefully slip it into my skirt pocket. Tuck the pendant in beside it.

With a final glance at the empty road, I head into the house.

ROSIE

6

We will be forced to close the trust.

There is no money left.

The words of the email whisper at me as I try to sleep off the fug of the early start. I shrug Mum away when she knocks on my door, offers me lunch. I can't sit there, with them, like nothing's happened. Why didn't they say anything in the interview? And what are they going to do to stop the trust closing before it's too late?

I feel sure nothing will come of the TV appearance now. Nothing but another chance for journalists to rake up old stories, for people to gawp at us on the streets, for someone to spray-paint 'The Parents Done It' on the wall by our house.

And then the other thought, the one I try to keep buried deep, deep down, because it makes me think of the last time this happened, and what it did to us then: what will happen to Mum, if it really does shut down?

In the afternoon, Keira messages me, asks me to go to a party. I rouse myself, agree, hoping that surrounding myself with people will drown all the other noise in my head, distract me from the urge to play with the soft skin on my abdomen, running the tips of my tweezers over it in fine cuts that'll heal by the time anyone would have reason to notice. I tell Mum we're going to the cinema, that I'm staying at Keira's. Better than having to answer twenty million questions.

She stops me anyway, as I'm on my way out of the door. 'You'll be all right, darling. After this morning? You're sure this is a good idea?'

I tighten my limbs. 'I just want to see my friends, Mum.'

She sighs. 'OK. You have your phone?'

'Yes, Mum.' I wave it in the air, training my eyes on her, searching for the hairline fractures in her perfect facade.

'And a charger?'

I nod.

'And you'll check in when you're done with the movie? And if there are any problems you'll call? I can always come and collect you – it doesn't matter what time it is.'

'I'll be fine, Mum.'

'OK.' She releases her hold on me, picks up her handbag from the hall table. Her hand emerges with a wad of notes. 'Take a cab back from the cinema. I don't want you getting the bus back in the dark.'

'Mum, it's not even that ...' I take the money, stuff it into my wallet. 'Thank you. I'll message you when it's finished.' Why bother arguing?

I meet Keira at the bus stop, and once we're settled at the back of the top deck, we begin a well-rehearsed choreography, swapping trainers for wedges, loosening shirt buttons and rimming our eyes in thick black liner.

Keira digs into her bag to reveal the neck of a bottle. She pulls it fully out, unscrews the top and hands it to me. The familiar red label shines up at me as I lift it to my lips and drink, and I inhale before the liquid reaches my throat, thinking past the acid burning my nostrils as I take a long swig. The vodka powers through me, hot, numbing.

When we get to the house the front door is open, and a group of people are clustered on the front lawn, smoking, and drinking from those thin plastic cups that always break if they're squeezed too hard. I brace myself for the whispers, the is-that-the-one's that usually follow me. Maybe this was a bad idea. Maybe I shouldn't have come.

I take the vodka from Keira's hand, take another gulp. Don't think about who I am. Don't think about the trust, or the increasingly dark circles under my mother's eyes, as each day brings us closer to the end of the month.

In the kitchen, every surface is lined with bottles and cardboard cartons of mixers. It's ultra-modern, all black granite surfaces and wide, chequerboard-pattern floor tiles. Apart from the debris on the surfaces, nothing else looks used.

'Hey, Jamie,' Keira calls out to a guy in a blue tartan shirt whose face I vaguely recognise. Jamie: I remember him now – he played Mercutio in *Romeo and Juliet*. Keira was the Nurse, bobbing around the stage in a pair of comedy boobs the drama teacher kept telling her were in no way necessary for the part.

'Hey, Keira. Great you could make it.' He kisses her on the cheek and then looks over to me.

'You remember Rosie?' she asks.

'Sure.' I can tell he's trying not to stare. The name. If he didn't recognise my face, the name would have done it. I wonder if he saw the interview. 'This is Adam, my cousin.' He jerks his head at the boy next to him, who's currently draining a bottle of beer. He salutes us with the bottle, then throws it into a well-filled black bin bag tied to the handle of the kitchen door. It lands with a clear clink.

Keira bustles past the boys, pours us each a glass of vodka and tops them up from a carton of cranberry juice.

'Here you go.' She hands me the glass of vivid liquid. Some of it splashes over the side and runs down her hand. She lifts it to her mouth and sucks up the juice, her lips puckering around the hilt of her thumb.

Jamie blinks, and I see him adjusting his stance. I know her moves have been intentional; she loves seeing what she can get away with. What would it be like to garner attention like that? Attention you've asked for.

'Catch you around, Jamie.' She grabs hold of my arm and propels me to the living room, where Rihanna is blasting out so loudly that the sound system has a deep, low fuzz to it. People are draped over the grey leather sofas or sitting cross-legged in little clusters. The room is a long rectangle, covered in edgy black-and-white photography in thick black frames: a huge eye, zoomed in so just the pupil and the hint of lashes are visible; an empty street scene, dominated by a Victorian street lamp which casts an elongated shadow on the pavement. 'Art', apparently.

A couple of wooden bowls of tortilla chips sit on the glass coffee table in the centre of the room, which I can see is already sticky from spilled drinks. Multicoloured pools of alcohol dot the surface, like melted Skittles. We each grab a handful of crisps as we spot a couple of girls from school sitting on the arm of a sofa; we head across the room to greet them.

A boy I don't recognise nudges a mate and jerks his head in my direction as we walk past.

I feel my face going hot, and stare intently into the pink liquid slopping in my glass. When we sit, I drain the cup.

Keira raises her eyebrows, but says nothing.

I enjoy the dull fug as the alcohol slips into my system. Keira was right: this is just what I need. Not to feel, not to think. The girls are talking about going on a trip, after exams are over. I don't know where to. It doesn't matter, I won't be allowed to go anyway.

How many people here watched me in their living room this morning, marvelling at my family's plight over the crunch of their morning cereal?

If they close down the trust, is that it? Are we just supposed to give everything up for good?

Some boys come over and ask if we want to have a joint outside. I shake my head: I don't like the smell, or the dizzy feeling it gives me. But the others pull themselves to their feet.

'Do you mind?' Keira looks down at me. Her voice is sincere but her eyes are hopeful, wide.

'Course not.'

On my own, I wander into the kitchen and mix myself another drink. Our vodka is already empty, but I find another one – heavy, two litres. It sloshes out too fast as I tip it over to pour. The ice is all melted by now, and there's no cranberry juice left, so I top the glass up to the rim from an open can of Coke, slurping it from the countertop until it's empty enough to lift. The thud of the party fills my ears, turning my thoughts to white noise.

'Nice tekkers.'

I turn to see Adam, one of the guys in the kitchen earlier, popping open a family-sized bag of crisps. He empties them into a bowl and they make a satisfying rustle as the smell of salt and fat sharpens the air.

'Thanks.' I raise my glass in cheers. 'Call me the gold medallist of cup diving.'

He laughs, and I take him in more carefully. I wouldn't call him good-looking, but his face is pleasant enough. He's tallish – not that it matters when I'm so short – and he has tousled, curly hair that's so dark it's almost black. He's wearing an 'I Heart NYC' T-shirt, which he notices me reading.

'It's meant to be ironic.' He pulls at the bottom, reading it upside down. 'I went with my parents at Easter. It was either that or "Make America Great Again".'

I laugh.

'Hey, I don't think we were properly introduced before.' He sticks his hand out. 'I'm Adam, Jamie's cousin.'

'Rosie.' I take his hand, which has residual crisp crumbs on it.

'I know who you are.'

'Right.'

He sizes me up, and I wait for it: the inevitable comment or question. In the silence I take a large gulp from my glass. Instead he reaches over for the vodka and a bottle of flat-looking lemonade, and pours himself a glass. 'So, cheers then.'

He raises his glass out to me and we both down our drinks. The alcohol hits me in the pit of my stomach. There wasn't that much Coke left in the can.

'Another?'

I shrug. Why not? It's not like Keira to leave me alone for so long, but she's not my babysitter. I lean against the counter, vaguely feeling a steel cupboard handle butting at the base of my spine. The vodka seems to have softened my edges but thickened my skin.

He hands me back my glass. I wait for him to speak, bracing myself again for the predictable question, but instead he says, 'So, you go to school with Keira?'

'Yes, that's right. Year Eleven. You?

'Lower Sixth.'

My phone vibrates against my hip. 'Sorry,' I mumble, pulling it out. Mum's face flashes on the screen: *Mum wants to FaceTime.*

I mash my thumb onto the screen, hitting decline, but then swiftly text her back, knowing she'll just try again if I don't. *In the cinema.*

Sorry, comes the immediate reply. *How is it?* I roll my eyes. She's one step away from checking in when I go to the loo.

Good thanks.

I start to put the phone back, but she's already sent a reply. *Everything OK?*

Yes, Mum, fine. Have to go now. Love you. I press send and stick the phone back in my jeans. 'Sorry—'

A guy with braces and a red zip-up hoodie bursts into the room and starts riffling through the fridge. 'Tequila shots!' He jiggles a yellow net bag of limes and clears a space on the counter to cut them into wedges, knocking empty beer cans and bottles aside as a group of people spill into the kitchen and crowd around him.

'What do you think?' Adam jerks his head towards them.

'Yeah, sure.' Why not?

The energy of the party seeps into me. I can do this. For tonight, I'm just one of these people: clasping a sticky lime between my thumb and forefinger, running my tongue over the patch of skin between them, pouring salt onto it and feeling the tickle of crystals as they escape down my arm. I hold the neon-green shot glass in my right hand and a wave of petrol flies up my nose.

'One, two, THREE!' someone shouts, and we raise our glasses to the ceiling, then simultaneously lick the salt off our hands and shoot. Adam gives me a lime-wedge smile, and I do the same, pulling my lips apart to expose the green skin.

I think I see him making eyes at someone over my head, then cock his head in my direction, but I brush it off.

'It's really noisy in here,' he shouts to make his point. 'Want to go somewhere quieter?' He reaches out his hand. I take it.

I feel a little unsteady as we head up the stairs. The cream stair carpet is marked with splashes of liquid, and ground-in crisp crumbs, and shoeprints. We pass a boy who fists-bumps Adam, and whispers to him, 'Is that …?'

'Yu-huh.'

I wince, even through the fog of alcohol, waiting for the conversation to contine, but the boy just raises his eyebrow and carries on down the stairs.

Still holding my hand, Adam edges along the landing past staged family photographs that get younger the further along we go, towards a white panelled door at the end. He raps softly, and when no one answers he pushes it open and switches on the light.

We're in a guest bedroom. Identical side tables with identical lamps flank the bed, made up to perfection with a turquoise towel folded neatly on the end. As Adam shuts the door, I flick on a bedside light, running my finger over the spines of the books set very deliberately next to it: *Anna Karenina, Infinite Jest, Crime and Punishment.* The spines are new, uncracked.

'This is where I normally crash when I stay here.' Adam comes up behind me and looks over my shoulder. 'And now I think you've officially had more interaction with those books than I have.' I feel his arms slip around my waist.

In some dim, forgotten corner of my mind I feel a vague sense of unease. I try to ignore it. He brushes the hair away from my neck and plants a kiss on the soft skin where my neck and shoulder meet.

'Hey.' I spin around to face him, and sit very cautiously on the bed. 'Didn't you want to talk?'

It comes out wrong, like I'm flirting; like I'm a tease. I start to feel out of my depth. But at the same time, there's something dangerously thrilling about being here with him. Somehow this is what I need to do, to block out my family, and the interviews, and the anniversary, and the email, and the thought that somehow – somehow – there is something I have to do to stop it all. Even though it seems impossible. Even though I've never tried; even though I've spent my whole life trying *not* to be a part of it, to just be like everybody else.

'Talk. Sure.' Adam's voice has an edge of huskiness in it as he parks himself down on the bed. The mattress springs give a dull squeak as they bounce to accommodate the change in weight. He strokes the skin on my forearm; leans in and pulls a strand of hair away from my face. His pupils are dilated, but I can't tell if it's because of the alcohol or because of me. He smells of tequila and crisps and too much aftershave: sharp and somehow vegetal. His lips smash against mine and instantly I feel the smooth, wet tip of his tongue nudging into my mouth. His body presses mine back onto the bed and I feel a hardness pressing against his jeans as he reaches over to click off the bedside light.

I lift my face towards him and he doesn't wait for an answer. I wonder distantly, *Is this what I want?* but I already feel his hands searching for the hem of my top, and then the tips of his fingers warm against my rib cage.

With his mouth still on mine, he guides his hands upwards and around my back. He tugs in frustration at the clasp of my bra and then laughs into me. 'Sorry, would you?'

I reach back, search for the two metal teeth, and feel the spring of release against my chest as it comes undone. He's instantly there, pushing the bra aside, kneading my flesh under his palms. I wonder if he'll notice the scratches on my stomach, if he'll say anything, but his hands have moved down now, to the silver button on my jeans, which he works open with his thumb and forefinger. I try to give in, to forget everything but this moment, but it's all there – Emily, the email, Mum, Emily, the email, Mum – and panic begins to rise inside me. Nothing I can do will make it go away.

'Wait.' I try to push his hand away, but he either doesn't want to know or doesn't hear me. His fingers are on my zip now, and I hear the metallic tear of it opening. 'Wait,' I say, louder, more insistent.

'Come on,' he murmurs, pushing harder against me. 'I want to see what it's like to fuck Emily Archer's sister.'

The sound of her name is like a shooting star, exploding me into life. *'Stop.'* Palms outstretched, I force him off me and roll onto the floor, clutching my clothes and myself into a ball by the side of the bed. Tears spring into my eyes as I slam on the bedside light, plunging us into brightness. 'Were you ever interested in me?' I ask. 'Or just my sister?'

He doesn't answer.

My breath catches in my throat as I wrench myself off the floor and stumble out of the room, down the stairs, blindly feeling my way with arms reaching out as I knock against the walls, skewing photographs and tripping over empty cups. I clamp my fists over my ears, voices fuzzing indistinctly around me.

In the open air, I push past the people spilled out onto the front drive. The street is quiet. There are a few lights on in the surrounding houses, but most are dark. All that can be heard is the indistinct *whomp* of music at my back, mingling with my own dry heaves. I force my hands against my mouth, muffling the hurt and the anger that desperately want to escape, squeezing my eyes tight shut to force the tears from them. I lash out at a lamp post, kicking it so hard stars of pain dance up my leg.

Footsteps behind me. A hand on my shoulder.

'Rosie? What's the matter? What happened?' Keira.

I open my mouth to speak, but can't stop the primal wail that escapes instead.

'Oh, Ro.' She pulls me to her. I struggle to breathe – my lungs feel like they're squeezed between two fists – and I open and close my mouth wildly, trying to force the air in. And Keira does nothing but hold me, not saying anything, not moving, as I press my face against her, tears and snot streaming from my eyes and nose and wetting her shoulder.

Eventually the shaking subsides and I start to regain control of my body, my breathing slowing to ragged huffs. Keira strokes my hair and pulls away from me, the worry scored into her clenched lips, her knotted eyebrows. 'Rosie, you have to stop doing this to yourself.'

I hang my head, feeling the alcohol and the pain fighting biliously in the pit of my stomach.

Mum. The trust. Emily. Three balls juggled in the air, and I can't catch any of them.

'I know.' A residual sob, like an aftershock, cracks in my throat. 'But what other choice do I have?'

ANNA

7

We walk to church. Lately, Mamma believes it's the only true way to arrive there. *Didn't Jesus walk, after all?* I don't point out that this has only been a recent occurrence, since her car broke down, and that surely even Jesus would have been annoyed by the lack of bus routes.

The walk lasts about an hour, but it feels longer in the heat. Even though it's early, the sun beats down on our backs and saps our energy as we stride past the fields and farms that line our trail to the United Methodist church.

I do my best to forge a path between garnering information and alerting Mamma to what I've uncovered so far. All night, I was certain that the pendant would shine its light through its hiding place beneath a loose floorboard under my chest of drawers, and expose itself alongside my other bank of treasures – the Astroland entrance ticket, the card – and I kept waking to check if it could be seen.

Once upon a time I'd never hide anything from Mamma; now my secrets, like these objects, grow numerous by the day. Half-formed thoughts and half-filled memories flicker then extinguish, like the candles on a birthday cake Mamma would think it too frivolous to have. I parse each one. The voice, *Emily? Emily?* The carousel spinning, then slowing to a stop. And then something else: a hand reaching out, a blue whirl of cotton candy. I take it. The voice fades. Someone replaces it, leans towards me, and I breathe in something that reminds me of bubble baths, and something else, something sharp and chemical, that now, at the thought of it, pulls at some indistinct recollection. And then they come closer, and I see the flash of a pendant dangling on a chain: a cross, encircled with a flower. A lily.

'Mamma ...' I tilt my face into the sunlight, try to keep my voice smooth as a bird on the breeze, 'where did we live before here?'

'Georgia, Anna.' She gives me a stern look, picks up the pace. 'You know that.'

'I know but ...' I scurry to catch up. 'Where, exactly?'

'Why are you asking this, Anna? You were barely three years old – why does it matter?'

'I just ... wanted to hear more about what it was like when I was little. Like ...' I'm teetering dangerously close to the edge now, but I can't help myself, 'where did we go to church?'

Mamma stops so abruptly I nearly slam into her, her face so close I can see the beads of moisture forming on the pale hairs on her upper lip. 'Anna Montgomery, stop this pestering. I don't want to talk about the past.'

'Sorry, Mamma.' I bow my head, and seeing this Mamma gives a small sigh.

She huffs, 'You know I just can't talk about that time – there are things that happened that I don't want to remember. That I don't even like thinking about. You don't understand – that time, that period of my life was ...' She falls silent, and I think about coaxing it out of her, even mentioning something about the pendant. But then she stiffens, speeds up again. 'Come on now, we're going to be late.'

When we arrive Mamma is puffing, and I can see the darkening patches of sweat forming like ink blots under the arms of her navy shirtwaist dress. She even accepts a glass of water from the outstretched arms of one of the church wardens, despite inspecting it before she allows the rim to touch her lips.

'It's a scorcher today, Mrs Montgomery, isn't it?' The woman, who is about her age and who I dimly recall is called Glenda, gives her a friendly nod.

'Yes, yes,' Mamma says, draining the glass and setting it back on the round wooden table. She gives her a terse nod, then walks into the main body of the church. Mamma doesn't like small talk, or the cheery congregation members she calls 'busybodies'.

I take my seat in the choir stalls, and my body feels heavy in the pew, as if at any moment I could sink off the smooth wooden seat, fall to the ground and rest my head against the floor's cool flagstones. Last night's broken sleep, and the blistering walk, are catching up with me.

The air is cold, despite the dappled light that floods the room from the stained-glass depiction of the Annunciation, and I suck it in, hoping the rush of oxygen will power me through the service. From my position in the choir stalls I look across at her, seated far enough away from the nearest congregation member that there is no chance their body will touch hers. Her hands are folded neatly in her lap, and she wears the same look she always gets in church: blue eyes imploring, dewy and wide; lips open in a silent gasp, head tipped upwards, as if her whole self is begging to receive the Holy Spirit. I've always assumed this anxiety is simply Mamma's yearning to demonstrate her faith to the Lord, but now I can't help but think there may be something else at play here. Emily, the lily cross, Astroland – could they somehow be connected?

Pastor Timothy delivers a sermon on forgiveness. His voice is deep and tuneful, commanding a powerful spell over the listening crowd. I can sometimes pick out his particular lilt above the swell of the congregation's hymns and know that's who William must get his pleasant singing voice from.

'Let us pray; and remember the Lord, in His infinite wisdom, is always open to forgiveness.'

As I bow my head, I watch Mamma fervently clasp her hands in her lap as her lips begin a silent prayer. Do I forgive Mamma, for keeping me both at arm's length and never far from her side? I'm sure any other girl would just tell her about what happened, ask if she knows what it means, but the threads of it all are still so frayed – where do I even begin?

'Amen,' Pastor Timothy concludes his prayers, and motions to the choir. We rise, and the opening strains of 'Guide Me, O Thou Great Jehovah' swell from beneath Bob Hanson's fingertips on the battered piano in the corner. As we sing, I search the wide walls to find some trace of Him; someone or something that could guide me through this. The Bible talks of the Holy Spirit working within you; of it acting or speaking to believers in their time of need. Internally, I search with careful fingers for the edges of my soul. Can I tug on it? How do I know if it's there, if it will guide me now?

My solo approaches, and I fear I won't be able to find my voice; that I'll have forgotten the words or that they'll come out a jumbled mess. I manage to force the words out across the pews; thin at first, but growing stronger as I allow the lyrics to carry me, their beautiful melody stirring my heart.

> When I tread the verge of Jordan,
> Bid my anxious fears subside;
> Death of death and hell's destruction,
> Land me safe on Canaan's side.

Songs of praises, songs of praises,
I will ever give to Thee;
I will ever give to Thee.

Mamma loves me. Even if she doesn't say it, I know. I catch her sometimes, staring into the very core of me. Whatever this is about, whatever I discover in the mess of my mind, I must remember that. Even if she sometimes makes it difficult to.

After the service, Pastor Timothy stands on the lawn, his back to the modest white church's facade as he greets the congregation. His family are gathered with him: William's mother, Hilary, in a blue frock the colour of the sky peeping through clouds; his twin sisters, like a short chain of paper dolls, identical in starched dresses, neat plaits tied with sharp white bows. William stands a few feet apart from them, embarrassed by all the attention on his family. The congregation come up one after another to shake his father's hand and glean a few words from him, commanding his attention for as long as they can.

His mother spots us, and gives me a wave of her fingers, calling us over. Mamma seems intent not to say a word to me, hasn't done since the abrupt end to our conversation, but I know she won't give up the excuse to speak to the pastor's wife.

'Anna, honey, how nice to see you. Mary, thank you for coming.' She pulls me into a hug and I try not to flinch. To Mamma she extends a hand. Hilary shows affection without even thinking about it, but even she knows how to read my mother.

I watch Mamma's visible discomfort as she accepts Hilary's hand, wondering how she'll react. She won't like the unprecedented touching of flesh, but she won't want to risk offending her; not The Wife Of The Pastor. Sure enough, as their fingers unclasp, her arm falls stiffly to her sides, her hand held away from her dress, as if she is afraid it might now be contaminated. I see her steeling herself, the stiffening of her spine as she wills herself to overlook it, and then she mumbles, almost shy, 'It was an excellent service, Mrs Sail.'

'Why, thank you!' Hilary beams at her, flashing perfectly formed teeth. 'I'm sure that Tim will be pleased to hear it.' She looks across at her husband, engrossed in a conversation with an elderly couple, each touching a patch of his upper arm, as if in doing so they are touching godliness. 'And you'll be joining us for dinner tomorrow night, Anna? Your birthday celebration. I haven't forgotten.'

Her words suck all the moisture out of the air. My body prickles cold, as if someone has blown out the sun and plunged us into winter.

I forgot to ask Mamma about dinner.

I glance over at her. The expression on her face seems placid to the casual observer, but I know well enough to see the rigidity carved into it; the smile is a little too fixed, her eyes just that bit too glassy. Hilary's expression falters, and I can see her working through what she could possibly have said wrong. Mamma's opinion is voiced in her silence. Hilary's gaze flickers to Pastor Timothy, as if she's hoping to catch his attention to relieve her from the conversation.

'Mamma, would it be all right if I have dinner with Mr and Mrs Sail tomorrow night?' I bleat, finally, the sentence stretched out in a single, desperate breath.

Mamma's voice comes out of the ether, mechanical and flat. She doesn't look at me. 'Why, yes, of course, Anna.'

I can see Hilary doesn't buy this resolution. Her mouth opens as if to say something helpful, but then she appears to change her mind, and instead gives me a weak pat on the arm. 'Great. Well, come over as soon as you can; we'll be waiting.' Then she leans across to Pastor Timothy and touches him lightly on his back. 'Tim honey, look: I think Mr and Mrs Jones want to talk to us about the fundraiser and they'll be wanting to get back.' She gives us a bright smile, mouths 'Excuse me', and then expertly manoeuvres herself and her husband away from us.

Her disappearance creates an open path between me and William. He motions as if to come towards us, but I give him a look and the subtlest shake of my head, and he backs off. *Don't make it worse than it already is.*

'Come, Mamma, let's head home.' I want to take her hand, to link an arm into hers like I've seen other girls do with their mothers. Instead I wait, and when she moves I follow.

Mamma is silent on the walk home. She huffs as she pounds her feet on the dry ground, forcing herself to keep up a racing pace as I half walk, half skip to stay beside her. When we arrive at the house she goes straight through the kitchen and then out into the backyard with her gardening tools. I hang back, wondering what course to take, before scrubbing my hands at the kitchen sink, grabbing my gloves and rubber boots from the plastic tub by the back door and joining her.

Outside, she's already bent over the geranium bush, a pair of clippers in her hand. I hear the rhythmic snip before I see her, a pile of pale pink petals surrounding her feet – their tips tinged beige as though they've been dipped in tea – expertly pruned away from the healthy heads.

You'd think, perhaps, that someone who adheres so strictly to cleanliness would have little regard for gardening. But it's as if, out here, she has complete mastery over the dirt and earth. Each petal, each frond, is bent to her will, and to her exacting perfection. It is her ultimate expression of control, and the result is breathtakingly beautiful. Compared to the relative plainness of our home, out here, at any given time of the year, the backyard erupts in a blaze of colour. As I've got older I've learned their names and forms by rote: cheery yellow swamp sunflowers and burnt orange daylilies and pop-star-pink calliandra (also known, so poetically, as 'fairy's paintbrush') were my own way of learning the colours of the rainbow, and of trying to find a way to get close to Mamma. I often tell her she should enter her flowers into competitions, or leave her job and become a professional florist. But she always says she doesn't want the attention. In fact, she is always looking to escape unwanted attention.

Mamma's fingers move deftly through the bushes like a harpist plucking strings, searching out the rotten flowers and dispensing with them with a precisely timed cut. Silently, I open up the refuse bag in my hand and move around her, cleaning up the dead heads. She doesn't acknowledge me, but neither does she turn away, so I take this as a tacit agreement that I can stay.

I often help her like this, receiving a very small allowance in return, just enough to save up for occasional treats, such as the bicycle which ferries me about now the car's bust, when I'm not required to walk. Now I hope that by performing this ritual I'll somehow dispel the ill will from earlier.

We work in silence as the afternoon moves on. My stomach rumbles. We ate breakfast before we left for church, and normally we'd grab a light lunch at home after, soup, maybe, or a salad, but Mamma doesn't mention it so neither do I. The sky knits together overhead and turns a purple-grey, and I can tell it's going to storm. I had a good idea that it would be coming: the thickness in the air needs to break, and although it's not yet hurricane season, it's not unusual to get one or two early reminders.

When the first thick droplets begin to fall, I look over at Mamma. 'Why don't I make us something to eat?'

She doesn't speak.

I pick up my sack, motion encouragingly towards the house. 'Come on, it's going to storm.'

'Anna, leave me be.' Her voice is as sour as the brightly coloured candies William loves to keep in his car.

With a sigh I hurry inside. By the time I reach the back door, the rain is falling from the greying sky in a thick sheet.

'Mamma, you can't stay out in this,' I call from the open doors. 'Please, come inside.' I see her shoulders knit together, and then slacken as she eventually rises. She stalks past me through the kitchen, pausing only to drop her gardening things into the basket. Puddles of water mark her exit upstairs, and I zealously dry them, as if her unseeing eyes will be moved by it. I do the same to my hands, driven by layers of guilt to scrub them clean under scalding water until they are satisfactorily red and raw.

Giving in to my clenching stomach, I prepare us both something to eat – ham sandwiches cut into meticulous triangles, and a fresh green salad, and glasses of milk filled just so – and sit at my place opposite her empty chair, coiled as a grass snake, my ears trained on the sound of her footsteps on the stairs. She emerges, eventually, and takes her seat.

Grace is perfunctory, but at least she speaks. Then her blue eyes fix themselves on the midpoint between our plates, where her gaze remains for the rest of the evening. The sound of chewing is the backdrop to our silent meditation.

It's when I rise to clear our plates that Mamma reaches out for the vase of tulips and, almost as if choreographed, hurls it across the room in one fluid movement.

The vase hits the oven door full on its side, and sprays across the floor in a mass of colourful petals and liquid that quickly pools along the stone tiles. The noise shatters through the silence. Mamma is poised, half sitting, half standing, with her hands resting on the tabletop and, surprisingly, a look of serenity on her face.

It happens so rapidly, so unexpectedly, it feels like I've been plunged into cold water. Fear grips at me with icy fingers, but I force myself to meet Mamma's eye.

'Go to your room.'

As my foot touches the first tread of the stairs, I hear the whispering of incantations from the kitchen. I turn back to see Mamma, seated at the kitchen table, her eyes tight shut and her hands clasped together so fervently that I know if I look closer the knuckles will be white. There is a gentle sway to her movement as she recites, in a voice that rasps like scratches on wood, 'Pure in mind, in word, thought and deed, I ask You, Lord, to pay me heed.'

It's a curious prayer; one I've heard her say many times before, but that seems to have no source in any book of psalms or hymnals I've ever come across. As soon as she gets to the end, she starts again, faster and more ardent. The rasp becomes a hiss. I go upstairs without daring to look back.

When I open the door into the darkness of my room, the light from the hallway casts a beam onto the cushion Mamma gave me, pride of place on my bed. *I prayed for this child, and the Lord answered my prayer.* The words seem to mock me now.

I pull it to me and, denying myself the luxury of a light, crawl into the corner between the dresser and the door, rocking back and forth with my cheek pressed against its rough weave, sobs moving in waves through me. Masochistically, it feels good to cry, to give myself over to the pain and confusion that have been pursuing me like some unseen gadfly.

What are you trying to tell me? I silently demand of the pendant, hiding beneath the floorboard. *Who are you?* I beg of the anonymous ink of the card, of the white-suited man who disappeared too quickly for me to register him. Why am I so meek that I didn't run after him when I had the chance? *What does it mean?* I plead with the Astroland ticket, as the rush of the whirling carousel looms again into view.

Emily.

The name shimmers at me like a silver thread, begging to be pulled on. Outside, the storm shrieks through the trees with a voracity that means it's directly overhead. I imagine it taking up my anger and confusion, shaking the branches and blowing up violent winds that rattle the windows in their frames.

Later, when the gale has lessened, leaving only the methodical trickle of rain on wet leaves, I feel calmer, more rational. William is right: there must be some reason behind all this; there must be a way to find out what it is, without upsetting Mamma.

Mamma.

I think I know at least part of the source of her anger this afternoon. She fears me slipping away, leaving her, as I edge towards adulthood. The fear grows more pronounced the older I get. Sometimes she keeps me so close I feel like I'm drowning in her. In this house. In this life. But could it be there's another, deeper reason she won't let me go?

I crawl over to the dresser, peel up the floorboard and draw out my secrets.

I take the Astroland ticket between my fingers, smooth it with my thumb. The green turrets of the castle are etched in the background, and I imagine the carousel, whirling just out of sight.

Emily? The voice gets clearer, and I can just make out the faint impression of a woman: a mass of curly hair; something – a freckle? a mole? – on her right cheek; sunglasses; a red top. But as soon as I turn my head towards her, something or someone pulls me away.

Why that name? Why now? I pick up the pendant, squeeze it tight, as if, maybe, holding it will draw something out further. I see it in my mind's eye, swaying again from a neck. But whose neck, and why, I can't say.

I replace the trinkets, edge open my bedroom door. I have no idea how long I have been in my room, but now the house is silent and dark. Down the hall, a ray of light under Mamma's bedroom door. Her presence hangs in the air like the smell of her lavender perfume. I tiptoe down the stairs, careful to avoid the third step from the bottom, the one that creaks.

The kitchen light is off, but the moon throws a pool of pallid yellow light across the floor. The dinner things have been cleared away, but the vase is still there, untouched. Splinters of glass shimmer against the white tiles, and the tulips are already crisping, turning brown at the edges. A can of corn has rolled across the floor, remains wedged against the bottom of the refrigerator. I ease across the room in the thin light, cautious of the water and broken glass, and pick up the can. It's dented but unbroken; a welt sears across the Jolly Green Giant, severing him at his jolly green neck. I place it back in the store cupboard, nestled in precision next to the others, their labels all meticulously facing outwards.

I fetch a broom from the closet in the hallway and begin to sweep.

ROSIE

8

When I dare to crack open an eye I wince. A dull and constant throb makes its way across my temples. I remember that I'm at Keira's house, and stretch for my phone to look at the time. It's nearly eleven o'clock. I rouse myself, sitting up against the wall and pulling the blanket up to reach me. As I do, my fingers brush the side of my body, and the acrid memory of Adam's hands on my rib cage rises within me. I draw the blanket around me tighter.

I hear the grind of the doorknob, and the door is butted open with the edge of a brown wicker tray. Keira sets it down on her desk by the window and nudges aside the debris of make-up and lever arch files scattered across it. A grey light takes over the room as she rolls up the blinds with a steady sweep. It's rained in the night; the window is speckled with droplets of water, and beyond it the trees shudder miserably in the wind.

'Oh, good, you're up. I brought you breakfast.'

The mattress wobbles underneath her as she sits cross-legged at the other end and hands me a glass of sparkling vitamin C, the tablet still fizzing at the bottom and turning the water a darkening shade of orange. Next come a couple of aspirin, builder's tea, and a plate with four slices of Marmite toast.

'I have to find out what happened to Emily.' The words leave my mouth before I have time to process them. They're the first I have said today, forcing themselves out through my arid mouth. Without warning, I feel my face start to crack, sobs erupting from my chest.

I ball my fists, trying to force the tears away, but through them I can see Keira looks horrified. I don't think she's ever seen me cry before, and now it's twice in twelve hours. Instantly she's crawling across the mattress and wrapping her arms around me. I breathe in the smell of butter and Marmite, and the hint of last night's vanilla-sweet perfume mingling with the last strains of weed, and something else which is just 'her': biscuity and warm and familiar. I wipe my face with the neck of my T-shirt and I open my mouth to speak but my thoughts overwhelm me again and I choke on hiccups and tears and snot.

Keira hesitates, then asks, 'Is this because of what happened with Adam?'

I inspect the corner of a nail, the white ridges of torn cuticle. 'I thought it would just stop my thinking about it. But it didn't work. It never works.' I stare down at the blanket, following its colourful swirl with the corner of my thumb. I swallow thickly. 'I found an email.'

She listens, stroking a spiral of hair by her ear, as I tell her about the email, the lack of money; the timing; how impossible it all seems, even with the anniversary, that we'll be able to keep the trust going. At last she sits back, folds her arms, sighs. 'And they haven't said anything to you?'

I shake my head.

I feel her searching my features, trying to see how carefully she should tread. 'And you're worried ... because of last time?'

Last time. The time we don't talk about. The time before, after the ten-year mark, when they all told us it was impossible. When the money in the Emily Archer Trust really did run dry, and it was only at the eleventh hour, with an anonymous cash injection from some millionaire donor, that it survived. When there were arguments and shouting and crying. And Mum became no longer my mum, but a limp rag wrung dry, not eating, not speaking, barely leaving her room, let alone the house. And Dad tried so hard but nothing he could do would fix it. And then one day when I woke up she was gone, and Auntie Sally was there in her place, all fixed smiles and why-don't-we-have-pancakes and Mummy's-gone-for-a-little-rest. And nobody would tell me where she'd gone, or when she'd be coming back. And I wanted so desperately to know.

That was the first time I hurt myself, the day Mum went away. Secreted a pair of nail scissors from Mum's sink – I was just looking for something that smelled like her – and found myself locked in their bathroom, sitting on the loo and without really meaning to tracing a barely there squiggle on the top of my thigh, enjoying the burn it produced. When Auntie Sally questioned it, seeing it peeking from my pyjama shorts, I told her I'd scratched it on a tree in Highbury Fields. I learned to be more careful over the years: certain things, like the broken knuckle, invite more trouble than they're worth; the poking and the prodding inevitable with a 'child who has experienced trauma'. I'm not trying to kill myself or anything, but God, sometimes it feels nice to have control over my own pain.

And Mum came back, after a month or so. Wore a smile every day, even though it didn't quite go as far as her eyes. And I stopped doing it, for a bit. And nothing was ever said about where she'd gone.

These are the bits no one really wants to know, when they ask what it's like. They want to hear about the TV crews, and the endless gory theories, and what it was like to meet Barack Obama. Not the bit that makes them feel truly awkward and uncomfortable. Not the bit that feels too real. Which was why I decided, after that, to stop talking about it altogether; to try to pretend it didn't exist. Because if no one wants to know the actual truth, why should I say anything about it at all?

Keira keeps her arms around me, not saying anything, giving me the space I need to collect my thoughts.

'I have to figure out what happened to her,' I say, finally. 'Before the money runs out, and everyone just forgets. I have to do something, before ...' I inhale slowly, 'before it destroys my family more than it already has.'

Keira pulls away from me, holding me at arm's length so she can read the smallest expressions on my face. 'You really want to do this? To start looking for an answer?'

I nod.

She pulls her laptop from her desk, places it on her lap as she scoots next to me and tucks her legs under the blanket. The base is warm, it heats our legs beneath the covers as she flips open the lid. The screen whirrs into life.

She moves the cursor to the URL bar, types 'TheHive' with the fingers of her right hand, and taps the enter button with a short, sharp click.

'Then this is the place to start.'

I know this site, although I've never had much reason to visit it before. It's a gossip search engine: a place where Internet sleuths and people who've watched too much true crime pore over unsolved mysteries and share rumours they think'll help solve them. I heard Dad once refer to them as 'scum of the earth', and I know he tried to ban them from mentioning Emily's case when the site first launched a few years ago. He couldn't do anything about it though. Freedom of speech and all that. But he doesn't want us trawling the Internet, seeing the crazy theories. It's not that it's forbidden – it's more of an unwritten rule.

I've seen it all, of course. Read what people have written about us in the comments section of articles. On the sidebar of shame. I can easily imagine the sort of thing that could be written. That Rob and I are overprivileged. That we're wasting taxpayers' money (even though, if they bothered to actually look into it, they'd know that any public funding dried up a year after she went missing). That Mum and Dad ought to just give up and get over themselves.

The site's acid-yellow home page loads, bearing The Hive's childish logo – a cartoon bumblebee holding a megaphone, with the words 'What's the buzz?' looping out of it in black cursive.

'Have you been on here before?' I ask Keira.

She stares down at the keys and I see a pink blush darkening her caramel cheeks.

'How often?'

'I just like to ... keep an eye on things.'

The home page lists the most popular stories, voted for by the Hivemind – the site's readers – by clicking the little bee icon at the corner of each post. Tapping on a header topic brings up a new page, under which readers can comment. Under the logo is a search bar, with the most searched for topics listed underneath.

On the right-hand side, Keira deftly flicks down the list of topics, delving further into the subtopics until she reaches a page bearing Emily's frozen-in-time grin, next to a bold yellow heading, 'Astroland of Horror'. I look up at Keira, who quickly scrolls past it. 'Ignore that. That moderator's a dick. And likes being sensationalist.'

The screen loops through a series of subtopics, each with its own dramatic heading:

Was Emily Archer the victim of a prank gone wrong?

Archer still buried in the park.

Prey of the Florida State Killer.

I look on in silent amazement at the endless theories and conspiracies, some of them with hundreds of comments attached. Keira mutters about this one or that, praising one commenter, snorting at another.

I stop her. The cursor is blinking next to 'Archer parents did it'.

I force myself to look away from that one. There was a period, I know, in the beginning, when they were treated as suspects. You can hear the disgust in Mum's voice, even now, if she ever mentions it.

'How well *do* you know all this, Keira?'

She avoids making eye contact. Her finger hovers over the trackpad as she tries to find a way to answer.

'I don't mind – I just want to know.' But I *do* mind. I know that other friends will read things and have their own opinions about what happened, but I've always thought Keira would ask.

I feel a tweak of shame in my rib cage. I'm not always the easiest person to ask. I suppose it must have been difficult, all these years, to be so close to it all and not feel she could talk about it.

'I guess … pretty well?' she finally ventures. Her index finger loops around on the pad, moving the cursor in a figure of eight on the screen. 'I first went on it about four years ago. But it's been going more like ten. I heard from someone at school that there was stuff about you guys on there. I just wanted to have a look, and make sure no one said anything bad about you, and since then I've just been … checking in. Seeing the theories, what people are saying.'

'And …' I swallow, knowing what the answer will be, 'have they been saying anything about *me*?'

She looks up at me from beneath a tangle of hair, taking my complicity to mean I've forgiven her snooping. 'Not bad stuff. There's a few pictures, now and then, of you growing up. Some commentators like discussing whether you guys look alike. There's a thread run by someone called KittyMum09 which sketched out which parts of each of you are like each parent. It was interesting, actually. I never noticed before that you have your dad's nose.'

I feel as if the thin blade of a scalpel is running over my face, parcelling each of my features into one box or another. Mum. Dad. Emily. Will there ever come a time when my family aren't specimens of public curiosity?

'OK …' I breathe out slowly, resisting the urge to gouge my fingertips into the heels of my hands. 'So, where do I go from here? Did my parents really do it?' My voice is light, jokey. I know enough to understand that there are a lot of sickos out there, people who come up with stupid theories just for kicks. But seeing it all on there, all the crazy speculations, just makes me realise how public my life is; how open to anyone's pulling apart.

Keira relaxes. She shifts her weight on the mattress, balancing the laptop on the cross of her knees, and idly scrolls down the screen. 'Obviously a load of these are bollocks. But there are a few key threads and core Hiveminders who seem to genuinely know what they're talking about.' She glances at me again, as if for reassurance. I nod, and she clicks deeper into the web, eventually bringing up a thread called 'Astroland Hank'.

The heading looms at the top of the page. Beneath it, a small circle depicts an avatar: a cartoon drawing of a woman holding a magnifying glass – the author of the thread. The cursor blinks over her name, 'MissMarple63'.

'MissMarple63 has a theory that Emily was snatched by a man named Hank Wilson, who was a worker at a nearby construction site. Witnesses say they saw Hank on the day Emily went missing, in the park.' Keira flicks through the dense jumble of words my brain can't process.

'But why would he have anything to do with Emily? What's his motive?'

She's silent.

'Keira, what?'

'Sorry, Rosie – it's weird, suddenly relating it all to you.' She sighs and gnaws at the skin around her thumb. 'Hank was convicted of raping two girls in the Florida area about ten years ago.' Keira puts a palm on my hand, squeezes it. The skin is moist where she's been chewing. 'There's nothing to link him directly to Emily, but witnesses came forward after he was convicted to mention similar incidents with him, and someone picked up on the fact that when he was on the construction site he used to spend a lot of time hanging around the park.'

My throat feels dry and scratched from last night's vomiting. I swallow. 'I see. And what happened to the girls?'

It's the question she must have been waiting for, and one I had to ask. 'They're both still alive.'

I blink. 'So, OK then.'

'That's why the police dismissed it as a lead. They said it didn't connect up, and obviously when they spoke to Hank it was years after Emily's case, and they couldn't find anything to pin it on him.'

She pulls up something MissMarple63 has posted, a black-and-white photocopy of a newspaper article. In the centre is a picture of a man I assume to be Hank. He's heavyset; you can tell by his jowls, and the width of his shoulders beneath his creased cotton T-shirt. His hair is fair, and thinning on top, forming two inlets of bare skin either side of his temples. He has a goatee, bristly and clipped short, and creases around his mouth that place him in about his mid forties. I search his eyes, trying to find some definite sign of misdemeanour. He looks like a creep, but did he harm my sister?

'Show me another.'

Keira sighs, but turns back to the screen. 'This one's a bit out there, but you have to bear with me.' She pulls up an image of the infamous carousel, the one Emily was said to have disappeared from. Above it are the words 'No Death in Dreamland'.

'Ouch.'

Keira shrugs. 'I warned you.' She touches a finger to the screen, where the name Astro7402 occurs again and again, popping up in speech bubbles in dispute with other commentators. 'This person had a theory that something went wrong on the ride, and an Astroland employee got rid of the evidence before anyone noticed.'

I blink at the words on the screen, trying to make sense of the blocks of text. 'What on earth are you talking about?'

'Astroland was brand new,' Keira explains. 'When you guys visited, it had only been open a few months, and there had already been several reports of glitches with the rides.' She scrolls through the messages and comments, pausing to pick up subheadings:

5 witnesses come forward to claim major injuries.

Park forced to delay opening by 3 months due to issues with rides.

Leaked employee handbook claims "No deaths allowed in Astroland".

'So you're saying something injured my sister on the ride, and nobody noticed? And then, what, they just … smuggled her away?'

'I'm not saying anything, Rosie.' Her voice is suddenly sharp. 'I'm just showing you the theories that have got the most traction here.'

I hold my hands up in submission. 'Sorry, sorry. Carry on.'

'Apparently there were problems with the rides; several malfunctions and a number of employees injured. In the leaked handbook, there's a statement from the park owners saying that employees must stay alert to injuries at all times, and that in the event of an incident, guests must be removed from the park as quickly and as quietly as possible, to avoid there being a death on Astroland property.'

Photocopies of the leaked document appear on the screen. The offending lines are highlighted in red pen by an unseen hand. Next to them, Astro7402 has typed, *Time from carousel to exit: 2 minutes, 34 seconds, slower when considering the additional weight of carrying a three-year-old child.*

I feel like I've been drawn into some terrible made-for-TV movie. 'Keira, this sounds ridiculous. Do people really believe this?'

'Dude, you should see some of the other theories.' She hits the back button, and scrolls through the list of main articles. 'Serial killers, witches, aliens. It's got it all. Astro7402's got sound evidence and a strong case. Plus, Astroland tried to get the thread shut down, threatening a libel suit, which is why they haven't posted anything in five years.'

She goes back to the page, and pulls up the last entry on it, typed in pillarbox red by a moderator.

We at TheHive attempt to maintain integrity and freedom of speech at all times. However, due to circumstances beyond our control, we are unable to permit the continuing population of this Hive thread. To review TheHive's Thread Posting Guidelines, please click HERE.

Keira gestures at the screen. 'It just sounds dodgy – that Astroland would lawyer up and stop people discussing it, and yet the park's never been shut down, or investigated seriously. They got a rap on the knuckles for the handbook, and that was it.'

She can tell by my raised eyebrow I'm not buying it. I reach out for my mug of tea, which now has that grey tinge to it that means it's stone cold. I swirl it around into a mini tornado, then drink the remnants down in one gulp. I scrabble to the end of the mattress and rest against the wall, cool where it touches my head. I feel like a soft toy, stuffed full to bursting with cotton-wool thoughts.

'One more, Kiki. Show me one more and then let's stop. It's too much.' My head is truly pounding now; my eyes feel as though all the moisture has been sucked out of them. The combination of the crying and the stories and last night's excesses have left me red raw.

Keira reaches an arm around my shoulder and pulls me in close. How many times have we sat like this, on the air mattress on a Sunday morning, with her laptop across us, watching silly YouTube clips or not-so-legally streaming movies? It seems so normal, and yet, so not.

'One more,' she agrees, clicking a final link.

This page is different from the others. I notice it right away. There are no shouty block capitals amidst the text, demanding attention and answers; no reams of images; no newspaper photocopies. Instead, there's just a single, grainy image, looking as if it's from CCTV, with a red arrow drawn over it by hand, pointing to a blurred-out figure. The heading reads 'The Woman in the Navy Dress', the author's name a simple 'MikeD'.

Keira scrolls down, but the page is blank. Her mouth folds into a frown. 'That's funny.' She refreshes the page, taps at the keys. 'I haven't looked at this one for a while – it didn't really get updated that often – but it definitely had stuff on it about a few years ago.' She hits the back button. 'The site must be down. Anyway, this Mike guy says that there were reports of a woman in a navy dress that could have been connected, but that no one ever followed it up.' She tries again. The page remains blank. 'Sorry, Ro – I really thought that was a good one.'

I push back onto the pillows and groan deeply.

Keira's face looms over mine. 'What are you thinking?'

'That it's just so pointless.' I run my hands over my face and through my hair, trying to make sense of it all. Images of the park cram into my mind, and at the centre of them is that stupid carousel, endlessly turning, one minute bearing my sister, the next not. In each revolution, I see a different scenario: snatched by some horrible man; the looming figure of a Astroland staff member; and now this, the random shadow of a woman with nothing more than the fleeting suspicion that she may or may not have been seen with a child. 'This is the first chance I've had to find someone who might have worked out what happened to her, and it's a mess.' I nod towards the laptop, which Keira's now shoved onto her bed. 'This last woman; I mean, I'm not surprised no one followed it up. You could make similar statements about hundreds of people who were there that day. What makes her so special? Why would she have anything to do with it?'

'This is just the surface, Rosie.' Keira lies back next to me so our heads are twinned on the pillow, her hazelnut curls tangled with my own oatmeal strands. 'If you want to know more you need to go one stage further: you need to meet them.'

'Meet them?' I echo, eyeing the laptop screen, thinking about the endless anonymous voices who have poked and prodded at my family's history. 'How will we even find them?'

'Come on, Rosie.' I hear a whisper of adventure in her voice as she reaches up to her bed and grabs the laptop again. 'This from the girl who managed to work out from Instagram that Miss Jenkins is seeing the new history teacher?'

Her fingers scuttle across the keyboard, and then she presents the laptop back to me.

There is an icon in the left-hand corner of the screen, the outline of a head and shoulders with the words 'new user' next to it. Under that, a name: 'ROAR2001'.

'Your user profile is complete.'

I wrinkle my nose. 'Why "roar"?'

'*Rosie!*' Keira smacks her face. 'RO-sie AR-cher. Come on – I was so pleased with that.'

'OK, so now what?'

'Now we can contact them. On the site.'

My chest tightens. I think of my parents' disdain for all the amateur detectives out there; their brushes with the obsessive theorists who have appealed to them over the years, convinced they've found the answer. 'What if they're all lunatics?'

'We'll steer clear of the lunatics.'

'What if we can't find them?' I ask.

'We *will* find them, Rosie,' says Keira.

'What if they don't want to talk?'

'We—'

A knock at the door interrupts whatever pithy answer Keira has to offer, and Keira's mum Caro pokes her angular face in, a paisley silk scarf tied around her head. 'What are you girls doing lazing around in here, eh?' she asks in her brusque South African accent.

Keira snaps the laptop shut and performs a deliberately casual stretch. 'Nothing, just playing on the Internet.'

Caro pushes the door open fully and stands with her hands on her hips. 'Well, enough already – get some air in here. This whole room smells of alcohol and weed.'

We spring from the air mattress, but Caro's grinning. 'I thought that would make you get a move on.' She comes over and kisses me on the cheek. 'Don't worry, Rosie, my lips are sealed.' She zips her thumb and index finger across her mouth.

For the first time – perhaps ever – I am desperate to talk about Emily, but we don't get a moment alone for the rest of the day. We sit side by side at the big pine kitchen table, working on our last biology project before exams, as Keira's dad Tom potters around us making Sunday lunch. He asks me if I'd like to stay, and I text Mum quickly.

Of course, darling, comes the speedy reply. *What time will you be home? Call if you need a lift.* If I can't be at home, the safest place Mum can think of me being is with Tom and Caro.

We eat beef and roast potatoes and the fluffy Yorkshire puddings that Tom always says are his speciality, even with the box of Aunt Bessie mix in full view on the counter.

I observe them, this tight-knit family of three – Caro smacking a kiss on Tom's cheek as she sits down beside him, or Tom squeezing Keira's shoulders as he gets up to steal another potato from the bowl beside her – and think, *This is what normal looks like.*

Tom drops me home in the afternoon – me in the front, Keira in the back. And when he double-parks the car in the road, Keira jumps out and gives me a hug goodbye. As she grabs me, she presses a piece of paper into my hand, its hard edge grazing the inside of my palm. Then she jumps into the passenger seat, her hand on the door handle. Just before she shuts it, her mouth forms the words, 'We'll find them.'

As the car pulls away, I look into my palm. Three names are written on the ripped-out piece of notepaper, the black ink scrawling through the feint-rules. 'MissMarple63. Astro-7402. MikeD.' I stare at it for a second, then fold it tightly and tuck it in my jeans pocket.

And then they're gone, and it's just me and the piece of paper and the empty road.

I turn and walk towards the house.

ANNA

9

Mamma's face twitches into a smile when I come down for breakfast; she asks me if I want some cantaloupe melon with my cereal. A fresh bunch of flowers sits on the kitchen table. The weather outside has cleared, and so, it seems, has Mamma's frost. It's as if Sunday never happened.

I want to ask her something – anything that could give me some clarity. I glance up at the picture of my parents' wedding day, and a thought niggles at me. I search for a way to form the words, fearful of upsetting the careful balance of Mamma's mood.

Eventually, as I am holding my cereal bowl in the sink, washing it two, three times until no trace of breakfast remains, I turn to Mamma and force the words out: 'Mamma, are there any pictures of me as a baby?'

I flinch in anticipation. She pauses, dishcloth in hand, and I swear she turns a shade paler. But then in an instant it's gone: the corners of her mouth twitch tight and she straightens herself up.

'Anna, you know this: all the baby pictures got lost during Hurricane Wilma; they were in the garage and got soaked.'

I have vague recollections of this storm; one of only a few to have hit Alachua County before Hurricane Irma last year. I remember reports on the news about a zoo in Palm Beach that had to move all their small animals and birds into restaurants and restrooms to keep them safe, and thinking it was cute that the animals were getting a taste of what it was like to be a guest there. I remember too, because we had no relatives and nowhere else to go, that we went to a hurricane shelter with bags of saltines and our comforters, and I played cards with some of the other kids and thought that must be what it was like to go on camp. Mamma snatched me away from them; told me I didn't know what diseases they may have, and burned the comforters and all our clothes in the backyard once we were out.

I don't remember the photographs.

In class, Ms Abrams, the wiry, red-headed English teacher, lectures us on the role of the word 'matter' in *Othello*. I sit in my usual seat in the farthest corner of the class, speaking only when I'm asked a question and praying we won't be asked to work in pairs.

I try my hardest to contemplate Desdemona, quivering in the face of her husband's wrath, but my mind keeps wandering back to the photographs. Did I ever see them? Could they really all have been destroyed? My right hand mindlessly begins sketching the wedding portrait of my parents, as if each scratch of my pen can unlock a clue.

And that's when I see it.

My fingers slacken. I lose the grip on my pen and it falls from me, landing on the floor with a clatter that makes the rest of the class look up and me to redden in shame, before the horror of what I've realised overrides all other emotion.

That photograph. Perhaps the only one of Mamma I've ever seen.

Around her neck. She's wearing a lily cross.

Ms Abrams catches me, gives me a funny look. 'Is everything all right, Anna?'

'May I ... could I please go to the bathroom?'

The wave of nausea washes over me like a visceral thing and I don't wait for permission to go.

Just in time, I duck into the restroom, where the content of my breakfast upends itself into the nearest toilet bowl.

'Hope someone's not pregnant.' I hear a giggle from outside the stall, and freeze.

Whoever it is makes no sound as if to leave, so I reluctantly edge out to find two girls I don't recognise leaning against the sinks. They burst into laughter when they see me come out, hiding their faces in mock shame. They have the window open a crack and they are passing a cigarette between them. I head straight for a sink, eyes down, and splash cool water on my face, lifting handfuls to my mouth to wash away the taste of bile.

'Sorry, we'd offer you one, but smoking's bad for the baby!' one of them snickers as I reach for the door.

I race back into the corridor, head down, just as the bell rings.

'Anna!' Ms Abrams stops me before I walk straight into her. 'Is everything all right? I was worried.'

I shuffle my feet, trying to imagine how I can possibly summarise how not-all-right everything is. I can barely feel my mouth to speak. 'Yes, Ms Abrams,' I choke out. 'It must have been something I ate.'

She cocks her head to the side but doesn't dismiss me, which makes me blush and turn my eyes back to the floor.

Ms Abrams is so young she must have only finished college a couple of years ago, and could almost pass for a student. She is kind, never pushing me to volunteer in class, never asking why my grades are so good and yet I never raise a hand to answer questions. She's trying to encourage me to major in English Literature at college. I haven't found a way to explain to her that I won't be going to college.

'Are you planning to go to prom, Anna?'

The question takes me by surprise. 'I ... hadn't thought about it.'

'It seems a shame not to.'

I feel her eyes on me, trying to coax me to look up. I inspect a beige scuff mark on the toe of my shoe. 'I know … but it's not really the sort of thing I'm comfortable going to, Ms Abrams. Besides, my mom would never allow it.' *Please, please, let me go.*

Her thoughts hang heavy in the air. 'You're dating the Sail boy, aren't you? The son of the pastor?'

'Yes, that's right. William.' *I have to be alone. I have to think.* The image of the pendant on Mamma's neck is burning behind my eyes.

'Hmm.'

She doesn't say anything else for so long that I am tempted to look up. She is watching my face. Suddenly, she glances over to the clock on the far wall, twists her bag off her shoulder and deposits the textbooks in her arms inside it. She nods down the corridor. 'OK, Anna, I won't keep you any longer; you can go.'

William's house is a forty-minute cycle ride from the high school, which is over in Newberry, near the church. His family live in a small, unincorporated town which is practically all brand new, picture-perfect clapboard houses, and a ten-screen cinema complex. It seems so shiny to me, so bright compared to the dullness of home; like staring straight at the midday sun.

My gears are a little rusty, and although the storm has blown over a slick of water remains on every surface, so I press forward cautiously. As I make my way onto West Newberry Road something catches my eye: a flash of white, a man with a neat grey ponytail staring hard at me as I pass. It's the suit that makes me notice him: white, like the man I saw from the mailbox. It's enough to make me pull my brakes tight and turn around, but when I look again he's gone. Or perhaps he was never there.

My mind won't let me settle.

There is a steady stream of commuters making their way through all the little towns that make up Alachua County, but the evening is still fairly light, and the humidity that has been pendulous in the clouds has blissfully dispersed, leaving behind a crisp breeze, and the aroma of wet leaves and fresh soil.

I try not to let my mind wander as the steady hum of my wheels lulls me with their rhythm. Instead, I mark the way to myself, very deliberately taking note of the familiar signposts along the route. There's the Equestrian Show-place, where I know some kids go in the afternoon to play with the horses, which Mamma says all have fleas. There's the entrance to the vast Dudley Farm, the historic pioneer house, often the scene of class trips. I remember those trips: how fun it looked dressing up in period clothing, and learning to work the old hand pump; how I'd keep in the back, arms by my sides, praying I wouldn't get called on to volunteer. I should be grateful Mamma let me go, at least. Further on, I spot the plant nursery where she buys most of her cuttings, and which to me used to seem like the most magical place on earth. All that colour. All those smells—

Mamma. The pendant.

I've never seen her wear it before. Who could have taken it from her, and why have they sent it to me now?

Don't think, just ride.

I reach the town centre and turn right down to the Sails' road. A group of kids are shunting scooters along the sidewalk as I pull up at William's house and lean my bike against the fence.

Ally, one of William's sisters, spots me and bounces out of the group. 'Anna!' I brace myself as she rushes into me with a hug, trying to relax my shoulders and accept her tactility. I can smell the rainwater on her, kicked up by the wheels of the scooter and leaving muddy brown splashes on her bare legs. 'Hey, Kate!' she shouts over to her sister on the other side of the road. 'Look, it's Anna!'

The twins are nearly twelve years younger than William, and are adored by their family, for all their sassy behaviour: measuring out each temper tantrum with infectious giggles, and the perfectly timed bear hugs I am learning to accept. The girls are moon-eyed over William, the only one who can truly tame then, and in return he treats them with all the gruff affection a big brother should. It makes me wonder what it would be like to have siblings; to have anyone apart from just me and Mamma.

Ally grabs my hand and propels me towards the front door with a dismissive wave to her friends. Across the road, Kate, the softer and less bold of the two, kisses each one in turn and then shunts her scooter over to us.

They push open the door, which has never been locked in all the time I've known the Sails, and kick their shoes off into the open hallway.

'Hi, Mommy,' their duplicate voices chime at Hilary in the kitchen, bent over the oven with a large dish between her gloved hands. The smell of roasting chicken and baking pastry permeates the air, and I realise that she's making chicken pot pie. She made it one of the first times I came around to visit, and I told her how much I loved it. My heart swells a little at the thought that she remembers.

The girls lean over her bowed form and give her simultaneous kisses on the cheeks with easy affection, then Ally tugs on her apron and sticks a pointed finger out at me, lingering in the doorway. 'Look, Mom, we found Anna.' Her finger moves to point at my left foot. 'She cut her ankle. It's bleeding.'

I glance down and, sure enough, a sticky, deep purple line of blood is smeared across the outside of my ankle, just below the hem of my skirt. There must've been a loose wire at the back of my bike; I hadn't even noticed. Now I focus on it, an itching pain swells from the source, and I feel faintly queasy. I've never been good with blood.

'Oh, honey!' Hilary shuts the oven door and scurries over to take a look. 'Grab a seat. Katherine, get the first aid kit.'

Kate scampers out of the room as Hilary pulls out a chair for me from around the circular dining table. She kneels in front of me and gingerly takes my foot in her hands, turning it to get a better look at the wound.

Ally leans over and her snub nose wrinkles into a disgusted sniff. 'Gross,' she declares it.

'Ally, don't be a nuisance.' Hilary waves her away and accepts the green first aid box from a returning Kate. 'The two of you get washed up for dinner. You smell of mud and the grass stains I'm never going to be able to get out.'

She gives Ally a pat on the butt, then turns her attention to my foot as the girls clatter away and up the stairs. 'Well, it's not deep.' She angles it towards the light to get a better look. 'It's just a little jagged. Here, let's clean it up.'

She pulls an antiseptic wipe out of the box and rips it open. A spritz of alcohol hits my nostrils as she rubs it over my ankle, then she scrumples it and places it beside her on the white tiled floor. Its centre is now stained a rusty orange. I peer down to assess the damage. The cut is rendered a pale, crusty line, flecked with congealed blood. I'm both disgusted by it and compelled to prod it to test the parameters of the pain.

'Am I going to need a tetanus shot?' I ask as Hilary clicks the case shut and stands to throw the wipe in the trash. I'm surprised that this is it, that there is no further dressing or administration required. I remember once falling as a child: I was in the garden, playing with a rake which was far too big for me, twirling around and singing. I tripped on the end of it, banged my head and burst into immediate tears. Mamma was there, and she raced me straight to the bathroom to assess me. I escaped unscathed, but she warned me that if I'd fallen and cut myself on the rake end, I would have caught tetanus – such a frightening, alien word – and bacteria would leak through into my body from the cut, and release toxins that could cause suffocation or, even worse, death. I was quietly cautious during playtime from then on. No rakes. I never did need that tetanus shot.

I stare dubiously at the untended ankle. 'Maybe a Band-Aid?'

'Oh Anna, I shouldn't think so. It's really barely a graze. The cycling probably just made the blood flow faster to the cut, which makes it look worse than it is.'

I will myself not to press her further at the risk of sounding fussy, but as she clears away the box I am compelled to wash my hands, to rid myself of any potential areas of infection. I feel her eyes on me as I set the tap to hot and lather my hands with the liquid soap next to the sink, but she says nothing. I wonder how much William has told her about my life at home, or how much she will have gleaned from her brief interactions with Mamma.

'We're home!' The sound of the front door slamming turns Hilary's attention off me as William and Pastor Timothy appear in the hallway, returning from the church, where, once a month, William helps his father with the youth group meeting.

'Daddy!' The twins, with their ceaseless energy, bound downstairs to greet them, as Hilary and I follow in more measured pursuit.

I can't help notice, standing among them, how alike William is to his parents. They are the parts of his whole – his mother's hair, his father's eyes, her chin, his height – such that he may not look solely like either one of them, but it's easy to see where the original has spawned the replica. I try to visualise that photograph of my father, hanging in the kitchen at home: is there any aspect of him that I can truly claim as mine? I see nothing definite, but something lingers: fingers holding mine over the keys of a piano, measured singing as each note is pressed, *twin-kle twin-kle li-ttle star*, and then it's gone, like a cloud of sand being kicked up underfoot.

What part of Mamma is me?

Dinner is loud and warm and energetic. It's so noisy I want to cover my ears to soften the reverberation of their easy chatter in my head – everyone clamouring to be heard at once. Timothy and William go over the events of the meeting, and enter into a long debate about the dwindling numbers of the youth congregation, and ways they can attract more young people to church. Feeling bold, I dare to suggest, 'Movie nights?' And Pastor Timothy tells me that's a great idea, and writes it down.

William reaches for my hand under the table and squeezes it. I squeeze back.

Hilary brings out a birthday cake, not home-made ('What do I look like – Martha Stewart?' she asks in mock indignation) but fresh from the bakery in town, and alight with pastel-striped candles that I blow out as everyone at the table sings – messy, out of tune, happy. I can't remember if I've ever had a birthday cake before. The flames flicker across the piped writing – *Happy Birthday, Anna!* – and I'm sure it can't be just that causing my face to feel hot, for a glow of warmth to overtake me. Is this what it's like, for everyone else?

I want to linger over the washing-up for ever, but then the last piece of cutlery is put in the drawer and there is nothing left for me to dry or tidy away. 'Will,' I murmur, edging close to him in the guise of wiping the countertop, 'please, I have to speak to you. Alone.'

His lips pinch together and he nods his head, once, twice. 'Dad, would it be all right if Anna and I hung out upstairs for a little while? Just to spend some more time together?' I see his parents exchange glances over our heads. I wonder if they'd be more appalled or less if they knew the real reason for our seclusion.

Pastor Timothy looks at his watch, and then nods his approval. 'OK, William, but not too late: Anna has school tomorrow. And with the door open please.'

In the silence of William's room, we look at one another across his navy tartan throw. His room is large, with a wide bay window overlooking the back garden, but some-how it feels airless. I haven't realised it until now, but I have been dreading this moment.

'Anna, what's going on with you? I've never seen you so jittery. Is this about the park?'

I play with the edge of the throw, winding the woollen tassels around my fingers. Words gather and dance away from me. I don't want to go there. I don't want to think about it. I want to go downstairs where it's warm and safe; where my memories don't frighten me and thoughts aren't creeping into my head that I'd rather keep far, far away. I breathe in so deeply my lungs constrict, and then I look up at him, the throw forgotten as I knot my fingers together, over and over.

'I've always felt as if there were some parts of myself that didn't quite add up. It's like – it's like, you know when you're in the bath, and the surface is covered with bath foam, so thick you can't see through, but occasionally a part of your body will break through to the surface: a knee here, or a toe there? And it's as if you're not a whole at all, but pieces, broken up?' William's eyes narrow. My words are heavy, stumbling. 'I feel like that's me. Like I'm parts of a whole, but that there's part of me that's missing.'

My throat tightens – even as the words form I feel foolish – but I force myself to continue. 'And then there's this dream I've always had. A voice. And I know how stupid this sounds, and that you don't believe that dreams have meanings, but I've always felt there was more to this. That there's something I need to remember. Then we went to Astroland, and there it was: the missing piece. Not the whole thing, but something that convinced me it wasn't a dream at all. It was a memory.'

A sigh heaves in my chest. My cheeks feel hot; William's room dances in front of me. His hands on mine: cool and rough; his voice, soft but urging. 'Anna, what is it you remember?'

I close my eyes, and with a rush I am back there. The carousel looms in front of me. I see the flashes of pink and green and yellow, and the bobbing pattern of the horses on their endless route to nowhere.

And I'm not looking in. I'm looking out.

The horses are surrounding me, and the outside world spins in a sea of crowds and rides and concrete. I am trying to get the attention of someone, waving manically at them, but they're turned away, not noticing me, and then they wander off, and I kick the horse in frustration, as if trying to race towards them. 'Giddy-up,' I whisper into its mane. The ride is slowing down, but whoever I'm trying to reach still hasn't seen me, and instead I feel someone's arms on my sides, helping me down, coaxing me off the platform, onto concrete, and then hurrying me away along a shadowy path.

As we move further from the carousel, I glance up at this stranger taking a subtle but firm hold. And I see it: the pendant, dangling from a neck, the lily's stem curled like a serpent's tail.

In the present, a choke rises in my throat. It overwhelms my body with shakes and I gasp for air as I bounce between hot and cold. I feel like I'm drowning in it – all these memories, all these images, all this truth.

And so, if only to escape it, I open my eyes. 'Will, I think someone took me.'

ROSIE

10

On Monday night my parents fight. It always happens this time of year, despite the lengths they go to the rest of the time to pretend that everything's all right. It's as if they spend their year stuffing all their thoughts and feelings into a drawer like unwanted clothes, but eventually it gets too crammed and bursts open.

I know the real reason, though; I've paused on the stairs, one foot hovering above the next tread, and heard the late-night whispering from behind their bedroom door. I've seen glances across the room when I've tried to dig, to mention the trust. I know they're both spiralling towards the end of May. I know there's no news. I know they're terrified. And they still haven't said anything to me or Rob.

So it's not surprising that they blow up. What's surprising is that it's Dad who starts it.

We're in the kitchen. Dad has just got back from work and Rob and I are at the table, Rob on his phone and me on my laptop, writing notes on the causes of the French Revolution for History. The perfect picture of domesticity.

Dad says he wants to hold a party, to commemorate the anniversary of Emily's disappearance, and to thank all the people around us who've been involved in the case. Mum loses her temper, tells him that she doesn't think a 'party' would exactly endear us to the press, who already use any opportunity they can to show us 'cavorting' in our celebrity. The venom with which she says 'party' would make you think Dad has suggested that we charter a yacht and ask the media to fund it.

'Just what they want, David: "Archers Spend Taxpayers' Money to 'Celebrate' Daughter's Disappearance". You're mad.'

Dad fights back, says it's the proper thing to do, and accuses her of kowtowing to the press; of caring more about what they would say than about the people we should be thanking.

And then Mum hits him with the sucker punch: 'You weren't watching her.' She says it quietly, almost a whisper, and even as the words are emerging I can see she regrets it. And it's as though the whole room freezes – I swear, even the dishwasher pauses.

Dad turns very white, and his lips go all thin and his fists clench, and then he chokes out, 'Fuck you.' The violence of it infects every corner of the silent room.

And then Mum slams down the wooden spoon she's been holding, and turns to Dad full-on. 'No. Fuck you. You weren't watching her. You were on the fucking phone.'

As if there is some sort of unspoken agreement, Rob and I slip out and go to our rooms, and the shouting recedes behind us.

We'd been to a parade that day – the day Emily disappeared – and then a character signing at the castle. Emily was getting tired and fractious, but then she saw the carousel and became completely entranced by it. We waited in line for an hour, and when we got to the front, Mum realised I needed changing. There was no way Mum and Dad were going through the queue again, so she took me off to the bathrooms. Dad would go on the ride with Emily and we'd all meet up after. But Emily was stubborn, wanted to be the only one actually riding the horses, barely wanted him on the ride at all, and so as a compromise he stood on the revolving platform, along with several other reluctant, jet-lagged parents.

Dad was working for a big international record company then, all fast-paced and no-nonsense – not his sort of place at all. When he told them he needed to take this break, they'd given him a mobile – new and so expensive at the time – and told him in no uncertain terms to answer it if it rang. So, when the phone buzzed in his pocket, he was terrified not to take it. He couldn't quite hear the caller's voice over the blaring music, so he walked a little way off. When he finally rung off, the ride was slowing down. It ground to a halt just as Mum came back from the loo and was scanning the crowd to find them. It was then that he saw the empty carousel horse. And it was then, in that single moment, that everything changed.

There was the initial, gentle panic. The thought that she'd just wandered off, perhaps mistaken someone else for Dad, and was now working her way back to them. Then the escalating alarm with every call of her name. And then the park authorities called in. The closing off of the park. Police. Helicopter and ground searches. The ensuing fifteen years of appeals and investigations that have led nowhere.

In those dark, early days when the press were grabbing on to any angle they could, I know Mum had actively spoken out against their wildly insensitive claims – that Dad was neglectful; that they were bad parents, for allowing Emily to ride the horses herself; that that's what they got for taking such an elaborate holiday. I know she could have only brought it up today out of desperation, rather than any deep-seated conviction.

Even so, I stay in my room, out of the way, as the argument dulls and fades, and I hear the slam of their bedroom door.

On my desk, the piece of paper lies open. I have folded and unfolded it so many times now that deep creases have formed in the folds, and the paper now fails to stay flat. MissMarple63. Astro7402. MikeD. A hole is beginning to niggle into the centre of the list. The cracks in the paper seem to be echoing the cracks in my own family: if I don't do something soon, they'll both fall apart.

There's a knock on the door, and Rob's head appears around it. His hair is tousled, and his face looks blotchy and dry, as if he's been rubbing it profusely with a towel. I don't embarrass him by asking if he's been crying.

'Hey.' I discreetly fold up the piece of paper and secure it in my tracksuit pocket. 'You OK?'

He nods, and then he lowers his eyes to the ground and leans on the door frame, all gangly-teenage-boy limbs. He's gone through a growth spurt in the last year, already taller than me, and it's as though his brain hasn't quite connected with his body yet, to master how to accommodate the extra length. 'I'm hungry.' It comes out like a whine.

'Are they ...?'

'In their room. With the door shut. The chilli's burnt.' He crosses his arms, but I see his lower lip wobble.

My stomach grumbles. It's gone nine o'clock. Dinner was the last thing anyone was thinking of. 'Come on.' I slide off the bed, nod towards the stairs.

We order two pizzas. And potato wedges. And a bottle of Coke. It seems both decadent and necessary. We eat it on the living room floor, yanking the slices off so fast that thick strands of melting cheese drip down our forearms, burning our lips and tongues as we race to fill our empty stomachs. This, at least, is easy to fix.

We don't hang out much, Rob and me. Part of me thinks it's the guilt, like we'd be leaving her out, like it's not fair. But it's nice, sitting like this, on cushions stolen from the sofa in the other room. Rob drops a circle of pepperoni on his cushion, and looks at me in horror when he removes it to find an oily red stain remaining.

'Don't worry.' I haul myself up and grab fabric cleaner from under the sink in the kitchen, returning to dab at the stain with a wodge of kitchen roll. 'It should be fine. We'll just turn the cushion the other way around. They won't notice for ages.'

I see his shoulders relax a little. It's a move that is uncannily like Dad. 'Thanks, Rosie.' He sits back on the wood floor and nibbles on a potato wedge.

'That's OK.' I feel like a proper sister.

Rob loiters on the stairs as I'm about to head up to my floor. His movements are oddly shifty, and I realise he's thinking of hugging me. We haven't hugged since we were little kids, forced to make up when one of us made the other cry. I lean over and wrap my arms around him. I feel him stiffen, as if he's embarrassed about such an overt display of affection, but I hug him tighter.

'It's going to be all right, Rob. You'll see. I bet you it'll all be back to normal tomorrow.' Or whatever passes for normal here.

In my room, I listen for signs of Mum and Dad, but the house is silent. I pull up the window and look out over jumbled parcels of gardens and terraces and tower blocks. A couple of lights are on, but not many. If I look past them into the distance, I can make out the blinking lights of the City. On a clear day you can make out the very top of the Shard, rising in a sharp point into the sky. I wonder at all the thousands of people between me and there. Could one of them be MissMarple63? MikeD, are you out there now, asleep in one of those tower blocks?

I open my bedside cabinet, feel for the back of the bottom drawer where Mum never looks, and take out a squashed rectangular packet. On the cover, a grey, moon-like pupil stares out at me, accompanied by a stark white message, telling me I'm 'increasing the risk of blindness'. I open the packet, pull a cigarette out, then edge around my desk to lean over the window ledge and spark it up, watching the orange tip glow fiercely in the dark.

I inhale, dragging in the crisp night air, and blow out an unconvincing smoke ring that quickly dissipates in the breeze. I imagine the little curlicues of smoke wafting through my mouth and down into my lungs as the familiar fuzziness fills my head. I don't even like the taste, but something about it just feels viciously good. Plus, it gives me something to occupy my hands with. When I'm finished, I stub the cigarette out onto the side of the house, and reach around to feel with my fingertips for one particular loose tile, tucking the butt underneath it. I sometimes worry that something, a pigeon maybe, will work it loose, and I'll have to explain away a rain of cigarette ends on the garden below. I creep downstairs to the bathroom, brush my teeth and wash the tips of my fingers vigorously. Mum's never been able to tell.

In bed, I lie in the dark, feeling the presence of the piece of paper resting on my bedside table. MissMarple63. Astro7402. MikeD. Their names have begun to feel like incantations to me, as if by saying them I'll somehow conjure them up, and everything will be solved.

MissMarple63. Astro7402. MikeD. Could one of them really hold the answer?

My whole life has been a push and pull between knowing too much, and not knowing anything at all. I know what Emily receives every year for her birthday, because Mum will always buy her something – just a little trinket – and make a point of telling us what it is, as if this year, if she picks right, my sister will be returned to us. But I don't know the sound of her voice. I know what colour her room was, because it was kept exactly the same until I turned twelve, when Mum finally relented, painted it blue and moved Rob in there. But I don't know what she dreamed about, or the way she smelled. I know that, in reality, the only person who truly knows the answer to her mystery is the person who took her. My concrete, ineffable sister.

Which is why I have to find her. I think of the endless theories on TheHive, spiralling out and all coming to no conclusion. If these three come up blank, will I keep going, until I've crossed off every lead?

The thought of it makes my brain pulsate inside my skull. I reach across to the bedside table for a glass of water and, finding none there, reluctantly crawl out of bed to get one. I pad downstairs in the near darkness, feeling out the edge of each step with my bare feet. It's only when I turn into the kitchen that I notice the faint sound of someone there, breaking through the stillness.

Mum is sitting at the kitchen table, her head in her hands, crying.

I pause in the open doorway, caught between letting her have her private moment and wanting to comfort her, but some maternal sense must alert her to my presence, because she raises her head from her hands and looks up at me.

'Rosie?' Her voice is cracked and thick.

'Mum.' I go to her; pull back the kitchen chair next to hers and sit.

'Darling, you shouldn't have to see me like this. I just needed a moment. I'm sorry.' She pulls herself up and presses the heels of her hands into her eyes, wiping away the tears.

'No, I ...' I feel utterly helpless. 'Let me get you some water.'

I get up and turn on the tap and reach up to the cabinet above the sink to pull down a couple of glasses.

'Is there anything I can do?' I ask, setting a glass down in front of her.

'Oh, my sweet girl.' She takes my face between her two hands and plants a kiss on my forehead. I can feel the moisture from her drying tears as her cheek brushes mine. 'Just be here. That's all.'

'I am.' I wonder if this could be it: the moment she'll confide in me, tell me the truth I've already discovered. 'Mum,' I prompt, 'I'm sorry. About all this.' I gesture pointlessly into the darkness, as if I could even begin to encompass the depths of our family's pain within an arm span.

She gives a tired sigh. The corners of her eyes fill with tears again, and I see her forcefully blinking them back. 'I'm sorry too, Rosie. And I'm particularly sorry about tonight. I should never have said those things to your father. It was awful. Unforgivable. I know we try our best to go on, but this time of year dredges up all that panic and horror all over again. It's like I'm trapped in a nightmare where I'm reliving it over and over. Only with a nightmare, at least you get to wake up.'

I reach across the table with my hand. She takes it, giving me a grateful smile through the tears that are now rolling down her cheeks. 'Dad knows I was just speaking out of frustration and anger. I could never blame him. Whatever happened, it was just horrible, horrible luck. There's nothing we could have done or planned for that would have made it any different. And I guess, in a way, that's even worse: we're just pawns in the hands of fate.'

'*We are merely the stars' tennis balls, struck and banded. Which way please them.*' The quote has loomed up at me from the marked-up copy of *The Duchess of Malfi* sitting in my backpack by the door. Through her sadness, Mum manages an impressed eyebrow raise. 'See, I do pay attention in school.'

We take simultaneous sips from our glasses. I swirl the cool water around my mouth, distracting myself from the silence as Mum sets her glass down with a soft clink.

'It's late, Rosie.' Her chair makes a scraping sound against the tiles as she stands and takes our glasses over to the sink. 'We should get to bed. You have school tomorrow.'

'Mum,' I venture, seizing my chance before it's too late. 'What do you remember about' – I choose my words carefully – 'that day?'

I hear her sigh, and in the dim light I can just make out the rise and fall of her shoulders. 'Rosie, we've been through it all so many times. Do you really want to hear it now?'

'I want to hear it from you. Please, Mum. One more time?'

'OK.' She comes back over to the kitchen table and stands behind me, resting her hands on my shoulders.

'We'd flown from Miami to Jacksonville late the night before. We knew the wedding was likely to go on quite late, so we'd planned a deliberately relaxed departure. The party had been wonderful. It was on the beach, and there were lots of other children, so Emily was in her element. I'd bought you both the most gorgeous dresses – white with capped sleeves and tiny sequins on the skirts.

'Emily fell in love with hers from the moment she put it on and insisted on twirling around in it all day. I remember watching her on the beach, running around barefoot and trying to mimic some of the older children doing cart-wheels, with you fast asleep in the pram next to me, and thinking how lucky I was to have my two perfect, beautiful girls.'

Her voice cracks, and I hear her tearful sniffs. I reach a hand back to touch her arm, confused emotions twisting and untwisting themselves in the pit of my chest: guilt at being left; anger at whoever did this to our family; grief for my lost sister; the knowledge that there is nothing I can do to take this pain away from my mother.

She pats my hand. 'It's OK; I shouldn't have taken myself there. Anyway, we got into Jacksonville very late the night before, and were all exhausted and managed to sleep in late – even you. The next day, we set off after breakfast for Astroland, which was about an hour's drive west. The moment we stepped foot in the park ... Oh Rosie, you should have seen her. Emily's eyes just lit up! The whole place was magical – it's hard to admit that now, but it's true – and we all walked around in a sort of daze all morning, just taking it in.

'I had you strapped to me in a papoose and you were perfectly content, watching everything. We had a novelty pushchair for Emily, shaped like a mini rocket, but she was too excited to sit still and kept clambering out, so eventually we gave up and made her hold on to the side of it instead. We stopped at a shop and she begged us to buy her a souvenir T-shirt; green, with the logo on it in silver.' Her voice softens, remembering. 'I can't help thinking that was my first mistake: practically every child in the park was wearing one. Maybe if I'd insisted that she stayed in her own clothes it would have been easier for us to find her.' She stops, lost in her thoughts now.

'Mum,' I say gently, partly to stop her blaming herself for every little detail, partly to urge her on: I've never heard her talking about it all so intimately before and am rapt, sickly fascinated to hear my own history playing out in such great detail. 'I—'

But it's as if that has broken the spell. She steps away from me, breaking our contact, and flicks on the overhead lights, plunging us into a sudden brightness that makes me squint.

'You know the rest now, Rosie. Come on: let's go to bed.' Wearily, she opens the dishwasher and places the empty glasses inside.

'OK, OK.' I grab her by the forearm as she starts to make her way out. 'Just one last question: did you ever try searching yourself, or speaking to all those people who think they know what happened?' I ask this nonchalantly, but something in my voice must alert her, because she stops dead and grasps me by the shoulders.

'No.' There's a note of warning in her voice. 'And neither must you, Rosie. I mean that. We have the best people possible working on the case. If anyone ever finds out what happened, it'll be them. Don't even think about poking around into any of these so-called "theories".' She practically spits out the word. 'They're all lunatics. The lot of them.

And not just that: some of them could be downright dangerous.' I can hear an edge of panic in her voice. She grips my shoulders even tighter, and forces me to look directly into her eyes. 'Promise me, darling. Promise you won't even think about it. I can't lose another child.'

'I promise, Mum.' I speak slowly and deliberately, all the while feeling my heart beating with a deceptive thud in my chest.

'Good.' She hugs me to her with an almost violent urgency, pressing her lips to my cheek with a kiss. 'Now, off to bed with you.'

But I can't sleep; my mind is alive. Blinking up at my ceiling, I follow a crack of moonlight shining through the curtains and onto my desk, and I know what I have to do.

I open my laptop, navigate to TheHive, to MissMarple-63's page.

It's all still there: Hank Wilson's lazy eyes staring vacantly out of the screen; a drawing depicting the distance between the construction site and the park entrance; the layers of comments from other users, agreeing with or protesting the evidence. I read it through again, to remind myself, all the while silently repeating, *Please don't let it be him.* Whatever happened to Emily, this is amongst the most heinous of possibilities.

I realise this is how my parents must have felt at the beginning, when each day brought a new and more terrifying lead: both the hope that finally they'd have an answer, and the sickening thought of what Emily's fate might have been. They have been forced to think the bleakest thoughts it can be possible for a parent to have; and they have both confessed in their darkest moments that if she had been interfered with in any way, they would rather my sister was dead than having to suffer further. What an inconceivably awful choice to have to make.

Nausea wraps itself around me and squeezes at my ribs like a boa constrictor. *Hank Wilson, you bastard*, I vow, fixing his image into my mind, *if you have hurt my sister, I swear I will find you, and I will kill you with my own hands.*

Those hands now hover over the keyboard, trying to determine my next course of action. There are no contact details for MissMarple63 – no helpful email address on her profile page, or background information that may lead me to her. Only her profile handle, and the detective avatar. For all I know, she might not even be a woman. I scroll through her posts, which are dotted sporadically during the ten years of TheHive's creation, getting thinner in number as they become more recent. My heart sinks when I see the posts dry up at the end of last year, but then to my surprise I see there's been one posted only last week, to mark the fifteen-year anniversary: *My thoughts are with the Archer family, still searching for their lost daughter. Hope springs eternal.*

I quickly open a new comment box and begin to type.

ANNA

11

I open my eyes, allow myself to take William in; to fully understand the truth of what I have remembered. 'Will, I think ...' I swallow air, forcing the reluctant words up from the base of my chest, willing them to be false. Knowing them to be truth. 'I think I was taken. From the park.'

I wait.

His face is oddly sterile, the expression fixed on it as though it's got stuck halfway between one thing and another. At last I see a slight shake of his head, and his lips move to an awkward half smile. 'Anna, what do you mean, "taken"?'

'I think ...' I breathe. 'I think that a long time ago, I went to Astroland with another ... another ...' My throat clenches around the words. 'With other people. I was someone else. And somehow, I was taken from them. If I'd never gone to the park with you, I may never have put it together. But I have.'

Opposite me, William exhales.

'You don't believe me.' I feel my face go hot, embarrassment flying through my system. 'Why would you? It sounds ridiculous. But Will, I'm *telling* you.'

'Anna, please don't get upset.' Another long, careful breath escapes from him. 'You know I love you. You know I want to believe you. But this is all jumping to a lot of quite irrational conclusions.' His voice is calm, as if he's trying to reason with a small child. 'I wasn't going to bring this up now, but when I left you on Saturday, I went home and did some research.' He pulls his computer into his lap and starts to type, opening a page and holding it out for me to read. It's from an online psychology journal. The title says, 'False Memory Syndrome'. The article reads:

False memory syndrome, or FMS, is a condition whereby a person strongly believes an event or events to have occurred, despite this being factually incorrect. The syndrome can have deep-rooted consequences for the individual, who believes so vehemently in these mistaken memories that they can become impossible to correct.

I press the lid of the laptop shut.

'So you think I'm crazy.' I fix my gaze on my hand, resting on the laptop. The skin at the top of my splayed fingernails is torn where I have bitten at the cuticles; a habit easy to fall into, when frequent handwashing often makes the skin dry and cracked.

'I don't think you're crazy, Anna. I just think you're a bit confused; like maybe you've read about this kind of thing happening before, and remembered it when we got to the park, but that it didn't actually happen to you. Like your mind fused the two things together.'

'Then how do I explain the card?' My teeth are clenched so tight I can barely get the words out. I think of my secrets, hidden under the floorboard in my room. If only I'd brought them. If only I had told him before, then he'd have to believe me.

'What card?' I can hear the sigh under his words.

I tell him, but even as I'm speaking I see his features change; the corners of his eyes softening as he takes my hand in his and pats it gently. 'Oh Anna.' He strokes my skin, ignoring the cracks in the palm of my hand. 'That was probably just the kids at school messing with you. You remember what happened last summer?'

Last summer.

I am so used to being invisible at school. Passing through the corridors with barely a glance from anyone. So I don't know why they decided to pick me.

The red. Spilling from my locker in a thick, viscous wave. Splashing my face and running down my clothes as the bucket perched inside clattered to the ground. The laughter echoing around me. The note pinned inside, calling me 'Carrie'. I didn't understand, had to ask William to explain. A book, he said. And I tried to block my ears when they called me that name for the rest of the school year.

William watches me. 'Someone probably thought it would be funny,' he says softly.

'No.' A tear escapes and rolls down my left cheek. I wipe it away with the back of my fist. 'It's not that. It doesn't explain it. What about the pendant? I remember seeing it, that day. And Mamma ...' I steel myself. I don't want to think about that part. Instead, I say quietly, 'If it was someone at school, how could they know that?'

William pulls me closer towards him. 'Anna, I wish you'd just hear me out. You know how badly you wanted to go to that park. And you know how vehemently your mom stopped you from going. You know how she can be. Can you just entertain the tiniest possibility, even for a second, that maybe you could have been misremembering? This syndrome: these false memories can just take root in you. It's not even something you're actively doing, it's the way the ideas can be stored in your brain, so you become utterly convinced that they're real.'

'No,' I insist. I replay it in my mind again: the carousel, the voice, the lily petals folding outwards from the cross. 'I want to go home.'

'Anna ...' William cajoles, stroking the centre of my palm.

'Please,' I say. 'I need to get out of here. I need to think. It's late anyway. Mamma will worry.'

He rakes a tired hand across his temple.

'Please, Will.'

'OK. I'll drive you.'

Outside, blackness. The only light is the flash of other cars that pass us. The car smells sickeningly of the pine-scented air freshener that dangles from the rear-view mirror. I bought it for William myself only a few weeks ago, complaining that his car reeked of sweaty basketball kit. The scent of manufactured resin intrudes into my nostrils and I eventually yank the little tree off and stuff it into the glove compartment.

William reaches across the stick shift, finds the top of my knee across the distance and gives it a tentative rub. I stiffen. His hand lingers there, but he says nothing further.

When we pull up in the driveway, there are no lights on. William suffocates the engine and opens his mouth to speak, but before he can I put my hand over his and say the words I've been mulling over in my head for the duration of our silent drive: 'I think it would be best if we don't see each other for a while.' I speak slowly and efficiently, hoping to numb myself from the pain of their meaning.

'You can't mean that.' I hear the hurt in his voice, and wish it could be another way, but I know for certain that I can't do this right now, have him doubting me, making me doubt myself, until I can find a way to prove it for sure.

'I do.' I swallow; I can barely look at him. 'I know there's church, and choir. I know we have to see each other. But apart from that, the best thing for me right now is to be alone.'

'Anna.' He clutches for me in the dark but I brush him away.

'No.' I unbuckle my seat belt and reach for the door handle. 'If you love me the way you say you do, you'll respect me when I say I need to be alone. Even if you don't believe me, you can at least respect that.' As I speak I am fighting against the trembling in my voice.

William slumps against his seat. 'I do. I love you, Anna. You know that. And I would do anything to make you happy. That's the only reason I'm fighting you on this: because I think you could be causing yourself a whole lot of unnecessary pain.'

'And if you truly believe that, I understand. But I have to know for certain. For me. Do you understand?'

I sense him reaching carefully for his words. 'I do,' he concedes. 'I do understand. And when you're ready, you know I'll be waiting for you.'

We each step out of the car, and William lifts my bicycle down from the rack on the back. We stand awkwardly, the bicycle wedged between us, unsure of what to do. Feeling the finality of the moment. I move it gently aside, throw myself into him and bury my face in his familiar chest. His arms come around me tightly, and we stay like this, swaying ever so slightly with the force of it. Eventually I wrench myself away from him and say, 'You should go.'

He nods, climbing back into the car.

'Not for ever,' I add, watching him through the open window. My words sound hollow, but I want desperately to mean them.

'Not for ever.' He exhales wretchedly, and the car revs into life. 'Goodnight, Anna.'

'Goodnight, William.'

And then he's gone.

Mamma's voice calls me from the living room. I have no choice but to go to her. She is sitting on one of the two overstuffed floral armchairs that take up most of the space in the room, lit only by the strength of one side lamp and the white beams from the television, which is broadcasting one of her favourite television preachers. A gardening magazine is on her lap, the open pages blooming with pastel-coloured plants.

The voice of the preacher booms from the television set – 'And at times our faith may be tested, and we must say unto ourselves, have faith; and trust in the Lord, and that trust will be rewarded' – and he holds his arms wide to his remote audience, as if embracing them.

Mamma nods her head emphatically, reaches over to the side table for her one and only vice: her nightly tincture, two fingers' worth of Wild Turkey bourbon, cooled with a single ice cube. I search her neck, hoping and not hoping to catch sight of the pendant. But the skin is bare, as I've always remembered it, allowing me to cast the thought from my mind.

She takes a sip of bourbon, and only when the glass is set down does she incline her head to me. I quickly shift my eyes down.

'It's late, dear – was everything OK at Pastor Timothy's house?' she asks.

'Yes, Mamma, I …' I struggle to think of some way to explain the hour, and realise I have the perfect thing. 'William and I have decided to take a little break. I told him I needed to concentrate on school for a while.'

Mamma's features seem to soften in the yellow light, and the corners of her mouth curl into a barely perceptible smile. 'Well, that seems very mature of you, I must say. I did think you two were getting too close. You've clearly earned your eighteen years. I'm proud of you.' She lets out an approving sigh. 'I think that deserves a small prayer of thanks for guiding you to this decision, don't you?'

'Now?' I stiffen in the doorway.

Mamma gestures authoritatively to the other armchair, and I reluctantly sit and take her outstretched hand. She lowers the volume on the TV, though the pastor continues his sermon in mute. She shuts her eyes. I try to do the same.

'Dear Lord, we thank You for leading Anna through this path to maturity, and for giving her the strength to make an important decision that will only be the best for her. Your wisdom has guided her from when she was but a tiny baby in my arms' – my ears prick up at this – 'to the woman You see before You, and we pray that You continue to guide her as You see fit. Please grace her with the sense to make good decisions, and to open her eyes and her heart to Your way. To You we pray. Amen.'

'Amen,' I say quickly. Now I seize hold of the door Mamma has left open for me before she shuts it tight: 'Mamma, what was I like as a baby?'

Mamma opens her eyes sharply, and I think I see her shoulders flinch. Could this be it? Have I caught her off guard, unable to prepare a suitable reply? 'Anna, if this is about those photos again, I told you: they all got lost in the storm.'

'No, no, it's not that.' Suddenly it occurs to me how terrified I am of taking a wrong turn. If I'm mistaken about all this, what a terrible daughter she will think I am. If I am right … I sense the closed living room door behind me. Adrenaline courses through me, as if preparing me to run. I try to keep my voice neutral. I give her an encouraging smile. 'It's just that, now I'm eighteen, I'd love to hear more about myself when I was growing up. You don't really talk much about when I was a baby, when Daddy was alive.'

'Anna …' Mamma turns the television off mute and the preacher's voice once again fills the room, 'why can't you understand? You know I find that time very painful.'

'Just any little detail,' I say. 'I promise I won't ask again.'

Her finger pauses on the button, then the preacher's face is extinguished into blackness. 'Anna, you are going to make me very angry.'

I teeter on the edge, desperate to push her further, terrified of pushing too far. 'Please, Mamma,' I say softly, 'tell me about when I was born.'

'Anna.' I see her resisting, her finger still poised on the remote. But then her features shift, as if she's looking elsewhere, to some long-forgotten time. She swallows. I hold my breath, worried that any sound will spoil the moment, make her change her mind. But then she speaks.

'You were a beautiful baby. People say that babies are all shrivelled and grey at first, but I swear to the Lord you turned out pink and perfect. It was a difficult birth. I laboured for nearly thirty-six hours, and they were worried that your heart was getting weak. Mason was traditional, so I was all on my own, and terrified I was going to lose you. I begged them to fetch me a Bible, and I prayed and prayed, begging the Lord not to take you away from me. And then, when you were finally born, and placed into my arms, and I saw just how flawless you were, I knew that He had heard my prayer, and I vowed to always have faith in His guidance.'

Mamma's eyes close, and she folds her arms neatly into her lap like she is telling herself a bedtime story. 'I had a name all picked out for you: Hannah. It means "grace of God", and I loved how tidy it was, spelled the same way backwards and forwards. The perfect name for the perfect baby. But then, when your father saw you, the first thing he said was, "She looks the spitting image of my mama." Her name was Annie, and so we compromised ... Anna you became.' She frowns in her reverie, but then seems to shake the thought out of her head, resting it against the back of the armchair. 'I didn't mind, really. My own family were ... his parents were all we had. Besides, you were mine, and it didn't matter what you were called. You were truly a special baby. You barely ever cried. You slept well. You took to feeding easily. You smiled early and made everyone who saw you smile.' Her lips purse as though she's sucked on a lemon. 'Almost everyone.'

In an instant it's like the door I have been holding so tentatively ajar crashes shut between us. She opens her eyes with a start; the look of tranquillity on her face disintegrates, and her face pinches meanly.

'But it's the middle of the night. You should be in bed. Have you even ...?' She casts her eyes down to my hands. 'For heaven's sake, did you even wash your hands when you came in?'

My palms feel as though they could betray me at any moment, so I'm already halfway off my seat when I say, 'No, Mamma, I didn't have a chance.'

'Then get upstairs right this second and wash up for bed. Lord knows what germs you've picked up today, in school or on that bike of yours. If you get sick it'll serve you right. I regret what I said about your maturity – you are clearly still a child in need of scolding. Go.' She points a rod-like arm towards the door.

'Sorry, Mamma. Sorry,' I fluster, hurriedly picking my way around the chairs and towards the door. 'I shouldn't have asked. I won't do it again.'

I loiter in the doorway, hoping for some final word of forgiveness, but instead she turns the television back on, and holds her thumb firmly on the volume button until the preacher's voice is booming through the room.

'Goodnight, Mamma.' My voice is barely a whisper.

She doesn't look round.

In the blackness of my room I toss and turn beneath the covers, trying to piece together the opposing facts the evening has presented. I don't think I have ever heard Mamma tell that story before. The way she told it, it seemed like such a clear memory. How could it not be true?

Scrunching my eyes tight, I try desperately to conjure up some image or story that will validate her tale. My paternal grandmother – the shadowy figure after whom I am named – did I ever meet her? Not that I can recall, but then I know Mamma has said before that we lost touch with Daddy's family after he died. I imagine they still live in Georgia, like we did. I don't know where exactly, but it's conceivable enough that we wouldn't go to visit there. As far as I know, I've never even left the state.

As if taunting me, the carousel revolves into my mind. The neon horses loom at me, and I feel the breeze fanning my face as I am pulled into their orbit. A shadowy figure is beside me, helping me down from the horse and off the ride. It's a game, they tell me, like hide and seek. The pendant, flashing in the sunlight. I hold their hand and look up into their eyes, and I see ... I see ...

Something is wrong. Like a flat note in a piece of music – this isn't something tangible, but simply something I can feel. And what's more, someone else knows it too. My secret gift-giver, my shadowy letter-writer: what part does he play in all this? What is he trying to tell me?

I have to find out who he is.

I have to find out what happened. And why.

And if I have any chance of understanding any of these things, I have to begin with Mamma.

ROSIE

12

The party will go ahead. White flags have been waved. My parents smooth a clean sheet over their argument and pretend nothing ever happened. And in the meantime, I receive an answer from MissMarple63.

It's not instantaneous: by Saturday, with still no word, the curiosity is eating away at me. I go for a run around Highbury Fields, thinking through the possibilities, whether I should nudge her further, whether my initial request was too vague – *I would really like to speak to you in greater detail about your theory about Hank Wilson. Is there a way I am able to reach you?*

Still flushed from my run and damp with the remnants of peach shower gel on my skin, I find myself sitting at my desk, with the home page of TheHive staring back at me.

Cautiously, I retrace my path, and find myself staring at MissMarple63's page.

Underneath my first comment I write, *I think we could learn a lot from speaking to one another, and I have some information that may be of interest.*

Nothing. I don't know what I was expecting; I don't even know if she's in the same time zone.

By Sunday I've refreshed the page so many times I'm surprised I haven't broken my laptop. I stagger through an essay with one eye trained on the browser, using any excuse I can to look up something online, so I can bring up the page, refresh, scroll. I am about to give up and go downstairs for a sandwich when a dull ping from the vicinity of my desk halts me. There it is: a reply.

I don't know what this is insinuating, but if this really is of interest, here is the address you can email me on …

I can't stop the tremble of my hands as I open up a new email and hurriedly tap out a reply.

Hi there,
This is going to sound a bit out of the blue, but I just got your message on TheHive and I want to talk to you more about Hank Wilson.

What else can I possibly say? Looking at the stark black-and-white message box, I realise my identity is going to be an instant giveaway: I have my name in my email address. Hastily, I add,

If you can't tell already from my email address, I'm
Rosie Archer.

As soon as the message sends I pathologically begin
checking for new mail, waiting for a response. Barely five
minutes pass before an alert pops up on my screen.

One new message.

I never expected such a quick response. I feel a tiny bit
sick as I click it open. What if Mum's right and MissMarple-
63's a psychopath? Or, even worse, a journalist who's
going to leak my enquiry to the press. Mum's going to
kill me.

Hello.
If this is a hoax, I am not very impressed. Anyone
with half a brain can create a fake email address.
However, if I were to give you the benefit of the doubt
and agree to pursue this further, I'd like to ask for
some sort of proof, and also your reasons for getting
in contact.
Kind regards,
Jane

I glance around the room, looking for inspiration, and
my eyes land on my Spanish notes from last night, and the
date scrawled on them in the top right corner. I pull out a
clean sheet of paper, writing today's date in the centre in
neat black letters. Unquestionable. Then I reach for my

mobile, hold up the paper, and create the ultimate proof of identity: a selfie.

Giddy with a sense of action, I attach the picture, hit send. If she feigns to have any interest in my family, she'll know what I look like. I stare at the screen, wishing I could somehow reach into that black hole and grab her reply out myself.

Once again, nothing.

In the kitchen, I crash about making a ham sandwich, keeping my phone out on the counter so I can check for messages.

Dad and Rob come in, hot and red-faced from a game of tennis.

'Want one?' I ask Dad, pointing to the open loaf of bread as Rob trudges upstairs to the shower.

'Thanks, sweetie,' Dad says, running the tap and gulping down a glass of water. 'That would be lovely. And Rob too. Extra ham: I couldn't even take a set off him; he'll be in need of meat.'

He observes me as I move about the kitchen, spreading mustard on the bread, layering on pink slices of ham. 'Someone important?'

I look up in alarm. 'What?'

'Your phone. You keep checking it. Must be a boy.'

'Don't be silly, Dad,' I reply lightly as he waggles his eyebrows knowingly. I move off the topic as quickly as possible: 'Just waiting for Keira to tell me what time the film starts tonight.'

Rob comes down, and we eat standing up against the counter, sharing a bottle of Diet Coke I find in the back of the fridge. Mum's at an art exhibition with a friend, so it's just the three of us. We've stacked the plates in the dishwasher before I manage to steal another glance at my phone, and nearly choke on the last of my Coke when I see Jane has replied. I shove my empty glass in the top rack and dash out of the room, shouting at them that I need to call Keira.

'Boy stuff,' I hear Dad tell Rob confidently.

Upstairs, my fingers fly across the keyboard as I pull up her reply.

Rosie! I'm sorry I had to doubt your validity at first, but as you can imagine, you get all sorts on TheHive. I'm thrilled and slightly nervous that you've got in contact with me. I hope nothing I have said has offended you and your family; I wish you all nothing but the utmost respect. Please, tell me more: I'm intrigued.

Kind regards,

Jane

I read and reread the email, unable to believe this is really it: the first step. A bombardment of questions invades my mind. Why is she so convinced that Hank Wilson did it? Why, if she's so certain, does she think he hasn't been convicted? The answer to it all seems so tangibly close.

I am suddenly very, very nervous. I have spent so many years avoiding the search – and now Mum has emphatically warned me against it. *Promise me, darling. Promise.* What if they're all freaks and lunatics, like she says?

My index finger hovers above the reply button.

But then, isn't it Mum I'm doing this for? The thought of that time, of her going away again, rises like bile in the pit of my stomach.

There are two paths on the road in front of me: one the same flat line I have always been on; the other a steep hill, with who knows what on the other side. I have already stumbled partway down one, but if I want to turn back, the way is clear; I can go back, forget about all this and take the easy path. Or I can begin to climb.

As if some invisible hand is guiding me, a breeze blows through the open window in front of me and ruffles the piece of paper with Jane's alias written on it.

Three emails later, a date is set: in two days' time – 1st May – officially one month to go – I will meet MissMarple63.

I arrange to see her, with Keira in tow, at the cafe in the British Library at five. Mum thinks I'm at a netball match.

I couldn't believe it when Jane told me she'd be travelling down from Edinburgh, so eager is she to meet me.

It's really not a problem, she said in one of her later emails. *I have a brother in Clapham I can stay with overnight; it's a good excuse to see him and the kids.*

Keira insisted on coming along, not so much in a detective capacity but in fear that this woman is going to turn out to be a psychopath. 'You might need me for backup,' she said, forming her fingers into an imaginary gun. Thinking of Mum, I allow her.

We took the bus to King's Cross, sitting for so long in the painfully slow traffic on the Euston Road that I was convinced Jane would think we were a no-show. By the time we got here I'd chewed my nails down to the quick.

'Are you nervous?' Keira asks now as we stare up at the library's monolithic red-brick facade. I am as tightly coiled as one of Keira's curls. I say nothing, but she loops an arm into mine all the same. 'Don't be.'

We've been to the British Library before, but I've forgotten how vast it is: all polished white stone that ricochets the sound of footsteps around the entrance hall, and light streaming through from the balconied tiers reaching skyward.

I can't help the rising thud of my heart as we head up the escalator to the first-floor cafe, the excited voice whispering in my mind, *This is it*. The thought of Mum, when I tell her the news: *I've done it, I've found the answer!*

Jane spots me before I've even stepped onto firm ground, shouting 'Rosie!' from across the hall, so that the other people in the cafe turn around and stare. 'Sorry,' she whispers exaggeratedly when she reaches us. 'I just can't believe it's really you. I've seen pictures, and that interview a couple of weeks ago, but it's so strange seeing you here in the flesh.' I see her taking me in. 'It's true, you really are like your dad.'

'Sorry we're a bit late; the bus got stuck in traffic,' I mumble, trying to move off the subject, and stretch out my hand to her. 'This is my friend Keira.'

She gives my hand a hearty shake. 'Don't be silly – you're here now. Come, sit down. I have tea.' She stretches an arm around each of us and steers us to a table in the corner. MissMarple63 turns out to be a very short, very fat Scotswoman, with hair the exact rusty shade of red as my nan's old cocker spaniel. She's originally from Glasgow, she tells us, but now lives in Edinburgh where she owns a bookshop and café near Princes Street.

'Hence my love of the great British Library.'

Her lilting accent and incessant need to mother us, fussing as we settle and insisting on getting the full blackboard's worth of cakes, gives her the air of a nursery school teacher, rather than the discerning sleuth after which she has named herself. I can't quite work out how she became so invested in my family, and she must read my mind, because it's the first thing she tells us once we're settled at the wooden table with our coats barely off.

'I remember the day it all hit the news,' she says, pouring tea in a steady stream from one cup to the next. 'It was just so awful. That pretty little girl, and your poor, poor parents. My sister lost a child when she was young.' She swirls the milk slowly into her cup. 'Thirty years ago now. I don't think she'll ever get over it. Having seen her go through it all, I couldn't even begin to imagine what it must have been like for your parents, the not knowing, the constant publicity. And for you, for that matter, growing up under it all.' I look up, my teacup poised at my lips. 'Agatha's other daughter, Kirsty, was only a baby when Laura died. It was very difficult for her, growing up with the testament of her older sister to look up to. It was always "Laura was so beautiful", "Laura would have been so clever". It's hard on the ones left.' She puts it into words so succinctly, the constant pressure of being number two. It makes me warm to her.

But she doesn't hang about: as soon as our cups are drained, she unzips the suitcase that has been sitting beside her chair, spreading the contents out in front of us – reams of files and paperwork – running her hands across it all like she's presenting the opening of a magic trick. 'There we go: this is everything.'

I hesitate. This obsessive cataloguing of my family seems just a little bit creepy.

But I pull a lever arch file from the stack, wary of unsettling the whole lot. If I've come this far, there's no point turning back now. It's full of newspaper cuttings, I see as I flip through the pages. Neatly folded, and pressed into clear plastic envelopes, like some sort of black-humoured school project. The first is an article about the case from one of the national papers, with a sentence marked out in neon highlighter. *Investigators are looking into reports of a nearby construction site for a possible link to the disappearance.*

'At first, they wanted to search the site for a possible location for a …' Jane catches herself, and gives me an awkward look, mashing her lips together in a grimace so that the red lipstick she's wearing blends over her Cupid's bow.

'A body,' I finish. 'You can say it. I've heard it enough times before.'

'A body, then. But, as you know, they didn't find anything. So, instead, they obtained a list of all the construction workers on site that day and interviewed them one by one. However, nothing unusual came up.'

She flips to the next page, a local Floridian paper. It looks as if it's been photocopied – I can see where the sentences have been cut short, where the paper hasn't quite fitted in the machine. The words 'CONSTRUCTION WORKERS CLEARED IN KIDNAP CASE' are splashed across it.

'I had it sent to me from a library in Jacksonville,' she explains as she sees me running my fingers over the truncated phrases. 'They've been very helpful, over the years, feeding me bits of information that might be useful. The head librarian and I have built up quite a friendship.'

On and on the story goes, each one revealing a tiny piece more of the puzzle: there's a gap of several years, and then, five years after Emily first went missing, a man is being questioned over his involvement in the case. Then, finally, his name and face are revealed: Hank Wilson, construction worker and now a convicted child rapist.

I want to throw the file away from me when I see those words. It's a shock, even though I knew it was coming. Instead, I politely close the file and move it to the side, then ask in a wavering voice, 'What's in the others?'

Keira jumps in, 'This one looks like it's in some sort of code?' and I know she can sense my distress.

Jane takes the book from her. It's a notebook, like an ordinary school book; a faded red cover of mottled, recycled card. The lined pages are filled with words and scrawled signs in hastily written pen. 'Transcripts,' she says, opening it up. 'From conversations. Conversations I had with Hank.' She gives me a guilty look.

'You spoke to him?' I ask as Keira speaks over me: 'What language is it in?'

'It's shorthand.' Jane looks gratefully at Keira, happy to explain the easy question first. 'I was a journalist many moons ago.' I can tell she's stalling, running her fingers over the pages. She catches my eye, speaks through a sigh. 'Yes, I spoke to him, Rosie. Still speak to him.'

I say nothing.

'Like I said, I've always had an interest in Emily's case. I followed the story from when it happened. When Hank was first connected, he was already on trial for those two little girls. It was one of his co-workers at the time who brought up the connection to Emily – Alan … something or other. He said he'd always been surprised that no one had pursued Hank further. Hank is ... he's a little odd. He has some learning difficulties. He lived in a trailer on his own in the middle of nowhere. And then, when he stood trial for the girls, it just made sense. It got leapt on, of course, and they started trying to bring a third case against him, but there wasn't enough evidence for him to stand trial. He got life without parole for the girls – only escaped the death penalty on the grounds of his mental health.'

She looks up. 'And now you're both probably wondering, even more, why I would want to go speaking to a man like that.' She's been worrying the corner of the notebook back and forth with her thumb and forefinger. Eventually it comes loose and breaks off in her hand. She brushes it to the floor; the little triangle of red lands on the black tile. She stares intently at it for a second, before carrying on. 'My marriage was breaking down, around the time that Hank's case started to be reported over here. My husband ... wasn't a nice man. He wasn't very kind to me.' She rubs an uncomfortable hand up her left arm.

'Once the divorce went through, I picked up and moved to Edinburgh. I found myself on my own in a new city, without many friends or ties to speak of, and I became fixated on Hank. It was as if all my anger over my marriage somehow transposed itself onto him. I needed desperately to make him confess.' She pauses, takes a breath and pours herself a glass of water from the carafe in the centre of the table. 'I wrote to him, at first saying I was a journalist. It wasn't exactly an outright lie, more a bending of the truth.

Eventually he wrote back, and after about a year he agreed to a phone interview.' Her hands work through the collection of files until she stops at a yellow speckled one. 'The letters are in here, if you want to go through them.'

She hands the file over to me, and, barely glancing at it, I take it. Thinking of her speaking to him, this man who could be my sister's killer, has sucked all the moisture from my body. I clear my throat, willing the words to form. 'What ... what was he like?'

'Angry, at first.' She nods. 'And eventually remorseful. We speak maybe twice, three times a year. I was eaten up by it.' She gestures to the files. 'I was convinced that I was going to crack the case; that I'd be the one to get a confession out of him. It can get quite addictive.' She shakes her head in a flurry of reddish-brown curls.

Something isn't right here. 'And now?' I ask, although I already know the answer.

'Rosie, I'm so sorry.' I'm surprised to see a tear escape from the corner of her right eye and course down her cheek. 'But I don't think Hank did it.'

'What?' Beside me, Keira slams shut the file she is holding, causing the people at the next table to flinch in surprise. 'But all of those posts ... all of this ...?'

I can only look on, waiting for the explanation to come.

'I know; I know what a horrible person you must think I am, for hounding that man all those years. But the more I've looked into it, the more I'm convinced it couldn't be him.'

'How?'

'The ages, for one thing. Those girls were ten and eleven – nowhere near the same age as Emily. And they were girls he knew – there was no predisposition for going after strangers. Plus, the fact that they're alive when ...' She flinches. 'Well, with Emily, we just don't know. But most of all ... most of all, I know he didn't do it because he has convinced me he didn't do it. I can't quite explain it, but when you speak to someone in that situation, where there's no hope of freedom, you develop a certain degree of honesty between you. After all those calls, over all these years, I've got to know Hank. And whilst I absolutely believe he is where he deserves to be for his other crimes, it wouldn't be fair of me to saddle him with the blame for something I'm sure he did not do.'

'Then why is it all still up there?' White-hot anger burns through my veins and grits my teeth. All this time wasted. All the hope, and the anticipation, and the excitement of meeting her and maybe, maybe finding something, something the investigators missed or overlooked, has fizzled into nothing. I push the files away from me. One of them falls off the table and lands on the floor with a thud, but I leave it there, refusing to pick it up. 'You're a liar. You're a fantasist who gets off on thinking they're some great detective. But this isn't an Agatha Christie novel. This is my family. And my sister. It's real.' I stand, pulling my jacket up from where it's draped over the back of the chair. 'Keira, let's get out of here.'

We've taken barely three steps before Jane's voice stops us. 'Rosie, wait.' The tone of sadness pulls me back. 'You're right. I'll take it all down, as soon as I get back home. I think maybe it became a bit of a lifeline for me, at a time when I needed it. And a bit of me is still addicted to that rush – being a part of it all, feeling like I was making a difference. You must understand, Rosie, I really did think I was helping. But I'm glad I met you. Seeing you here now, I realise I need to let it go; move on. I should never even have replied to your email. It was foolish of me; but I just couldn't bring myself to pass up the opportunity to meet you, after having felt so involved for so long. I ... I'm sorry. But before you go, there's just one last piece of information I want to give you ... if you'll let me?'

I make no motion of acquiescence, but I can't quite bring myself to turn away from her. She seems to take this as consent, because she reaches into her purse, pulls out a folded piece of paper and places it on the table in front of her.

Cautiously, I find myself reaching across, picking it up and unfolding it, unsure of what else she can possibly tell me that will be of use. All that's written on it is 'Michael' and a phone number.

I look up, confused.

'You may know him better as "MikeD"? It was stupid of me to ever think I could help you. But he might.'

ANNA

13

There must be something in the house. Something to tell me who I am. For over a week I am haunted by this chant.

I go to school. We go to church. I help Mamma in the backyard. I go to choir practice, where I am polite and courteous with William but refuse his offer to drive me home. Ascension Sunday is coming up, and we rehearse 'Hail the Day That Sees Him Rise', whose lyrics are all about glory and triumph. I pray harder than I ever have in my life for some sign to tell me when the time is right.

And on Tuesday night, an opportunity presents itself.

'There's a craft fair in Cedar Key tomorrow morning. I'm going to collect some supplies.' Mamma sets down two bowls of box mac and cheese. 'Mrs Murray is going to give me a lift in on her way to work, so you'll have to take my packages to the post office before school. And make sure the Anderson package goes Priority Express: her daughter's

171

getting married on Sunday and she'll need the dress by then.'

I imagine her weighing up the better of the choices: admitting she really does need a car, or having to share one with Mrs Murray. But then a greater thought seizes me: if Mamma is leaving early, then she won't be around to see me off for school. I say a silent thank you to whoever is up there, as the seeds of an idea begin to take root.

The next morning, when I wake up, instead of getting dressed for school, I scurry downstairs and dial the school office number from the phone in the kitchen. 'Hello?' I ask gruffly when the receptionist answers, giving a little cough for good measure. 'This is Anna Montgomery; I'm in Mrs Baker's homeroom.'

'Yes?' I hear the slurp of coffee; imagine her in her grey office chair, going through the motions of another ordinary day.

'I'm sorry but I'm not well. I don't think I'll be able to attend classes today. My mother's already left for work, but I can bring a note in tomorrow?' This last part is a terrifying bluff – I've heard other students boasting about forging their parents' signatures for one excuse or another, but it seems to me to be just one deception too far.

I hear the clack of fingernails on a keyboard. 'That won't be necessary at this stage,' the voice meanders. 'You've had no other absences this year, and you're a senior. Only absences of three days or more require written documentation. If you're off for more than five you'll need a note from your doctor.'

'Oh ... well, OK then.' I've never been off sick before, as far as I can remember. I've never had the need to know what the procedure is. 'Thank you.'

'Byeeee.' I imagine her phone already halfway to the receiver. 'Get better.'

I hold the phone in my hand, the dead tone ringing dully from it. If I hoped for some sort of hiccup or hindrance, I have been thwarted: it's all gone completely according to plan. And so now the real work begins.

If there is anything that will tell me the truth about who I am, I know it lies within this house. Mamma is too particular, too cautious, to bury her secrets anywhere else. My thoughts turn at first to the attic, which is accessed via a short flight of wooden steps by Mamma's room. But I've been in there recently, and it's practically spartan: Mamma's neatness won't allow for much more than the old wrought-iron bed I slept in as a child, a chest of drawers we've been keeping up there to repaint, and a couple of boxes of winter coats and sweaters, all neatly folded and packed away.

It would be far too easy to stumble upon a clue in the living room or kitchen, and there's no way I'll find anything in my bedroom.

Which just leaves Mamma's bedroom.

I've only ever glimpsed the inside of her room before. As a child, if I had a nightmare, I would knock softly on the unpainted pine door until Mamma's face appeared in the doorway, when she would spirit me back to my own room with barely a backward glance, soothe me there until my bad dreams dissipated, and return to her room's obscurity. I try to recall, now, what sort of dreams would wake me with such violent sobs. My hand touches the cool gold metal of the doorknob.

As the door releases, my heart is beating so wildly I'm sure I can see it thumping in my chest. I almost jump as the door shuts with a bang behind me, but I wipe my sweaty palms on my pyjama shorts and allow myself to look at Mamma's sanctuary properly for the very first time.

In a way, I am relieved to see it is exactly as I pictured it: no print or pattern to claim an identity; the bed sheets – plain – are heavily starched, their edges forming sharp lines against the mattress; nothing but a stern wooden cross to save the eyes from the starkness of it all. Two pine side tables sit almost bare either side of the bed. There are no lights apart from the single bulb in the ceiling. On the right-hand side – the side she sleeps on, I see, from the whisper of a depression on the pillow – there is a copy of the Common English Bible, the same version I also own, its burgundy-red cover standing out against the monochrome of the room.

I feel myself compelled to go to it, to see if there is some special verse or chapter she has marked or highlighted, but the pages are crisp and unadorned. Feeling brazen, my fingers coil around the handle of her bedside drawer.

A note, perhaps, from my father? A birth certificate? Something secret and special that she'll want to keep close at hand. Resting against the rough wooden interior are a black-toothed comb, a red pencil with a rubber at the end, and a little vial of the lavender oil she makes herself from the bushes in the garden. Nothing more.

The other side is even worse: so empty I doubt it has ever even been opened. My eyes scour the room for inspiration.

The wooden dresser opposite the bed is almost identical to mine; so much so they could be a pair; but whereas mine is neatly adorned with a mirror, hairbands, combs and a stack of books, Mamma's holds nothing. I am overwhelmed with sadness for her little life.

Pulling out the first drawer, I am hit with the saccharine smell of lavender drawer liners; I can see the pattern of purple paper poking out from underneath the meticulously folded T-shirts. My first instinct is to reach out, to feel underneath them for a potential hiding spot, but as I stretch my arms out in front of me, I become aware of my own incriminating hands; their ability to muss up or crease something that could leave tangible evidence of my break-in. Will Mamma's keen eyes be able to spot her tainted T-shirts, marred with my touch?

Holding my breath, I flatten the palm of my hand and press it ever so gently against each stack of T-shirts. I repeat this with two more drawers, through the discomfort of seeing Mamma's puritanical bras and panties on display, rooting through each exactingly twinned set of socks that sighs under my touch, but leaves me empty-handed. And then, as I tug at the bottom drawer, something jars. I pull again, harder, and it frees itself entirely from the dresser, landing in my lap with a force that throws me backwards onto the hard wooden floor.

The drawer is empty. But in the space where it sat, I see a stack of papers.

I hold my breath. Outside, a cloud passes over the sun. I reach over and take them in my hands.

They're identical, each about the size of a postcard, and, as I take the first one out, I realise I've seen them before.

A watercolour spray of lilies, their petals reaching for the edge of the page.

Inside, the neat, looping cursive that not so long ago spelled out my twinned names.

And here, a message, printed with almost exact precision in the centre of the page. *Remember The Lilies.*

And there, a signature. *Father Paul.*

I turn over each card, but every time they say the exact same thing. *Remember The Lilies.* Again and again. Ten, twelve, fifteen times.

Father Paul.

The man in the white linen suit. My silent pursuer has a name.

Mamma must know him. He must somehow be connected to it all. But how, or why, I can't say.

Remember The Lilies.

Feeling light-headed, I turn away from the chest of drawers, throw open Mamma's spartan curtains and heave open the window, gulping in the clean air. I stare across Mamma's blooming backyard, willing the flowers to give me inspiration.

And then it strikes me: the lilies.

Since I was big enough to wield a trowel, I have known my way around Mamma's backyard, learning from her sure hands which plants will flower with which, how to weed and deadhead, which shrubs need care and attention, and which will bend to their own will. I have scraped and scratched every inch of that fertile ground. But there is one area I am absolutely forbidden to touch: the white Easter lilies that grow in a vast terracotta pot at the far end of the yard.

It makes no sense: why would she trust me implicitly with every other leaf or stem, only to bid me, should I venture near the lilies, 'No, Anna. Not there'? I carefully restack the notes, replace the drawer, shut Mamma's bedroom door behind me with a soft click and make my way outside.

The day is still early, not even 9 a.m., and a soft breeze licks at my legs, bare in my pyjama shorts, as I stalk towards the back of the yard, trowel in hand. The grass is wet with dew, and makes an even crunch under my galoshes as I walk. In the distance, there is the occasional chirrup of a bird, but apart from that, all is silent, as if every creature in my vicinity is entranced by my steps.

The lily bush waits for me in its ruddy pot, sat atop a rectangular stretch of flagstones next to the curved wooden bench Mamma likes to sit on with a cup of tea, her face yearning towards the sunlight, on the fleeting occasions she allows herself a break. The flowers are in full bloom, unfurling their silky white petals like a room of debutantes twirling at a cotillion.

My first thought is to see if there is something in the base of the pot, but I can see that's impossible. There is no way of getting through the soil without dislodging the flowers or pulling them up without it being noticed. I give the earth a dissatisfied poke with the edge of my trowel, but it's all easy and yielding; nothing hidden beneath its depths that I can find. And then my eyes flicker to the flagstones.

Memories return. Those odd, sidelong looks in the direction of the stones. I've always just put them down to her concern for the lilies' growth. The time I found her out there, hands pressed to the ground, the look of ashen terror that crossed her face when I called out to her. And now I play again the scene from my childhood where I fell on the rake. It was there, wasn't it? In that part of the garden. I landed right by the pot. I remember now the feel of the rough earthenware rubbing at my back through my thin T-shirt as I butted against it. And how she shouted, above my infant sobs, almost without thinking, 'Get away from there! Don't look under it!' At the time, I was too struck with the injustice of my own pain, but even then I thought it a strange phrase. *Look under where, Mamma?*

Answering my silent question from long ago, I look.

Using all my strength, I hold on to the edges of the pot and roll it onto the grass. A damp ring marks where it has sat on the paving stone; a dark soiled circle which suddenly feels like my very own 'X marks the spot', because soon I can see that, unlike the other flagstones that line this section, the edges of this particular one are loose, they haven't been cemented down – which means that at some point or another it has been lifted up.

With trembling hands I feel my way around the cool grey stone, finding a convenient edge to grab hold of; trying not to think of my gloveless fingertips and the dirt they are accumulating, or the worms and earwigs that lie beneath. I do my best to pull up the slab but it refuses to budge. Frustrated, I reach out for the abandoned trowel at my feet and, working in tiny incremental movements, force my way around the square perimeter, like I'm opening a jar of beans that has been stuck fast. At last I feel a give, and the slab starts to loosen. Abandoning the trowel, I grasp the corners with my fingers, and slowly the stone comes away.

Carefully, I rest the stone aside and look at what lies beneath. The smell of moist earth chokes me with every ragged, fearful breath.

To the uninquisitive eye, there seems to be nothing worth noting. The black soil is moist, but undisturbed apart from the writhing pink bodies of worms traversing through it. Suppressing the wave of acrid bile that rises in my throat at the thought of them on my bare hands, I reach down and press my fingers through the earth. It's soft, but I can't tell if this is from where it has been disturbed by the removal of the paving stone, or from more frequent activity.

And then, as my fingers press down to my knuckles, I feel the distinct cool surface of metal.

I snatch up the trowel, brushing the earth aside as neatly as I can without disturbing the clean paving stones surrounding it. It's difficult: the soil moves aside for a split second, but then slips back down to cover the object, but eventually I can tell it's some sort of tin. I manage to clear a wide enough space to tap the top, and it replies with a hollow knock. Feeling around its perimeter, I can tell it's circular, and as I brush the dirt aside I make out a red-and-white pattern on the front: a drawing of fruits, trailing around the rim, and people, their faces now blackened with dirt as if they've spent a day at the mines. Then I make out the letters at the top – 'Pilgrim Fruit Cake'– and I realise I know this tin. Mamma has another one. She keeps it in the living room on the coffee table; it holds buttons and thread for her sewing and mending. I asked her once where it came from: she said it was her father's favourite thing to eat, but they were only allowed a tiny piece of it, once a year, after church on Christmas Day.

With shaking hands, I grasp hold of it and feel it yielding from its grave, ready to be pulled into my waiting arms. I feel like an archaeologist – except the only bones I am searching for are my own.

I almost can't bear to open it.

But then, as if guided by some force external to myself, my fingers reach for the rim, and pull.

Every fibre of me is on edge. I can feel every blade of grass; smell the soupy, wet earth and the sharp metal of the tin that has been hiding beneath it. I can hear each rustle and squawk of the birds in the trees, each discrete buzz of the bees, sucking sweet nectar from the yellow acacia flowers; each beat of my heart as it gets faster and faster and the lid comes looser and looser.

And then it is open, and I stoop over to see what lies inside. And I know in an instant what I am looking at.

That green. That unmistakable, lurid green.

Even now I recognise it.

It's the colour of the gift bags my classmates waved at school on Monday mornings, handing out blue candies and showing off treats. It's the colour of the ticket I held in my hand less than two weeks ago, and of the looping logo I walked underneath.

The T-shirt is small, clearly a child's, and as I run my fingers over the silver letters 'A-S-T-R-O', a sob rasps at my chest and I pull it to me, breathing in the fabric as if it can somehow help me suck the memories harder into myself. It smells of nothing distinct: the ground and the tin. No hint of perfume, or a wave of sunscreen that will help me form a clearer sense of the voice that has always tickled at my ears, but whose face has remained in silhouette. Why can't I see her?

I want my mommy.

I lay the T-shirt on the ground beside me as gently as if it still contains the body of the child I once was. Underneath it, a flash of silver. I pull out a pendant, looped on a metal chain. The twin to the one I received not so long ago: a cross, the swirl of a lily wrapped around it.

Remember The Lilies.

Then I reach inside the tin once more and take out the last item inside: a swirl of multicoloured fabric nestled into a ball.

And that's when I hear the unmistakable rumble of tyres rolling up the drive.

At first I think it must be William, so unused am I to the sound of a car on our property. But as the noise gets closer, I know it can't be William. It must be Mamma.

My heart seizes in my chest. Hurling the T-shirt and pendant back into their hiding place, I leap up and stuff the fabric absent-mindedly into my pyjama pocket. Hurriedly grabbing at the dirt, I start piling the earth back on top of the tin, hating having to once more cover it up. As quick as I possibly can, I pull back the paving stone and haul the terracotta pot back into place. The trowel I hurl far into the bushes, hoping to recover it later.

Barely thinking, I run back into the house, pull off my galoshes and toss them into the bucket by the door, and then I am up, up the stairs, driven by a mindless energy towards my room. My pyjamas, flecked with soil, I wrench off and push under the bed as far as they will go, and then I am down the hall and into the bathroom, turning the shower on full before I've even finished stepping into the tub.

And then I am scrubbing. Every inch of me, hard. My muddied legs. My forehead, where a soiled hand may have accidentally rubbed against it. The elusive spots under my nails where an unnoticed speck of dirt may give me away. Adrenaline pulses through my body, and that, plus the hot water raining down on me, makes me dizzy and light-headed. Through the cascade of water, I hear the distant thud of the front door, and I know it won't be long until she finds me, and this makes me scrub faster, harder, lathering the soap on my body in thick white clouds. Surely she will know; she will guess in an instant where I've been.

Footsteps on the stairs. And then a pause. 'Anna?' The bathroom door pushes open, revealing Mamma's concerned face.

'Mamma.' I'm sure I must shriek it. I instantly go to cover my naked body with my arms, ashamed of her bald gaze.

'What to goodness is going on?'

I close the taps, reach for a towel and step shakily onto the bath mat. 'I ... I ... don't feel too good.' It isn't a lie. As I rest myself on the edge of the bath, I feel my limbs go shaky and limp, and the dizziness from the hot shower overwhelms me. 'When I woke up this morning, I felt all weak and kind of fluey.' The lie tumbles out of me in a subconscious act of self-preservation. 'I didn't want to bother you, but I thought it best to take the day off school, and rest up. I was hoping a shower would make me feel better but ... but ...'

I hang my head in my hands, the events of the morning and the fear of discovery weighing down every inch of me.

'Oh Anna.' Mamma comes to me, towels my forehead and rests a cool hand on it. 'You do feel warm. Let's get you back to bed.'

And I allow myself to be led, glad to be mothered; to have myself dried, and dressed in a cool, clean nightgown, and tucked into bed.

'You're never sick,' Mamma tuts, smoothing the sheets down around me a little tighter than is comfortable. 'I warned you, didn't I? It's all this upset, over that boy. And you're lucky I happened to come back home ... That idiot woman talked at me so long this morning I left my purse on the hall table. Lie back now. Mamma will look after you.'

Paralysed with fear, I train my eyes on Mamma's hypnotic movements as she steps around the room, pulling the curtains even tighter shut, and straightening the things on my dresser. She leaves the room, appearing moments later with a glass of water and two round blue pills.

'Oh, but Mamma, I don't think ...' I struggle to sit even as she's pressing them into my palm.

I picture Mamma's medicine cabinet, an exercise in cautious paranoia: Band-Aids by the packet-load, sealed in their wrappers; murky brown vials of iodine; bottles of aspirin and cough syrup and Pepto-Bismol. The armour Mamma uses in her daily combat against disease. Often-times, when I was little and scared of the demons whose faces are now hazy to me, Mamma would give me the corner of one of these blue pills and promise me all would be well.

'Take them, Anna,' she says now. 'They'll help you sleep.' She holds the glass to my lips, watching as I swallow.

Before she's even left the room, I feel my eyelids pressing down and my head go heavy on the pillow. I hear the soft click of the door, but before sleep can claim me, I remember the muddied pyjamas beneath me, the last secret of the tin in their midst.

I wrench my woozy limbs from the bed and stretch a leaden arm underneath it. My unseeing fingers excavate the pyjama pocket, curl around the multi-coloured fabric, tug.

Looped around my middle finger and thumb is a bracelet: the sort of thing you see them making at stalls in the centre of the mall. Strands of brightly coloured threads – fuchsia pink and kingfisher blue and marigold yellow – all woven together in an intricate pattern. But the colours alone mean nothing next to the white beads plaited into it.

I feel the pills working their magic on me, blurring my vision and begging my body to sleep. But I fight against them, turning the beads with my thumb and forefinger to reveal the five white letters as they start to form a word.

And there, in my weary hands, rests the incontrovertible truth. Because even if Mamma denies me the truth of our life before, or the pendant, or even the hidden tin, I know, in my drugged state, what these letters mean.

An E.

An M.

I.

L.

Y.

The letters spell out Emily.

ROSIE

14

The day of the party the weather is clear, so Mum opens up the French doors that lead from the main living room into the garden, sniffs the air, and declares we'll host everything outside. 'It won't feel so claustrophobic.' She fiddles with the necklace Dad bought her for their tenth wedding anniversary, a pendant with two gold rings intertwined, pulling at it like it's a noose.

She remains tensely skittish all morning. Tidying things that don't need tidying. Moving objects from one place to another, then back again. I try to keep her company, but I feel like I'm underfoot – sitting on a sofa when she's just puffed up the cushions, setting down a glass without a coaster – so instead I hover, my hands fiddling at my waist, until she sends me upstairs to change.

I stare at my open wardrobe, trying to decide what, exactly, is appropriate to wear to a party celebrating my missing sister. I dig out a pleated skirt in a deep shade of coral that I know Mum likes, and match it with a white blouse that has ruffles down the centre. I practise my smiles in the mirror – *How nice to see you. Thank you for coming. Yes, exams are really soon* – as I rim my eyes in black.

My hand hovers over the pair of tweezers in my make-up bag. How I would like to score a line on some soft part of my flesh; the skin just above my knee, the knobbly line where my hip bone meets pelvis. How like scratching an itch. Instead, I chew at a fingernail until I've exposed pink rawness.

In my bedside drawer, Michael's number remains folded up and uncalled. I've read and reread Astro7402's page, but I feel frozen, inert. Jane's false lead has left me bruised and broken. The thought of doing it all over again, of building up all that hope and then having it destroyed, makes me wish I'd never started. But I know time is running out. Today, it's just over three weeks until the end of May.

Downstairs, a girl in a starched white shirt and an expression that says she has no idea what she's here for, and doesn't really care, has been stationed near the door, with a tray of half-filled plastic champagne glasses and a bottle in her hand.

'Can I have one please?' I point to a flute. She must be in her early twenties, and I see her wrestling with the decision, but instead she shrugs and tops one up for me.

In the garden, finger sandwiches have been laid out on a table, next to two big bowls of Eton Mess that Mum made up fresh this morning. The fruit is haemorrhaging into the cream. With no one looking, I stick my finger in and scoop a dollop into my mouth. I crunch on meringue with my back teeth, feeling the sugar condense and stick. And I can sense it: Mum's desperation, in this dessert, in this manic desire to make everything good. And I know I have to keep going.

Three weeks left to find an answer. To find Emily. To save Mum.

In the kitchen, she's tidying away the last of the debris, stuffing the empty sandwich trays into black bin bags as Dad sits at the kitchen table, simultaneously stacking napkins and plates into a tower and reading off a sheet of paper in front of him. 'And so, in short, this is a celebration as much for Emily as it is for all of you: the people who have touched our lives, and indeed hers, in so many ways. Without you, we could not have gone on. So, I would like to raise a toast, to Emily. And to you all.'

'It's great, David.' She kisses him on the top of his head, holds his hand just a little too tightly.

'You think?'

'Honestly, I think it's perfect.' She sees me coming in and smiles. 'Hi, darling, you look very pretty. I do love that skirt on you.' Her eyes flick to the champagne in my hand, but she says nothing. The atmosphere remains light, upbeat. We're spreading a picnic blanket over the mud today; there's no room for arguments.

The doorbell rings, and Dad looks at his watch. 'Gosh, is it time already?'

Mum turns grey, hurriedly stuffs the bin bags into a corner and starts upstairs.

Showtime.

Auntie Sally is at the door. She takes a glass from the tray and pulls Mum into a hug. She catches sight of me – 'Rosie ... goodness!' – and then bursts into tears. I stand there awkwardly, feeling the extremities of my body harden as she dabs at her eyes with a cocktail napkin the waitress hands her. Mum's jaw has tightened, and she's doing her best to pat Auntie Sally on the back, but all the while I can see her blinking forcefully, fixing her gaze on the spines on the bookshelf in the corner.

Dad saves us. Propels Sally into the living room and murmurs, 'Celebration, Sal, remember?' as he turns the speakers on, floating soft choral music into the room and out through the open doors.

When I turn back around, I catch sight of Mum's feet as she disappears upstairs.

I ache to go after her, but then people start to arrive, and I'm swept along on a stream of hellos and how-do-you-dos. There are some faces I recognise – family, obviously, and Aunt Pam, who's not my real aunt but an old friend of Mum's – but there are others, too, who have made up various factions of the Emily machine over the years. Mark Alcott, the 'family spokesperson'; John Buck, a private investigator; several members of Scotland Yard; journalists – the few who've garnered my parents' respect. And then I see Sarah Brown, the director of the Emily Archer Trust. The one who wrote the email. She's talking to someone, a glass of champagne in one hand, throwing her head back in laughter. And I want to storm over there right now and confront her. Demand to know why she's trying to destroy everything. Force her to take it all back.

But then Mum appears, the shadow of a smile pinned so forcefully to her face. And I can't. Instead, I head back over to the doorway, top up my flute. That sandwich and that bit of meringue is all I've eaten today, and I knock it back, letting the bubbles fizz through me and dissipate my anger. Keira arrives as I'm topping up a third time, flanked by her parents.

Caro eyes the glass in my hand, and I see her and Keira exchange a look. I wonder how much Keira has told her about the party. I think she's going to say something, but instead she kisses me on the cheek and pulls Keira's dad past us into the house. 'Nice to see you, Rosie. Tom, let's go find Susie and David. We'll leave you two to catch up.'

'You on the fizz already?' Keira nods to my champagne-filled glass. I give a weary sigh, but she loops an arm around me, nudges her shoulder into mine. 'Hook us up, then?'

We take a couple of glasses into the garden, where a greyness has blanketed the sky, and it's starting to spit. It looks, at first, like everyone's going to be all British about it and ignore it, but then it soon becomes apparent that it's not going to let up, and suddenly it's all hands on deck, moving the sandwiches and paper plates into the living room, running to cover up the Eton Mess, and whipping off the tablecloth, which is now speckled with wet splotches.

'So much for the weather,' Dad says, to no one in particular. I can tell he's starting to feel nervous about his speech, fiddling with his top shirt button, doing and undoing it as his eyes roam restlessly around the room.

I hear the doorbell ring, but the waitress has left her post to help with the food, and with no one else around I reach out for the latch and open it.

Standing on the topmost step is a man of about my dad's age, with hair a fading brown like a squirrel's fur, and a short, peppery beard. He's holding a bunch of flowers that look sort of mournful, their heads drooping down, and he himself has an odd, embarrassed expression on his face, as though he doesn't really know how he got here.

'Can I help you?' I ask when he makes no move to introduce himself or come inside.

'Oh, ah, yes.' He looks up, and there's something intelligent in his eyes, an alertness that suggests he's constantly assessing his surroundings, as he does with me now. 'Rosie.' He blinks, taking me in.

'Yes.'

'These are for you.' He holds the flowers up like he's glad of the barrier between us. 'Well, for your family.' As I take them he skulks inside, but before I shut the door he seems to glance around the street, as if he's looking for someone coming up behind him. 'Listen, I can't stay long. I really shouldn't be here at all. I'm not even strictly invited, but an old colleague told me about the celebration, and I wanted to come and pay my respects to your family. To say … to say … Sorry, where are your parents?'

I point into the living room, and he scuttles off with barely another word, still in his long, grey overcoat. I frown at his departing back. I don't recognise him. He has a gravelly, plummy tone which suggests to me he might be some sort of lawyer or detective, but if so he's not one who's been involved within my memory. There's something so odd about his manner – his twitching movements, his nervous speech – but I can't work out whether it's something about today, or whether that's just what he's like.

I follow him down the hall into the living room but soon lose sight of him in the crowd. Keira spots me, and together we meander through the damp guests, picking equally damp sandwiches off the trays that have begun to recirculate. I want to tell her about him, to ask her what she thinks it's all about, when a hushed conversation to my left stops me.

'Did you see Michael Davis is here?'

'No. Really? Where?'

'Over there, by the window. But don't stare.'

'Jesus, I haven't seen him for three or four years now. Why was he even invited?'

'I don't know – maybe because he wrote for *The Times*? He did publish a couple of articles about Emily, didn't he? Maybe Sandra invited him – she was features editor then, wasn't she?'

'Yeah, maybe. Just seems odd. What's he doing now?'

'I think he moved to Chesterfield. Works for the local paper there.'

'Poor bloke. He was a good journalist. I don't really understand what happened to him but it really messed him up. Said he needed a new start.'

'I never really got to the bottom of what it was about. Something to do with a woman in a navy dress – he thought it was connected to all this. Surprised he even showed.'

I clutch Keira's shoulder, and she jumps so abruptly that the champagne jerks in her arm, and a cloud of bubbles fizzes over the rim.

One of the group catches my eye, and hesitates on whatever she was about to say. 'You must be Rosie.' She beams at me, and holds out a hand. 'I'm Helen Daly, from the *Mail*. I did the exclusive with your parents about the Emily Archer Trust, when it was first started.'

'Pleased to meet you.' I hurriedly take the proffered hand, then I grab Keira's arm and pull her towards the stairs. 'You will excuse me, won't you? My friend needs to borrow something from my room … it's … talk to you later …'

'What's going on?' Keira asks as I push open the door to my room and grab my laptop from the desk.

'Did you hear who they were talking about just now?'

'No.'

'Michael Davis.' I go to TheHive, and almost sub-consciously my fingers hit the keys to find the page I am looking for.

'Who's that?'

I pull up the page. The heading looms on the screen – 'The Woman in the Navy Dress'. Underneath it, I see the avatar my eyes have skimmed over hundreds of times, of what for some reason I thought was a line drawing of an organ, but now realise is an old-fashioned typewriter. I turn the laptop towards her. 'MikeD.'

Keira peers at the screen. 'What?'

'Didn't you hear them, Kiki? The man who just came in: they said his name was Michael Davis; that he was a journalist, and that something happened – something that scared him. And they mentioned a woman in a navy dress.' I scan the page, trying to find something that will confirm it, but just like before, it remains blank. 'It has to be the same person. When I spoke to him, there was something in his voice that sounded ... I can't explain it ... almost frightened.'

Frustrated, I navigate away from TheHive and start searching frantically. At last I find the page I'm looking for, and click it open to show Keira.

'MIKE DAVIS JOINS THE CHESTERFIELD BUGLE.' There's a picture there: grey-haired, and slightly leaner than he is now, with the same short, speckled beard, and an almost uncomfortable way of avoiding the camera's eye. He looks kind of handsome, in an old-man sort of way.

We're pleased to announce the appointment of Michael Davis as features editor for the Chesterfield Bugle, *the short paragraph reads. Mike has recently moved here from London with his family. He joins us from* The Times, *where he was a news reporter.*

'I'm right. It's definitely him, Keira. Here, in my house. I have to talk to him. Maybe there's a reason the page is blank. I have to find out what he knows.'

That familiar feeling builds inside me, the same way it did with Jane. The chance is too good to be true: that he could be here this very moment, ready for me to take up the search. I toss the laptop aside and pull Keira behind me, back down the stairs.

I scan the living room for him, trying to pick his grey coat out across the room. Nothing. The rain has reduced to a drizzle and a couple of people have chanced it outside, but he's not there either. I'm about to check down in the kitchen when I see it, a flash of charcoal wool moving across the hallway, and I realise in horror that he's heading for the door.

I dart across the room, nearly crashing headlong into a man with flushed pink cheeks who splashes champagne and says 'Wotcha!' as I wrestle free.

I get to the front door just as it clicks shut behind him. I struggle on a pair of trainers and throw myself into the open air.

'Mike!' I call to his retreating back, moving fast and already halfway down the street. He doesn't hear, or pretends not to. 'Michael!' I shout louder, picking up the pace as I hurry after him. 'Hey.' I eventually catch up to him, tapping his shoulder so that he flinches and turns around.

'Rosie?' He looks at me quizzically. 'Did I leave something behind?'

'No, no.' I catch my breath, taking him in. Trying to get my thoughts in order. 'It's just ... you're Michael Davis, aren't you?'

The corner of his mouth twitches. 'Yes.'

'MikeD?'

His shoulders seem to close in on him. He turns his head away. 'I don't want to talk about that.'

'Wait,' I scramble, seeing he's poised to take off. 'Please.' I reach out helplessly, catching hold of the sleeve of his coat.

'Rosie, seriously, let me go.' He jerks his arm away, setting off again down the road.

'I don't understand! Just tell me why you're leaving?' I call out to his departing back, desperate to run straight after him.

'I shouldn't have come.' He stops suddenly, whirls around to face me. 'Like I said, I wasn't even invited. It was rude of me to show up unannounced. I don't know what I was thinking. Lying to Rebecca. Coming all the way over here. I just wanted to see if you were all doing OK. To convince myself that you didn't need my help, that I'd made the right decision to leave it all alone. It was a terrible idea.' He's speaking more to himself that to me now, muttering under his breath and waving his hands erratically.

'I do need your help.' I bite my lip, searching his face for some kindness, some sign that he's listening. 'I've seen your page on TheHive. The woman in the navy dress. I know there's nothing on there now, but my friend saw it. I want to know more. Maybe ... I don't know ... maybe there's something you've found that no one else has. I spoke to Jane – Jane Thomson – and she thought that perhaps ...'

'Jane,' he snorts. 'That woman's a conspiracy theorist. Way too much time on her hands,' but then his voice softens, and he touches a hand to my shoulder. 'Listen, I'm so very sorry about what happened with Emily. I wanted to come here today to say that, but that's as far as it goes. I can't tell you anything more about the woman in the navy dress. It's over now. We shouldn't be having this conversation. I can't risk them finding out I've been here. I have no idea who might be listening.'

'Who's "they"?' I ask.

'I said no, Rosie.' I'm taken aback by his sudden forcefulness. And then he whips his head around, like he's expecting to see someone watching, and pulls me in closer, his voice fast and low. 'I'm sorry. I don't mean to be rude. There are factors beyond my control here. Things that could put my family at risk. Both our families. And I don't want to get involved with it again. I told him I wouldn't get involved again. I have too much at stake.'

My mind fizzes, trying to find something to say or do that could convince him to stay.

'I've said too much already.' He removes his hand from my shoulder. I haven't realised until now how firmly the tips of his fingers were pressing into it. 'Just trust me, Rosie, you're better off not getting involved. He's not someone you want to mess around with.'

He gives me a final, apologetic look and heads off down the street, his head bowed low into his coat, as if hiding his face from some external threat.

'How can this be better off?' I scream at his back, fighting the tears that dance around my eyes. He doesn't turn around.

In the living room, Dad has already started his speech. Mum gives me an irritated look as I slip into a space next to Keira. 'Bathroom,' I mouth back, turning my eyes quickly away. But I can barely concentrate.

'Where did you go?' Keira asks as the applause starts and the audience begins to break up.

'To talk to Michael.' I shake my head. 'He wouldn't talk to me, could barely even look at me. It's like there's someone following him. And I think that's why he's cleared his page on TheHive. I think this person, whoever they are, stopped him. Made Michael leave London, leave his job, scared the shit out of him. But I can't let it go. I need to find out who this person is, and how they're connected. Keira,' I look up at her, clenching my fists as I realise my next move, 'Mike says he won't talk. But if I want to find out what happened to Emily, I'm going to have to convince him.'

ANNA

15

Images invade my drugged sleep, edging themselves closer to memories.

Snatches of the green T-shirt; the feel of it beneath small, sticky fingers. Those fingers gripped by another hand, guiding, urgent, as the carousel fades into the distance.

I clutch tightly to the mottled rainbow of string, a thread joining me to who I am. I strain to see the face of the person leading me, trying to force any other scrap of memory to rise to the surface. Where did we go when we left the park? Why did nobody stop us, or find me? Why didn't I scream or try to run away?

Mamma keeps me off school for a week, and I allow her to, giving myself over to the illusion that I'm just sick, that all I need is for my mother to make me better. But I can't fool myself forever.

On Tuesday morning I hover at the threshold of the kitchen, eyes parched and cheeks puffed from restlessness. I swallow down the vitamin pills that are resting on the counter for me without committing to sitting down. 'Mamma, I feel much better today. I'm going to go to school early; there's a Spanish test I need to prep for.'

The bracelet grasps at my pocket. I don't look at the wedding photograph as I turn to go.

The whirr of my bike against the tarmac is the sound of relief, each turn of the wheel bringing me further from the house. And yet the further I am from it, the more my restless mind clamours for attention. I should go to the police. I should ride over there right now, slam open the doors and scream, 'I know!' But what is it I know?

I beat the pedals faster.

After school, I walk my bike over to church for choir practice. I know I'll see William there, and the thought squirms inside me. I have a desperate desire to go to him, to tell him what I've discovered, but I hear the distant echo of his dismissal, and my hurt makes me guarded.

I have never thought of myself as a lonely person, but now, with no William and no Mamma to turn to, my tiny world has closed around me.

I missed practice last week as well as church. Mamma will have told them I'm sick. And so I hesitate, as I open the door to the church, bracing myself for the questions.

But Sam the choirmaster gives me a precise, well-timed nod as I enter, murmuring, 'Good to have you back,' before pulling distractedly on his earlobe, turning his attention back to the group. 'All right, everybody, please turn to page number twenty-five. We've got a lot to get through this evening.'

But then, in the break, there William is, pushing past Phillip's vibrato belly and Jenna's high-pitched gossip as they pass around jugs of water, seeking out the space beside me. His hand brushes against the sleeve of my shirt as he picks up a glass, and I shrink away, unable to help a shiver as his insouciant touch pulls at the fine hairs of my forearm.

'How are you feeling? Your mom told Dad you were sick. You're never sick,' he asks steadily, pouring me a glass of water and grabbing a cookie from a plate of chocolate chip.

'Fine, thank you. It was just a bug.' I feel the rest of the group go quiet; my cheeks grow hot. I don't want to be the subject of their Chinese whispers.

Sam clicks his fingers together, and I gratefully take my place.

When he finally dismisses us – 'Good job, everybody. Same time next week' – I sneak out the door without saying goodbye; secrete myself in the restroom until I hear their chatter fade and die, and know I am alone.

Outside, I head over to the railings next to the graveyard, eerily silent under this grey sky, and start to unlock my bike. There is a wind picking up. It disturbs the branches, tugs each little leaf in its sway and sweeps through my hair, dragging strands across my forehead and into my eyes, so I have to keep brushing them away as I bend towards the lock. The wind pulls with it the unmistakable scent of white jasmine that clings on to the walls at the back of the church, and I feel a ghost of rain on my neck. I draw my cardigan in closer, cursing myself for not bringing something with a hood. If it really starts up in earnest, I'll be soaked through by the time I'm home.

I fumble, lose my grip on the keys and drop them on the gravel. As I bend to pick them up I hear a crunch of footsteps, and rise to find a man standing by me, so close I can smell the medicinal notes of cloves on his breath. He is in his early fifties, with a deeply lined, handsome face and bewitching, glacial blue eyes. He's wearing a light cream suit, immaculately pressed, and his hair, a soft grey, is pulled tight into a ponytail that reaches just past his collar.

Silently, he takes a finger to his jacket, removes a barely visible thread from the cuff, perusing my features so deeply I raise an involuntary hand to my face, as if his fingers are prodding inside my skull.

'Can I ... can I help you?'

There's a barely imperceptible twitch to his top lip, before his features smooth. 'You tell me – did you receive my gift?' He steps towards me, his face clarifying, and I instantly take a step back, my insides lurching, as if I've been dropped from the peak of one of Astroland's roller coasters.

But this is far more terrifying than any ride.

I've seen him before: walking away from my house the night of my birthday; on Newberry Road – just a glimpse, before he folded into the trees.

'Father Paul.' It's not a question.

A pause. 'Yes.' His expression is as cryptic as his cards. Is he surprised? Impressed? 'Remarkable.' He clicks his teeth, observing me. 'How very like her you are.'

I visualise his looping handwriting, the bundle of cards in her bottom drawer. 'Mamma?'

His eyes laugh at me. 'Her too.' The veins in my legs prickle, ready to run if he gets too close. His calmness has an edge to it, setting my senses screaming.

'What do you want from me?'

He opens his mouth, lets out a low rumble halfway between a laugh and a growl. 'My dear, it was never about you.'

Danger stalks the hairs on the back of my neck, but I force myself to meet his gaze, wrap my arms tight around my torso. 'I don't understand.'

'*Anna* ...' he crows, breaking my name into two chastising syllables, 'or is it Emily now?' There's a lick of delight in his eyes. I try not to flinch. 'Don't tell me you haven't asked your mother about my card?' He tuts. 'And I thought you were so close.'

My hands, still holding the lock and key, clench. 'What do you want from us?'

'I know this must all be very confusing to you,' he says, 'but you're intelligent enough: surely you must have figured it out by now?'

I shake my head, as if ridding my ears of the words. Half of me is desperate to know, for him to tell me straight out. But the other half can't bring myself to ask.

'Anna.' He steps closer, his voice deepening. 'You must realise. I know you are a good girl, I see it in your eyes; the way you're holding yourself now, keeping yourself closed off from potential threat. And I know you care for Mary, regardless of who she is and what she's done. But you're an adult now. It's time you realised the truth.' His voice beats at my temples, makes me want to close my eyes and block out the thoughts I don't wish to have.

Despite my thin layers, I can feel the sweat pooling at my chest, the nape of my neck, the warning rippling through me, *Don't listen! Get away!*

'No.'

'Listen to me.' He's so near now that the smell of cloves is overwhelming, as is the clean, talc scent of his finely pressed suit. A pristine exterior disguising what lies beneath. 'You have to face up to the truth. She's done a wicked thing, Anna. There are people out there who will lock her up and throw away the key, if they find out. But you don't want that, do you?' His eyes bore into me as he shakes his head, the grey ponytail swaying side to side. As if under his power, I find myself mimicking him, the strain of my neck as my head moves from side to side. He reaches into his pocket, drawing out a little white envelope and holding it out to me. 'Good girl. Which is why I need you to give this to her. To your mamma.'

Instantly I pull myself back; the cool metal railings bite the back of my knees. The tease in his voice; the way he says 'mamma'.

'No,' I force out, my voice small. 'No, I'm not giving her anything from you.'

I see him flinch. He waves the envelope at me. 'Anna, don't be silly. I need you to give this to her.'

I look away, biting back tears. 'I won't.' His words have run rings around me, as confusing as they are clarifying. But I will not be the conduit for whatever plan he is enacting.

His features corrupt, the sheen of composure at last breaking. This isn't a man used to being disobeyed. He snatches at me, grabbing my sleeve at the elbow and pulling me into him. I can see the strata of his irises, the way they're not the blue skies of Mamma's, but so clear they're almost grey. I clench my teeth, force myself to stop trembling.

'Now, you just listen here.' His voice grows thorns. 'Your mother has had her folly long enough. It's time she's back where she belongs. I need you to give this to her. I am the only one who can protect her. She won't hear it from me, so she'll have to hear it from you.'

'Get off of me!' My forcefulness startles him, and I use the flicker of distraction to wrench my arm away. 'I won't let you do this to me. I won't be part of it. Stay away from me. Stay away from us.'

I grip hold of my bike, adrenaline pulsating through my veins and readying me to flee. The rows of tombstones grimace beside me. He tries to reach for me again, but I twist my body from his grasp.

'*I said leave me alone!*'

I kick the bike into gear. Fear makes me dizzy, pumping blood in my ears as I focus on the road ahead, on getting as far away from him as possible.

'You stupid girl,' he snarls at my retreating back. 'You don't know who you're dealing with.' His frustration rips through the air behind me, and I will myself not to look around as his voice roars despite the increasing distance between us. 'The past will catch up with you both! *And when it does, you'll see it won't be me who takes the fall!*'

I power the pedals down the nearly empty road as his voice fades into the air, replaced with the sound of my own laboured breathing. The weather is an unfinished promise: no rain yet, but a lash of wind against my back as I race through the dark streets. It seems to be calling me; I can hear the whispered sound of *Anna, Anna* whirling through the trees. And then I don't know exactly how it happens, but I find myself turning into William's street, juddering to a halt outside his house, the nerve endings in my legs pinging in response.

His face, when it appears at the door, is mottled with concern. 'Anna?'

I'm so relieved that it's him who's answered that I half collapse into him. 'Are your parents home?' My thudding heart negates politeness. I stumble through the hallway, searching for any sign of them.

'No, they're at Kate's recital. Anna ...' He stalks behind me, takes hold of my elbow. 'You're shaking.'

I feel a momentary beat of respite, knowing that we're alone. 'I need you to look up the name Emily. And Astroland.' Decisive, I turn towards the stairs, start to lead the way to his room.

'Anna, is this ...?'

'Emily. And Astroland.' I don't turn back.

In his room he pulls his laptop onto the bed and opens it. Each clack of the keys seems to thud in my ears like a hammer on drywall.

Emily.

Astroland.

I hold my breath, watching Will's eyes narrow, blink, grow wide. I may not be entirely computer literate, but even I understand what the stream of results that populate the screen means.

He clicks the first one and a headline flashes up, stark, indelible type: 'EMILY ARCHER, MISSING FROM ASTROLAND, APRIL 2003.' A child with blonde hair, short in a bob and held back with a headband, and large brown eyes the colour of maple syrup, beams into the camera. She is wearing a cloud-blue sundress, with frilled sleeves and a pattern of yellow and white daisies, and has a hand raised to the camera in a half wave. There is another image next to it: a 'forensic artist's impression', the caption underneath reads.

The child in this is older, ten or twelve; the hair is darker and the smile less, and a plain blue T-shirt replaces the daisies. It's not exact, but it's a good enough approximation of how I remember myself looking at that age. Next to that, she's older and more serious, her hair frozen in the same bob but her features somehow uncertain, blurred. *As she would look today, 2018,* the caption reads.

Emily Archer.

I whisper it, my lips barely moving, like I'm scared to wake up my long-forgotten self too soon. As if in answer, she stretches; uncurls; reaches out the invisible limbs that fit with such perfection into mine.

Yes?

I wait for William to say something. I sense his eyes flitting between me and the photographs.

'Well?' I ask in the face of his silence.

'I mean …' He shrugs, casts his eyes to the ceiling.

As if this new self has now taken root, I feel the skin on my face start to burn and an unfamiliar anger lick like fire at my core. I wave my hand at the laptop. 'Can't you see? Doesn't she look like me?'

He is collecting himself. His face is too open to hide his thoughts; I've always joked he'd be a terrible poker player. He swallows, licks his lips. I can almost see his mind whirring, finding a way to answer. 'In that she is a blonde, white girl with brown eyes. Yes, I see that.'

His denial clenches around me. 'William, it's me!' I snatch the laptop from its cord and hold it up next to my face. 'Look!' I shake it, forcing him to bear witness. 'My eyes, my hair ... my face. Why can't you see?' Hurt cracks my voice. I turn my head, not wanting him to see the tears threatening to fall, and reach into my pocket to feel for the curl of woven thread, lay the bracelet on the bed, the white letters grinning at me like tiny teeth.

William's mouth hangs open. 'Where did you ...?'

'The backyard.' I breathe the smell of his room's air freshener so deep into my lungs that its synthetic brightness hits me right in the back of my ribs. 'With another pendant – same as the one in Mamma's photograph, same one that was sent to me. And a T-shirt, from Astroland. A child's T-shirt. And this bracelet, Will. A bracelet with the name Emily on it.' I let the words settle, feeling William's muted attention beside me. 'There were cards. In Mamma's room. From a man – Father Paul. He was there, just now, at the church. Waiting for me. He wants to use me to get to Mamma – I don't know why. And I think ... I think ...'

He lets out a long, slow whistle. 'Anna, are you saying ...?'

I can't bear it. To speak the words out loud.

I run a finger over the smooth surface of the letter E. And I picture it, tied to my wrist. My hand outstretched, fingers curled around someone else's, someone leading me through crowds, into the back seat of a car. And I picture myself straining forward, catching a glimpse of them in the rear-view mirror. I work my way up a long, pale neck. A pointed chin. Round cheeks that rarely see colour. Thin lips that have never seen more make-up than Chapstick.

Fair hair that's most comfortable pushed back with a headband. And then I place the final piece of the jigsaw puzzle. Those blue eyes. The ones that crease in the corners and can flit between warmth and anger in a breath.

And I see their face in full. *Her face.*

My silence betrays me.

William sucks in his cheeks, mutters 'Shit' under his breath. 'You're sure?' he asks again. But then he looks at the bracelet and shakes his head. He scoops it between his fingers. I hear the *clack, clack, clack* as he moves each letter in turn.

'Lord, Anna, we have to do something.' All of a sudden he's a flurry of movement, setting the bracelet down and slamming the laptop shut. 'We've got to go to the police. Now.'

'No!' I reach out for him, dragging him back down onto the bed.

'Are you kidding me?'

What will happen to Mamma? 'I can't go to the police, William. I don't know why Mamma ... there must be a reason. She's never harmed me. She's raised me like a daughter. But this man – there's something wrong about him. I sensed it. What if he's involved? What if he's trying to hurt Mamma, or threaten her? I need to hear it from her.'

'You were *abducted*, Anna.' I flinch at the word, my fingers tensing against the tartan comforter, twisting it beneath my hands. 'This isn't a joke,' William says. 'You have the evidence right here: you have to go to the police with it. I know how you feel about your mother, and I know that you would never intentionally want to hurt her, but you have to understand that she has done something very, very wrong. And besides, you don't know who this Father Paul is, or how she knows him. He could be dangerous. They could both be dangerous. They could be in this together. They could—'

'*I said no!*' I spark. William's mouth opens and closes, a grouper underwater. 'I need just a little more time,' I say. I ball into myself, press my head into my hands. I feel exhausted, weighed down. 'I need to work out what to do. I can't think right now. It's all too much. You have to respect me on this.' I uncurl enough to look at him, hard. William has always lived his life by right and wrong; he believes any problem can be solved by someone in authority. It's who he is. But I'm only just beginning to learn who I am, and I'm starting to understand that life isn't like that.

He swallows, but at last he holds his hands up in a gesture of submission. 'I do. I do respect you. I just want to protect you.'

I pick up the bracelet. The letters leer at me. I stuff it back in my pocket.

'I don't need protecting. I know what I'm doing, William. I know *her*. I know her quirks, her habits and her moods. She must have been driven to do what she's done. I have to understand why before I do anything else; I at least owe

her that. Do you trust me?' He stares wordlessly at the
ceiling, but nods. 'Take me home now, please?'

He squeezes his eyes tight, and nods.

The car has reached a reluctant halt at the top of my road.
William remains in his seat, fiddling awkwardly with the
keys in his hand. 'I can't just let you go like this.'

'I'll be fine,' I say. 'You have to trust me.'

'I do.' He blows air from his cheeks, a long, exaggerated
breath, and then reaches into his pocket and holds an object
out to me. 'Take my cell.'

'What?' The black rectangle feels cool against my palm
as he sets it down.

'I'll tell Dad I broke it – I'll find a way to get another one.'
He wraps my fingers around it. 'I want you to keep it on,
and with you, at all times.'

'O-K ...' The object weighs against me as I turn it over in
my hands. I barely know how to use one, and yet I have to
admit that having some sort of lifeline out of the house is a
quietening thought.

'And I want you to call me on it, any time, day or night.'
His hands are back on mine, pressing them into the phone.
'If you feel anything's not right, or you think you're in
danger ... Promise me, Anna?'

'I promise.'

'Because I wouldn't be able to live with myself if—'

'Nothing's going to happen to me, William. I promise.'

214

'Well, OK then.' He sits, frozen, rubbing his keys distractedly on the side of his jeans.

'Thank you, for the lift.' I open the door and race round to unclip my bicycle from the rack, making the decision for both of us. He reluctantly clambers out of the car to help. 'I'll see you on Sunday?' I say, clutching the handlebars. 'At church?'

He hangs his head. 'Yes.'

'So … goodnight?'

'Goodnight.'

I turn to go.

'I still love you, Anna,' he murmurs at my back.

'I know,' I tell him.

But I don't turn around.

I tense as my key turns in the lock, sure my new knowledge must be evident in my face, the way I hold myself, even without saying a word. I hear the thud of her footsteps as she flies from the kitchen: 'Where have you been?'

Anger is etched into her face, but I can't help myself scouring it for similarities. Some tiny signal to prove to me that I'm wrong, that there's some unmistakable element that proves we're related. I've never paused to question it before. Why would I? Our base features are similar enough that it wouldn't have thrown me off guard: we're both fair; we both get freckles on our noses when we spend too much time in the sun; we both have two eyes, a nose and a mouth. I have friends who are always being told they look 'just like your mother'. Why did I never stop to think it was odd I wasn't told the same?

I swallow. 'I'm sorry, Mamma ... practice ran over.' The lie skitters out. 'I should have called.' I turn my eyes to the ground, worried that just by looking at me, she'll read Father Paul's visit all over my face, and my visit to William's. I think of William's own warning: how do I know I can trust her?

I can feel her assessing me. 'How did you ride home without getting wet? It's pouring with rain out there.'

I dimly acknowledge the dusting of moisture over me, from the short walk from the car. 'I got a ride home.' I am sure she can hear the beating of my heart.

'From who?' Mamma's voice peaks, instantly on edge.

'Jessica Willis.' Surely she can read the lies written in the creases of my forehead. 'You know, the pre-school teacher who lives over in Jonesville? She was visiting her mother in High Springs, so she dropped me off en route.' I think this will put her at ease, but she remains where she stands, blocking my path into the house.

'I thought perhaps William ... or someone else ...?'

'No, Mamma. It was Jessica,' I say quickly.

'And how *was* William?'

'I barely spoke to him. It was a busy session.' I don't know where these words are coming from. It's as if another force is guiding me, speaking before I have a chance to think.

'You better not be lying to me, Anna.' With no warning, she grabs me by the wrist and marches me to the kitchen sink, where she turns the taps on full blast. 'You know full well that lying is a sin; that liars will go to the *lake that burns with fire and sulphur.*' She stretches for the soap, rolls up my sleeves like I'm a child, lathering me right up to the elbows.

When my arms touch the water, I yelp – hot water scalds my skin and I try to pull them free. 'Ow, Mamma, you're hurting me!' I cry out, shrinking away from her.

'You've been riding around on that bike all day, Anna; stop acting like a child, you need to wash your hands.' She holds me firm as I try to wriggle away from her. 'The Lord wants you to remain righteous, and pure, and I'm the only one who can make sure of that. It's the only way.' She scrubs so hard her nails scrape into my skin. 'Only then will He see fit to show you His mercy and His grace. Do you understand? Righteous, and pure.' Scrub, scrub. The water splashes up from the sink and lacerates my cheeks. 'That's why I have to protect you. Why can't you see, Anna? I'm saying this for your own good.'

'I haven't done anything wrong, Mamma,' I insist. 'Practice ran over; I got a ride with Jessica!' Lies, lies.

'I have to protect you, Anna, to keep you safe. If you're pure, if you're good, nothing – no one – can take you away.'

'I *am* good, Mamma! I am!' I moan, praying for it to stop.

As quickly as she grabbed me, she releases me. I grip hold of the sideboard to steady myself. 'I know you are,' she says. I examine my hands, my water-bloated fingers. My skin is pink and shiny, as a newborn's. 'I'm sorry, Anna.' There's a huskiness to her voice, and she turns away from me to close the taps, almost as if she's embarrassed to show me her face. 'I don't mean to hurt you. I just need you to understand. Everything I've ever done has been to keep you safe. If I didn't have you … if you ever left me, I …' She bites her lip, silences herself. Whatever she was about to say evaporates into the walls. When she looks back at me, there's a softness in her eyes, pleading with me. 'I had a call from that Ms Abrams at work today. She told me that there's a school dance on Friday.'

I blink up at her, trying to keep up with her fickle rhythm. 'Oh?'

'She said that she was worried about you.' Mamma takes a kitchen towel from the drawer and pats gently at my arms, nursing them, as if she weren't the cause of their initial injury. 'She thinks you're working too hard, and that the stress of finals might have been what made you unwell. She said that she strongly believes the dance would be good for you. That you'd be missing out if you don't go.' She sighs deeply, and in the silence between us I can feel her weighing up whatever she is about to say next. 'So,' she eventually says, carefully, an eyebrow cocked as if she's about to regret it. 'What do you think? Would you like to go?'

Does she see this as some kind of peace offering?

She moves towards me, and I can't help my natural reflexes, my muscles flinching at the potential hurt she might inflict. Instead, she strokes my cheek, brings a finger under my chin so my face is tilted in her direction.

'I want you to be happy, Anna. I know sometimes it may not seem like it, but everything I do, I do for you. If this would make you happy, I want you to go.'

'Mamma ... I ...' My thoughts tumble together like a ball of twine. It's just like her, to throw kindness and meanness at me in equal measure, so I'm never sure whether I'm coming or going. How can I possibly think of going to a dance, with Father Paul waiting for me, for us, around every corner? When I don't know what harm, if any, Mamma might bring me.

But if I say no, if I reject the gift she's so keenly handing out, who knows what questions will start to arise.

If I am in danger, I should get out now. Slip out of the house in the dead of night and run to William; run away from it all. But if Mamma is in danger, how can I leave her to face it alone? And how can I leave without knowing what happened to me; and *why*? I have to press on until I get those answers.

'Yes,' I say quietly, pulling my injured hands into myself.

'Then it's settled.' She looks relieved, almost pleased. 'I'll speak to Mrs Murray. She has a grandson of about your age; Jonah, I think he's called.' I realise a beat too late that she won't expect me to go with William. I know Jonah, why Mamma picked him: she knows there's no danger of him whisking me away anywhere.

Even still, I thank her, quickly.

'Good girl.' For a second I think she might kiss my cheek, but then she straightens. Her features close up, and I know any momentary softness was just that – a moment. 'You see, Anna, I'm your mother. I know what is best for you. Now, why don't you go to your room and read over your Scriptures? You'll find Ephesians 6 particularly elucidating this evening.' She folds up the kitchen towel, places it delicately on the dirty laundry pile. Like me, another object she has neatly put away.

Ephesians 6. I know without looking why she's picked that chapter.

Children, obey your parents in the Lord, for this is right.

ROSIE

16

The party wraps up by early evening: most guests tore into the champagne from the start, and are complaining of burgeoning hangovers by the time they leave. Dad's speech was such a success that it brought a number of the guests to tears, so that we've had to work hard to rally the mood before it descends into melancholy.

I let it lie for a week. Let the dust settle. Hoping, partly, that something will come of the party, or that perhaps enough distance has passed from the interview that someone will uncover something of note. But the world remains inert, whichs means I have to act. I ask Keira over on Saturday night. In the morning, we ring the *Chesterfield Bugle*.

It's surprisingly easy, it turns out, to find a journalist's home address.

'Hi there,' I say pathetically when the receptionist's chirp answers the phone. 'I was wondering if you can help me. I'm calling from Il Salvatore, and I believe that a Mr Michael Davis, who is a journalist for your paper, left his credit card with us when dining here last night.'

'Right?' she answers.

'Well, I was wondering if you can give me his address, so we can give it back to him?'

She sighs. 'Sorry, unfortunately I am unable to give out personal information for staff. If you've got a pen, I can give you our address, and you can send it back here.'

'Oh no ...' I force a slight wobble into my voice. 'Please, is there any way you can find it out for me? You see, it's my fault that he left his card in the first place. I forgot to give it back.'

'Look, I'm only the weekend receptionist, so there's no one around to confirm this. I'm just supposed to cover the phones.'

'Oh, please,' I say. 'I know it's a Sunday. That's why I need his home address. My manager's going to fire me if I don't get it back today. He says Mr Davis is a very important journalist from London, and I need to personally hand-deliver the card to him today, otherwise I'll lose my job.'

Keira holds a pillow over her mouth to stop herself from laughing as I lisp into the phone. I can imagine the girl thinking it over in her head, then eventually she groans into the receiver. 'Oh, all right. I wouldn't want you to lose your job. But if he asks you how you got the address, don't say you got it here. Otherwise it'll be my job instead of yours. Did you say you had a pen?'

The train to Chesterfield leaves from St Pancras. It takes over two and a half hours, and there's one at half ten, which means we'll be there just after one. I check the balance of my savings account: birthday cheques, the hoard from my summer job last year at the coffee shop down the road. Even with railcards, the tickets are fifty quid each. Keira sees me wince and offers to pay her way, but I shake my head. 'It'll be worth it.'

In the kitchen, Mum's making a pot of coffee, plunging the top of the cafetière, a pan of milk warming on the hob. 'Hi, Mum.' I walk over and kiss her on the cheek.

'Hi, darling. Hi, Keira, did you sleep well? Coffee?'

I search her face, seeing the bags under her eyes, the telltale signs that she hasn't slept. 'Actually, Mum,' I say, 'we think we're going to head out.'

'Head out? But it's barely past ten o'clock.'

'I know, but Keira's going to revise in Regent's Park. I thought I'd go with her, seeing as it's such a nice day.' Now I'm doing the Well-Behaved Child bit.

Mum folds her arms, observes us. 'So conscientious. To think, I remember feeding you chicken nuggets and chips and having to bargain with you both to eat your peas. All right, I'll see you later then. Keira, you're welcome to stay for dinner, if you fancy?'

'Thank you, Mrs Archer,' says Keira. 'I'll probably head home though.'

'Of course.' Mum pulls at my arm just before we duck out the door. 'Have fun, darling, and, you know ...'

'I know. "Be safe." Don't worry, I will.' For a moment, I consider telling her. Maybe she'll give me her blessing. Maybe she'll even help. I imagine myself sticking my head round the door: *Oh, by the way, I'm just popping off to Derbyshire to stalk some weird guy I think might know something about Emily, only he seems really freaked out and, like, really scared of some man who seems to be following him.* Yeah, good luck leaving the house for the next ten years.

When we arrive at Chesterfield station it's raining. Neither of us has brought an umbrella, and we huddle together by the taxi rank with our bags over our heads. Next to us at the station entrance is a bronze statue of a man holding up a small train – at an angle that makes it look as if he's giving future passengers the middle finger.

Keira bops me with her hip. 'Insta?' She jerks her head at the statue and mimics his gesture.

'No,' I say, 'Aunt Pam's on there. She might see it and say something to Mum.'

'Fine,' she says reluctantly, pulling her mac tighter around her.

'Visiting someone, are we?' the taxi driver asks as we give the address and haul ourselves into the back seat.

'Yes ... my uncle.' I barely miss a beat.

We wend through the centre of town, where the driver points out a church with an oddly shaped, crooked spire – 'The Leaning Tower of Chesterfield,' he says, laughing at his own joke – and then the houses thin out, interspersed with dark green fields dotted with tangle-haired sheep and mournful black cows. Eventually we pull into a paved driveway, facing a white, flat-fronted detached house. My eyes scan the drive for cars, and with a sinking heart I see there aren't any. I didn't think about that. What if he's out for the day? Or, worse, on holiday?

I try the doorbell, but as expected, there's no answer.

As the driver revs off, I turn to Keira. 'Now what?'

She sticks her bag on the ground and sinks down beside it. 'I guess we wait.'

When it gets to half an hour, we take out the sandwiches we bought at the station and rest them on our laps, our hands fighting for the bag of crisps we wedge between us. When half turns into full, I look at what time the next train is, and then realise, stupidly, that we don't know the number of a taxi.

As the time creeps towards two hours, I'm about to suggest we give up and go when the soft rumble of a car makes my ears prick up. We stiffen as we watch a deep-green Mini turn into the drive, then we hastily stuff our rubbish back into our bags, and stand. The car judders to a stop; my breathing gets shallower, and my throat gets drier, and I begin to feel very, very nervous.

The passenger door opens and a woman with dark hair and a confused expression starts towards us. Seconds later the back door opens, and a little boy of about four or five leaps out and clings to her legs.

'Excuse me, can I help you?' she asks, but before she's got even halfway towards us, the driver's door opens, and Michael Davis's grey head comes into view.

'Rosie.' His tone is brusque, and I see a snarl of irritation knot his features.

'Hi, Michael,' I mumble, feeling suddenly embarrassed.

'You know this girl?' the woman asks, a fractiousness creeping into her voice.

'Not exactly.' He shuts the car door sharply, comes closer. 'Rebecca, it's Rosie Archer. The sister of Emily.'

'What?' Instinctively, the woman takes the little boy by the hand and pulls him into her.

'Nice to meet you,' I say, hanging my head and wishing there was a way I could scrub out this whole day – and yesterday as well, when I first had this stupid idea.

'Becs,' he speaks deliberately, not taking his eyes from me, 'why don't you take Hugo up for his nap. I'll be in soon.'

She gives us a long look, but then bounces Hugo onto her hip and says with false cheer, 'Come on then, Huggers; why don't you come and choose a story for me to read, while Daddy chats to his friends.' She pushes past us without giving us so much as a second glance.

'You shouldn't have come,' he says plainly as soon as the front door has clicked shut.

'I—'

'*No*, Rosie.'

I look up, surprised by the sudden sharpness. 'What do you mean, turning up here like this?' He has a richness to his voice that is striking in its power; I can imagine how he must have been, the commanding journalist he once was. 'I thought I made it quite clear yesterday: I just wanted to pay my respects; to see how you all were. I told you I didn't want to be dragged into it any more than that. I can't. This is my *home*, Rosie. My *family*. I can't have you here, risking their safety. What if someone saw you? What if they think …?' His head whips up and his eyes search the landscape around us, as if someone may be watching, right now. '*What if they think I'm helping you?*' I see his jaw set, his shoulders stiffen – a decision made. 'You have to leave. You have to turn around now and go back home; forget you ever saw me.' He places a hand on my shoulder, physically trying to propel me out of his driveway. 'Come on, let's get you back to the station. There are trains back to London every hour. I'll even give you a lift.'

I hear a rattle of keys as he fumbles with his jacket pocket, moving towards the car. I can't bear the thought of this being it, of having come all this way and having to turn around again. My hands clench into fists. He knows something – I can feel it. I can't just go back, watch everything shut down, watch my family collapse, Mum disintegrate, if there's even the smallest, tiniest chance that I could have done something to stop it.

'They're closing down the trust!' I choke out, wrenching myself away from him.

'Sorry?' He stops, keys in hand, just short of the car door.

'The fund to find my sister.' I slow myself, gathering my argument. 'They're closing it down, Michael. And when they do, that's it.' I bear my empty hands to him, like a magician vanishing a coin. 'We'll never know what happened to her.' I feel Keira's hand on the small of my back; reassurance.

'Last week, at the party, you said you wanted to see if we were doing OK. Well, we're not.' I take a step towards him, not pleading exactly, but coaxing. 'We've been in limbo for fifteen years. You don't know what that's like. You don't know how it felt, as a kid. You come to a stop on the swings, and when you turn around you realise it's because your mum's staring at some blonde kid in the sandbox. Every Christmas, the wish at the top of your list, praying that surely you've been so good this year Santa will find her. Every holiday, apologising if you've ducked out of sight for the smallest millisecond; the guilt, for the rest of the day, at seeing the fear on their faces. Never, ever able to feel totally pleased with the smallest fucking achievement, because you know that nothing you do will be enough to wipe out the pain of losing her.'

I feel the back of my throat thickening, the threat of tears, and wipe my hand across my mouth, forcing them back. 'I know you want to protect your family, and I get it. But don't you think you owe it to us to tell us what you know? If there's even the smallest, tiniest chance that you know something that could help us, don't you see what that would mean? You wouldn't just be saving Emily ... you'd be saving all of us.'

Michael's hand is frozen on the door handle. I see the tension in his shoulders; the urge he has to pull it open. But then something in him slackens. He turns, resting his body against the car and raking a tired hand over his head, grabbing a fistful of hair. For a moment there is silence. Nothing to be heard but the occasional rumble of a car, or the rustle of a rabbit or pheasant in the undergrowth. And then, at last, he speaks.

'OK,' he says, squeezing his eyes shut, as if looking at me will make him change his mind. When he opens them, I see a million thoughts running through them: fear and apprehension, but also a tiny shred of hope. 'You're right.' He steps away from the car and stalks towards the house, the keys jangling in his hand. 'I'll tell you what I know.' He looks wearily over his shoulder, and beckons us with a nod of his head. 'Come inside – quickly.'

ANNA

17

The dress is almost the exact coral shade of the inside of a conch shell. When I turn to see my reflection, the gauzy skirt fans ever so slightly around me, as if mimicking the very frills of a conch's edge. 'Mamma,' I breathe as the fabric twirls around my legs, and I stroke my hands over the soft material.

For the past few days, an equilibrium has draped itself over the house like the swathe of fabric Mamma has cut and stitched and shaped. Each night, long after I've gone to bed, I've seen the light on in the living room and the whirr of the sewing machine. Even in the mornings, there she's been, desperate to prove her love through the hem of a sleeve or measure of a zipper.

I have done my best to keep up the pretence, to carry on as normal until I am brave enough to make the next step.

But my mind has not been able to rest; I have been waiting for the fabric to slip.

'I never got to go to my own prom.' Mamma stands behind me and looks over my shoulder at our twin reflections. 'I'd left school by then, to help on the farm.'

The farm is part of the few hazy details I know about Mamma's past: where she lived, before she got married; before me. Hearing her offer up this glimpse into it, I can't help a fleeting hope that maybe she really did have nothing to do with it all, and that somehow Father Paul – who had the air of danger lingering on him so thickly I could almost taste it – drove her to it.

I could ask outright. Looking back at her in the mirror, I see, properly, the lack of commonness in our features. I can feel the words shaping themselves like the pattern of Mamma's scissors against the coral fabric: *Why did you do it? What does Father Paul want?*

Bad, good, pure, evil … which side does Mamma fall on?

'Mamma?' I begin. And then I see the softness in the corners of her eyes, taking me in. Feel her hands on my shoulders, hands that have fed me and clothed me and mothered me.

'Yes, Anna?'

The doorbell chimes, and a flutter of panic seizes at my heart as it has at every ring since my encounter with Father Paul. It's only a matter of time before he comes again, and

I know time is running thin. I am going to have to act, one way or another. Confront Mamma, or run. Indecision calcifies me.

I answer the door to find Jonah standing on the porch, dressed in a pressed black tux, his hair greased away from his forehead. In his hands, a clear plastic box. He's actually not that bad-looking; underneath the unfortunate pimples that speckle his face he has those soft, all-American features I know some girls find charming. But he's not William.

'Good evening, Jonah.'

He holds out the box. 'This is for you.' Inside is a cluster of peach ranunculus bulbs, spray roses and green berries, tied with a coral-coloured organza ribbon. I imagine Mamma orchestrating it. Even in this tiny detail, she has mastery over me.

'They're lovely, Jonah. Thank you.'

He scoops the corsage from the box to tie on my wrist, but Mamma is already beside us, taking the flowers and tying them on herself. I wonder if she is already regretting her decision.

'There.' She executes a neat bow and then stands back to take us both in. 'Now, don't you two look smart?'

'Well, we should be on our way, Mrs Montgomery.' Jonah tips his head deferentially towards Mamma. 'What time should I have her back?' He speaks over me, as if I'm a small child he has custody of for the night.

Mamma's lips twitch in satisfaction.

*

When we arrive at the high school, the place is already heaving. Dance music thuds from the building, and dozens of students are making their way up the grass to the entrance in brightly coloured formal wear. I can tell lots of them are already drunk: the guys seem louder than usual, fist-bumping and bellowing into the darkening night sky, while a couple of the girls are swaying on their feet; one even sits down on the grass bank, and has to be pulled up by a friend.

The party is held in the school gymnasium. The theme is 'Happily Ever After', and already I can see hints of the prom committee's handiwork when we enter the room: tawdry crêpe paper roses and a cardboard cut-out of a pumpkin carriage. At the far end, a band on a small stage is blaring out covers of pop songs against a backdrop of multicoloured stage lights. A small group of early adopters jerk along in front of them in time to the beat, the girls hiking up their skirts and swinging them rhythmically, while the guys loosen their ties, letting the ends dangle down their shirts.

Over by the punch bowl, I feel a tap on my arm and turn around to find Ms Abrams is behind me, looking elegant in a forest-green dress, her red hair swept into a neat chignon. I've never noticed before that she's pretty. 'Anna, you made it! And don't you look nice?' I see her looking from me to Jonah.

'Thank you, Ms Abrams.' I turn reluctantly to Jonah. 'This is Jonah, my date.'

Ms Abrams' smile becomes a little forced, but then she holds a hand out to Jonah. 'A pleasure to meet you, Jonah.' I see her hesitate, wanting to say more, but instead she gives us a little nod and motions to go. 'Well, I suppose I'd best be off chaperoning.' As she slips away, she touches me lightly on the arm and murmurs in my ear, 'I'm so pleased your mother listened to my advice, and let you come after all. She did tell me about you and William though; I was so sorry to hear it. Your first heartbreak is always difficult.'

Jonah and I move across the room, which is slowly filling with people. A row of chairs lines one side of the gymnasium. I glance across at them, eager to rest my already aching feet, but instead Jonah nudges me towards the stage. 'Want to dance?'

I hesitate, but follow. At least if we're dancing we won't need to talk.

Jonah's movements are angular, jerky. He stands the right distance from me to convey that he is most definitely my partner, without actually being in physical contact with me. My body is awkward. I can feel the rhythm of the music, but I don't know how to move like my peers, to twist and turn my limbs in the way that seems so natural to them. Where do they get taught this? I sway on my feet and take a long sip of my drink. It tastes as pink as it looks.

I see some girls I know; they look curiously from me to Jonah. One of them tells me she likes my dress, and when I say thank you, that actually my mother made it, her face creases into an indulgent expression, eyes unnaturally wide, lips slurred upwards. 'That's so neat,' she says, sugar-sweet as the punch. 'My mom can't even sew on a button.' She smooths a hand down the hip of the figure-hugging black dress she's wearing, and merges into the crowd.

Jonah unexpectedly takes hold of my arm: 'Hey, let's—' He upsets my already tottering balance, unsteady on charity shop heels, and my glass of punch jerks towards me, tips. I watch as a rivulet of bubblegum pink makes its way down the centre of my dress.

Jonah claps a hand to his mouth, his eyes round O's in his face. 'Gosh, I'm sorry, Anna. I honestly didn't mean to ...' He holds his empty arms out towards me, useless in their lack of comfort or napkins.

I look down at the ruined silk. 'It's OK,' I say, 'it was an accident. I ... I better go clean it up, before it stains.' I turn to leave, pushing my way through gyrating bodies to the exit. The gym is almost full now, and I feel as though the very walls are pulsating with the noise that thuds inside my skull.

The double doors swing shut behind me, suffocating the sound. In the restroom, I dab at the dress with a wad of paper towels, watching the pink fade, to be replaced with dark coral water spots I'm not sure will ever fully disappear. The edges of the room are slightly fuzzy, and a warm, tingling sensation spreads across me. I think back to the punch, to its sickly-sweet taste. Could someone have spiked it? I've heard rumours of such things happening. Perhaps this is what it's like to be drunk? And I've barely eaten anything today. As a wave of dizziness overwhelms me, I hold on to the sides of the sink, feeling the cool Formica beneath my hands, and look into the mirror.

Who did I think I was fooling, playing out this fantasy? The ruined dress says it all: there is no place for me here. I have been moulded and shaped by the way Mamma has raised me; I don't know any other way to be.

I cup my hand under the tap and bring cold water to my lips, drinking thirstily. When I look up, I allow myself to inspect my reflection in the mirror. I'm pale, despite the warm weather; my eyes are muddy and wan, dark circles forming underneath them; cheeks a little sunken on their bones. How different I look from the morning of my birthday. But then, I am different. A different person.

Emily Archer.

Do I look like her? The question shivers into my head. I find myself compelled to look deeper, to see her, to try to remember the fading images of the girl I saw on William's computer. There is nothing. No friendly freckle or birthmark to help me on my way. It'll take more than just my face to prove who I am.

I move to the hand dryer, severing my reflection in two. Whether I've banished the Anna or the Emily, I can't say. In the half that remains, I try out one of those laid-back, carefree smiles I see my classmates performing with such ease. 'Hey,' I practise saying to Jonah, with a coy nudge of my shoulder. 'All sorted now. No harm done.' My half-reflection remains unconvinced.

I head back out into the hall with renewed resolve. I am so focused on my intent that I fail to notice the figure I find myself walking into head first.

'William?' I stare up at his familiar form, taking in his long limbs, my body already responding to the feel of his hands on my waist. 'What are you doing here?'

'I couldn't get hold of you.' There's a note of panic in his voice. He hasn't quite let go of me, as if my physical presence is the reassurance he needs that he's found me. 'I kept trying the cell – why didn't you answer? You promised me you'd keep it with you, Anna, but I rang and rang and I got no answer.' I bite my lip, guiltily picturing the phone, lying in its hiding place in my room. How could I have possibly taken it with me, without Mamma noticing? 'I rang your home just to check everything was all right, and your mom answered. She told me you were here; she sounded … almost gleeful about it. Anna,' his eyes dart around, almost as if he expects Mamma to be right there behind him, 'I have to tell you something. We have to go somewhere we can talk. But we can't discuss it here. Not like this.'

He grabs hold of my hand. I try to unpick my thoughts. 'What about Jonah?'

'Anna, you're not listening to me.' He tugs harder. 'We have to go – now. Tell him anything: tell him you're sick, that a friend's giving you a lift home. But do it now.'

I take in the wildness in his eyes, the urgent way his fingers press into my wrist. Slowly I nod, leave William in the hallway as I make my way back into the gymnasium, which now seems twenty degrees hotter, reeking of hair-spray and sweat and stale perfume, their cacophony as loud as the noise level in the room.

I spy Jonah at the punch table, talking to a couple of boys I recognise vaguely from the football team. I approach them, catching Jonah's eye as he takes a swig from his glass. 'Hi,' I say. He sways slightly. The punch must definitely be spiked.

'Hey, I was starting to get worried about you. Anna, this is Jacob and Sam,' he slurs as he points to each one in turn. 'Guys, this is Anna. My date.' In an unprecedented move, he reaches a hand around my waist and tugs me into him so our hip bones smash together. I politely disentangle myself, and exchange the briefest possible pleasantries before turning towards him.

'Jonah, I'm so sorry, but I have to leave.'

'Leave?' He screws up his eyes, as if trying to process what I'm saying. 'But we only just got here.'

'I know, but I'm … not feeling well. I think it was something I ate. I have to go home. Now.'

'But how will you get home?'

'A friend is going to take me. But I don't want you to worry about it. Please, stay here and have a good time. I'm sorry, Jonah. I haven't been a very good date.' Rather than allowing myself to linger, I lean over and give him a fleeting kiss on the cheek. And then, before he can say anything else, I extricate myself from the group and go out to meet William.

He starts the car, and I know without him saying a word exactly where he's taking me.

Watermelon Pond is a short drive from the high school. It's not really a pond any more, it's almost completely dried up, but it's a pleasant place to hike, full of blackberry bushes and Florida rosemary and draping yellow jasmine. I know William likes to come here to think. It was one of the first places we went to, when we started dating.

We park up. The sand is deep and soft underfoot, and I am suddenly alert to the fact that I'm still in my formal wear. 'Will?' I look down at my satin sandals, already speckled with grains of sand.

He ducks into the trunk of his car and appears seconds later with my hiking boots clenched in his hands. I forgot I left them there – before all this began. With the boots on, and his jumper draped over my shoulders, I pick my way with him past the entrance and into the park. It feels illicit doing this now, skirting our way past the bird house that faces the kiosk.

In the silence, only broken by the occasional bird call, we find a patch of land by a tall loblolly pine. It's already dark, but the moon is high in the sky, illuminating us with a bright silver glow.

Only now does William speak. 'I've found some things out about Father Paul. Some worrying things.'

'Will, I don't care,' I say. 'I've already decided—'

'No, listen to me, Anna. I've done some research. He's the leader of a church – The Lilies, that's what that means.

I asked a pastor about it. Don't freak out,' he holds his hands up, seeing the panic seize my face, 'someone from our old church in Texas. He was really concerned when he heard the name. He said they were a Christian sect, with some pretty extreme views. A lot of them, they sounded just like your mom: the puritanism, the cleanliness, the order.' He presses his palms together, holds them to his chin. 'Anna, I think your mom might have been mixed up with them; for all we know, she still might be. It could be the reason that she ... for what happened to you. He said he'd heard things – rumours, mainly, about strange goings-on there, aggressive behaviour, severe punishment. I don't know why this Father Paul is seeking you out now, but you have to get away.'

'Where?' The hollowness of this thought punches me in my core. All I have is Mamma. Without her, I am Alice, falling down the rabbit hole.

'Marry me,' William says.

A brutal laugh escapes me, ripping through the silent night in a ragged gasp. 'Now you're the crazy one.'

'I'm being serious. You must have known I always intended it, eventually. We'll go to my dad, right now. He won't ask questions; he trusts me. He'll do it right away.' He clutches me to him, and I can feel the desperation build in him. 'You're eighteen. You're free to marry who you please. Your mother has no hold on you. Marry me, and we'll face her together. We could find a way, maybe, of protecting her from Father Paul. And then we'll go away, just you and me.' I say nothing, but he pulls himself into me harder, burying himself into my neck and murmuring, over and over, 'Please, Anna, please. I can't let anything happen to you.'

It's too much, too overwhelming, everything within me conflicting and vying for attention. And in that moment I want to hate Mamma. Hate her for doing this to me; for making me choose, and giving me no choice at all.

Before I realise it my mouth is on William's, hungry for the comfort I have so desperately been missing. We sink to the ground, and the rough sear of sand rubs against my back. My skirt has risen up my thighs, and I recklessly nudge my bare skin into him. It feels wrong, so terribly wrong, to be doing this, but at the same time I am overcome with desire; for William, yes, but to punish Mamma too, the way she has punished me, and transgress the bounds she holds so dear.

Besides, what does it matter now? What does anything matter?

'Anna, are we doing this? Are you sure?' William murmurs, even as I feel his warm hands against my flesh, moving along the length of my body. I can feel the strength of him on top of me, powered by an animalistic urge that, now unleashed, doesn't seem to want to stop.

We dive into each other, all hands, and lips, and limbs. We are fumbling and awkward, neither quite knowing whether to lead or be led, but we somehow stumble our way into a rhythm that eventually makes us both cry out.

Afterwards, when we are still and quiet, our bodies cooling in the moonlight and William's arms wrapped around me as I lie against his torso, I am the first to break the silence. 'You're right, Will. I have to let Mamma go. But not tonight. Please. Let me go home to her. Let me pretend everything is all right. I just need a little time.' I stare into the distance at the oaks and trails surrounding us.

'OK.' He pulls me closer. 'I will.'

In the car home, I don't need to tell him: he stops at the top of the road. I kiss him deeply on the mouth, part of me not wanting to let go.

'I need you to swear to me you won't do anything until I tell you.' I hold his face up to me, boring the promise into him. 'If we're going to do this, I have to know I can trust you.'

He rests his left hand over mine, traces the lines of my fingers in the dark. 'You can trust me.'

From the top of our long driveway, the house looks quiet. It's a quarter to eleven. Mamma will be in bed, listening for the door. She'll be worried about falling asleep and missing me, so I picture her propping herself up, her ears pricked up for the sound of my footsteps on the stairs. Once she knows I'm back, I imagine her settling into her pillows, and falling into a comforted sleep.

I open the front door into total blackness, edge out of my shoes and then creep up the stairs so I don't wake Mamma unduly. I open my bedroom door with a creak, and turn to switch on the overhead light.

When I turn around, I seize in shock. Mamma is sitting on my bed. Wide awake. Waiting for me.

'Mamma!' I clasp my hand to my chest, nearly jumping with fright.

And then I look properly at the bed, and at the objects beside her. A cell phone. A ticket. A bracelet. The pendant. The card.

A magpie's trove, unearthed.

'It was the strangest thing,' she begins as my eyes slowly turn to meet hers. 'I heard this incessant buzzing sound, coming from your room. And I thought to myself, there must be a bee, trapped in there somewhere. I was scared, in case it stung you in the night. So I looked all around, and there it was again. Buzz, buzz, buzz. Coming from your chest of drawers. And I thought, aha, the bee must be trapped in there. So, I opened it up, and guess what?' I shake my head, tears stinging my eyes. 'Well, there was no bee, was there, Anna? No bee at all.'

'Mamma, I can explain.' I come towards her, thinking frantically what I can say or do to rectify the situation.

Something hard and heavy flies through the air from Mamma's hands, and lands square on the side of my head. The last thing I see, before my world becomes blackness, are the strangled stems of wildflowers, and the flash of a vase beside them.

ROSIE

18

It's not like I've spent much time considering what MikeD's house might look like, but as soon as we enter, something about it rings true. It's very clean with lemon-fresh polished wooden floors and stark white walls hung with framed posters from art exhibitions and theatre productions. Off the hallway there's a living room, with one of those leather corner sofas and a bookshelf that lines the entire length of a wall, crammed with books.

'We're both big readers,' Michael says, seeing me staring. I give him an awkward half smile, happy to have his small talk as the backdrop to my gently calming mood.

'Tea?' he asks when we're seated in the country-style kitchen. The wall is covered with a child's drawings stuck on with Blu Tack. I hear the flick of the kettle switch. He opens and closes cupboard doors, taking out mugs and spoons and tea boxes. 'I don't think we have anything more imaginative than regular breakfast or Earl Grey, but I think there may be some peppermint somewhere if you like?'

'Breakfast is good for us.'

'Right then.' He doesn't look back, keeps moving around the kitchen. Stalling, maybe?

'Sorry it's not much.' He brings over three mugs and some biscuits, sits, says nothing. I glance at the clock on the far wall. It's edging on four o'clock. If we want to be back in time for dinner, we have to get a train at five. I take a loud sip of tea, as if the act will urge him into speaking. He sucks his top lip, looks down at his mug. 'I'm afraid I don't really know where to start, Rosie. What do you want to know?'

I press my tea-warmed hands to the sides of my face. 'Whatever it is you can tell me. Who is the woman in the navy dress? How did you find out about her? Why do you think she's connected to Emily? We've travelled three hours to get here, Michael; please, just tell me anything that could help me find my sister?'

He bows his head. 'OK. I'm sorry. I know you're frustrated.' He loops his hands tighter around his mug. 'I'll tell you everything I know, but you have to understand that the reason I've kept this to myself is because it's not safe—'

'I get it, Mike,' I interject before he gets a chance to talk himself out of it. 'But I have to know.'

He nods, understanding. 'I guess it all began when I met my wife.' He glances away from us, and his mouth curls into a guilty frown. 'My first wife, Angela.' He takes a long sip of tea, letting the sentence hang in the air. 'When I first started out – gosh, more than twenty years ago now – I was an investigative journalist. Lengthy, painstakingly researched pieces about human life: an exposé on what it's like to be a prison guard, MPs' expenses, a profile piece about a celebrity chef I'd heard was terrorising his staff. I was doing pretty well.' He shrugs. 'I wrote for lots of the nationals. I wrote a couple of pieces for the *New York Times*; I even won an award for a piece I wrote about a drug cartel in Jalisco. I was spending a lot of time in the States, and that's where I met my Angela.'

I start to build a picture of him, before whatever made him slink away into the shadows happened. He's clearly sharp – it's in his manner, the way he holds himself. Could it be that this man has unearthed the key to what happened to Emily, when so many others have failed?

'Angela was American. Her parents lived in Georgia. About six months after we got married, her father got sick, and she wanted to move back home to be near him. They lived in a little place right at the border of Georgia and North Carolina. It's very quiet there, proper small-town life: one bar, a diner, a mayor who knew most people by name. I was quite content, starting to cobble together ideas for a book. I began to find that so-called "Southern charm" quite irresistible.'

'How does this relate to my sister?' I urge him on, but he raises an eyebrow.

'I said I'd tell you everything. This is everything.' He continues, 'Around the time Angela's father got sick, her mother became involved with a new church. She started going quite regularly: Sundays at first, and then twice a week, later more. I think she found it comforting, with her husband sick like that.' Michael gives a heavy sigh, and I can see him placing himself back in that time.

'Almost overnight, something changed. As I understand it, they were never a particularly religious family. But suddenly it was "the Lord" this and "the Lord" that. Soon, she was fascinated with this idea of "good" and "evil", and "purity" versus "sin". She became obsessed with dirt. She fretted over Bill. They gave her the crazy notion that his illness was the result of some imperfection, some sin within him that was working its way out. The man had stage-three cancer,' he spits, 'and they were telling him to confess his sins.' I see his knuckles tighten around the handle of his mug. 'It was about that time that Angela got pregnant.

'Ruth began to ask Angela to come to church with her. It started out just as light nagging, but she wouldn't let it rest. Eventually, Angela couldn't take it any more, didn't want to be the cause of arguments when her father was so unwell, and so finally she agreed to go. As soon as she saw it for herself, she felt that there was something off about it. She told me she couldn't quite put her finger on it, but there was just something wrong about the place.'

'What?' Keira asks; she's trying to chivvy him along too. She's hooked her finger on the handle of her empty mug and is drawing it round and round in a circle. The mug makes a dull scraping sound against the tabletop, and I give her a nudge with my knee.

'She found it hard to describe at first,' Michael answers. 'It just gave her the creeps. The church was about a fifteen-minute drive from us, set back from the road in a clearing next to a river.' He pauses, looks up. 'They called themselves The Lilies.' From his place at the kitchen table, he lets his words hang in the air, searching our faces for any sign of recognition. We stare blankly back at him. *'As a lily among thorns, so is my love among the daughters,'* he quotes, tickling a faint recognition in my brain.

'Oh,' I say. 'That's from the Bible, isn't it?'

He nods. 'The lily is a symbol of purity in Christianity. Angela said they started off every meeting with this weird ritual: they'd dress in these long, white robes, and wade into the river to "wash" themselves of their sins whilst one of the leaders would quote Scripture at them. Angela said it was the most bizarre thing, these grown men and women standing about in nightdresses like some sort of adult baptism. There were other things too: a sort of "confession" session, where they'd take turns admitting something they were guilty about, and then everyone would chant, "Unclean! Unclean! Unclean!" at them whilst they scrubbed their hands in a bucket of diluted bleach until a leader pronounced them cleansed. They wanted Angela to do some sort of special purification ritual for the baby, but on that she absolutely put her foot down. And then there was the money.'

Michael leans back in his chair, drags his hands across his face and gives his head a slight shake from side to side, mentally readjusting himself. And then he continues. 'Cancer treatment is expensive, especially in the US; the insurance, the lack of a nationalised health service. Bill and Ruth didn't have much to cover the bills, and Angela and I were hardly in a position to help out. Bill's doctor was suggesting a new drug trial ... and that was how we found out that Ruth was giving money to the church. Small bits, in the beginning, at least. But it was her talk of the church leader, Father Paul, that made me really uneasy. Ruth's eyes would get all kind of twinkly when she'd talk about him. Soon it was "Father Paul says this" and "Father Paul says that". It was like, to her, he was God incarnate. And then she wanted Bill to stop having treatment. "Father Paul says he doesn't need treatment," she'd quote in this pious tone. "He just has to believe."'

Michael sucks in his cheeks, breathing the air into himself before he next speaks. 'And then Angela lost the baby.'

I'm not quite sure where to look. 'I – I'm so sorry.' Next to me, Keira murmurs the same. I awkwardly reach out a hand to him. Surprisingly he acquiesces, and pats mine gently in response.

'It was a very sad time. She was about five months along. There wasn't anything out of the ordinary about the pregnancy. But with the stress of her mum, and Bill ... it was just all too much. That was when things started to get really bleak. Bill was so weak. Ruth was becoming more obsessed by the day. When Angela lost the baby, Ruth told her Father Paul said it was because she was "impure", and the Lord had seen fit to take it from her. He wanted to do some sort of cleansing ritual on her, to *cast the evil out of her.*'

I can see the anger building inside of Michael. His nostrils flare; his hands grip his mug so hard I think he might snap the handle off.

'That was when I lost it. I got straight in the car and drove over to that vile place, and asked to speak to Father Paul. When he finally deigned to emerge from his office I already knew what I was going to say. "If you know what's good for you," I told him, "you'll leave my wife and my family alone." I accused him of brainwashing people, stealing their money. And he took it all in without saying a word. Just as I was about to drive off, he tapped ever so lightly on my window, and when I opened it he said, in an utterly calm, knowing voice, "You can take Ruth away from The Lilies, but know that no one ever truly leaves. The church will always have ways of finding you."'

I can picture exactly the sort of man Father Paul is. Charismatic. Dangerous.

'After that,' Michael says, 'I told Angela we couldn't stay in town any longer. None of us could. We left for Atlanta the next day. I found us a place to rent – Angela, Ruth, Bill and me – with the last of my savings. We discovered quite soon after that someone had torched her parents' house – it was razed to the ground. I couldn't prove who did it, but when I went to look at the damage, there was a single lily planted in the rubble. I never told Angela, or her parents, and somehow they started to build their lives back. Ruth – it was like she was slowly waking up from a dream; the longer she was away from that place, the less she talked about the church. Then Bill passed away – it must have been two or three months later – and it was as if the effect of that completely overcame her, and she never mentioned the place again, to the best of my knowledge.'

He clasps his hands above the table and strokes his thumbs together as a look of immense sadness drops over his face, pulling his features down. 'Angela and I were broken, though. All of that turmoil, the miscarriage, then Bill dying … we just couldn't get past it. We separated. I moved back to New York. And then we divorced.' He shrugs, a lonely, almost childlike gesture. 'The States lost all magic for me, as did my writing. And so I moved back home, to London. But it turns out I'm not really good at anything else, so I became a hack news reporter. And I would have had nothing to do with The Lilies again if I hadn't seen the woman in the navy dress.'

All my senses sit up, alert. This is what I've been waiting for. This is what the whole journey has been for. 'And that's how we come on to Emily?'

Michael slowly nods his head. 'Yes. That's how we come on to Emily.'

ANNA

19

A pounding pain in my temple throbs me into wakefulness. I try to reach out to place my palm against it and realise with a dawning alertness that my wrists are tied either side of me. Panicked, I open my eyes more fully. I am lying on a bed that's not my own. And then I hear it, a whispered, trembling voice, chanting the same thing over and over: 'Pure in mind, in word, thought and deed, I ask You, Lord, to pay me heed ...'

I gradually take in my surroundings. Everything around me is white. The sloping walls; the sunlight streaming through a slanted window; the bed sheet that rests over my body, which, glancing down, I see has been draped in a white nightdress. It's stifling, airless – the sweet, muddy scent of mothballs so thick I can taste them in the back of my throat.

The attic. I'm lying on my childhood bed, my arms tied to its wrought-iron frame.

'Mamma?' My voice is hoarse.

The pulsating in my skull clogs my thoughts, and I try to dilute them. The dance. The images drift across me: the dress, Jonah, the punch, William. *William*. Memories of the pond resurface – what we said, what we did there (I blush inwardly) – and then returning home and—

Sluggishly, I turn my head against the pillows to meet Mamma's eyes.

She knows.

I don't know what I expect: for her to lash out at me, to reveal the truth in all its glory and then … and then what? Instead, she rises tentatively, crosses the room from the wicker chair she's been sitting in by the door. I recognise it now – the one from the bathroom. Mamma must have dragged it up here while I was out cold. 'Anna,' she bends over me, 'I didn't mean to hurt you. Honest, I didn't. I was waiting for you all that time and I … I … I panicked.'

My tongue feels thick against the roof of my mouth, and as I try to swallow the dryness away, a taste of something lingers, sharp and vaguely chemical. William's words come rushing back to me. If only I listened to him. Acted when he told me to. I said I needed time; well, look what time has brought me.

'What have you given me?' I try to sit up, but the ties around my wrists hold me down like an invisible extension of Mamma's force.

'I just needed a way to make you stay.' I hear a tinkle of water; feel a coolness on my forehead as a rough flannel presses against it. 'I knew you'd try to run. And I can't lose you, Anna. You don't know what I've done, to keep you here.' She sits on the side of the bed, and I am gently rocked as it sags under her weight. 'Please. Let me look after you like when you were a little girl. You loved me then, didn't you? You didn't want to go away from me.'

Panic sparks around, but I try to keep my voice calm; ignore the thickness in my head. 'Mamma, I'm not going to go anywhere. But you can't keep me like this. Why can't you at least untie me, and I'll prove it to you?'

'Shhh ...' Mamma dabs zealously at my head. 'There now. We're safe here, you and me. Don't worry, Anna. You can stay here with me and no one will hurt you. I'll protect you – no one can get to us up here.' There's a breathless quality to her voice, unnaturally high and bright, as she turns her head to the attic door.

Slowly, I follow her gaze. The padlock. The only door in the house with one. In case of skunks, Mamma said.

'Mamma, you don't need to do this. I promise you I won't leave you. I ...' I try to shake my head from her grasp, but she only presses the cloth against me more firmly. And then she takes my face between her two palms and bores those bright blue eyes directly into mine; I see a mixture of desperation and urgency.

'Pray with me, Anna, please?'

Her fingers press against the bottom of my jaw, and my pulse thuds rapidly against them. Confusion turns into fear, and I swiftly close my eyes in obedience.

'Dear Lord,' she begins, as if the power of prayer has calmed her, 'we pray that You show us guidance, in our time of need. We know that we may have erred, but we trust in Your wisdom, to show us the true path, and to help us weather the storm. Lord, as Anna's mother, help me teach her forgiveness, and give me the strength to protect her, to keep her safe from harm. In Your name we pray. Amen.'

'Are you my mother?' The words are out of my mouth before I've even had time to process them: the whispered thought I've been trying to block, even from myself.

I watch her body petrify, her limbs becoming hard and stiff as a look of pure terror washes over her. But then something happens: like the white sheet draped over me, her features seem to mask themselves, her mouth unknotting itself and her eyes calm, unblinking. Her hands slide away from my face. 'Why in heaven's name would you ask me that?'

She stands, busies herself with something out of sight. I hear drawers opening and closing, and a foggily familiar clicking sound. 'You're sick, Anna. You're not thinking clearly.' Too late, I realise why I recognise the noise: it's the sound of a child safety cap twisting on a bottle. She pushes a spoon at my mouth, filled with a gummy green liquid. 'Perhaps when you're feeling better, you'll be kinder to me.'

Before I have a chance to think, I taste the cold bowl of the spoon between my lips, and then the minty green liquid fills my mouth. Mamma screws on the cap, and places the bottle back down somewhere with a clink.

She steps towards the door, and I hear the deep chink of the padlock followed by the thud of her footsteps on the stairs.

And then silence.

I lie for a long time trying to process what has happened. Mamma is in some sort of reverie, flitting between what she wants to believe and what's real. I want to trust in the fact that she would never truly hurt me, but right now, drugged, bruised, tied up, how can I be so sure? And I remember Father Paul – his threat to return. How long will it be before he claims us both? The thoughts toss and turn in my head as my eyelids grow heavy. I try to fight it, but a warm fuzz descends over me, and it's like my body is being forced down, down against the mattress.

I sleep.

The noise of the padlock stirs me. The pain in my head has lessened, but in its place is a vague grogginess, like all my edges are rounded off. The heat in the room has swelled, coursing through me, and even without being able to touch it, I can tell my nightdress is stuck to me with damp: when I move my legs against one another beneath the sheet, they're covered with a thin film of sweat.

'Mamma,' I croak as she steps into the room. My throat is paper-dry, coated with the sickly residue of the medicine.

When I run my tongue around my teeth, I feel the rough lining of sugar.

'How are you feeling, dear?' Mamma says with white brightness, setting a tray down on the wicker chair. She's holding something else, busying about the room, and I hear the rasp of a drawer being pulled out, from the old chest of drawers in the corner. Something lands inside it, heavy, leaden. And then the drawer shuts, and she's back in my eyeline.

'Mamma.' I can't help the tears that sting my eyes. How long has she kept me here? How long will she keep me here? 'Please. Could I have something to drink?'

It seems to please her, hearing me call her Mamma, asking for her care; she leans over the bedside, supporting my head as she puts a glass to my lips. I gulp thirstily, nearly choking as the cold water floods my mouth, and she snatches it away again. 'Careful, Anna. You have to move gently with a patient, to avoid overwhelming them. That's what it says in the books.'

She crosses back to the chair, sets the tray down on one of the cardboard boxes by the wall and sits, picking up an object from the floor beside her. From my position on the bed I can just make out the dahlia-red cover of her Bible. She opens it out onto her lap, and her fingers move methodically through the pages. 'I thought we'd do some Bible study, while you're still feeling unwell. What do you think?' Her lips fix into a vacant grin. 'Do you have a favourite chapter or verse you'd like to begin with?'

'Why are you doing this to me?' I ask. 'How long are you going to keep me here?'

'Keep you here?' Mamma's fingers don't rest as they trill through the pages. 'Anna, you're in your own home. All I'm trying to do is protect you. You just need to stay here a little longer, until you're well. And then we can go anywhere you please.' Her fingers pause, and in a low, agitated voice she reads, *'Is anyone among you in trouble? Let them pray. Is anyone happy? Let them sing songs of praise.'*

'Go? Where will we go?' The word prickles against me. Will she try and take me away – into hiding perhaps? I think of those girls, the ones found in that basement in Ohio – what if she locks me away for ever? I realise I know so much about her outward character, but virtually nothing about her inner mind.

'Is anyone among you sick? Let them call the elders of the church to pray over them and anoint them with oil in the name of the Lord.'

'Mamma . . .' I try softly, hoping to reason with her, to make her see sense. But she beats on, relentlessly, her voice growing louder but unbroken in its rhythm.

'And the prayer offered in faith will make the sick person well; the Lord will raise them up. If they have sinned, they will be forgiven.'

'Mamma, please, listen to me—'

She carries on, as if I am nothing but the buzzing of a fly in her ear.

I squirm against the bed, trying to release my wrists from the ties that bind them: garden twine, I realise, feeling the burn of it against my skin. 'I'm not sick. I don't need you to heal me. You have to let me go.'

There is a wildness in her eyes now, the same religious zeal I see in her preachers on television, a loose smile on her face, as if she truly believes she's doing the will of the Lord. 'Why aren't you hearing me, Anna? I've told you: you're not well. All I'm trying to do is take care of you, as the Lord commands.'

Anger sears at my insides. 'You're not my mother, are you?'

Her finger, poised over the Bible, stills. Words get snarled in her throat. She places the book on the floor, then she stands, comes over to me and slaps me clean across the face.

I gasp, swallowing air in shock. My cheek stings, and there's a ringing in my ear where her hand caught it.

'How dare you disrespect me like that?' She turns towards the door. I know if she goes I'll be locked in here again, alone.

'Please, Mamma, don't leave me here,' I cry out, trying to reach out for her with my tied wrists.

She pauses, cocks her head, and turns to assess me. 'Everything I've ever done has been for you, Anna. Perhaps you should think on that, before you upset me again.' She pushes open the door, but right before she ducks her head through it she gives me a tight smile. 'Rest now, daughter.

Remember your Scripture.' She nods. 'You'll feel better soon.'

The padlock turns. And once again I am alone.

She doesn't return for a long time. From the bed, I watch the light gradually darkening outside the attic window, retreating and eventually fading completely from the room. I place myself at Saturday evening. That means I must have been here nearly a full day.

My thoughts drift to my childhood. It seems so long ago, those innocent times. We were happy, weren't we, Mamma and I? Growing flowers, singing hymns, a family of two. I should never have gone looking. I should have forced myself to believe that it was all just a misunderstanding. I should have thrown Father Paul's gifts away.

I wrench my arms against the twine, trying to break loose. If I can only get free, I can go to her, ask her what Father Paul wants from her, and how I can help her make it all go away. Before I get away from her.

Father Paul. Mamma. Their figures dance and converge in my mind, shadow puppets in some ancient fable of good and evil. But which represents which?

I work my wrists back and forth against the loops that circle them, hoping to loosen them enough to slip my hands through. But although this does seem to release the twine's grip just the tiniest bit, the straw-like material clutches at my skin and makes me cry out in pain such that I can't bear to keep going. And I can feel a bruise now, forming where first the vase then Mamma's wrist hit me. When I move my mouth, the skin by my cheek is stiff and achy, and when I close my eye, the area around it feels puffed and thick.

I hear the dull click of the padlock, see the door slowly open to reveal Mamma's tall frame, and am instantly frozen. One look at her face and I know that reasoning won't work. In the past, I've always thought of her height as admirable; strong and commanding. Now I only see the menace. The blackness of the room casts an elongated shadow against the wall behind her, as if revealing the true nature that lies within her.

She flicks on the switch just inside the doorway, and the bulb over the bed plunges me into fluorescent white light. Instinctively I screw up my face, sheltering my eyes from its beam. Wordlessly she stalks over to me, placing a rough hand to my forehead. Her fingers press into the tenderness of my temple. She tuts, brings water to my lips, allows a few measly mouthfuls to trickle down my throat. The sound of my desperate swallowing cuts through the silence.

'Mamma?'

She doesn't reply.

I hear a new sound now: plastic, popping. Her fingers probe my mouth, and I feel the circles of two pills resting on my tongue. 'It's late. Take these, they'll help you sleep.'

I try not to swallow, to move them off to the side of my tongue and hide them in the corner of my mouth, but they're already starting to dissolve. Bitterness and chalk flood my mouth.

'I don't need to sleep,' I say. 'I want you to let me go.'

'Don't argue with your mother, Anna.'

And then she's gone.

I sleep, dreamlessly, the pills dragging me down to the centre of a black hole. It's pleasant there, and part of me wishes I could stay, let the blackness take over.

When I wake, it's already light out, and Mamma is back in the chair. I wonder how long she's been there. It makes my skin crawl, the thought of her silently watching me.

'How are you feeling, Anna dear? Better rested, I hope?' She has an uncanny expression on her face, her eyes wide and hopeful. And then in an instant it dawns on me: it's Sunday.

'What about church?' Each word feels heavy in my mouth. Mamma may not socialise with her fellow church-goers, but her presence is as constant as a ticking clock.

'What do you mean, Anna?' She bustles around me, plumping up the pillows behind me. 'I've been to church.'

I crane my head to see the sky through the attic window. The sun is high – I notice now, the way the beams hit the bed sheet. The heat has risen again – the cool relief of the night has passed – and brings with it a sickness in the pit of my stomach.

'I've been and gone,' she continues, moving about me to seek out any little imperfections in the room she can find to tidy, smoothing the crumpled bed sheet, adjusting the angle of the chair.

Her lavender-and-Lysol scent – an empty comfort – curls across the room and licks at my senses, heightened by my lack of sustenance. 'It was a pleasant sermon. All about faith, obedience and the perseverance of the Lord. It was really very moving.'

She allows me the indignity of a bed pan she must have bought from I have no idea where, and I let the mortification of this be washed away by the relief that at least she doesn't expect me to lie in soiled sheets.

Then she stops, holding a damp flannel half folded to her chest. 'That William was there. He gave me the strangest look; went quite pale and asked me where you were. Apparently he was with his father in the church all morning; a pipe burst and flooded into the offices. I told him you were all right, just a little under the weather.' Her face wrinkles into a frown, and she slaps the flannel down on the bed. 'I wish he'd listen to my advice and let you be. You need to understand, Anna: your relationship with William wasn't right. You don't know what boys his age want. He wants to lead you down an unrighteous path. He wants to lead you away from me. But if you're pure, if you're good, nothing – no one – can take you away.'

William. Hearing his name kindles a spark inside of me. I'm not alone. There's someone for me to fight for. Someone to fight for me.

'I love him, Mamma.' I speak slowly and carefully, dragging each word out through my dry lips. 'We're going to get married.'

'Anna, don't be ridiculous,' she brushes it off, 'you're only a child,' but I can hear the quiver at the edge of her voice. I'm encouraged: I think I may have found a chink in her armour. Years of living with Mamma have me attuned to the tiniest of her tells.

'It's true,' I say. 'He asked me, and I said yes. We're going to get married, Mamma.' A tiny part of me relishes it, the chance to twist the knife in deeper. 'It's not just you and me any more. You can't keep me locked up here for ever.'

'Stop saying that. You're not marrying that boy. You're not leaving me. I won't let you.' Mamma is shaking her head, turning away from me.

I was right. I've got her. 'Mamma, come on now.' I speak forcefully, but with caution. Now I've taken hold of her, I can't afford to set her free. 'Look at me. Look at what you've done to me.' I hold up my wrists, tense against their bonds. 'You can't keep me here like this; it's not right. I know that whatever drove you to this, you must have had good reason. I want to understand what that is. And I want to try and help you, to protect you. But to do that, you have to tell me the truth, and you have to let me go. I'm not your little girl any more.' I swallow, delivering the blow I know will devastate the most: 'I'm not your little girl at all.'

She presses herself against the padlocked door, holding her hands over her ears to block out my voice. 'No, no, no, no, no.'

'Please, Mamma. Tell me. Tell me the truth. I'll listen.'

'No, no, no, I won't listen. You're *my* daughter. You're mine.' She rocks back and forth.

'We both know that's not true, Mamma. You have to face up to it. It's a lie. It's all a lie.' I thrash my wrists. All the hurt, all the churned-up feelings of the last few weeks rise inside me, and I need to know who Mamma really is: my mother, or my captor? 'You took me. You tricked me. Why did you do it? What drove you to it? Let me go. Tell me, and I swear I'll understand.'

'*No.*' There's a storm in her voice. In a flash, she is beside me, standing over the bed. I try to look into her face, to find some semblance of the mother who raised me. 'I won't let you go. I have to keep you safe. I have to keep you pure. I won't let him take you from me again, Anna. He took you from me once, but I won't let it happen again.'

'*Who*, Mamma?' But I know the answer already. I picture his face, leaning towards me, the dazzling whiteness of his suit.

Her whole body is trembling. She looks wildly around the room, as if she's afraid someone is going to burst in and attack her.

'It's Father Paul, isn't it?' At the sound of his name she cowers into herself, an animal struck. 'It is, I know it. Mamma, I met him: I know he's a dangerous man. I understand why you're scared – he could hurt you, hurt us both. But if you let me go, together we can stop him.'

She turns to me, her eyes hollow in her head. 'I can't stop him, Anna. I never could. There's nothing we can do.'

ROSIE

20

Michael rises from his chair, places the empty mugs in the sink. With a brief jerk of the head bidding us to follow him, he makes his way into the hall.

'This next bit makes more sense if you see it for yourself.'

'Your sister's disappearance happened maybe five or six years before I moved to the States.' He leads us into the living room and gestures to the sofa. We both sit, poised on the edge. Michael moves around the room with ease, pulling files from a shelf and flinging them onto a glass coffee table, rummaging through the drawers of a desk that faces French windows that open onto a small, perfectly manicured garden. 'I remember the initial burst of news – the search for leads, the backlash against your family. At the time it wasn't of that much interest to me; it wasn't the sort of thing I covered, and by the time I'd moved to New York, there was the Crash, Lehman's going under, et cetera, et cetera – enough fruitful material right in Manhattan alone that some kid going missing in Florida wasn't really front and centre—' He catches himself, the storyteller and the host clashing. 'I'm sorry – that sounds crass. It's not to say it wasn't important, it's just ...'

'I know.' I nod that it's OK to continue.

'But once I moved back to the UK, I'd lost whatever it was that made me write. I couldn't make arse or end out of a story. Nothing excited me. I managed to get a steady stream of work as a freelance reporter, but I was a mess. Living in a shitty flat with a roommate I couldn't stand. Drinking more often than was good for me. And then the ten-year anniversary of Emily's disappearance rolled around.

'The last few years had been pretty doom-and-gloom in the UK – we were still feeling the recession, the coalition happened, student riots. And amidst it all was this adorable little blonde girl, snatched from Britain's hands by Evil Corporate America. It was like she became the hope of the nation. Like finding her would make everything right. Suddenly, every journalist I knew was trying to find their own angle on the case. And seeing them all fighting for scraps, I became consumed with a desire to beat them; to prove myself as the great journalist I once was.

'I met Jane on the TheHive, and she passed on some of the contacts she'd made, including one of the private detectives your parents had hired, Rosie. I found the pub he went to, started hanging around; you know, not too often to look weird, but enough to become a familiar face. One night I sat next to him up at the bar, and offered to buy him a beer. Told him he reminded me of someone and in fact, wasn't he – oh yes, he was! – one of the detectives I'd seen on TV, who'd been involved with the Archer case?

'He sussed me out straight away, of course.' Michael snorts, giving us a roll of his eyes. 'But he told me he'd give me one thing, off the record: recently they had gone back through the CCTV footage to look for anything unusual that could be connected with any of the new information that had come to light.'

Michael fiddles with a cushion, pulling it into his lap and working a corner back and forth as if he'd rather focus his attention on that than on either of us. 'I'm not proud of what I did next,' he says. 'I had a grandmother who'd died, left me some money. I promised him a decent chunk if he'd let me have copies of the stills. He refused at first, said it was unethical. But I kept hounding him, and eventually he agreed. And the time after that ...'

He reaches to the debris on the coffee table and plucks a brown cardboard folder from the pile. We crane our necks to look over his shoulder as he splays its contents across the glass. There are hundreds of grainy photos, blown up to A4 – images from the park. Most of them contain lots of people, and many more are no more indistinguishable than blobs. I don't know where you'd even begin.

'I agonised over these for days.' Michael strokes his fingers over them. 'Most of them were useless. There was nothing I could identify, without police records or any other files, that would give me any leads. And then I saw this.' I already know which picture his hand is about to pick. It's one of the less crowded images, the familiar green towers of the Astroland castle in the background. Judging by the position of the castle behind her, I guess she must be walking towards the carousel. She's alone – no kids beside her, no bags or souvenirs that I can make out – and she looks tall, with broad shoulders and light-coloured hair that's held back with an old-fashioned Alice band. She's not that old, maybe in her early twenties – it's difficult to tell exactly with the quality of the picture – and the dress itself is unremarkable; short sleeves, buttons down the front, not much by way of shape. I know this is her: the woman in the navy dress. What I don't know is why she caught his eye.

'I don't understand,' I say. I gesture hesitantly at the picture, pausing my hand inches from it. 'What made you think this woman was more remarkable than anyone else?'

'Nothing, at first.' He places his finger on the centre of her throat, where I can just make out something around her neck. 'Except for this.'

'A necklace?' I squint dubiously, bringing my face closer.

He reaches across the table, and pulls up another piece of paper. This one looks like a website printout: the name 'The Lilies' loops in white cursive on the left-hand side, underneath that a welcome message, and hyperlinks for

'Who We Are', 'What We Believe' and 'Where We Meet'. On the right, next to a photograph of a group of people holding hands, laughing into the camera, is the outline of an elongated cross, its edges bowed, fanning slightly outwards. Wound around it, its leaves twisting around the base, is a flower. A lily.

I follow Michael's finger as he traces a pattern around the throat of the woman in the CCTV still, and then again with the cross in the printout.

'I don't know.' I shake my head. 'I'm not sure I could make out if that was one cross or any other.'

Keira, next to me, reaches out for the piece of paper and holds it inches away from her nose. Then she shrugs and puts the paper down. 'Sorry, I don't buy it.' I know what she's thinking – the same thing as me: all this way, all this time, and he's just another Jane after all. 'And even if it was,' she says, 'why would the two be connected?'

But Michael doesn't seem perturbed or embarrassed. He rustles through the documents again, and pulls out a different folder. Inside are dozens of images of the same thing: close-ups of the woman's neck, zoomed in to different points, some of them almost blurred beyond recognition. He takes one in particular, where he's drawn over the points of the cross in black ink, and holds it next to the web printout.

'I wasn't sure either, at first. After looking through hundreds of images, I couldn't see the wood for the trees; started to think the whole thing was a complete waste of time. But something about the cross's shape made me sit up. I went back to the detective, and convinced him to get me access to more images, closer up. I think he decided that it was easier just to give me what I wanted to shut me up – I was pretty persistent. I don't think he believed I'd actually find anything worthwhile.

'As soon as I got hold of the close-ups, I was convinced it was the same symbol. I remembered Angela's mother wearing one – I hadn't thought about it at the time; after all, it's not so out of the ordinary for people to wear crosses – but then I remembered something else. The day I went to visit Father Paul, they'd all been wearing them. I must have noticed it, logged it in some corner of my mind, but once I saw it again it came back to me. I remembered thinking it was quite uncanny, seeing them swinging from people's necks like that, all exactly the same. And I thought to myself, isn't it awfully odd for someone from The Lilies to be wandering around a theme park like that on their own? They hardly share a common love of roller coasters. It didn't sit right with them at all – their beliefs, their eccentricities. I looked at the website, but there wasn't a church I could find in Florida. From what I knew from Ruth, they didn't tend to travel far from the church, unless they were looking to start up somewhere new. And then I looked at a map. Florida is only one state over from Georgia: perhaps that was all it was; Father Paul was looking to find a spot in Florida. But that wouldn't explain why the woman was on her own. Or in Astroland.

'This woman: could it be that there was a more sinister reason for her presence? That she was connected to the disappearance of Emily? I wondered, what if I were the one to break the case? Not the Americans, not Scotland Yard, not some private detective or even a Pulitzer Prize-winning journalist, but me. I stopped drinking. I lost two stone, moved into a place of my own. I was up every night, researching. Even when I was sleeping, scenarios would develop in my dreams: how I'd unmask Father Paul, how I'd find out the truth about Emily Archer, how I'd honour Bill and get closure for Ruth and Angela. And finally, my mind was made up: I couldn't let it drop. I had to go back to Georgia.'

ANNA

21

Father Paul and The Lilies. The names that have been haunting me since this all began, reverberating around the attic walls. I process them as I watch Mamma across the room. I see something inside her melt. Imperceptibly at first: the sag of her shoulders; the drawing down of her eyes and mouth, pulled by some unseen force. Then, wordlessly, she sinks into the wicker chair, her arms lifeless at her sides. Whatever they are to her, their names alone have the power to change her before my eyes.

'Mamma, who is Father Paul?' I speak sotto voce, afraid of upsetting the balance. 'Why does he have such a hold on you?'

Her mouth puckers. She steers her face away from me like a toddler refusing food. 'I can't explain it to you. If I do, you'll leave me. You'll never be able to love me again.'

'There's no turning back now, Mamma – it's too late. Tell me from the beginning. Pretend you're telling me a story. I'll listen.'

A bead of sweat snakes down her forehead. The air in here is stale, dead. My body is drunk on sleeping pills and medicine. But I am alert. I have to know. At last, Mamma wipes her head with the back of her hand, exhales so deeply I can almost feel the breeze on my face. There is nowhere else to go.

'I was a good child,' she begins plaintively, turning her chin to the shaft of light spilling through the attic window. She's turning back to the beginning, to where it started. 'I was quiet and obedient. Kept myself to myself. We lived in the very north of Georgia, in the foothills of the Blue Ridge Mountains. Just Daddy and me. On a twenty-acre farm that belonged to him, and his daddy before that.' She squints into the sunlight, as if trying to picture the place in the shape of the clouds. And then her mouth moulds itself into an ugly ball. 'I hated that place. Hated the leaking roof, and the windows that rattled every time the smallest of vehicles drove past it. Hated the sickly-sweet smell of hogswill, and the constant squabbling of the broiler chickens, and the way even breathing near the hay made you feel its dryness scratch the back of your throat.' She snorts.

I try to picture her, Mamma as a young girl, her sturdy form among the muck and muddle of farmland. Knowing her as I do, it's not hard to see why she disliked it.

'Mamma died when I was just a baby, and Daddy hated me for it. He was strict. But it often felt like he was making up the rules as he went along, and the only way I knew a rule existed was when I broke it. I left school at fourteen,' she continues, 'to help on the farm. Daddy didn't see the point in a "dumb girl" like me staying on at school.

'I wanted to grow things – pretty things to brighten that bleak place – but every time I did he'd just rip them straight up. I found a kitten once – wandered into the farm; a darling little thing that must have lost its mamma. But it chased the chickens and got underfoot, and one morning when I came down for breakfast he told me he'd drowned it.'

'Oh Mamma.' I hurt for her, for this girl who had no one. How different would her life have been if she'd had someone to care for her? She looks down at her hands, and for a moment she is silent, remembering. 'Please,' I urge. 'Go on.'

'My only relief was on Saturdays,' she swallows thickly, 'when Daddy would spend the day getting drunk with the other farmers, and I'd sneak off to the library in town. If the weather was pleasant and not too hot, I'd pack myself a sandwich and an apple, and then I'd check out a book and go sit in the park under a shady tree, reading until it started getting dark. Daddy said fiction was the devil's tools. But he never found out.' There's a ghost of a smile on her face. I never knew she liked to read. All those books I've hidden from her. All those chances to understand her, for us to share something special in common.

'There was a boy there I'd see sometimes,' Mamma goes on, and her voice gets a softness to it, a certain lilt I don't recognise in her. 'We didn't talk to each other, but we'd smile across the way. I used to watch him and his friends out the corner of my eye, and think that if I were a different sort of girl, maybe I'd go up to them, say something casual. And then, one afternoon, a shadow fell over the book I was reading. He was standing right there in front of me, holding his hand to his forehead to block out the sunlight, and he said, "You read more than anyone I've ever met." He said his name was Mason and invited me to come sit with him and his friends. I remember the little prickle in my heart when he took my hand to help me up.'

Mason. My father.

'Mason had those wide, kind eyes and the gentlest smile, and when he looked at me I felt something stir inside me and thought, *So this is what all the fuss is about*.' I think of his picture in the kitchen. There was something placid in his face, yes, but there was also a tightness to his mouth, a solidity in his eyes, that suggested sternness. 'He wanted to know all about me. Where did I live? What did I do? Where did I go to church? And then, when we started talking about church, Mason patted my knee and nodded to his friends – there were four or five of them then – and he said that, funnily enough, church was how they all met.'

'So it was Daddy who …?'

Mamma nods. 'It was Mason who first told me about The Lilies. He said they'd come to town a couple of months before from Indiana; that their leader had started his mission in San Francisco in the eighties: to bring purity and righteousness to the world.'

'Father Paul?' I coax. I shift uneasily on the bed, feeling the snarl of twine against my skin, trying to ignore every sensation except for the sound of Mamma's voice.

She sighs. 'It was the first time I heard his name. And when I made to leave, Mason clasped his fingers around mine and said he thought I'd really like their church and would I like to go. I said yes.'

'But' – I try to cling to words, form a sentence from the thoughts that tumble from my mind – 'why?'

Mamma clasps her hands together, and there's a brightness in her eyes that sets off a creeping unease in me. 'The way Mason talked about him, it was like he was the Second Coming. You have to understand: I had nothing in my life. Nothing to divert me from my daily chores. But suddenly there was this man, showing me a new way to be.' I think of William, of the chance of freedom he has shown me, even before all of this, and I think I understand.

'The church was about half an hour's drive away from where we lived.' Mamma's fingers played idly with a corner of her dress, working a seam with the edge of her nail. 'It was set right next to the river, and the crystal water bounced the light off it and reflected right onto the church so it seemed to glitter white. As we got out of the car, Mason explained the river was one of the signs Father Paul looked for when assessing the grounds of a new church. He said they believed the soul must be continually baptised, not just at birth, in order to wash away the sins that stick to the mortal body from the outside world. He told me Father Paul was a blessed man; that he had been chosen by God, to deliver His mission on earth.

'Mason squeezed my hand and led me to the altar, to a tanned man in a white linen suit, with his hair tied back in a ponytail. He said, "Father Paul, I'd like to introduce you to Mary," and he presented me to him. Father Paul beamed at me – he had two rows of perfect teeth. He said, "Mary, welcome to our little church. We do hope you like it." He said they'd heard so much about me.

'I often think to myself, what would it have been like if I'd never met Mason; if I'd never gone to that church?' Her head shakes gently from side to side, and she fixes her gaze on the Bible on the floor beside her. 'Unfortunately, that didn't happen.'

She rises from the chair, crosses the attic floor. There is something fragile in her movements, despite her height and broad stature; a trembling, in the intricate bones of her fingers; an unsteadiness on those long legs.

I swallow. 'But what did?' I strain to catch her eye, but she stands at the window, looking out.

'After that first visit, it was so easy to fall into it all.' The back of her neck stretches as she looks through the slanted glass, over the treetops and parcelled fields that have always protected our little house from the outside world. In a way, she is as trapped in here as I am. 'There was a small fee, to join officially, to pay for the robe and the sandals, and other items necessary for my first baptism. I got an allowance from the work I did on the farm but I was always embarrassed that I wasn't offering enough. I started selling some of my trinkets – a necklace I inherited from my grandmother; my mamma's pearl earrings – and every time I was able to contribute a little more, it made me feel *good*, especially with Mason sitting beside me, squeezing my hand and telling me how generous I was, that I was truly a blessing on the church.

'I brought flowers I had grown, to dress the church, and when Father Paul saw them, he took me into his arms and told me it was clearly the will of the Lord that I had been sent to them; that I was special. No one had ever told me that before. For the first time, I felt like I was surrounded by people who treasured me, and admired my gifts, and valued goodness and truth. For the first time, I felt loved.'

I am mesmerised, captured by Mamma's story: a woman who seems to have been so devoid of love her whole life. I want to speak up, to ask if it could have driven her to do such a thing as this, but something stops me. Instead, I listen.

'After that,' she says, 'Father Paul began showing a particular interest in me. He gave me licence to plant whatever I wanted around the church, and I spent all my free time there, sowing seeds, my hands in the earth. I grew lilies, of course, great big white ones that the members would pin to their robes on special occasions, hoping for my good fortune to rub off on them. And white roses – the symbol of the Lord Himself; and wild purple *Passiflora*, each part a representation of the Lord's Passion and suffering; and they all blossomed and multiplied so fruitfully that it really did seem like the will of the Lord.

'When I was done each day, I'd scrub my hands until not a speck of dirt remained, to please Father Paul, to show how strongly I believed. I became so good at it, so meticulous, he would call me up to the altar, heralding me as an example to the congregation. "Look at your sister!" he would say, holding my hands out for the church members to inspect. "See how she toils the land; and despite this keeps herself pure as the lilies in the field? This, I tell you, is doing the Lord's work."

'But soon, I started running out of things to sell. My donations to the pot got smaller and smaller, and I became fearful, every week, that someone would notice, and say something. But Daddy was always leaving change around here and there, and there were little things I found to pawn, things nobody could notice, money that would benefit the church far more than our crumbling farmhouse. I felt bad, it's true; I spoke about it during the Confession Ceremony, and let the members shouts of "Unclean" swell around me, but afterwards Father Paul called me to his office, told me I shouldn't feel guilt for actions which would benefit the church; that The Lilies had a higher plan for me.

The way he looked at me, and touched his palms to mine, I felt certain he was right.'

Mamma's movements are hypnotic: the pulse of her eyelids, the jolt of her throat with each swallow, the repetitive smearing of her palms across her skirt. I can't tear my eyes away from her.

'Daddy complained about the missing money,' she says. 'I told him it was probably one of the farmhands, but he knew straight away that it was me. One night, Mason dropped me back home, and I found everything I owned strewn on the front porch. Everything trampled through the dirt.

When I walked in the house, it was so dark I almost missed him completely. But there he was, sitting at the head of the carved oak chair that his daddy had sat on, and his daddy before him, every inch the head of the household. And he told me I had to leave.'

Mamma's hands squeeze into fists, and her face twists in hatred. 'I spent my whole life being scared of that man. Everything about my life up to then was dirt and decay, from that wretched farm to my own father's soul: my muddied clothes were a symbol of that. Before, I was trapped – there was nowhere else for me to go. But now I had a choice. There was Mason. And Father Paul. And purity and love and happiness. *I made a choice*, Anna. I chose The Lilies. If you had two paths in front of you, one you knew was dark and the other had even the smallest promise of light, which would you choose?'

When she looks at me there is a ferocity in her eyes, an intensity bubbling up in her that makes me feel scared, yes, but also the tiniest bit impressed. 'I understand,' I murmur. And I do.

Mamma's face softens, and she comes over to me on the bed. I struggle against the twine, twisting my fingertips to reach for her hand. She notices, moves it towards me, and I clutch her fingers clumsily in mine. Would it have been different if she had had a mother; or someone who cared for her as she has cared, in her own way, for me? We remain motionless, listening to the faint call of birdsong and my own dry swallows. I think this could be it – the moment she'll come to her senses and let me go.

But then a noise intrudes into the silence. Low at first, but gradually getting louder. A repeated *thud, thud, thud*.

And a voice. A man's voice.

Mamma drops my fingers, and her whole body goes rigid, her eyes round as full moons. She races to the door and barricades it with her body.

She turns to me, her face white. 'It's him.'

ROSIE

22

Through the French windows, the daylight is mellowing into early evening. Michael seems to relax into himself, his body slackening against the sofa. Georgia. At last it seems he is bringing us closer to the woman in the navy dress. Closer to Emily.

It's quiet, Michael's home. I'm so used to the familiar grumble of traffic outside our front door, or the even patter of Mum moving through the house, or the soft chords of Dad's music, switched on as soon as he walks in the door. But here, it's like every living thing has left us alone, giving Michael the stage to tell his story.

'Stepping off that plane in Atlanta was like stepping right back three years. The lingering smokiness from mountain wildfires, the corporeal reek of the Bradford pear trees, that dry, scorching heat. When I was living there, they became so much a part of my make-up that they'd stopped existing for me, but distance made each scent fresh and new.

'I admit I was scared. Excitement and a fair bit of bravado had got me as far as border control, but once I entered Georgia proper I couldn't escape the feeling that Father Paul would somehow know what I was up to, and I half expected him to be there waiting for me as soon as I walked through the exit. It wasn't that I thought he was dangerous, exactly, it was more of an overall unease.

'I hired a car, parked in town; just walked around for a bit. I bought some food from a deli and went to sit in the park. There was a group of teenagers in the shade near me, and something in their manner, the way they moved, reminded me of Ruth. There was the careful way they sat on the ground, the cautious glances they gave to their hands, subconsciously checking them for dirt. When I spotted the pendants around their necks, I knew I'd found who I was looking for.

'I played the tourist card, told them I was passing through on a road trip with my wife and daughter, that we were heading through Georgia down into Florida, and might stop off at that theme park ... Astroland ... had any of them ever been? No, no, they all shook their heads, most of them had never been out of the state. They genuinely seemed like they didn't know why I was asking. Did they know that a girl had disappeared there, a little English girl, about ten years ago? That was when they began to get shifty, like maybe I was starting to go a bit off the beaten track. I told one of them that I liked her necklace. She was a pretty girl with white-blonde hair that hung in a sheet down her back. I reached out to touch the necklace but she pulled away and they all seemed to get up at once, said they had to leave. I was being stupid and erratic, but I'd come all that way and I was jet-lagged to buggery and thought this might be my only chance.'

Michael seems to hesitate, as if he's decided to say something else but then thinks better of it, because his cheeks puff and he sways his head a little before carrying on. 'I ate dinner with the owners of my B&B – a sweet old couple. I was the only guest, and the wife was keen to show off the best of her Southern hospitality. The husband told me their kids had all left the state, and that it was nice to have someone new visiting, so I let them coddle me. When I was released at last I sat in my room with its dusty floral bedspread and all those doilies, and I tried to piece together the broken fragments of the story.

'There was a knock on my door about ten o'clock, and Mrs Leary, the wife, peeked around it. She was sorry to be bothering me, she said, but there was a man there to see me. She'd said I might be sleeping, but he told her it was urgent.

'Even before I left the room I knew who I would find. Part of me feared it, but part of me realised this was what I needed all along. I saw his boots first, shined so high his reflection bounced onto you. And a white suit – not a crease, not a wrinkle. And that hair, so neatly tied. Father Paul was standing in the Learys' chintzy living room, under a wooden sign that said, "If Mamma Ain't Happy, Ain't Nobody Happy"—'

From upstairs there comes a distant wail, footsteps moving on the landing. Michael turns his eyes to the ceiling, then looks back at us. 'Hugo waking up from his nap.' He looks almost as though he's going to ask us to leave, and although I feel bad for forcing ourselves upon him, one look at the images scattered on the table tells me I can't leave, not yet.

'What did Father Paul say, when you saw him?' I ask, gently but forcibly pushing him back into his story.

He cocks his head towards the hall, listening for signs of his family. 'He told me I was an easy man to track down.' The noises upstairs settle and fade, so he turns reluctantly back to me. 'There was a sneer to his voice, the way he said it, as if to say, wasn't he so clever, to have found me. But now I think of it, I suppose I wasn't being awfully discreet: an Englishman poking around a small town, asking questions. Once those kids mentioned it to him, it wouldn't have been too hard to find me. He was very jovial, as seems to be his way. Asked me how my trip was, how I was finding the bed and breakfast. He asked after Angela, and Ruth. When I told him about Bill, he held his hands up to the heavens and said that was always going to be the way. He said, "Cancer like that – there's not much chance of coming back from it."'

Michael's mouth thins into a hard line. 'I think he was goading me. It was like he was trying to cut the small talk and get straight to the point, and I took the bait, like an idiot. I went for him. All that praying, and all that money, and he knew all along it was a complete waste of time. I told him he was a charlatan, and a con artist, and that I could have him locked up. And he just listened to me rant and rave, and when I finished he quoted as if by rote, that studies show that hope and prayer can have a powerfully healing effect. He said he wasn't touting anything that hadn't been written about by the modern, mainstream Christian Church. He was actually laughing at me, that scumbag, so I told him, let's cut the niceties, why not tell me how the church was involved in the disappearance of Emily Archer.' At the sound of her name my whole body tingles, and I sit up, convinced, suddenly, I'm about to hear the definitive proof I need.

'I thought I had him there, for a moment,' Michael says. 'He didn't speak, and his expression froze on his face, but then everything seemed to smooth itself out like an iron over one of his goddam white robes, and he said, "I'm afraid I don't know who that is," with a voice like silk. I was feeling cocky now, and told him I knew all about it – that I had the images of the woman from Astroland. I thought I had him pinned down: a park full of kids; the proximity to Georgia; a member of his church, there on her own. Why else would she be there? I made a mental leap: the park's exactly the sort of place Father Paul would despise: dirty, noisy, messy. I thought perhaps she'd been sent to kidnap someone ... I don't know ... for one of their purification rituals or something.

'I said I knew they'd taken her, and demanded to know if she was still alive and where they were hiding her, and what they wanted her for. That's when Father Paul really began to laugh. He told me I didn't know anything at all. He said they had nothing to do with the girl, and that I should learn to keep my nose out of other people's business if I knew what was good for me. And then he said, completely in control: "You should think very carefully before trying to involve yourself in matters that go way beyond you. You should go home, to your life in England." And he looked me dead in the eyes and said, "Look after your lovely Rebecca."'

Beside me, Keira puffs her cheeks and blows a stream of air through her lips. 'This guy sounds like a lunatic,' she says.

Michael nods. 'That's putting it lightly. It creeped me out, the fact that he used Rebecca's name. We'd only been dating about six months. But I didn't take him too seriously at first. Anyone with half a brain and access to Facebook would be able to find us. I kept my head down for the rest of the week, looking out for anyone who looked like Emily, spending a lot of time at the local library, reading through reports from the time and trying to find something unusual which could point me in the right direction.' Again he pauses, as if something has come into his mind he's considering mentioning, but again he shakes it away. 'But there was simply nothing to be found. So I went home.

'I didn't think much more about Father Paul's threat. I was still convinced I was on to something, even with nothing solid to go on, and that was when I started writing on TheHive myself. I mentioned the church, calling for information, anyone who knew what they were up to. I went back to that detective, the one who'd given me the images. But he dismissed me, told me I couldn't possibly have found something that wouldn't have already been checked out by the police. And then one day I came home and there was a card in the post. A watercolour on the front – of lilies, what else? When I opened it, a picture spilled out. It was a photo of Rebecca going in my front door. Just that. We'd just found out she was pregnant ... it wasn't exactly planned, but we were pleased all the same,' he mumbles. 'I'd asked her to move in with me.' He puts his head in his hands, and I feel the blood run cold in my veins.

'I looked at the envelope for some kind of clue,' he says, 'but it was plain brown, delivered by hand. I threw it away immediately, didn't say anything to Rebecca of course. But that was just the start. They sent letters to my work – I'd stopped freelancing by then. There was nothing direct: one was just a blank postcard, a picture of Atlanta on the front; another sent *Congratulations, great article! from The Lilies*, with a torn-out copy of my latest hack job; one was just a quote from the Bible: *Even a fool, when he holdeth his peace, is counted wise: he that shutteth his lips is deemed a man of understanding*. Each time, they seemed bolder. They sent a bunch of lilies to the house. Rebecca assumed they were from me and thanked me for being so thoughtful, and I had to put up with their cloying smell and have their brown pollen dust on my clothes every day as a reminder, until she finally threw them out.

'I was spooked. The way they were all so nebulous, that there was no identifiable sender. I kept everything they sent together – you can have a look if you like; they're in a box in one of my desk drawers – and when I looked at it all laid out, I realised each one was written in a different hand.' He shivers visibly. 'I started to feel like there were hundreds of unseeing eyes watching me, that there was some network of Lilies keeping tabs on my every move.

'I did some research and found out there was a branch of the church in the UK, in Slough: it would have been easy enough to orchestrate. And Father Paul is a powerful man; I didn't fully appreciate it until then. Each individual church is small, but there are quite a few of them. He has at least six in the States; one in Mexico; I think there's even one in Israel. And the money these people willingly fork out to him … God, it makes it easy to command attention with the right number on a cheque.' He addresses me directly, his face a mask of gravity: 'We're talking about a cult here, Rosie, operating under the guise of Christianity.'

He breathes then, heavily, and shifts his weight in his seat. 'Sorry. Would you mind if we stop for a moment, so I can get myself a glass of water?'

When he's out of the room, Keira pulls at my arm. 'What do you think?'

I raise my hands at the ceiling. 'I mean ... what's there to say really? It all sounds batshit crazy. This Father Paul is obviously some kind of religious lunatic, and I feel like Michael is a good guy, you know? And sane. Not one of the strange conspiracy theorists my mum is always so worried about. But,' I shrug, 'I can't see how any of this is connected to Emily. Firstly, I don't know what they'd want with her, and secondly, if they do have her, why hasn't someone spotted her by now?'

'Unless she's ...' Keira leaves the thought dangling. She doesn't need to finish it – it's the noise I've been trying to drown out of my own head. Could it have been some sort of religious ritual? How dark does this stuff really get? For all I know, they were into sacrificing children, and Emily was picked out as their next victim. I push the thought back down.

Michael returns – I hear the rattle of the tray before we see him. Along with the glasses are a couple of cartons of kids' apple juice, elderflower cordial, and a can of Diet Coke. 'I wasn't sure if you'd prefer something more glamorous than water,' he says.

He drinks slowly. I hear the glug of water as it passes through his throat. He finishes, puts the glass down with a soft clink on the table, and then rubs both palms of his hands over his forehead and down the back of his head. He looks tired, older than when he started telling us his story.

'Sorry,' he says eventually. 'I haven't dredged all this up in a long while. It wasn't a pleasant period in my life; not one I particularly relish retelling.' He folds his arms across his chest, takes a gulp of air which he holds, briefly, his shoulders nudging up to his chin. 'I kept all of this from Rebecca. I know it doesn't sound like it was the right thing to do, but at the time, with the baby, especially after what happened with Angela ... I just didn't want to do anything that would upset or frighten her. But it turns out all of my caution was a waste of time anyway.

'Someone stopped her on the steps to our house. She was about seven months pregnant at the time. She couldn't remember anything particularly outstanding about them: it was a woman, medium height, she said, medium build, brown hair ... about as bland as you can get. She asked her if she was Rebecca, Michael's girlfriend, and when she said that she was, the woman pressed a package into her hands and said, "Would you see that he gets this?"

'When I came home Becs was sitting at the kitchen table, with the package open in front of her. I don't know how long she'd been there; maybe an hour, maybe more ... just staring at it. She said she'd been curious, that once she'd shut the door behind her it did seem a pretty odd interaction, and she had a funny feeling about what was inside it.'

Michael pauses, and looks at each of us in turn, as if debating how to continue. 'It was a foetus. Of a mouse,' he quickly adds, as I feel my stomach churn. 'I can still picture it. It was probably no bigger than my thumb. Its skin was translucent peach, so thin you could see the spider of veins beneath it, and the little thing was curled in on itself, so that the tip of its tail pointed towards its beady, half-formed black eyes.'

I take a sip of water. I hear Keira do the same.

'I looked at her belly, at the child – our child – growing inside her. It wasn't hard to guess what they were trying to insinuate. It was one thing when they were threatening me, but now they were turning to my family, I ...' He pinches the bridge of his nose, swallows hard. 'Rebecca demanded to know what was going on – as she had every right to. She was crying and shouting and asking to know what it meant, why someone would send me something like this. And all the while that creature was on the table, its eyes staring up at us, and I thought, *You know what, Father Paul? You've won.*

'I told her everything, but I already knew what I was going to do. I'd already lost one wife, and one child; I wasn't about to lose any more. I wiped everything from the Hive profile – almost everything; I still hoped that, maybe, if someone else out there happened to stumble upon something, at least they'd know they weren't the only one. I started looking for a new job instantly. We needed to get away from the city, away from London. And then, when we were set and ready to go, I went on that website,' he points to the printout from the church he showed us earlier, 'found an email address, and asked them to pass a message on to Father Paul. He had his wish: I would leave everything alone; I wouldn't say another word about The Lilies, to anyone, as long as he and his minions left my family alone.

'To this day he's kept his side of the bargain, and I've kept mine, but I've never quite shaken the feeling that they're watching me. Which is why, Rosie, I didn't want to speak to you. The party – I only wanted to pay my respects. I felt so connected to it all. But as soon as I got there I knew it was a bad idea – if they were indeed keeping an eye on me, what might they do if they saw me there?' There isn't malice in his voice, but I hear the sting of his words all the same. I feel truly terrible now, for springing myself on him like this. For threatening the equilibrium he has created.

But it's actually Michael who seems to be sorry. He places a hand on mine, and the skin between his eyebrows pinches into a frown. 'I know you must think me a coward, and a let-down, for not pursuing this further, or telling the police or anyone else. But you have to understand: Rebecca and Hugo are my life. We're happy here, and each un-remarkable day that goes by takes us away from that time; from Father Paul.'

'I don't think you're a coward,' I say slowly, letting his hand rest on mine. And it's true. I can see where he's coming from. Is it really that different from what I was trying to do, before I started looking? We've both been trying to distance ourselves from our past.

I want to say more, but there's a sudden pelting of footsteps down the stairs, and then a little dark-haired body comes hurtling towards Michael's lap. 'Daddy!' he says gleefully, his head buried into his father's chest.

'Hello there, little one.' Michael ruffles his fingers through Hugo's hair, and plants a kiss on the top of his head. I can see the love in him, in the way he holds his son, protectively. I can see that nothing is worth risking him for.

Rebecca appears in the doorway. 'Mike, you said you'd take Hugo for the evening,' she says. 'I've got to finish reading that report.' Her eyes flick from me to Keira, her unspoken dismissal heavy in the air.

Mike raises a curled fist to his mouth and clears his throat. 'Sorry, Becs, you're right.' He gives us an apologetic shrug. 'Girls, can I give you a lift to the station?'

I can't help feeling disappointment that it's all over, but one look at Rebecca and I know we've long outstayed our welcome. Besides, I have what I came for: Mike has told me what he knows, even if he hasn't given me the conclusion I was hoping for.

In the car we're awkward, our truncated conversation tangible in the silence. As we pull into the station, Mike catches my eye in the wing mirror. 'I'm sorry … about Rebecca. It's nothing against you personally, it's just that she's scared about dredging all that old stuff up again. She's very protective of Hugo. She handled everything at the time so remarkably well, but I think, in the back of her mind, it really affected her.'

I tell him it's fine, that I understand, that my mum is the same, and I reach blindly for the door handle.

But just before I close the car door behind me he calls me back. 'Rosie, you have to believe me when I say these are dangerous people we're dealing with here. I know you want to find out what happened to your sister, but if I'm right, if Father Paul really is involved, then you have no idea what lengths they'll go to, to keep that secret. I know what it's like, at your age: you think you know everything, that you're invincible. But you're just a child. If you get involved with The Lilies, you could get hurt.'

'I understand.' I nod, push the door shut behind me.

What he doesn't know is that my decision's already been made. If I want to know if The Lilies took my sister, I'm going to have to find them myself.

ANNA

23

The low, repetitive beat continues. A muffled voice travels in from outside, insistent but indistinct.

'Mamma, what should we do?' My instinct is to reach for her, to let her lead me, as she always has done, but my ties prevent me.

Her eyes dart from me to the door to the attic window, her whole body pressed against the wall, like it's keeping her upright. Even from across the room, I can see she is trembling. 'We have to stay here,' she says. 'He'll go eventually.'

'We can't hide up here for ever, Mamma. We have to do something. Shouldn't we call the police?'

'Be quiet!' The snap in her voices shocks me, and I am silent.

The banging continues. I try to strain my ears to make out what the sound is, but it's too far away, too hard to hear clearly through the padlocked door. Mamma begins to pace; fists balled, hitting her temples like she's either trying to block out the noise or smack an answer into herself. Words muttered under her breath. I realise she is praying.

After what seems like an age, the beating falls silent. Mamma, her face slicked with sweat, gives a sob of relief and sinks against the door. 'He's gone.' She presses her palms together, looks heavenwards. 'I told you, Anna. You must have more faith.'

She stays like that, unmoving, the only sound her panicked breathing slowly reaching equilibrium. I say nothing, hoping this will be my chance: to convince Mamma to set me free, to give us a chance to escape him. But then I hear the click of a bottle cap, see her pouring the viscous green liquid onto a spoon. 'Oh, Mamma, please no.' I can't help the whimper in my voice as she moves towards me.

'Hush now, honey. It's been a long day, for both of us. Why don't you get some rest?' I squirm away from her, but I can't stave off the metal butting between my teeth, or the medicine trickling down my throat. Mamma takes a flannel and wipes almost tenderly at my mouth, where I can feel rivulets of green running down my chin. 'There's a good girl,' she soothes, her voice as syrupy as the medicine. 'Trust in me. I'll protect you. I won't let him get you.'

*

I wake panting, and for a moment I've forgotten where I am. I see the beams of sunlight creeping their way across the bed sheets and it comes back to me: the attic.

The air is heavy with heat. I am soaked in my own sweat, blood pulsing in my ears. How long have I been here? Is it two days? Three? My world has turned upside down.

I suck my cheeks in, seeking out moisture, but tasting only the acrid remnants of the medicine that gums to my teeth and the roof of my mouth. I try once again to loosen the fastenings on my wrists and think I may finally feel some sort of give, when I hear footsteps outside the door, followed by the telltale sound of the padlock, and I force myself to stop. If I am going to free myself, Mamma has to be with me, not against me: I can't let her think I'm trying to escape.

When the door opens, I almost weep with relief when I see she's carrying a tray with a glass of water on it. I fall on it as she props me up and I gulp down the cool liquid, but before I'm even halfway through she pulls the glass away. 'Careful now, you'll make yourself sick.' Her tone is brusque, and there is something in her manner that seems closed now, shut off. She won't make eye contact with me. She sits, stiffly, in the wicker chair, and pulls her Bible onto her lap. The arrival of Father Paul has destroyed whatever openness we cultivated before. We're back to square one.

She draws a forefinger around the Bible's sharp corners and listlessly flicks the tips of the pages, then stops, opens the book fully. 'I thought, seeing as you missed church yesterday, that we'd do some Bible study today. It'll be good to take your mind off being ill.' She begins to read, and I recognise the chapter almost instantly: the parable of the sheep and the goats, from Matthew: *'Come, you who are blessed by my Father; take your inheritance, the kingdom prepared for you since the creation of the world. For I was hungry and you gave me something to eat, I was thirsty and you gave me something to drink, I was a stranger and you invited me in, I needed clothes and you clothed me, I was sick and you looked after me, I was in prison and you came to visit me.'*

Her voice gathers its familiar intoning lilt, and slowly I start to piece together the days. If church was yesterday, Sunday, then today is Monday. That means I've been here more than two days. How much longer can she keep me here, acting like her story was a dream, like Father Paul was never here? I know I have to break through this fantasy. If Father Paul came once, he'll come again, and I have to get her to free me before he does, if I have any chance of saving us both. I have to make her go back; to confront what happened. If she faces it, maybe she'll let me go.

'Mamma,' I say tentatively, when she pauses between readings. She doesn't answer. 'Mamma, tell me what happened once you left your father's farmhouse?'

Her eyes don't move from the page. 'Why do you want to know that, Anna?' she says. 'It's not important.'

I clear my throat, trying to break a path through its claggy dryness. 'Please, Mamma. It might help me understand.'

'Understand what, Anna?'

'What happened between you and Father Paul? Why does he want you to go back to The Lilies? What does he ...' I choose my words carefully, 'what does he want with me?'

She huffs, but remains silent.

'I have a right to know.'

For a moment I think she's going to turn and leave me here. She rises, looks to the door, then back at me.

'Let the wise hear and increase in learning ...' I say. I direct my gaze at the Bible in her hands. Reluctantly she sits, placing the book on the floor beside her. *'Let the wise hear and increase in learning and ...'* I prompt, hopefully.

'... and the one who understands obtain guidance,' she finishes, nodding wearily.

'Try, Mamma. Try and help me understand. What happened when you left your father's house? Where did you go?'

She closes her eyes, gathering her thoughts as I cling to the silence, waiting for her to fill it. 'There was only one place I *could* go: Mason. I walked out of that house, gathered everything up from the porch, and never looked back. It was pitch black outside. I walked an hour, maybe two, stopping every once in a while to set down my bags and suck the breath back into me. It was the middle of August, and even in the depths of night the heat clung to your face like you were breathing through cheesecloth. His parents' house was near the church. I remembered the way. I must have given them the fright of their lives when I knocked on their door. When they saw who it was, they sent for Mason. By then I was crying so hard I could barely tell my right from my left, but he put his arms around me, held me till I was quiet, and told me, "You have a new family now."'

Mamma lets out a sharp laugh, like a cat scratching its paw against a tree. 'I went from being a daughter to being a wife overnight. We moved into an apartment close by. Mason found a job at a local bank, and I managed to bring in a small income from selling bunches of flowers to a nearby grocery store. We lived simply. We donated most of our money to the church. We didn't want for much else.' She looks down at her hands. 'But soon after we were married, everything changed.'

She closes her eyes, drawing herself back. 'I remember the first time he said anything. I was pruning roses in the back of the church and felt a shadow fall over me. I turned around, and Father Paul was standing, watching me, an odd smile on his lips.' She sighs heavily, and I picture him, his silent presence forcing itself upon her, like it did that day with me. 'He asked to see me in his office the next day, in my baptism robe. He said he had a very special role for me. Something about the way he said it made me feel uneasy, but when I told Mason, he was proud; said I should feel honoured that Father Paul had taken a special interest in me.'

I hold my breath, wanting and not wanting to hear why. Something about the way she says it fills me with dread; a sixth sense that nudges me, hinting at where this may be leading. I don't know if I am strong enough to hear it.

'What happened in his office, Mamma?'

'I arrived the next afternoon, dressed in my robe, like he said. I had only been in his office a couple of times before. I remember it was very cool, and the smell of new leather and clean carpets was so strong it gave me a headache as soon as I entered. He was sitting at his desk, and when the door was shut behind me, he bid me to take a seat; not to be scared. Father Paul had a way of telling you something that made you feel both calm and terrified at once.' Mamma's voice has dropped so low I have to strain to hear it. My stomach spins.

'He told me . . .' Her words catch in her throat, as if each one is stuck in mud. 'He told me that I had been brought to him, to the church, for a purpose.' She wets her lips. 'That my purity and commitment demonstrated the role I was destined for, and that the Lord had chosen me to be a vessel for the church's mission.' *A vessel*. The word hangs heavy in the air, cumbersome and odd. 'He . . . he came around the desk.' She hesitates, rubs the heels of her hands on her knees, and I know she's reliving it entirely. 'He pressed the palms of his hands into my shoulders – I can still remember the feel of them, pinching my neck, the smell of his aftershave, the sweet cloves on his breath – and he asked me if I knew what he meant.' Mamma looks mortified, her gaze fixed on a floorboard in front of her. I could tell her to stop, tell her not to say any more, that I know what she's trying to say. My mind skips forward, but I wrench it back. I need to let her carry on. I need to hear it from her.

'He told me …' She swallows. I hear the gulp of saliva, thick in her throat. 'He told me that it was my duty to bring new life into the church.' Each word seems as though it might make her physically sick. She shakes her head. 'I still didn't understand: Mason and I had been married barely a week, and we hadn't … we hadn't yet had … the relations of a man and wife.'

Despite the strangeness of this situation, a blush crawls over her cheeks, and I know my own are blushing too. She shields her face from me. How strange; how completely out of body, to be hearing this from her now, when even talk of kissing would have been prohibited between us before. I want to block my ears, to beg her to stop. It feels cruel to let her carry on. But she presses her hands to her cheeks, driven to let the full revulsion of the scene play out.

'Father Paul's hand dipped between my legs, and when I faced him, he had this look in his eyes, glazed and wide, and I knew. It was a look I'd seen on the pigs in the yard; in my daddy's eyes after a day of drinking, when he'd come home hard and mean, and look at me oddly, before roaring for me to go to my room, where I'd lock the door and hide.'

'Mamma, no,' I say, desperate to offer her the sanctity to end this here. But something has been unleashed in her, and she can't, or won't, stop.

'When it was over, I couldn't help but cry.' Her voice grows hoarse, and I see a tear trickle down her cheek, an echo of the memory. 'Father Paul told me I should be overjoyed that I had been singled out for such a position, to bear the children of the Lord's chosen representative on earth. But secretly I didn't feel so certain. Surely, surely the thing we had done should be only between a husband and wife; wasn't this a sin?' Her hands wrap around her stomach, closing in on herself. 'He bid me come to him, almost every day, to repeat what we had done. But then he went away, to oversee the building of a new church in Mexico. He was gone almost a year, and while he was away, I found myself expecting.'

I try to hear her words, but I am thrown into confusion. A child? For the first time, a glimmer of hope surfaces.

'I didn't know what I was supposed to do,' she says. 'Mason was my husband. I had to honour that bond. Wasn't it the will of The Lilies "to grow our family like the flowers of the field"? And Father Paul had left no instruction as to what I was to do.

'She was a lovely baby; everyone said so. I would have sworn that she was a gift from God.' Somehow, despite the horror that has gone before, a small smile plays on her lips – sunshine peeking through clouds. But as quickly as it appears, it dissipates. 'Except for Father Paul. When he finally returned from Mexico, he could barely even look at her. There was no way she could have been his, and he knew it. He declared an edict, forbidding husbands and wives to have relations, saying it was the will of the Lord for us to remain pure in deed, as well as word. Only that edict didn't apply to his relationship with me. He began again, right where he left off. I tried, I prayed so hard that I could bear his child – in the hope that it would finally release me from my duties to him – and a little over two years later, I finally found I was expecting again.'

Now I feel as if I'm seeing double. The twists of the story seem to confuse rather than clarify. What happened to these phantom children – and is one of them me?

'This pregnancy was different – I knew straight away, even from only having had the one. Something just felt *off.* I couldn't explain it. And then one night, when I must have been about six months gone, I went to the bathroom in the middle of the night with terrible pains in my stomach, and when I looked down there was blood everywhere. And I knew. *I knew.*' The pain in her voice is so raw I can feel it.

'Oh, Mamma ...'

'I felt sure this was a sign from God, telling me what I was doing wasn't right. Mason knew that the child was Father Paul's, but he had been brought up in the church; he believed Father Paul had a direct relationship with the Lord, and whatever he decreed was received from Him. And besides, even if he didn't agree with it, what could he do? Father Paul's word was absolute. But, for the first time since I joined, I was beginning to lose faith.

'It was nearly Easter, the church's most important festival, because the Easter lily itself is a symbol of Christ's resurrection. There was a ceremony held at midnight – the whole church was lit by candlelight, and the congregation processed through it, each with a lily in their hands, placing the flowers in the river and watching them float away, before wading into the water to be cleansed. I used to think it was beautiful,' she snorts. 'But that year, Mason and I fought. I had made up my mind: I wanted to leave, to get out of the church and start a new life, just the three of us. My body and my soul were broken, but I thought, perhaps, this was a chance to make everything right. I refused to go to the ceremony; told him to take the baby and go on his own.' For a moment she is silent, lost in the memory of that night. When she speaks again, it's as if her insides have been pulled out. Her voice is ragged, hollow. 'I would give anything now, to be able to take that back.'

A bad, bad feeling worms its way inside me, and I steel myself against what is coming next. 'Father Paul came to tell me himself,' she says. 'I was waiting up, but I must have fallen asleep on the couch: I woke up to the sound of him banging on the door. They'd been in a crash, coming back from the ceremony. The car hit directly into the driver's side. They had been trying to overtake him, and smashed right into him on a blind corner. Mason had been killed. But she was alive.'

Like the pulling back of a curtain to let in the first glimmer of dawn, I watch the tip of her head rising. Mamma's body stiffens, and as she turns her gaze directly to me.

'Anna was alive.'

ROSIE

24

It's barely dark when I get home from Chesterfield. I open the front door and the house comes alive. Dad has *Madama Butterfly* on at full volume, singing along as he manoeuvres the vacuum cleaner through the living room. I catch sight of Rob's feet, sticking over the arm of the sofa; his thumbs going *tap, tap, tap* on his mobile. Mum's in the kitchen; the clatter of pans.

At dinner she rubs my arm. 'You look tired, sweetheart. Is everything OK?'

I think of burying my head in her chest, letting her stroke my hair, like she used to when I was little. The moment is here – I could snatch hold of it, tell her everything. And then I see her pull at a streak of grey in her hair, tuck it behind her ear. Was it there a few weeks ago? What will telling her do? Cause more arguments. More upset. She'll ban me from doing anything further; or worse, dismiss the

315

whole thing completely: *Leave it to the professionals, Rosie*, she'll say. We'll never know.

And so I jerk my shoulders, up, down. 'Just exam stress.' I force a tight smile, take a mouthful of peas. 'Not long to go.'

Later, ignoring the drone of the TV and Dad shouting out the answers to a quiz show, I play back Michael's story, pulling it apart just as I did with Keira on the train home. If I can get to The Lilies, I feel sure I can follow the trail to Emily. Keira told me not to do anything stupid before we parted ways at the station. But she knows exactly what I'm planning. And she knows my mind is made up.

In the morning, I make a show of getting ready for school, threading my backpack over my shoulder before Mum can realise it's lighter than usual. I duck into the nearest coffee shop, exchange my uniform for jeans and a jumper and stuff it into my bag. The train to Slough is barely half an hour. I have netball first thing, then a free period, then break. I'll be there and back before anyone realises I'm gone.

When the train pulls up at the station, I'm struck by the urban-ness of it all. From the way Michael described it, I imagined The Lilies only existing in some sort of rustic farmland, far away from people and places; not nipping to Sainsbury's for their weekly shop. I'm surprised further when I arrive at the address I found on their website and discover that The Lilies' UK headquarters are nestled within a fairly commonplace stretch of residential roads.

But all that is stripped away when I see the building itself. It is starkly white – even on a beige day like today it gleams – and is striking in its simplicity, lacking the ornate windows and spires of a typical English church. It can't have been built more than fifteen, twenty years ago. Fifteen years ago: after Emily?

What do the neighbours think, with it plonked there in the middle of them? Or perhaps, I realise with a chill, perhaps they're all part of it. I whip around, half expecting to see someone in a white robe walking out of their front door.

I scan the frontage for something to confirm that I'm in the right place – a name or a banner – and can't avoid a tiny prickle of hope that I've got it wrong, that I can just say, forget it, I didn't find them, and give up. But as soon as I walk up to the high arched door, I see it. Carved into the wood, its leaves curling down the centre of the door, is a lily.

I press my hand to it, feeling the grooves of the pattern rise and fall beneath my fingers, willing the lily to give away its secrets. The wood is cold to the touch, tells me nothing.

Standing on the precipice, I am seized by a sense of vertigo. A wind has picked up, threading through the trees that line the pavement and dampening my cheeks with a wet drizzle. Until now I've never really thought about what

I'd say, what I'd do, once I got to this point. I've been propelled only by the furious need to get here. Now, all Mum's warnings whirl around me like phantoms in a nightmare: all the crazies, all the dangerous people she's been worried about me getting mixed up with; surely, surely, this is exactly what she means?

No. I shake my head, and the thought away with it. I can't turn back now. I put my ear to the door, listening for voices inside; perhaps a service under way.

And when I hear nothing, I push it open.

Inside, it's eerily quiet. The white walls bounce light across the room, highlighting rows and rows of empty pews. Encouraged by the emptiness, I take a tentative step forward, freezing instantly as the sound echoes into the air. I look down to find the floor is made entirely of white marble, shining in its spotlessness. Working each footstep slowly from toe to heel, I make my way across the room, breathing in the tart chemical smell of cleaning fluids. Like a hospital waiting room. Or a morgue.

With every step I feel my pulse quicken, my vulnerability increasing the further I get from the door.

In many ways, it's just like the churches I remember from our infrequent visits as kids: the occasional wedding, the once-in-a-blue-moon trip to a carol concert. There's an altar at the front. And an upright piano to the side of it, painted white. And casting a dappled shadow over the room is a huge stained-glass window, each jewel-toned panel polished crystal-clear. When I look closer, I see it's a depiction of Christ on the cross, a spurt of lilies wrapped around his ankles and trailing up the cross. They're clearly not ones for subtlety.

Feeling bold, I move faster, brushing my fingers against the tops of the pews as I try to think of how I could possibly extract the answer I am looking for. My foot slips on the polished floor, and I find myself clasping the air, my hand jerking in front of me to get some purchase. It lands with a clash on the piano keys, a cacophony of notes ripping through the silence, and I freeze in horror as I wait for an army of Lilies to storm in.

The notes evaporate into the ether. No one comes.

I spy a door off to the side and slip through it, finding myself in a window-lined corridor. Outside is garden, bare but for a couple of trees, and to the left of that a small graveyard with a cluster of tombstones like a toddler's gap-toothed smile. I wonder with a grey dread if it's possible one of those belongs to Emily. Beyond, right to the back of the garden, I can tell there's some sort of stream, and it makes me think of the ceremonies Michael talked of, their strange 'purification' rituals. And then with a start I realise there are people in it.

I quickly duck my head down below the window ledge, and creep backwards away from it in a crab-like crouch. My shoulders butt up against what I think is a wall, only I realise too late it's not a wall at all, but a door left ajar, and I find myself falling, back first, straight through it. I clamp a fist against my mouth to stop myself crying out.

When I pull myself to my feet, I find I'm in a study. Unlike the rest of the church, here it's not white at all, but more like an old gentlemen's club. The bovine reek of expensive leather hangs in the air, from the dark brown sofa in the corner and the swivel chair pushed against the oversized hardwood desk. The walls are lined from floor to ceiling in wood panelling, hung with black-and-white photographs. Photographs, I see as I step towards them, of The Lilies.

At first, I can't tell what the distinction between them is. Each one shows a group of people, huddled together with the briefest of smiles on their faces. They're all wearing the same thing: loose-fitting white robes that hang to their bare feet, their arms clasped in front of them just like we're told to do in school pictures. I scan their faces eagerly, convinced I'm going to spot Emily among them, but there are barely any children, and none of them are my sister.

In the centre of all of them is the same man, his smile the brightest and biggest of all. Unlike the others, he's not wearing a robe but a suit, and in his hands he clasps a copy of the Bible, a cross etched on its cover. This must be Father Paul. I can make out his ponytail, just like Michael described. I wonder how many secrets that satisfied smile is hiding.

In one of the photographs, I follow the line of his feet down to the centre of the frame, where I make out, printed in even, sans serif type, the name of a city, and a date. *Jerusalem, 1991*. Searching, I discover all of them have a similar stamp, the locations and years changing with the faces in each one: *Oaxaca, 1995; San Francisco, 1988; Rome, 2009.* They must be the locations of the Lilies churches. I scan the room, trying to find the one labelled 'Georgia'. There it is, deep in the right-hand corner: *Georgia, 1999.* The year before Emily was born. I press a finger to the glass, marking each face, trying to search out the woman from Michael's photo. But it's too hard: both Michael's printout and this photo are too obscure. Besides, in their robes they all look alike.

Frustrated, I turn away and focus instead on what the rest of the room may hold. There's a bookcase, filled mainly with religious texts and various copies of the Bible, along with tracts that have obviously been plucked from some sort of 'top books to look educated' list: volumes of Shakespeare, Dickens, Keats. None of them revealing anything that could tell me about Emily. A filing cabinet holds various bills and receipts: lighting, heating, none of them untoward.

Which only leaves the desk. Blood pumps in my ears as I step towards it. I think of the people outside. I don't know how long their ceremonies last: at any moment they could stop, find me here. Every second I hesitate brings me closer to being discovered.

The surface itself is meticulously clear, as I would expect from the little I know about The Lilies' scrupulous manner. One of those fancy pens that comes in a silver holder sits at an exact angle. Next to it, a brass paperweight the shape of an egg bears the engraving, *Blessed are the pure of heart, for they shall see the Lord*. The second I touch it, I leave the filmy depression of my thumbprint on it, and instantly regret it. There's a bone-handled letter opener, out of its sheath, and I think about pocketing it, just in case, but then my eyes drift to the drawers that run down both sides of the desk. I tug at the first, then the next, then the next, my movements getting sharper and more frantic as I realise with a quickening heart that they're all locked.

I scan the room, looking for somewhere a key could be hiding, but it's all so sparsely neat I can't begin to think. I run my fingers along the books, hoping, in the wildness of my imagination, that one will turn out to be a hiding place. I feel along the inside of the filing cabinet, hoping to find a groove I've missed, pull back the pictures, searching for a key taped to the back, and I am just about to give up when I feel it: an unmistakable bump. Carefully, so as not to leave a mark, I peel the picture from the wall.

Taped to the back, a piece of yellowing Sellotape on each corner, is a folded piece of paper. I look back again at the photograph and my breath shortens: it's the one from Georgia. Again, I scour the faces of the women in the photograph, trying to seek out my woman in navy. There's one next to him, next to Father Paul, her head slightly bowed as if trying to avoid the camera. It could be her, but then again, how would I know for sure?

Frustrated, I turn to the paper on the back, agitating the space between the tape and the cardboard backing, working it until it peels loose. I unfold it, and something falls to the ground. When I bend down to pick it up, my world comes undone.

It's a photograph. Formal, like it has been taken professionally: there's a brightly painted background, with writing in the right-hand corner: *Alachua County Fair*. A woman, her features plain but not ugly, staring unsmilingly into the lens like this wasn't really what she had in mind. Beside her, a child, beaming.

The child is Emily.

ANNA

25

'Anna was alive.' Mamma's fingers begin to dance a tarantella in her lap, and I see a bead of sweat snaking from the tip of her forehead down the side of her face. The sight of this liquid makes my temples throb in response, but the thought of myself, of my own body, seems insignificant in the face of this name.

My name.

The outside world has become a vacuum: all that exists is the attic, Mamma, me, this story.

'Father Paul allowed me that, right away.' She lets out a bitter laugh. 'But then he told me there was something else I needed to know. I was still trying to take in the news about Mason. I felt like I was in one of those circus fun houses: floor sloping at different angles under my feet, the walls of the apartment distorting as I tried to find my balance. Father Paul could see that I was near to fainting.

He caught me underneath the elbows, just before I fell, and helped me to the sofa. I remember noticing how there wasn't a single hair on his head out of place, and thinking, how is it that this pristine man is the one to throw my life into chaos? And then he brought his face right up close to mine so that I couldn't help but look at him, and he said, "Do you hear me, Mary Elizabeth? Anna is fine. Untouched, in fact." He told me that the crash had been severe. The impact had killed Mason instantly. But not a hair on Anna's head had been harmed. When they found her, she was still strapped into her car seat – thrown from the wreckage, managing to land completely upright – dazed, but undamaged.'

Every movement, every sound in here seems amplified. I can smell my own sweat, taste the salt drying on my lips as I try to piece together the story as fast as Mamma tells it. I know deep in my soul that this Anna can't possibly be me. But if she's alive, where is she now?

'Father Paul leaned towards me.' Her voice is teetering on the edge of breaking. 'So close I could see the scrawling lines of purple in his irises, which made his eyes appear sometimes grey, sometimes navy. So close I could smell again the cloves on his breath, the mint of his aftershave. And he said, "Doesn't that strike you as odd, Mary?"' She shakes her head. 'I couldn't think what he meant: the room was still a whirl around me, but he pressed himself closer. He said, wouldn't I say it was odd, that the crash was so severe that it killed Mason on impact, but yet Anna was untouched? Somehow my words found my lips, and I said, "It's a miracle." Father Paul shook his head from side to side, no, no, no. And his voice was low and mean: he said it wasn't a miracle, that he had prayed to the Lord, and the Lord had shown him the answer: Anna was unclean. "There is sin in that child," he said; it was clear to him now. He told me: "There is dirt, deep inside her, that has caused the death of her own father."'

A tremor runs down my back. 'How could he say that, Mamma?' I can't help but cry out. 'About a child!' Mamma's face has turned ashen. I see her struggling, wrestling with the memories of that night, and whatever self-realisation hindsight has afforded her. 'Why would he even think it?'

'He'd always found any reason he could not to like her.' She speaks through a fixed jaw, her voice low, resigned. 'As she was getting older she was becoming more high-spirited, especially during prayers. She'd shout out, in the middle of ceremonies, try to run down the aisles, so I'd have to pull her back. And she hated the water; she'd scream during every baptism, kicking her legs when we tried to hold her down. But I knew, still, there was a deeper reason that Father Paul hated her: she was a constant reminder that she wasn't his. She was the living embodiment of his failure – the proof that it was him, not me, who was incapable of producing a child.

'I tried to tell him it couldn't be true! But he pressed his lips together and then he got up from the sofa and looked down at me on the floor. He said, "I'm afraid it is, Mary

Elizabeth." There was a toy, a doll, wedged beneath the brakes, that prevented Mason from stopping the car when he swerved. He said she must have thrown it – *in her wilfulness*, he said. He said that if she were a child of God, she wouldn't have behaved in such a way, that ultimately killed a man. "We are the lilies among thorns, Mary: here to cleanse the world. And your daughter must be cleansed. Tonight."' Mamma's voice hangs pendant in the heavy air.

I picture the tawdriness of that living room, filled with the cheap possessions they could afford after the church had had its fill of their money. Father Paul, his whiteness marred by his wickedness. Mamma, barely more than a girl, grief-stricken and frightened, and so terribly alone. All this talk of purity and cleanliness? What wickedness, what monstrousness did this man possess, that he could twist and turn her vulnerability and her faith like that, with such preposterous reason?

'I followed him blindly out of the apartment,' she says, 'barely remembering to put shoes on. My confusion and my pain were like a cloud around me, suffocating my senses and pushing me toward wherever Father Paul was taking me. What about Mason, I remember asking. He didn't even bother to turn around.

'We arrived at the church in the half light. It must have been three, four in the morning at this point, but I don't remember feeling tired. I don't remember feeling anything. I dimly heard Father Paul call "I have her" as we made our way over to the river. When we approached, there must have been about ten of them there, senior members of the congregation, all dressed in their white robes. And as we got closer, there …' all the air seems to compress in her lungs as she fights to take a breath, 'there she was – her fragile little body dressed in white, held by the arms by two of the women …' Mamma stops, unable to carry on. A sound wrenches from her throat – like a cat being stepped on.

'Go on, Mamma, go on,' I murmur, her hurt cutting through me too. 'What did they do?'

She wipes a slack hand across her mouth, muffling herself, and then her head bobs, rhythmically, up down, up down, up down. 'I ran towards her. All I wanted to do was take her in my arms and breathe in her baby smell, but Father Paul gripped me by the wrists, held me back and whispered, "It wouldn't be a good idea, Mary Elizabeth." I stumbled dumbly along beside him towards the water. I hadn't noticed until then, how odd it was that he was already in his robe, rather than a suit. He waded into the water, up to his waist, and then he called to one of the women to give him the child. She saw me; she squirmed and tried to free herself to run towards me, her fat little arms writhing in the air, but Father Paul held her firm, and then he gave a signal to the congregation, and they made their way into the water.'

I can see it unfolding before me: the sea of people dressed in white, the child, confused and helpless, and Mamma, utterly powerless against the force of them. Something is knotting in the base of my stomach – fear and unrest twisting with my body's own sick and feeble state. Through clenched teeth, although some part of me already knows the answer, I ask, 'What happened in the water?'

Mamma stares straight ahead, eyes glazed over, not seeing me, not seeing anything but the memories. Slowly, her arm reaches out in front of her, as if she is trying to grasp hold of something, but whether she's trying to draw her thoughts forward or pull herself back to that moment, I can't tell.

After a long silence, she speaks. 'You have to understand, Anna. There were so many of them, and only one of me. I tried to go in with them.' Tears are streaming freely now down her cheeks and pooling at the collar of her shirt. 'If I had – I could have – I could have stopped it. But Father Paul shouted at me to stay away. He told me it was for her own good. He told me he would make her better. I had lived and breathed The Lilies for so long, I didn't know what to believe any more. And so I watched them.' Her voice cracks. 'My baby. My darling girl. And them.

'Someone had given him a Bible, and the two women were holding her again. She was crying and shivering in the cold water, crying for me, crying for Mason, desperately trying to get herself free. "You see?" Father Paul roared at me from the water, never letting his eyes leave her. "You see how dirt has taken root in her? A child of God would have nothing to fear, nothing to try and free herself from." And then he began.

'He addressed the people in the water. "You here before me, do you understand why you have joined me here tonight?"

'Yes, they answered, in perfect unison – proud of what they were doing. Proud to be pinning down a little girl. They said, "We are gathered on this night to save one of our own: Anna Grace Montgomery, who we believe to be unclean. With your help, and with the help of the Lord in heaven, we will cast the dirt from her, and return her pure soul to God."

'Then he asked if they were willing to do what was right, to make this unclean soul pure. And they said again, like it was nothing, like it was any other ceremony, "Yes, Father Paul, we are."

'You have to understand' – here she breaks away, not addressing me wholly, but for a second paying heed to a world outside her story – 'the purification ritual was central to The Lilies. For them, there was nothing different about doing it then.' She bows her head, and a tear skis down her jaw, falls from the point of her chin. 'I dare say if I was in their position, I would have done the same.

'Father Paul crossed himself, then dipped his hand into the water and drew his thumb down the centre of his forehead, anointing himself, and bid the others to do the same. I wanted so badly to believe this was right, that what he was doing was in the name of the Lord, but then one of the women wet Anna's head and she shook violently, calling out for me in such a wretched way that it was like a knife to my heart, and I knew it could not be the Lord's will. I sank to my knees on the bank. I was powerless. I can still feel the blades of grass beneath my fingers as I tore at them, steeling myself from wading in there and taking her away from all of it.

'He began with prayers,' she says, 'familiar ones I'd heard many times before, that we used for the purification ritual, and then turned to the Gospel of Luke, to the story of Jesus driving out the Devil. And then, finally, he spoke to Anna directly: "I command you, unclean spirit, to depart from this holy soul, whom the Lord has made in His image. For this soul belongs to the kingdom of heaven, found within earth in The Lilies. As He has blessed this holy water surrounding us, it is this holy water that shall drive the dirt out. Congregation of The Lilies, what say you?" And then the congregation shouted, "Unclean!"

'They held her by the arms and plunged her into the water: I can still see the false piety in their faces in the moonlight. She came up coughing and spluttering and crying. My baby, my darling little girl – she had no idea what they were doing to her.' Mamma clamps a hand to her mouth, her body racked with unbroken sobs that make her rock back and forth on her chair. I feel helpless, trapped by the bed, the attic, the story; unable to offer her comfort, and not yet knowing if I should. I am staring down the barrel of a gun, and I can't look away.

'Father Paul shouted to the heavens again, splashing his hands against the water, saying, "I adjure you, unclean spirit, to leave this soul to the Lord. For The Lilies protect it and have made it pure." And again the congregation cast her into the water, shouting that she was unclean, and that they were ridding her of the dirt that covered her. They held her down longer this time, and when she came up she vomited up liquid. I could feel her fear!' Her voice breaks through the sobs, and she thumps a fist against her stomach and chest. 'Here! And here! It was like I was being torn in two. And I *begged* Father Paul to stop. *She is pure, she is clean, please, please, leave her be.* I was starting to see him for what he was: a liar; a phony; not the Lord's word at all, just a man who was hurting my child. But he was raging now; his voice was like thunder as he called out, again and again, and they plunged her under, again and again, and their voices got louder and faster and angrier.

'And then something in them shifted. I didn't notice at first. I was beating my fists on the ground, crying out for Father Paul to listen to me, but then I looked up and saw that the congregation had all gone quiet. And although I could barely bring myself to do it, I turned to look at Anna.' As quickly as Mamma's voice rose to a peak, it has dropped to barely more than a whisper. And I know, suddenly, what is coming next.

'She was limp in their arms. It almost looked like she was sleeping, except there was something about the angle of her body, and the way she hung her head. I knew, instantly, that she wasn't asleep. One of the women called for Father Paul, but I was already in the water, ripping my daughter from their arms and pulling her onto the bank.' Mamma's hands rise to her mouth, but they can barely staunch the deluge of pain that is flowing from her. 'She looked so tiny there, lying on the grass, her robe tangled around her feet. Her hair, her soft baby hair I would stroke and brush and make neat, was plastered against her forehead, and her lips were already turning blue. I tried desperately to think what to do: pinching her nose and blowing onto those beautiful, baby lips; pressing her tiny chest with the palm of my hands, fearful I might break her ribs; slapping her face, wake up, wake up, wake up!'

Wetness on my cheeks. I am crying, too. The attic is drowning in Mamma's story.

'It was Father Paul who pulled me off her. I felt hands under my arms lift me off the ground and drag me away as I called out for her. I was kicking. The group closed in around her. Some of the women were crying. One of the ones who'd been holding her was saying she didn't mean to do it, over and over. But none of them were me, or my pain.

'When he finally let me loose, he had the strangest expression on his face: I can still see it now. There was no remorse, no fear. Instead, he looked calm. His blue eyes were clear and serene, and there was even a faint smile on his face. And I could see, now, that this was never about her. Father Paul wanted to punish me: for having a child with Mason; for failing to bear one that was his.

'He took me by the shoulders, looked at me dead on, and said the Lord was angry with me, that He thought I would be a vessel, that through me He would spread the message of The Lilies. But he said my soul was twisted and rotten; that it killed the hope of that when it killed his child inside me. And now, the Lord saw fit to punish me further.

'I screamed and beat my fist against his chest and told him that it was all his fault; that I would make him pay. I told him I would go to the police, to the national papers, to anyone who would hear me, and I would bring the church down around them, and him with it. But even as I was speaking, that smile bloomed on his face, like one of his wretched lilies, and he shook his head and laughed. He said, "That wouldn't play very well now, would it, Mary Elizabeth? Just think of the headline: 'Crazed widow blames husband's death on infant child and drowns her'." I started to argue, but he gestured to the crowd of people standing downhill from us and said he had ten witnesses there who would say otherwise; he pointed at the church, and said he'd have at least fifty more should he need them. He kissed the tip of his thumb, reached out and marked a cross on my forehead. Blessing me. And burning me.

'I was trapped. I saw no way to go, no way out. But then, like the heavens were opening to show me the light, I saw my opportunity. Father Paul stepped away from me, left me in a heap on the ground, and went to calm the congregation, worried they were hysterical, making so much noise someone would hear. And when his back was fully turned to me, without hesitating another second, I ran.'

She swallows, and I try to imagine what it must have been like: the overwhelming fear, the blinding panic, colliding in her head. But I think, too, of *her* – the original Anna. How could she leave her there like that, discarded like an old toy?

And if that Anna is really gone, what does that mean for me?

She must sense what I'm thinking, because she presses her palms to the sides of her face. When she looks at me, it's as if her soul is drained. 'It was the only way. She was gone from me, for ever. If I stayed, for her, I would only be killing us both. But that doesn't mean I don't think of her every day. I know I will have the Lord to answer to, in the end.

'I don't know what I expected to happen: for him to come after me, or send his minions to chase me down, but when I was almost out of sight and felt no one behind me, I turned around. There he was on the river bank, watching me. Smiling, but still. And when I turned to go he gave me a little wave, a nod of his head, and called to me. I've never forgotten what he said: "Run, Mary. Run away. But remember: no one ever leaves The Lilies. We'll always be watching."'

I feel it, suddenly: the barricade Mamma has created around us. Her cautious glances every time we leave the house. The drawn curtains. And those cards, the ones I found in her room: a constant reminder of Father Paul's promise. How she has lived every moment lying in wait.

And I am also aware, breathing in the stagnant air under the attic's roof, of just how small our world has become. Father Paul has delivered on his promise: he has watched, he is waiting. So what is Mamma's plan for me?

'I stumbled back to the apartment,' Mamma carries on. 'I don't even know how I found my way. In a funny sense, it felt just like the night I had argued with Daddy; I packed things, a change of clothes, our wedding photograph. Forgetting myself, I went to reach for some of her things, and had to force myself to put them down. What do you pack, when you have nothing left that matters? We had some money saved up, in the safe in the bedroom – we'd been planning to make a big donation to the church, to help fund a nursery, in the hope our fortunes would grow.

'I walked. Faltering, half-crazed steps. Got myself to the highway, and eventually, after half an hour of frantic waving, a truck driver stopped. From the look of me, he must have thought I was an abused wife, took pity on me. He asked where I was headed, as I pulled the door to. I could barely think. Where was he going, I asked. Florida, he said.

'What did it matter now where I went, or what I did? I stared up at the rising sun in front of me and agreed. Yes. Florida.'

ROSIE

26

I stare into my sister's eyes, trying to make sense of what it is I'm seeing. In the picture, she can't be much older than when she was taken; the chubby toddler's cheeks thinned a touch, the wisps of baby hair around her temples turning dark, but still unmistakably her.

She's alive, I whisper, stroking her face. But if so, where? Why hasn't she come back to us? Why is she *smiling*?

I can't help the clench of anger that sears through me. All the pain, everything my family went through, and here she is, grinning at a camera. How could she have forgotten who she was, and what could this woman have said to her, to make her want to stay?

I tear myself away from her face, and then, with shaking hands, I realise there's something on the back. I turn it over. Handwriting, meticulous and exact, but also childlike: rounded, carefully formed letters like a page torn out of a primary school workbook. A single line: *She called me Mamma.*

I clutch the photograph to my chest, tears streaming down my face. I've found her. I've found Emily.

And then I hear footsteps clipping down the corridor.

My body turns to ice as the room seems to grow cavernous around me, its neatness offering precisely nowhere to hide. Maybe they won't come inside, I try to rationalise, even as I hear the footsteps coming closer.

My arms and legs jangle, coursing with adrenaline. They're right outside the door – two of them; I hear their voices distinctly – and in a last bout of panic I throw back the chair and crawl under the desk, pulling my backpack in after me, grateful for the front panel that cocoons me inside. Quickly, I fold up the picture, stuffing it in my back pocket where I hope it'll be safe.

'So, we do this after every service?' It's a woman's voice, young. 'Even if he's not here?'

I stuff my sleeve into my mouth, terrified my very breathing will betray me.

'That's right.' It's another woman. She sounds older, more authoritative. 'Father Paul likes to visit all of his chapters throughout the year and expects each of his offices to be kept to the highest standard. I'll show you the routine the first few times, and then you'll be on your own.'

I shut my eyes and hug in my knees, as if making myself smaller will somehow make me less conspicuous.

'So, we clean everything?' the first woman sighs.

'That's right, top to bottom.'

'But how will he know from one week to the next, if he's not even here?'

'Verity.' The second woman sounds impatient, the softness of her voice faltering. 'In joining us, you accepted Father Paul as the voice of the Lord on earth. If you are to do His will, you must accept his authority without question.'

There's a pause, and I imagine Verity hanging her head. 'Yes, Johanna. You're right. Pure as The Lilies.'

'Pure as The Lilies,' Johanna repeats, and with a horror that drags through me I hear the door shut behind them.

The pad of their footsteps comes closer and I squeeze my eyes tighter, trying to trace their movements through sound. They're standing at the doorway, but I know that the moment they come near the desk I'll be discovered. I hear a soft thud of something hitting the ground – a packing box, maybe? – followed by what I guess is the thump of books filling it, so I'm sure they're at the book-case. They work methodically, just an infrequent grunt or groan as they lift and place, and an occasional directive from Johanna. 'We clear all the books, dust the shelves, then replace them. Then we tidy the filing cabinets, make sure all the papers are neat and in order. And then the desk. Don't touch the photographs though.'

The tinny scrape of the cabinet drawers tells me which one is finished and how many are left. And then, finally, I hear them moving towards the desk.

My thoughts go into hyperdrive, trying to find an excuse for what I could possibly be doing here. My mind is as blank as the church walls. I hear the tap of metal next to my head, a key in the desk lock – they had it the whole time. And then the noise I have been waiting for since they walked in the door: a scream.

Footsteps. The chair scraped aside. Hands clutch at my wrists, and I'm hauled out from my hiding place. Two angry faces are waiting for me, and the younger of the two is gulping in air, on the verge of crying from the shock of discovering me.

'What are you doing in here?' The older one jabs at my shoulder with a thick index finger.

'I …' I look from one to the other. I expected them to be in robes, but instead they're in ordinary clothes, albeit loose, shapeless things like the woman in Michael's photograph. Only their hair is wet, dripping beads of water down their cheeks and flecking their tops.

'Did you get sent from the council?' the younger one says. 'Is that why you're here? We've told you already: this is private property.'

'Don't be stupid, Verity, she's not from the council, she's a child.' The older one moves closer, wagging a witchy finger at me. 'Come on, then: where did you come from? Who put you up to this? A school prank? What do you want?'

'I – I …' I am reeling. A couple of days ago I didn't even know who The Lilies were, and now there are two of them right in front of me. The photograph burns in my back pocket. If they find it, if they realise what I know, it's over. 'I ...' I tear my eyes away from her fingernail and look at her. She's about my parents' age, if not a few years older, lines playing at the sides of her mouth, the corners of her eyes. What can I say that will get me out of here, and make me safe? I think of The Lilies, of the sort of people they must be to join something like this: lonely, in search of something. And then it comes to me: 'I was running away.' I hang my head, making myself look smaller, pitiful.

Their faces soften. Verity lets out a sympathetic 'Oh'.

'I'm so sorry for trespassing,' I gush. 'I honestly wasn't trying to do anything wrong. I was just looking for a place to sleep, and this looked like a church. I thought perhaps I could find somewhere warm. I wandered in here, but when I heard your voices, I panicked.'

'You were running away?' I feel the older woman, Johanna, appraising me, taking in my clean appearance. I don't necessarily pass for a runaway.

'I had an argument with my parents,' I say quickly. 'I haven't been gone for very long. But being here, you know, in the house of the Lord, I see now I was wrong. I should go back to them now. They'll be so worried.' I flutter my eyelids piously at Johanna.

She sighs. 'OK then. But you need to get out of here now. This is sacred ground; not just anyone is allowed in.'

With Johanna and Verity by my sides, I retrace my steps back into the blinding whiteness of the main church.

Johanna, I can tell, still isn't one hundred per cent convinced: her hand clutches my shoulder a little tighter than is necessary as she guides me to the door, and so I turn to her, pressing the palms of my hands together, and give her a weak little smile. 'Honour thy mother and father.'

With the door sealed shut behind me, I gulp in a lungful of cool, fresh air, feeling the dizzying weight of what I've uncovered.

And then I run, feet smacking the tarmac as I motor down residential streets. Just before I reach the station, a stitch twists at my side, stopping me, forcing me to double over. I allow a primal moan to rip through me, gasping for breath, my face wet with tears.

I pull the photograph from my pocket, reading once again the cryptic note. *It's all going to be OK*, I tell myself, allowing my breath to slow as the pain in my side eases. *We're all going to be OK*. I put it back in my pocket and walk into the train station, ready to reclaim my family.

Emily, I whisper silently, *I'm coming for you.*

ANNA

27

The light from the attic window is starting to thin. It must be around mid-afternoon, early evening. The pale light bathes the room in a creamy white glow, softening Mamma's features, the wrinkles at the corners of her mouth, the dark half-moons under each eye. I know every inch of this face so well: how could it have hidden all this from me, for so long?

She seems drained of energy. Her fingers twist, coiling endlessly over and under one another. But, conversely, my body is starting to reclaim itself. Mamma has been so focused on her tale that the medicine has gone untended, so although a thin film coats the back of my throat, and although my limbs are weak, my wrists cut, I am beginning to feel more like myself.

'I just wanted to see the children,' she says now, squeezing her eyes shut as tears roll out of them. 'That was all it was: I just wanted to see. I don't even know how it happened.' A guttural sob wells from the pit of her stomach, and she clasps her fists against her mouth as she forces it down.

'Go on,' I tell her. 'Please.' The more I feel like myself, the more I am starting to see how my own story fits into this mess. And the more I don't like it. What Father Paul did to Mamma was cruel, unbearable. But why is that burden now being passed on to me?

She carries on: 'The truck driver dropped me right by the state line. I think he was starting to get nervous, having me with him. Perhaps he thought some crazed husband would be coming after me and didn't want to get caught in the crossfire.' Her mouth lolls open in a crazed 'Ha!', flashing me the wet, pink wall of her throat. 'If only he knew. He dropped me at a diner in a small town just off the interstate, told me I should get myself something to eat. Ask for Jenny, he said – "she'll keep you safe. She knows a thing or two about no-good scumbags." I couldn't think of eating, so I wandered through the town, trying to make sense of it all, trying to find some sign or some direction, to tell me what to do next. I passed a second-hand car dealership, and somehow found myself the owner of a car. They didn't ask too many questions: a woman comes in alone, pays for a car in cash? You don't want to get involved.

'And then I got into the car, and I drove,' she says. 'I'd only been going for about twenty minutes when I started to see the signs, those bright characters smiling, telling me

Astroland was only a short distance away. Anna ...' At her name – *my* name – she looks up at me. Our identities wrap themselves around her, reminding her, in her foggy brain, of the truth that is being uncovered. 'She used to love those films. I'd put one on in the mornings when I was giving her her breakfast and she'd bounce up and down in her high chair as soon as she heard the opening theme music. Mason wouldn't allow the TV on when he was in the house, so I would have to wait until he was out. It was our little secret. So when I saw those signs, for the park, it was like someone, somewhere, was trying to tell me something.

'As soon as I stepped through the gates, I could feel it: all that love and warmth and happiness. The children in their costumes, dancing about; their sheer joy when they spied a character coming their way; the shrieks of pleasure from the rides and the smell of candy in the air. Somehow it filled me with hope.'

I can feel it. Because didn't I, too, feel that same joy only a few weeks ago? If things were different, I'd want to cry out, to reach for her. If only there was a way, in some alternate universe that the two of us could have enjoyed it there together. But there is no alternate universe. And at the thought of reaching out for her, the twine that cuts into my wrist reminds me where I am. Who has brought me here. Because wasn't it Mamma herself who tied these arms, physically preventing me from going to her? Good, bad, right or wrong – my faith in Mamma flips like squares on a chequerboard.

'I don't quite know how I ended up on the carousel,' she continues, leading us to the brink. 'Those whirling horses, the neon lights … they seemed to draw me to them. It was full to bursting when I stepped on it. I stood on the platform, as I saw some of the other adults doing, and felt the breeze on my face and the horses cantering up and down around me. That's when I saw you.'

Her eyes fix on me, and the truth finally hits me. Like a wave crashing, like a light bulb turning on, like every other cliché and more. I can't hide from it. I can't deny it. Mamma took me. And she's going to tell me why.

'You looked so like her.' The words cling to the back of her throat as the tears fall steadily now, wetting her cheeks and splashing in droplets onto her chest, her clasped hands. 'You had those same blonde curls, and the chubby cheeks, and you had the funniest, most intense expression on your face, just like hers, kicking your little legs and jerking your body forward, as if you were hoping that both you and the horse would take flight. And I looked to the heavens and I thought: this is my sign. I looked for whoever you belonged to, and I saw her, that woman, giving you a wave from the crowd on the ground and then turning her back – *turning her back on you* – as she disappeared into the distance. And then I saw him.' Her words are gaining momentum; louder, faster. '*He wasn't watching you*,' she shouts so violently that my body jerks in reaction. Her face morphs into a snarl, and I turn my head away. '*He wasn't watching you*,' she repeats, smacking the palms of her hands against the arms of the chair. 'I saw him look at the phone in his pocket and then wander off with barely a backward glance. 'I edged closer, and he didn't come back. And neither did she. And then I felt the carousel slow down, and the other riders were being helped down by their parents, and led off the ride, but where was he? Nowhere. And where was she? Nowhere. Neither of them cared.'

She rises from the chair, and begins to pace the room, calling out like one of her beloved televangelists. In the world of the attic, this is a different Mamma. But to me it's starkly familiar. For the first time, a bud of anger begins to swell inside me. Because whatever happened to destroy her life, what gave her the right to destroy mine?

'Neither of them thought it important to check on their precious baby girl. They were both more concerned with themselves, and their needs, than the needs of the daughter the Lord had blessed them with, the daughter who they should have been protecting with their *lives*.' Her voice crescendos to a shriek. 'To ensure that she was safe. *I* helped you down.' She jabs a finger into her chest. '*I* saw you safely off the ride, and told you that everything would be all right, and why didn't we go home now and wouldn't you like an ice cream, your favourite flavour. The closer we got to the park exit, the more I realised you were the sign the Lord had sent me. Because those people didn't need you. They had another one – I saw her – they didn't need two. It wasn't fair. Because I had one child, then two, and then none, and then, like a miracle from heaven, I had one again!'

She stalks over to me now, her face looming over the bed. Her eyes are wild in her face, roving this way and that, and her hair, usually so pristine, has come loose from its band and shakes ferociously about her shoulders. I see the trails of spittle on her chin. Mamma is coming undone.

'I loved you from the moment I saw you. My golden girl. My second chance. And we were happy, weren't we? You and me. And you loved me too, you know you did! Don't you remember, that trip to Alachua County Fair?'

I shake my head. I won't remember. I won't think back. Whatever version of love I have or had for her, it was built on lies.

'We drove around, that first year. I saved the money I'd taken as best I could, sleeping in the car, or occasionally staying in motels where no one knew or cared who we were. I didn't have a plan, or a place to go, but something compelled me to stay nearby, almost as if I were enjoying tempting fate, skirting the danger every time. We went past the fair, and you saw the horses, the Ferris wheel, and begged me to stop. I thought perhaps your confused child mind was getting it mixed up with Astroland, that you were hoping you'd be taken back to your parents, but then you looked up at me with those big, brown eyes and you said ... you said, "Please, Mamma?"' Her voice quivers. 'It was the first time you called me Mamma. It seemed like a sign, that we were finally home. I found the house, used the last of the money as a down payment, and got a job doing mending for a local lady. When she retired, I took over the business, turned it mail order. And everything seemed to just … settle.

'I knew Father Paul realised what I'd done. He had no way of contacting me, before the house, but all the same I knew. I'd get a sense, sometimes, of being watched. The same car following us just a little too close. When the first card arrived, I wasn't even surprised. But I wrote to him, promised I would never reveal what he'd done, if he'd only let me have you. And I've been true to my word, haven't I? I've been good. I've stayed quiet. I haven't talked. I've been a good mother. I've prayed. I've lived a life of purity and grace and asked for forgiveness every day for my sins. So why, Anna? Why now? What does he want from me? Why won't he let me be?' Mamma leans over the bed, grasping my shoulders, begging me to understand, to legitimise her narrative.

But something within me begins to break. Because I am starting to remember now, too, albeit faintly, those first few months. When we slept in the car and kept moving and driving, day after day. And I remember my infant frustration, telling her I was Emily, not Anna, and that I wanted to go back to my mummy and daddy. And her telling me to shush now, and giving me something that made me sleep, laced in milkshakes that were sweeter than anything I'd ever tasted, and sent a cold shock up my nose and eyes when I drank too much at once.

Then all at once, as if I've finally found the missing piece of the puzzle, I can see the face I have been longing to see but couldn't: the face that has been haunting my dreams, begging me to remember it. Her rich brown hair; the coarse feel of it brushing my cheeks as she bent down to kiss me. Her wide brown eyes, which always seemed to have a wink in them, as she pulled me into a hug and called me her sweet girl. The shape of her chin. Her nose. Her ears. My mother. I remember my mother.

A fury inside me grows like a fireball, burning from the pit of my stomach and sending flashes to the tips of my fingers and toes. I thrash my legs against the covers and pull at my bonds: *'Liar!* They *did* love me,' I spit. 'You stole me from them!'

I watch the full horror of my words play on her face. And then something in her seems to shift. Her body slackens, like the full weight of it is finally sinking into her, and she looks at me with a mixture of pain, and fear, and anger, and something else. Something that is undeniably love.

'I did.' She hangs her head, smears a sweaty hand across her nose and mouth. 'I took you, Anna. The Lord has judged me, and Father Paul is my punishment. He wants to take you from me, to punish me for what I did. All these years, he's been waiting to strike, to find a way to hurt me the most. I can never escape him, Anna. And I can't lose you.' There's something different in her voice – a resolve that comes over her. She steps away from the bed, out of the edge of my vision.

'You won't lose me, Mamma.' My words flail in the air, desperate to draw her back to me. I can taste the remnants of medicine in the corners of my gums. The bitterness fortifies me, strengthens my desire to be free from this. 'Let me go, and we'll escape him together.'

'I can't.'

'Come on, Mamma.' She has crossed to the other side of the room, and I crane my neck to see her. 'You have to let me go. He's going to come again – we have to get away from here.'

'It doesn't matter, Anna.' As she speaks, I hear a distant popping sound. 'Wherever we go, whatever we do, he'll find us.' She steps into view, and I see she's holding some sort of packet in her hand. *Pop, pop, pop.*

'Mamma, what are you doing?' I try to swallow down the panic in my voice. I recognise the packet now: the sleeping pills she's always so quick to dispense.

'Pray, Anna, and the Lord will show us the way.' Her fingers push methodically into the back of the packet. 'Pure in mind, in word, thought and deed, I ask You, Lord, to pay me heed.'

I see a pile of round, white pills growing in her hand. I feel sick. 'Mamma, what are you going to do with those? Put them down. We have to get out of here before he comes again.'

'Pure in mind, in word, thought and deed, I ask You, Lord, to pay me heed.' She empties the packet, tosses it to the ground. 'It won't hurt, Anna. It'll be just like going to sleep. Like turning off a light bulb. I'll be right there with you, and then no one can ever harm us again. We don't have to run any more. We can be together, you and me. No Father Paul, no Lilies. Together, for ever. And free.'

'Mamma, no, you're crazy. You can't do this.' I twist violently against the bed sheets as Mamma walks back to the bed, the pills in her outstretched hand.

Her prayers start up again, over and over, blindingly fast. 'Pure in mind, in word, thought and deed, I ask You, Lord, to pay me heed.'

'I said *no!*' I wrench my wrists against the twine, and whether it really is a miracle or simply blind luck, I feel a sudden whoosh of release as the twine snaps free from the bed.

We both stare at my freed wrists, incredulous.

But there is little time for me to enjoy my release, because a sound intrudes inside the attic walls – the thudding at the front door. Louder, this time, methodical. And his voice, angry, insistent. Father Paul is back.

Mamma's body goes rigid, her mouth gaping open on a silent scream. The pills drop from her hand and skitter against the floorboards. 'No,' she whispers, backing against the wall and cowering there. 'No, no, no, no, no. Not yet. It's not time. Not yet.'

'Mary!' This time his words are clear, his shouts echoing through the house. He crashes against the door so hard I'm sure it'll break. 'I know you're in there. Open up.'

My limbs tense. Now I am free, every instinct is telling me to flee, to get away from here, from her. Run, as far away and as fast as I can. But then I look at her. Really look at her. Every muscle in her is twitching with fear. Her body sways, up, down, up, down, as every shout from Father Paul makes her shrink even further into herself. I can't leave her to him.

'Mamma,' I say quietly, 'we have to get out of here. We have to go.'

She shakes her head, tears pooling once again in her eyes. 'There's nowhere to go.'

I look beyond her, to the padlocked door that leads directly to Father Paul. 'Mamma, we have to.' My eyes probe the corners of the room, searching desperately for an answer.

The crashing increases. It won't be long until he breaks through the front door.

'The window.' I look over to the skylight. It's high, but if we stand on the chair, we should be able to haul ourselves up onto the attic roof. From there, we can lower ourselves onto the roof below, use the drainpipe to help ourselves down and sneak into the bushes to get to the road.

My hands tremble. In my weakened state, I'm not sure I'll have the energy to hold myself up, but I have to try. We have to try. I'm already up, out of the bed, limping across the room to drag the chair up to the window.

'Mamma, come quickly. We don't have much time.' I stand on the chair, poised to force open the skylight.

Mamma is still backed up against the wall, watching me in horror. 'Mamma?'

She looks from the window to the padlocked door, and then to me. Her eyes pierce through me, a look of realisation and utter clarity on her face. 'No, Anna.' She speaks slowly, evenly. 'I see now. The Lord is testing me. I could have saved her once, but I didn't. This is my second chance.' She backs away from the door and comes over to me. 'You have to go.'

Tears spring to my eyes as I understand what she is saying. 'No, Mamma, I can't leave you to him. I—' I can hear the sounds of the door yielding to Father Paul, the splintering of wood as it bends to his will. It won't be long before he's in.

'Anna. *Now.*' Mamma addresses me with the force that once upon a time would have struck fear in my heart. But not now. Now I know she's doing it for me.

Slowly, I nod. Force open the window. When I turn around, Mamma is moving across the room, to the chest of drawers in the corner. She opens the top drawer, and I hear the same metallic clunk I heard before. Nausea runs through me. 'Mamma?'

She doesn't turn around.

Tears blur my vision as I pull myself up through the open window. The roof is slanted, fairly steep, but I take advantage of my bare feet to grip the tiles as I move in a crouch to the second level. I hear Father Paul fully now, his threats rendered surround-sound by the open air. I know if he sees me it's game over, but he's hidden from me by the porch, and once I lower myself into the backyard, I can pick my way through the bushes to get to the road.

I'm almost at the mailbox when I hear the gunshot.

I freeze, aching to turn around. But then I'm running. Trying not to let myself think. Trying not to contemplate the object in Mamma's hands, and what she has done. Earth splatters my calves and the bottom of my nightgown. The road rips at the soles of my feet. My lungs barely sustain me.

When I reach the double doors of the police station, I throw myself through, stumbling over my nightgown as I can already feel my body start to fail me.

'Miss?' I hear a voice call, distantly, and know that I am finally safe.

'Help,' I manage to whimper as exhaustion claims me. My vision starts to blur, but I can make out bodies, moving around me.

'Miss, what's happened? Who are you?'

'Help me. I'm … I'm …' My limbs turn to pools of water as I sink to the cold, hard ground.

I feel arms lifting me up, shouting to others to make way. And then someone pushes through; a familiar voice: William. 'It's her. I told you.' I see his face come into view, feel his hand squeezing mine.

'I'm … I'm …'

'Shh, it's OK. You're safe now. Everything's all right.'

And whatever I am about to say is given over to black release.

ROSIE

28

When I step out of the Underground at Highbury and Islington, I can't believe it's still light outside. It feels as though I've been away for days, not hours. The journey has agitated me, made me tetchy and impatient. I have in my possession a key to Emily's disappearance; the door that it unlocks still seems so far away.

When I walk into the house, I assume no one's home: Rob will still be at school, Mum and Dad at work. I power upstairs through the silent house, playing it through in my head: the woman in the photograph must be the one who took my sister; she must be connected to The Lilies. But why did she take her? And where are they now? How on earth will we find them? All notions of going back to school have dissipated. I need to gather my thoughts: the photograph, the image of the woman in the navy dress. I need to go to the police. I push open the door to my bedroom, fingertips tingling, ready to spring into action.

And there's Mum, sitting on the edge of my desk. Around her, spilled across the bed sheets, are all my notes. I can see my emails open on the laptop screen.

'How long has this been going on?' Her voice is a needle, pointing somewhere between exhaustion and rage.

'I can explain. I—'

'*No*, Rosie.' I blink up at her, silenced by the vehemence in her voice. 'I've been worried sick about you all morning. School called. They said you missed French.' I curse my bad timing. 'Apparently Keira tried to cover for you. They rang me at work to check.' Guilt pulses through me – poor Keira; she'll have got it in the neck. 'I tried your mobile – you weren't answering. I spoke to Keira myself. She mumbled something about some boy. But I knew that wasn't it. I could tell there was something she was hiding from me. So I came home to see for myself. And yes, I checked your emails.' Her anger is accelerating, gripping at her voice. 'I have a right to. I am your mother, however grown-up you think you are. And I found the emails from that Jane. And then – hands up – I looked in your bedside drawer – any mother would have done – and I found the notes, and the names. Not to mention the cigarettes.' My stomach lurches. 'That page – TheHive – it was still loaded on your browser. And this rail booking – Slough? What were you doing there? Who were you seeing? I want to know now, Rosie. No more secrets. '

'I – I …' My thoughts jumble together; I can't get them straight. 'Mum, you won't believe it: I found something. That journalist, Michael Davis – he came to the party; he gave me the first clue. I went to see him. He's been researching Emily's disappearance for years. I don't know how it adds up, but it does. Father Paul; these people called The Lilies. Somehow they're involved with what happened to her. That's where I was today. At one of their churches. Looking for something to prove it. And I was right! There's a woman, Mum. She took Emily. I don't know why, but we have to go to the police. Now.' The story tumbles out of me almost faster than I can grasp it.

I motion towards her, to spur her into action, but Mum seems to pale. 'Where did you say you were today?'

I realise I've spoken too soon. I should never have mentioned The Lilies without making her see first. 'Mum, I—'

'Rosie.' Her eyes harden.

I stare down at my feet. 'The Lilies,' I mumble. 'The church.'

Mum rises, her lips a scored line across her face. 'You're unbelievable.'

'But—'

'I can't even look at you, I'm so angry.' She storms out of the room without another word.

'Mum, wait!' I call after her but she's already halfway down the stairs. I can cope with shouting, but this white silence is terrifying.

I follow her down into the living room, where I hear the vibration of her phone, buzzing against the bottom of her bag. She picks up the bag, glances at the phone but ignores it. It's probably Dad. I wonder if she's told him.

'Please, just listen to me.' I hurry behind her as she moves through the house, taking her coat down from the rack. 'I know what I did was wrong. I know I shouldn't have skipped school, and that I should have told you what I was doing. But I knew you'd never believe me and—'

She shakes her head, picks up her car keys from the side table. 'Stop it, Rosie. Go put your uniform on. I'm driving you back to school.'

I feel the panic rising in my chest. I can't go back to school. Not now. 'Mum, please. I'm telling you, this woman took Emily. She was involved with some kind of cult. I think she's still alive. Out there, somewhere, we just need to find her.'

'Rosie, I don't want to hear this nonsense. Five minutes and we're leaving.' She starts putting on her shoes.

Her phone buzzes again, momentarily stuttering my thoughts. Mum huffs. 'It'll be your father, asking about dinner. I haven't even told him you were missing. Go. Get dressed.'

'Just hear me out.' I hover, back to the stairs, not quite ready to admit defeat. 'Michael knew it. He recognised the necklace the woman was wearing, traced it all back. You can talk to him yourself.' I try to keep my voice calm, hoping that reasoning with her will work better. 'And it's easy to see how it could have been overlooked, because the only reason Michael recognised the necklace is because he knew about The Lilies first hand. No one else would have known what to look for. And so I went there, to The Lilies. I snuck in. I wanted to see for myself, if there was something they were hiding. And I'm really, really sorry that I upset you. I know it was wrong, and that I should have told you. I realise how worried you must have been; but I was right – I found something! And now we can go to the police and it'll all—'

'*Enough, Rosie!*' The rage in Mum's voice stops me. Angry tears prick the corners of her eyes. 'I told you that these theories were all crazy, that the police would have already looked into any viable leads. And I *specifically* told you not to get mixed up with these people – these conspiracy theorists. Do you have any *idea* of the danger you could have put yourself in? I can't believe you've been so irresponsible. This Michael could have been anyone. He could have done anything to you – anything. And this church! What if they really were a cult, and he was mixed up in it all? What if this was all part of some sick plan? It's so thoughtless for your own safety, and to Keira, and to me … and … and …'

I can't wait a second longer. In desperation, I reach into my pocket and thrust the picture in front of her face. 'Mum, *look.*'

In an instant she freezes. Slowly, she holds her fingers out to it, trance-like. A silent gasp howls through her body; a storm through trees. '… *How?*'

And then the phone rings again. Mechanically she takes it out, holds it in front of her then presses it to her ear, never letting her eyes waver fully from the photograph.

'David?'

A wash of grey comes over her face. Her body starts to quake – I see her visibly convulsing – as she backs against the wall, slinking slowly down it until she's sitting in a heap on the floor, the phone still pressed to the side of her face. The photograph floats from her hand, falling to the floor beside her.

'What is it?' I ask. Nausea throbs through me. 'Is Dad OK? Rob?'

Mum isn't speaking, just making a rasping, dry heaving noise and pressing her free hand to her mouth, her cheek, her chest.

'Mum?' I ask again. 'What's happened?'

She shakes her head, unable to say anything, and holds the phone out to me with an unsteady hand. I take it, pressing it against my cheek.

'Hello? Dad? Is everything OK?'

'Rosie?' His voice is hoarse. 'You need to get in the car and come to the station now. They've found her. They've found Emily.'

ANNA

29

The wallpaper in William's parents' guest room has eighty-nine blue stripes on it. I count them from the bed – one, two, three – only, when I stare at them for too long, my eyes go funny, and the poster-paint blue seems to bleed into the white.

Next to the bed is a side table. And on the side table there's a glass lamp, whose base is filled with seashells. I press my index finger to it, trace the outline of the starfish whose petrified form butts against the glass. Ten lines, traced up and down, to make up the shape of a star.

It's much easier to distract myself with concrete facts like these.

I've been in this room nearly twenty-four hours. By now I know every inch of it by heart. William's parents convinced the hospital that I would be far better off cared for in their home, without the constant threat of reporters sneaking in – posing as a doctor, as one did last night, and nearly getting to my room before security stopped them. A small length to go to, for the sake of a story. Especially when that story is one of the Biggest Unsolved Mysteries Of The Last Fifteen Years, and it has finally been answered. This from the headlines in the newspaper one of the nurses mistakenly brought me with breakfast. Better all round for me to be with William and his family. Close observation at all times.

To my left, cool air blows from the window I have asked them repeatedly to stop shutting. I can't bear to be closed in. From it I can see the tops of the linden trees on the sidewalk opposite and hear the laughter of the children playing in the street – not the voices of the twins, though, swiftly dispatched to an aunt and uncle in Texas. Such normal, everyday sounds. So at odds with the world in my head.

From this same window I can also hear the clatter of the reporters who spill around the front door and catcall to anyone who steps in or out. Their incessant hum is a small price to pay for the pleasure of feeling the fresh breeze against my skin, after the dankness of the attic. Voyeuristically, I like to stand by it, shaded just out of sight by the calico curtains, and try to make out the individual voices, take in the weight of the fact that the person they are calling for is me.

The diamond on my left hands catches the light. I wear an engagement ring now. What excuse would I have not to, without Mamma to question it? It twinkles, unnervingly unfamiliar, on my finger when I tweak the corner of the curtain, seeking a closer look.

William bought it for me this morning. He thought I would be thrilled. I tried so hard to remember what that feels like. He sat beside me, trying to read my movements and my unspoken words, stroking the untarnished gold band in an endless loop; telling me it is the symbol of us looking towards the future. I can't explain how for me it feels more like a reminder of the tangled past.

He has apologised, over and over in pained, pleading tones, for not trying to find me sooner. He says he wanted to show he respected my wishes, to prove to me he was listening. But when he saw Mamma in church without me, he knew something wasn't right. He went straight to the police, but they didn't believe him: they laughed in his face, told him he'd been watching too many made-for-TV movies and that he should take the hint. When he came to the house that day – oh, the irony of thinking he was Father Paul, of letting salvation slip through my fingers – he returned to the station and refused to leave until they took him seriously. He was on the cusp of a physical fight with them – only interrupted by my staggering in at that very moment.

I forgive him, numbly, take his head on my lap and stroke his soft hair and tell him it's not his fault. What else can I do?

He doesn't call me Anna now. None of them do, not his parents, or Ms Abrams, who visits, distraught, with a stack of books whose titles swim before my eyes. To them, I am 'How are you feeling, dear?' and 'Honey, how about something to eat?' and 'Sweetheart, are you sure you don't want to close the window?'

The others don't either. The men in suits – and they *are* all men – who take my fingerprints and a DNA sample, and then later talk about evidence and hearings and statements. They stomp in and out of the house like little boys playing soldiers, talking through me as William's father mutters 'Uh huh, uh huh, I see' a lot, and Hilary scurries around them, making endless cups of coffee. They've appointed a spokesperson, a man with translucent skin and a protuberant Adam's apple and a 'please, call me Greg' smile, who stands at the threshold of the house and asks the press to respect the family's privacy at this difficult time.

I'm not a person, but a purpose: the answer at the end of a question.

I try to ask them what's happening to Mamma now, but they seem almost bothered by me asking; tell me I shouldn't concern myself about it, that there will be plenty of chances for questions later, that it's all being taken care of. They regard me with caution, as if the wrong word might break me or, if they come too close, they risk being infected by the same rottenness that surrounds me.

She's being held in a psych ward now, closely monitored, that much I know for sure. And I know, of course, that she'll stand trial, and will most likely go to prison for a long, long time. I know as well, from the snatch I heard from Hilary, that Father Paul is alive. The bullet entered through the top of his left shoulder, missing his heart. At least this means she won't be standing trial for murder. And that he will live to fight a series of cases against him, not least of which will include intimidation, money laundering, fraud, perversion of the course of justice, and, of course, manslaughter ... maybe even murder.

I wonder if they ever found her body.

The thought pierces through me, but it also brings me a strange sort of comfort. I think of her almost like a sister, twinned, in some twisted way, by our shared name and our shared parentage. I like to think that knowing where she's laid to rest will bring Mamma some peace. I hope she'll get a chance to visit, to say a proper goodbye.

I can't bear the idea of her being incarcerated. The thought tears at me as much as the twine that made the welts on my wrists. I can't get the image out of my head of her in a dank, dirty cell. I picture her pacing the four walls, lying on a cold, hard bed, having to wash her hands and do her business within the same few square feet. How will she stand it? Will they let her have a Bible? A bar of soap? How often will they change her sheets, or let her taste the fresh air?

Who will tend to her garden, with no one left to care for it?

I try to ask the nurse, the one who comes after they bring me back from the hospital. I grab her arm as she reaches to remove the drip that has been steadily pumping fluids into my body, and beg her, *please*. She's Caribbean – from the Bahamas, she tells me – with peppery hair scraped back into a bun, and a heavy bosom that jiggles up and down when she huffs and puffs around the room, packing up the equipment to go back to the hospital.

She calls me Emmy. 'Don't you be bothering yourself with that, Emmy girl.' She clicks her teeth, checking the IV line in my hand. 'She's where she belongs. That woman will never hurt you again.' But I hear her talking, whispering to Hilary when she thinks I've fallen asleep. 'I've heard of this sort of thing before – it's that "Stockholm syndrome",' I hear her tutting. 'That poor girl. What she's been through? Lord dreads to think.'

I know what Stockholm syndrome is. It makes me think of prisoners in cells, women kept in bunkers by awful men and forced to bear their children. But that wasn't me. That wasn't us.

In a funny way, it's here that I am captive most. I am not allowed out. These walls are my world, for now. The media swarms on the driveway, and, besides, even if I wanted to go out, where would I go? The thought of it rises in my chest, squeezing so hard on my lungs I feel I'm back in the attic.

There's a knock on the door, and William's head appears around it. He's holding a familiar green cardboard box: a Scrabble set, which takes me instantly back to sunny weekend afternoons, spreading a picnic blanket out under the shade of a tree and taking turns picking letters out of the green cloth bag. It has always been a thing between us: William will be losing, terribly, so I deliberately play badly until he eventually notices and demands I treat him like a grown-up. When I think back to those days, they're covered with a golden glow: how lucky I was, how much I would give to go back there.

He comes fully into the room and offers the box out to me. 'I thought we could play?'

I nod, and he curls up gently on the edge of the bed, removing the lid and opening the board out between us.

He hasn't kissed me once. Perhaps he's afraid to.

We play in amicable silence, punctuated by the clink of tiles as we rearrange them on our racks, and the occasional hiss from William, as I add an S to one of his words, or take the triple word square. But I feel his eyes on me, even as I keep my attention fully on the tiles, forcing the letters that swim before me to fight their way into my murky mind, and form the words I will them to.

'What?' I ask eventually, plucking a P from the bag and flipping an X and O around to make 'pox'.

'You know they'll be here soon?'

'May I swap these, please?' The cream tiles in my palm look like fragments of bone.

'Why won't you talk about it?' he asks.

I take the bag myself and concentrate on the rattle of pieces as I pluck out a new pair. 'Foxed.' I spread the letters out on the board. 'Double letter score on the X. Thirty-two points, please.'

'Honey. You haven't even mentioned your family since the call. What is it?'

I finger the remaining tiles on my rack. *My family*. I chew the unfamiliar words around in my mouth like a hard piece of gum.

The idea of this unit, fully formed, has existed for me only in some sort of alternate universe, something I didn't quite think I would actually grasp hold of. But now they are a reality. They are coming for me. And I have a sister. Rosie. And a brother. Rob. What would it have been like, growing up with them – being a big sister? Would I have argued with my sister? Got mad at her for stealing my clothes? Taught her how to wear make-up and how to flirt with boys? Would I have loved my little brother, like William and his sisters, or found him annoying and exasperating and told him to get lost? I try to insert myself into their lives, imagining scenarios with my newly formed family of five. But I can't seem to make the image stick.

I spoke to her. My mother. They held the phone to my ear and I heard her English drawl breaking through the hysteria that kept overwhelming her, but it was like there was a disconnect between the woman in my mind and the one at the other end of the phone, a disconnect that left me feeling strangely numb.

They tell me not to worry, that I'll see her soon, in person.

They don't know that I saw Mamma.

I knew she was there, in the hospital. I knew, from the fragments I'd gathered, that after she shot Father Paul, she'd gone back up to the attic, picked up all of those little white pills and taken them herself – every last one. She was slumped by the chair when they found her, the window still open. They got to her just in time.

So I waited, until there was no one around. Unhooked my IV myself, ignoring the spots of blood that made the bile rise in my throat, and slipped into the corridor, my presence camouflaged by the beeping machines, the dull smell of disinfectant. The cops sitting outside the door made it obvious which room was hers. They were both asleep; I could see it from the slow rise and fall of their chests, the way their arms crossed around themselves and their heads lolled against their shoulders. I came right up to the door and they didn't even move. Then I raised myself on tiptoes, pressed my face against the glass panel. And I looked.

She seemed so small, against all that white. I've never seen her look so small. The machines, the screens whose wavy green lines mark the weak passage between dead and alive, were so at odds with the woman whose strong arms have wielded rakes and pulled up weeds. Pointed a gun; fired. I thought that she was asleep, too, but then she turned her head and, as if the last thread of maternal instinct was tugging at her, she looked back.

'Go on.' William's voice intrudes. 'You know you can tell me anything.'

He watches me, expectantly, so I force out the hasty response, 'What if they don't like me?'

He takes me into him, stroking the back of my head, and planting long-held-back kisses on my cheeks and forehead. And I let him. 'Oh honey, how could you ever think that? How could they not?' He draws his arms tightly around me and my fingers flex and curl, resisting the urge to push him away.

Because I know this is what he needs: to overwhelm me with his affection, to suffocate me with love, to feel that he is helping. So there's no need for him to know the other thought, the one that stutters inside me and makes me feel like I am in the middle of the ocean.

Because I'm not just scared that they won't like me. I'm scared that it's me who won't like them.

ROSIE

30

It's amazing how quickly you can get to the other side of the world when the world wants you to get there.

A plane is put on standby. Bags are thrown together. Rob is fetched from school. We are on our way to Florida. We travel with Mark, our spokesman, and Sarah, the director of the trust, everyone high on nervous energy and talking in jagged, breathy voices.

It's all too weird for me to take in, the fact that I'm also flying long distance for the first time I can remember, let alone that I'm doing so in a private plane. Dad tried to tell them we'd be fine on a regular passenger jet, but Sarah touched his arm indulgently, 'David, we'd never get past the press.'

Various people have patted me on the head. Told me what a Clever Girl I Am. How Brave. The photograph is apparently a Key Piece Of Evidence; taken away to be logged. The place in the photograph: Alachua – I didn't realise that's what it was at the time – is where she is, where she's been all this time. Hidden in plain sight.

But I don't feel brave. A tiny, tiny part of me, a part that will never say so out loud, is disappointed. That I couldn't have done more; couldn't have found her myself. And yet found her we have. At least my discovery will ensure that the people who did this to her won't get away with it.

On the flight, Sarah gives Mum something to calm her down. 'My husband's a nervous flier; I come prepared.' She hands her a round blue pill from a box marked 'Diazepam'. That, plus the glass of whisky, sends her to sleep before we're in the air.

Dad folds and unfolds the paper without reading it, eventually throwing it to the side and spending the rest of the flight with his arms crossed, giving an occasional shake of his head and muttering, 'Right there, the whole time,' under his breath.

Fifteen years of searching, and she was only an hour or so away from where she was taken. I picture the place where Emily has grown up, north-west Florida, with palm trees and sandy beaches, until Dad does a Google image search, and we see springs and alligators instead. I can barely begin to imagine what her life must have been like; how different it must have been from mine in London. How do I even begin knowing her?

I ask Sarah, tentatively, if they've found the church leader, Father Paul. 'And what about the church, The Lilies?'

She gives me an indulgent smile over the laptop she is tapping away at. 'We don't know the full details of anything at the moment, Rosie sweetheart. We're just overwhelmed by the fact that your sister is alive and well.'

When we step out of the plane, I'm hit with a whack of humidity, and a sweet, grassy smell of plant life that lingers in the air.

'That old familiar Florida heat.' Mark steps out behind me, agitating his shirt collar.

We're in a small, regional airport, barely half an hour away from where Emily is staying. We're met off the plane by a member of the British consulate, a woman in a tight black trouser suit despite the heat, who flew up herself from Miami earlier today. 'Welcome to Gainesville. I'm Diana,' she says in a brusque Scottish accent, handing each of us a bottle of water and ushering us into a long black car that's waiting right there on the runway.

In the car, she is businesslike, talking through details, the proceedings, paperwork. I watch Mum trying to take it all in through the last of her medicated fug.

At last Dad holds up his hands. 'Do you think we could save all this for tomorrow? At the moment, we're focusing on seeing our daughter.'

Chastened, Diana pursing her lips together, puts her laptop back in her bag.

It's 9 p.m. in Florida, but it's two in the morning in London, and my head is swimming, not with tiredness necessarily, but with a foggy sense of displacement. My mouth is dry and has a tinny taste in it from the air conditioning on the plane, whatever air freshener they used. My eyes feel as if I've been in the pool for too long, raw and itchy.

Rob's been pretty silent since he was picked up from school, taking it all in with his normal stoicism. I give him an elbow from my seat next to him. 'You OK?'

'Yeah,' he yawns. 'Fucking weird though, isn't it?'

Fucking weird doesn't even start to cover it.

When the car finally comes to a halt, we're on a residential street that looks like something out of a TV show: identikit, low-slung houses with fenced-in front gardens and wide, tree-lined pavements. A few of the houses have lights on in them, and I wonder how many of them know what is going on just a few feet away. My question is answered as, abruptly, hands knock on the car windows, and faces try to peer in through the tinted glass.

'Bloody hacks,' Diana mutters.

Mark must see my body sharpen in alarm, because he suddenly leaps into control. 'OK, people,' he says, leaning forward and taking everyone into his eyeline. 'It's going to get a little crazy for a couple of seconds, but then we're going to shut the door and it's gone, right?'

We each nod, ignoring the shouts from the press outside, 'David, Susanne, is that you?' 'Do you have a statement?' 'How do you feel?'

Next to Mark, Sarah has her phone pressed to her ear, talking, by the sound of it, to someone inside the house. 'Mm-hm, on my signal.'

'So, everyone,' Mark continues, 'get your things together, then we're going to go: me, David, Rob, Susanne, Rosie, Sarah and finally Diana. Everyone keep your heads down; feel free to put a coat or a jumper over you if you'd prefer; and move straight towards the door. Pretend there's no one there. Are you ready?'

Yes, we all nod.

'Sarah?'

She nods and says, 'OK, we're coming. *Now*.'

'Go,' says Mark. He pushes open the car door, and the muffled voices become a sudden roar, battering me from both sides as we move as one towards the house, shielding our eyes from the flash of cameras, and our bodies from smartphones thrust in our faces. Looking up, I can see a door open in front of us, a figure propping it ajar, and I propel myself towards it until I am inside and press myself against the nearest wall, trying to get my breath back. My skin is damp with sweat, and adrenaline is pumping through me, making my arms and legs feel all quivery. The door shuts behind Diana, suffocating the noise like a candle being snuffed out, and our party look from one to another with wide, dazed expressions.

When the shock of the outside world has subsided, a woman comes towards us. She's tall and slim, with auburn hair tied back into a ponytail, a heart-shaped face and high, rounded cheekbones that immediately give a warmth to her features. She looks straight at Mum. 'Susanne?' She pronounces it Soo-zayne.

Mum nods. Without speaking, the woman throws her arms around her, pulling her into a thick hug.

'Well, it's an honour to meet you all; it truly is.' She steps back, but keeps hold of Mum's shoulders. 'I'm Hilary, William's mother.' Mum blinks, confused, as if she is mentally going through a contacts list of all the people we have met in these few short hours to work out who William is again. 'Her fiancé.' Mum breathes in a mixture of pleasure and shock. We knew this; we were told on the way here that Emily is engaged, and that it is his parents' house where she is being looked after, but the realisation hits her physically all the same. Hilary threads an arm through the elbow of a man next to her; he has an equally kind expression, and a quiet, confident air to the way his body moves. 'And this here's my husband, Timothy. He's a preacher over in Newberry.'

He reaches out and shakes everyone's hands. 'She really is a special girl,' he says, 'you're very lucky. We all love her to bits – especially my son, of course.'

I can see Dad is already tiring of all the pleasantries. He's moving from foot to foot, and glancing anxiously around the house as if expecting Emily to pop up from a cupboard at any moment. 'Excuse me,' he says, 'I'm sorry if this comes across as rude, but could we ...?'

Hilary clutches a hand to her chest. 'Lord, what on earth was I thinking? Go on, go! She's upstairs, second door to the right. Will might be with her, but he hasn't slept a wink since she was found, so he may well be having a rest. She's been awfully tired, the poor thing, but I know she'll be so overjoyed to see you.' She ushers everyone else with her, into the kitchen I can see off to the right. 'We'll leave you to your privacy.'

They're gone. And for the first time in what seems like for ever, we are alone again; for the last time a family of four. We stand for a moment in silence, staring at each other. Then Dad reaches out and pulls us into a hug. I feel Mum shaking beside me, a crippling mass of emotions.

'Are we ready?' Dad asks, and Mum gulps down a sob beside him.

'I've been ready for fifteen years,' she says, wiping tears away with the back of her hand.

Together, we climb the stairs. When we reach the closed door, second on the right, Dad, Rob and I stand back: we all know who should enter first.

The room is lit by lamplight, and I expect to see her lying in bed, but I cast my eyes around the room and instead find her seated by the window, looking out at the street below. She's thin – I can make out the points of her shoulders under the floral cotton bathrobe she's wearing – with mid-length blonde hair that's tied at the nape of her neck. When she hears the door, she turns, and I can't help but scrutinise her neck, her jawline, her face, finding hints of all of us within them.

She stands up, and I can feel Mum urging herself to run across the room and pull her into us, but instead she stiffens her limbs, letting my sister come to us. She walks slowly, as if it's still an effort for her, and when she moves I see bandages peeking out the bottom of her sleeves.

As she comes closer, she takes in each of us in turn, her eyes boring into us as she assesses our features one by one. I wonder if she is doing the same as me, looking for hints, for definite signs, that we really are her family. I try to read her expression. Her eyebrows have just a hint of a frown in them, and her brown eyes seem to be saying all kinds of things: curiosity, fear, maybe even a hint of anger.

It all seems so ludicrous. That she is really here.

My sister.

Pictures flash into my mind: the baby in the pharmacy, the toddler at her second birthday, the composite sketches that never quite grasped 'her'. All of them more familiar, somehow more *real*, than the girl standing in front of me now.

And I don't know if we can let go of all the trauma of the last fifteen years overnight. I am not so foolish as to think that this new, unimaginable present can whitewash over the past. But now, at last, we have a future. A future with Emily in it.

She is right before us. I can smell the lavender on her skin, fresh and powdery. And something else too –

something faintly chemical. We stand in silence, no one knowing what to do, or what to say.

Finally, I see her shoulders twitch. Her arm moves as if going for a handshake, but then she seems to think better of it, and it flutters back to her side.

Beside me, I hear the breath clutch in Mum's throat. And then she's rushing into the room, arms outstretched, closing the remaining gap between us and her. Strangled by sobs, she clutches Emily to her, squeezing so tight she may never let go. Dad encircles them both, kissing her hair, her cheeks, her ears.

And I watch my sister. I see the rise and fall of her shoulders, grappling against my parents' embrace. I see her eyes flutter open and close, her lips part. And then, for the first time in my living memory, I hear her voice.

'My name ...' she swallows, addressing all of us and none of us at once, 'my name is Anna.'

There once was a little girl called Emily, whose parents loved her very much. They took her on a trip, far away to a magical land where machines flew and emerald glitter sparkled in the air. But when they got there, the little girl was taken away; stolen by a woman who wore two faces, who gave the girl a magic potion, to make her forget who she was. And the potion transformed her into another little girl. A girl called Anna.

Over time, Anna's memories of Emily faded away. The woman who stole her became her world. And together they were happy.

But happiness is fragile, especially when it's built on secrets.

And so Anna had to be someone else entirely.

*

Learning and unlearning yourself is a strange thing.

I must approach everything anew; parse each decision or thought with the greatest intensity. The person I am no longer knows what I like or dislike, what I want or need. A simple question makes my palms sweat. An open one leaves me numb.

But they have all been so very patient, with their encouragement, and their aphorisms; their 'you're doing so well's and their 'one day at a time's.

And I am grateful. But I am drowning in their love.

I wake in the night, feel the weight of it pressing against my rib cage, filling my lungs. Choking me. Missing her. I want so badly to be what they want. Who they want. But who they want is Emily. And I don't know who Emily is.

And so I tell myself the story of my past. Because it is easier. Because it is the only thing I have that draws all the threads of my life together.

Mother. Father. Sister. Brother. William.

And her.

Mamma.

Emily, Anna, either, neither: whoever I am, I have been woven together from the scraps of their narrative. Her narrative.

Because she is part of my story.

She will always be.

Part of me.

ACKNOWLEDGEMENTS

A year ago, a phone call disrupted my morning routine in the most unbelievable way.

To the judges of the *Daily Mail* Penguin Random House First Novel Competition – Sandra Parsons, Simon Kernick, Selina Walker and Luigi Bonomi – thank you for believing in *My Name is Anna*, and for giving me such an incredible opportunity.

Selina, thank you for your advice and guidance throughout – indeed to the entire Cornerstone team, especially Emily, Clare, Khan, Sonny, Becky, Elle, Ellie and Rachel – for the hard work you have done and continue to do on this book. Alison Rae, my copy-editor – thank you for your sharp eyes and for flagging my complete inability to count dates; a saving grace!

I feel particularly fortunate to have experienced the skill and mentorship of my fantastic editor, Emily Griffin. Emily, *My Name is Anna* would not be what it is without your faith, counsel and complete dedication to Anna, Rosie and Mamma. You have shaped this book to be a million times

387

better than I could have imagined. I may not miss the drafts themselves, but I will truly miss the process of working with you!

Luigi – your boundless energy and passion for this book (plus your enthusiasm for minor serial killers and obscure cults) have brought such joy to this whole process. Your kindness and nurturing have been vital to a first-time author – I couldn't have wished for a better agent. Thank you to you and the whole LBA team – to Alison for Twitter chats and Dani for the cheery emails.

Maggie, Howard and my fellow writers at The CCWC – this may not be the book that came from our classes, but it certainly wouldn't exist without the learning, growth and advice of our countless workshops.

I am lucky to be surrounded by a truly wonderful group of friends who have been so delighted for me and such champions of this book at every step of the way. From Florence to Forte, Cambridge to North London (not forgetting ballet Wednesdays and the wolf pack), you know who you are, and your support has made me grow a dozen inches (which we all know I could do with).

Team Reynolds: Sheron (I hope this lives up to all our other book recommendations!), Richard, Archie, Ferds – thank you for being proud; it has meant so very much.

My family: Mummy (my continual cheerleader), Jamie, Clare, Issy, Lola – you guys are everything. Jamie, you are so much more than a brother – a teacher, a protector, a role model, a friend. Thank you for your counsel and your positivity … and for allowing me to prove I can do two jobs at once.

And finally, to my husband, George. Thank you for adventures that could fill a thousand novels; for a friendship founded on chianti and fava beans, and a marriage built on Will and Lyra's heartbreaking goodbye. Here's to the next chapter.